MICKEY FINN

21st Century Noir
Volume 3

Michael Bracken, Editor

MICKEY FINN
21st Century Noir
Volume 3

DOWN & OUT
BOOKS

Down & Out Books
3959 Van Dyke Road, Suite 265
Lutz, FL 33558
DownAndOutBooks.com

The characters and events in this book are fictitious. Any similarity to real persons, living or dead, is coincidental and not intended by the author.

Cover design by Zach McCain and Margo Nauert

ISBN: 1-64396-279-5
ISBN-13: 978-1-64396-279-5

For Temple
My Love, My Muse, My Everything

TABLE OF CONTENTS

INTRODUCTION

Noir. A bleak, cynical outlook is often the central element of noir, and many of the stories that follow adhere to that trope. Characters scraping the bottom of the barrel discover there's still worse to come while a scant few cling to a glimmer of hope.

I often wonder why we read, and some of us write, noir. Is it because noir matches our own fatalistic attitude toward life and we believe that, despite our best efforts, there is no escape from fate? Or, is it because noir allows us to explore a darker side of life that we've been lucky enough to have never experienced? Either way, the nineteen authors included in this edition of *Mickey Finn* have faced the darkness and have given us a look at places most of us never wish to visit.

As in the first two editions of *Mickey Finn*, I restricted the stories to the twenty-first century, challenging contributors to write modern noir stories that don't rely heavily on the technological restrictions of the past.

So, turn the page and begin your journey into darkness.

—Michael Bracken
Hewitt, Texas

HOME IS THE HUNTER
James A. Hearn

Under the wide and starry sky,
Dig the grave and let me lie.
Glad did I live and gladly die,
And I laid me down with a will.

This is the verse you grave for me:
Here he lies where he longed to be;
Here is the sailor, home from the sea,
And the hunter home from the hill.

Requiem by Robert Louis Stevenson

The outside of the hunting cabin was a shambles, a dilapidated ruin of sagging eaves, askew shutters, and broken windows. Tattered curtains stirred fitfully in the autumnal wind, yellowed ghosts beckoning to the old man in the truck parked out front. *You've been away for so long, Joe. Come inside and join us. See what fifty years of neglect has wrought.*

Joe Easterbrook sat in his Ford pickup, weathered hands on the steering wheel, bleary eyes swimming with memories. He cut the engine and stared at the brambles crawling up the cabin's

3

walls and the weeds sprouting between the porch's floorboards. For a wonder, his father's hickory rocking chair was still by the front door, its slow back-and-forth motion sending a chill down his spine.

Joe roughly wiped a tear from his cheek. *Crying again, old man? For the second time in as many days? You didn't even cry at your mother's funeral.*

As a boy, the cabin had seemed as strong as the red oak trees overshadowing it. He and his father had built the cabin from the ground up, using white pine timbers harvested from the surrounding woods. On a nameless mountainside of West Virginia, on three hundred acres of family land bordering the Monongahela National Forest, a young Joe watched as How-ard Easterbrook imposed his will on the land.

Upon a foundation of exposed bedrock that seemed ordained for the purpose, father and son began by constructing a fireplace of white river rocks. Around the chimney and spacious hearth at its base, they laid solid wood floor joists, erected four log walls joined by saddle-notch corners, and finished with scissors-style trusses overlaid by planks and a galvanized steel roof. It was a small but sturdy structure, three hundred square feet of comfort.

During construction, Joe and his father had slept in a tent beneath the splash of the Milky Way. Meals were supplemented with game roasted over a firepit or fresh-caught golden rainbow trout from a stream behind the cabin, its water as clear and cold as the mountain air.

That was the summer of 1966.

Fifty-five years later, the once stalwart cabin looked like a strong breeze could knock it down, and the sight smote Joe's aging heart. He popped his last nitroglycerin pill under his tongue, let it dissolve, and washed out the burning taste with the dregs of a warm Coors Banquet.

Joe crumpled the can, then took out a flip phone and switched it on. He'd picked up the burner for cash at a Korean market on Detroit's east side, in the hours before the disastrous shootout with the Jamaicans. That was yesterday morning and a lifetime ago.

Joe held up the phone and watched the screen expectantly. No signal, roaming or otherwise. Just as he'd hoped. Smiling, he switched the phone off and put it in the glove compartment. It was a paperweight now, a useless assemblage of circuits and plastic that had no meaning out here. If his heart gave out, if he fell from a ladder and broke a leg, there would be no rescue from the outside world. Only the wolves would hear his cries for help.

No one owned this land anymore, not really. It was in the middle of nowhere, down miles of dirt roads that were marked only on paper maps—driving apps couldn't navigate roads where there was no signal. But Joe hadn't needed a GPS navigation app or even a map. He had found the cabin purely from memory. *Turn left at the abandoned windmill; after crossing the wooden suspension bridge, take the next right; five miles up the logging road, turn left.*

The land had passed out of the family the day Saigon fell, when Joe's stepmother donated it to some nature conservatory. The act was her punishment for Joe's voluntary participation in what she called "an illegal war of American imperialism." At least Shelby Watson Easterbrook had the decency to die before he returned from the jungles of Vietnam.

A brain aneurysm had saved Joe the trouble and expense of burying his querulous stepmother, though he had been dismayed to find her grave beside his father's. Howard Wilson Easterbrook—retired schoolteacher, huntsman, craftsman, veteran of the Second World War, and the best father a boy could hope for—reposed in eternal slumber between his two wives.

What are you waiting for, Joe? "*Wait*" *broke the wagon down.* That was his father's favorite aphorism whenever he saw his only son idling about.

With an audible creak, Joe eased himself out of the pickup and rubbed futilely at the ache in his back. Eleven hours behind the wheel had been murder on his arthritic joints, and he'd stopped only once for gas at a one-stoplight town east of Columbus. While filling up, he'd half-expected to see black Hummer H2s pulling up behind him, then grim-faced men with guns emerging into the flickering sodium lights. Would young Hector Ortega be among the men sent to kill him? And if so, would Joe's aim falter in the ensuing gun battle?

But William Donovan's assassins had not followed him from Detroit in the dead of night. They'd never stop looking for him, Joe knew, not after what he'd done. They'd find him; maybe next month, maybe in five years.

In the meantime, there was work to be done.

With a deep sigh, Joe went to his trailer and unlatched the back. He'd get no work done tonight—the sun was sinking behind the mountain, and the temperature was starting to drop—but he could at least set up his work area for tomorrow.

Joe unloaded a generator, filled it with gasoline, and plugged in a lantern. The gloom settling around the mountainside was pushed back a few yards, a tiny spark of civilization in an otherwise desolate wilderness. Insects drifted in and out of the light as Joe staked a canvas canopy, unfolded a table and chair, and then laid out his father's tools. They'd been in storage for decades, undisturbed, as if waiting for the day he returned to West Virginia.

In the moments after yesterday's shootout, as Joe stared at the six bodies around him—four Jamaican gangbangers, William Donovan's worthless nephew Sean O'Connell, and the pregnant girl the idiot had casually shot for seeing his face—Joe had considered leaving his father's things behind. Just grabbing his emergency cache and leaving Detroit as fast as possible.

But that seemed wrong. Cowardly. So he'd taken the time to go home, grab his money and guns, hitch his trailer, and drive as calmly as he could to the storage unit.

By the time Joe unloaded his equipment and supplies, it was well past midnight. He looked up at the countless stars in the sky, his breath steaming in the September air. There was Jupiter passing into Aquarius, and winged Pegasus taking flight. So beautiful. With a satisfied grin, Joe set up his tent and switched off the generator and the lantern.

Tomorrow morning, he'd go into the nearest town and buy everything he needed. He might go to several towns, so as not to raise suspicion by spending thousands of dollars in cash in one place. Yes, that would be best.

Before turning in, Joe looked again at the old cabin, now a dark shape silhouetted against the deeper darkness of the mountain. How strange to feel such a bone-deep sadness over times gone past, the innumerable hunts through the wilderness tracking deer and other game. Those were happy days of youth growing into manhood, of learning what the mountain could provide.

Inside the tent, Joe unrolled his sleeping bag and eventually drifted to a fitful sleep, his Winchester Model 1892 lever-action rifle within easy reach. Carrying the Glock 19, his preferred firearm for so many years, just didn't seem right anymore. Not after yesterday, and certainly not in these sacred woods.

Joe's last thought as he listened to the wind sighing through the boughs of the red oaks was disquieting, yet oddly comforting: *This place is as good a place as any to die.*

"The old man ain't here, Hector. We're wasting our time."

Hector Ortega didn't look up from the desk drawer he was rifling through. He hadn't found much of interest in Joe Easterbrook's quaint home on the outskirts of Detroit, besides some letters and a few Polaroids.

The letters were from the '60s and '70s—something the writers called a "Round Robin" that was apparently circulated via snail mail to family members in an endless chain. As for the Polaroids, one with a lean man holding a lever-action rifle caught Hector's eye. The rifle had a short barrel and no scope, the kind John

Wayne carried in a hundred Westerns. A buck lay at the man's feet, a blue mountain landscape behind.

Hector studied the picture and said, "*Isn't.* The old man *isn't* here. And we are not wasting our time, Blinky. We are looking for clues to where Easterbrook may have gone."

Blinky Simons opened a closet door and rummaged around half-heartedly, a frown on his square face. The big man was an aging street tough who followed orders without question, and Hector suspected he was along to ensure that if they did find Joe Easterbrook, Hector would actually kill his former partner.

As he had sworn to do.

"Clues?" Blinky said. "It's hard to know what's a clue when I don't even know what I'm looking for."

Hector closed the drawer and slipped the letters and the Polaroid into a pocket. He brought a slender hand to his dark beard and studied Easterbrook's home. He'd never been here, despite working with Joe for years.

The home was Spartan bordering on austere, everything arranged with a military precision. Even the leftovers in the refrigerator were labeled according to contents and date. There was nothing, aside from a vintage record player, to say what kind of man lived here. But that was a clue in itself, wasn't it?

"Easterbrook's been here," Hector announced. He went over to the record player and opened the plastic dust cover. John Denver's *Poems, Prayers & Promises* lay on the turntable, flipped to Side B. Interesting. Hector picked up a stack of records and began flipping through them.

Blinky scratched his bald head. "How do you figure?"

"It's what we *haven't* found that's important. No cash. No guns, ammo, or personal effects. He took his pillows from the bed but left his phone charger behind. He came home after the…incident with Sean. Grabbed his emergency cache, a few personal items, and left."

Blinky cracked a beer he'd found in the fridge and was helping himself to leftover fried chicken. He sat down in a recliner opposite Hector and said, "Incident? Killing the boss's favorite nephew ain't—I mean *isn't*—an incident. It's suicide."

Hector put down the records. More country artists: Waylon Jennings, Johnny Cash, and Willie Nelson. Outlaws. But no new country, none of the synthesized pop-trash Nashville churned out nowadays. That said something, too.

"Get me a beer, Blinky."

"Sure. Can we watch some TV?"

"No TV," Hector said. "I need to think for a few minutes."

Blinky set a Coors Banquet in front of Hector and a plate with more fried chicken, then returned to his recliner.

Hector cracked the beer and took a long swallow to steady his nerves. Yesterday, for a moment, he'd thought Joe would actually shoot him the way Joe had shot Sean. But the older man stood motionless over Sean's body and the dead pregnant girl, his face unreadable.

Hector went over the scene in his methodical mind, point by point. He had waited for the Jamaicans in an out-of-the-way alley for a supposed drug buy, while Joe and Sean hid behind concrete stairs, guns drawn.

The Jamaicans arrived wearing surgical masks, hands open. Hector pulled up his own mask and waved them over. Come closer. We're friends. When the men cleared the stairwell, Joe and Sean stepped from the shadows and opened fire, dropping them in moments.

For good measure, Sean O'Connell kicked the bodies and spat upon them. The boy always seemed like he was hopped up, but Sean never touched the poison he peddled. Whatever the demons were that fired his brain, they came from within.

Some people were naturally rotten, Hector supposed.

After the gunfight, Joe and Hector had to grab the animated Sean by the arms, pulling him away from the bloody scene and toward the street. As they turned, all three men stopped dead in their tracks. There was a girl standing in the mouth of the alley, a dark figure with a swollen belly.

The mother-to-be was maybe nineteen, an evocative silhouette against the brightness beyond. To Hector, she looked so pretty in her red dress, a bag of groceries clutched to her chest. Though a mask covered her mouth, pleasingly color-coordinated to match her purse, Hector could clearly see the "O" of surprise on her lips. She was looking right at Sean's face.

Sean, who wasn't wearing a mask. According to him, masks and vaccines were for *sheeple*, and the pandemic gripping the planet (the Kung Flu, as Sean called it) was part of some nefarious world government scheme. It had something to do with chemtrails in the sky and sterilization and taking people's guns.

"She's seen my face," Sean said, as if this were the girl's fault. Before Hector knew what was happening, Sean shot the girl three times—once in the chest, then a double-tap to the head when she was down.

An instant later, Joe's Glock 19 spoke at point-blank range, inches from the base of Sean's skull. The boy fell, his head caved in on itself like a rotten melon.

As Sean's body thudded to the ground, Hector found he couldn't move. There was a dead civilian, the kind to make police and politicians scream for blood, and there was Sean beside her. Granted, the world was a better place without him in it, but there would be a reckoning for him, too. A more severe reckoning.

And there was Joe holding his Glock, his eyes on Hector. Fight or flight waged war in Hector for a split second. Run? Draw my Beretta? Joe's quiet calmness decided the matter; Hector ran for it. Before he rounded the corner, he caught sight of Joe bending over the girl's body, head bowed.

"This chicken's tasty," Blinky said. "Can I turn on the TV?"

Hector sighed and stared daggers at the other man. Why not shoot this simpleton, like Joe had done to Sean, and disappear? It would be so easy and quick, three seconds, tops. But the man's perpetually red-rimmed eyes unnerved Hector, and he let the moment pass. Blinky was an ironic nickname, like calling a fat man Slim or a bald man Curly. The big man never, ever blinked.

"No TV. How about I play a record for you?"

"Like what?"

Hector went to the phonograph. "John Denver."

"Huh. I didn't know Gilligan was a singer, too."

Hector shook his head and didn't bother to correct Blinky. He sat back down on the couch and listened to "Take Me Home, Country Roads" while he drank his beer.

There was something significant about this album, Hector thought. For one thing, it didn't *belong* in this collection with the others. John Denver was no country music outlaw like Waylon and Willie; he was a bespectacled folk singer, a favorite of his beloved grandmother. There was personality and nuance in these lyrics, a longing for things past.

A homesickness.

Hector pulled out Joe's family letters and began to read them. Pecan pie recipes. The baby kicked today. Mundane details, tears, and quiet triumphs. His mind began to wander, and he thought of William Donovan standing over him, fat fists clenched.

"Your partner killed my sister's boy," Donovan had told him. "And you didn't do a thing, Hector. You ran like a coward and let Sean's killer go free."

Hector hadn't dared to rise from the floor. He was thanking his lucky stars to come out of this with only a beating.

Donovan delivered a swift kick to his ribs and said, "You're going to get justice for my Sean. You will find Joe Easterbrook and kill him. Or your precious grandmother will die."

The first time Joe saw the dog, Joe was on the cabin's roof with a bucket of mortar and a trowel. He'd been sealing up cracks in the chimney, enjoying the sting of cold air in his eyes, when he sensed someone—or some*thing*—watching him.

He glanced around warily, cursing himself for leaving his Winchester by the ladder. There. Down the winding dirt road, at the foot of a gnarled oak, a ragged-looking dog sat on its haunches. It was the wrong color and shape to be a coyote, and it was certainly no wolf. A hound of some kind, by the look of its floppy ears, and it was far from home.

Slowly, Joe put down his tools and descended the ladder. The dog continued staring at him, but its ears were back now, and a low growl sounded deep in its throat.

Once on the ground, Joe spread his hands to show they were empty. "Easy there, fella. Easy. Nothing here to hurt you." He took a cautious step forward, but the dog bolted into the woods.

The next evening, Joe saw the dog again, this time sitting much closer to his camp. A male beagle, Joe noticed, probably nine or ten years old from the white in his face. Had a hunter met with an accident in the wilderness, leaving his faithful dog to fend for himself? Or had some heartless bastard dumped him by the roadside?

Regardless of where he came from, there was dried blood at the dog's throat, and the tip of his left ear ended in a jagged line.

This time, Joe did not approach the dog. Instead, he maintained his seated position by the firepit, where a rabbit was roasting on a spit.

"You look like hell, old timer. But from the blood around your mouth, you gave as good as you got."

The beagle's tail thumped the ground once.

"By the fur stretched over your ribs, you could use a meal," Joe said. "Hungry?"

The beagle leaned forward, brown eyes flicking from Joe's face to the rabbit. Back and forth, back and forth. Joe could almost hear his thoughts.

Joe took the sizzling rabbit from the spit, placed it on a wooden plank, and carved it with his hunting knife. The beagle's tail betrayed his hunger, for it began to thump the ground repeatedly.

Joe sliced off the hind legs for himself, then held up the remaining carcass. The beagle was on his feet now, his entire being focused on the meal in Joe's hand. "This is for you, old timer. Eat hearty."

The beagle caught the carcass before it hit the ground, then tore into the meat with a will.

Joe laughed aloud for the first time in weeks. "Now I'll never get rid of you, I suppose."

The dog wagged his tail as if agreeing with this statement, though he retreated to the woods once his meal was done. Their relationship continued this way for another few weeks. At dinnertime, the dog would show up at camp and watch Joe cook his one meal of the day, then eat whatever Joe threw to him: rabbit, fried bacon and eggs, venison.

Joe continued his work on the cabin, the dog watching from the woods. He'd started outside first, working from the top down. For the roof, he'd mortared the cracks in the chimney and caulked any holes in the galvanized steel. Replacing the eaves proved tricky for one man to do, but Joe managed it by positioning multiple ladders beneath his work area to prop up unsupported boards. After clearing away the climbing brambles from the walls, he vigorously cleaned the white pine timbers and resealed them. Finally, he rehung the shutters and replaced the loose boards on the porch.

Inside, the damage was not as bad as he'd feared. Aside from some boards that had popped loose from their joists, the cabin's floor was solid, its construction fundamentally sound. It was just utterly filthy.

Joe began by sweeping away the cobwebs and animal nests, a process that gagged him with the stench of rat urine. The surgical grade masks he'd picked up in town kept his lungs clear of dust, animal dander, and feces stirred up by his broom.

All that remained was to clean and disinfect the floor, repair the loose floorboards, replace the broken windows, hang new curtains, and reseal the floor. The work was exhausting but refreshing, and there were times he forgot about Detroit.

Then one evening in late October, when a waning gibbous

moon was cresting the eastern horizon and the wind had died to nothing, something wonderful happened. As Joe sat before his cooking fire and felt the peace of the West Virginian wilderness penetrate his soul, the beagle walked up and put his chin on Joe's knee.

Joe scratched the dog's ears, and the animal closed his eyes and seemed to relax. "Your name," Joe said after a moment of deep contemplation, "is Old Timer."

The dog's eyes snapped open, and the two locked gazes. This was the primal bond, Joe thought, bred in the bone, a friendship between man and beast since the world began.

"Old Timer."

A playful bark, and Old Timer's paw came up and worried at Joe's hand. *Keep scratching me.* After dinner, when both had eaten all the roasted grouse they could, the beagle curled up at Joe's feet and went to sleep before the fire.

Joe sighed contentedly. "That's the ultimate show of trust, isn't it? Whether it's between two lovers or a man and a dog. You can fall asleep beside me. We are pack, now."

Old Timer kicked his legs in a dream.

"Chasing a rabbit?" Joe asked. "Wish I could sleep as deeply, as peacefully. But I keep seeing a dead girl's face when I close my eyes. She reminds me of something I've tried to forget." Whether it was in a Detroit alley or a rice paddy in Vietnam, the bodies of civilians looked the same.

"I was my best self here, Old Timer. In these woods, with this very rifle. Before I went to war to defend my country. Before Dad died and the family land was sold out from under me."

In the dying firelight, Joe spun a tale for his new companion. He told the dog how he'd gone to war and learned to kill, then returned home to a country that hated him. Spat on him. With a heavy heart, he left West Virginia and hitchhiked to Detroit, where he perfected his trade on the streets—murder. Joe left nothing out, confessing everything—the men he'd killed, the women he'd loved and ultimately disappointed. A cheap life of money, booze, and decades wasted in the service of evil men.

Wolves howled in the distance as night covered the mountain like a shroud. Joe looked into the darkness beyond his fire, his hackles rising. Sound was a funny thing out here. The wolves might be just over the next ridge, or miles away.

Old Timer raised his head at the howls.

"They're out there, all right. The wolves are always out there." Joe took up his Winchester and checked the action. The weapon had a twelve-round capacity, and the only ammo Joe used was Winchester's 100 Years of John Wayne; in his vest pocket above his heart, Joe kept another thirty-eight rounds in the box bearing The Duke's likeness.

As a kid, Joe imagined riding the range with his rifle at his side. The gun had no scope, but that was no matter; the buck-horn style rear sight and the front sight dovetailed into the twenty-four-inch octagonal barrel were all Joe needed. Chambered for .44-40 rounds, he could still drop a deer—or a wolf, if need be—at 150 yards.

The wind shifted, blowing from the north. Joe threw another log on the fire, held out his hands to the flames. It hadn't snowed yet, thank God. The first snow usually fell by mid-November, but it was not unheard of to have snow in late October. A man caught outdoors in a snowstorm might freeze to death by morning.

"Soon, maybe next week, the cabin will be done. We can sleep with a roof over our heads, build our first fire in the fireplace, and cook our meals inside like civilized folk. What do you say to that?"

Old Timer snored in reply. *Whatever you say, Joe. The hearth sounds nice and warm.*

Joe looked to the cabin. In the dancing light of the fire, he could discern his father's rocking chair on the porch. He had a vision of himself in the chair, his guitar in hand and an Irish whiskey on an upturned barrel, with Old Timer asleep at his feet.

When my labors are done, Joe thought. *When the cabin is fully restored to its former glory.*

* * *

La vida no es justa, Hector told himself as he drove the Hummer H2 past an abandoned windmill. That was his grandmother's favorite saying, and Hector agreed. Life wasn't fair. It wasn't fair that a heart attack struck down his father in his prime, or that his mother succumbed to breast cancer the following year, leaving Hector as a burden to a loving but aged grandmother.

It wasn't fair that he'd been pressed into the service of a drug lord to pay the family's enormous medical bills, or for Donovan to seek vengeance for the death of a monster like Sean O'Connell.

And it wasn't fair that ten men were coming to kill one.

"Beautiful country," Donovan said from the passenger's seat. The middle-aged Irishman had insisted on coming to witness what he called *justice.* Whatever this was, it wasn't just. "Take me home, country roads." The man began humming John Denver's ballad to West Virginia.

"It's colder than a penguin's turd," Blinky said from the back seat. The big man wore a thin jogging suit like he was Vladimir Putin about to go for a run. The other men in Donovan's entourage were dressed no better. They would be out of their element in these woods.

"You should've worn something warmer," Hector chided.

"It was fifty degrees in Detroit," Blinky complained. "Can we turn on the Thanksgiving game? The Lions are playing. I want to hear the score."

Donovan's eyes flashed. The man was irritable at the best of times, and the cross-country drive had not helped his mood. "Shut up, Blinky. Find the score on your phone."

"No signal out here," Blinky muttered. "Just trees."

Hector drove across a wooden suspension bridge, praying to God that it would support two Hummers and ten men, then took the next right. His map called this the Old Logging Road, and it twisted for miles into the mountains. Somewhere ahead, they'd find Joe in the middle of a wilderness.

At least, that's what a private investigator named Rainsford promised—a man who specialized in finding people in so-called witness protection programs. Hector had supplied the man with a starting point based on Joe's family letters and the Polaroid picture. Rainsford had done the rest.

Up the Hummers drove, higher and higher into the mountains, on meandering dirt roads. The air was thinning out, Hector felt, and the temperature was dropping. The bright sky overhead—at least what he could see through the pine trees—was clouding over.

Maybe they wouldn't find Joe, Hector hoped. Not that he felt any special kinship for his former partner. Between jobs, they drank together and spoke of trivialities, of women and football. No, it wasn't friendship holding Hector back, and it wasn't quite fear, either.

There was a Greek word for it, something he remembered from high school when reading about Achilles and the Trojan War. When mere mortals dared too much, tried to go beyond the boundaries set by the gods. And the gods struck them down for pride. What was the word?

"Something troubling you, Hector?" Donovan asked.

We are coming to Joe's country. His turf. The sun's about to go down, and the weather report is bad. Men will die today. But Hector kept this to himself and said, "Nothing." He pushed the accelerator.

Old Timer heard the Hummers coming before Joe did. The beagle had been relaxing on the porch by Joe's feet, listening to Joe pluck Johnny Cash's version of "Ghost Riders in the Sky" on his guitar. The cabin was done at last, and the sun was sinking behind the mountain. Above, dark clouds told of a coming snowstorm to mirror the song.

Suddenly, the beagle raised his head, alert.

Joe stopped playing. "What is it?"

The dog growled, his eyes trained on the road, as if he

smelled a wolf. Then Joe heard an answering growl, mechanical in nature. An approaching vehicle, perhaps several, and they'd be here within minutes.

Joe put down his guitar and belted the last of his whiskey. Then he put on his warmest coat and hat, grabbed his Winchester and a pair of night-vision binoculars, and sprinted to the woods as fast as his heart would tolerate. Old Timer followed soundlessly. About 150 yards up the mountain, there was a tree stand Joe used for hunting deer. And it had a perfect view of the clearing in front of the cabin.

Hector stood by the H2, his Beretta drawn. He didn't like the look of the cabin in the gloom, with its windows like eyes staring accusingly at the trespassers. Smoke was curling out of the stone chimney, and inside was a half-eaten dinner on the hearth. On the front porch, they'd found a rocking chair, a guitar, and an upturned rain barrel with an opened whiskey bottle.

Joe's truck was here, but apparently its owner wasn't. Had he gone for a walk in the woods? Was he fishing somewhere up that stream?

The other men were nervous, even Blinky. But not Donovan. The ruddy-faced man was drinking Joe's whiskey, a haughty look on his face.

"He's trapped up here, gents," Donovan said. "Oscar, slash the tires on that truck. Jamal, pass out the flashlights. Ramsey, give me your jacket."

"Boss, it's getting cold," Ramsey whined. Hector watched a single snowflake hit the burly man's face and melt like a tear. More snow began to fall, a gentle but steady drift.

"Exactly. That's why I need your jacket."

"Joe knows we're here," Hector said. "We should take the H2s and fall back. Get away from this cabin."

Donovan drained the whiskey bottle and said, "Don't worry about the cabin, coward." He nodded to a gas canister beside

Joe's truck. "Blinky, get the gas can by that generator. Torch this place."

The big man hesitated. He glanced apprehensively at the trees and said, "What about forest fires?"

"Smokey Bear can kiss my arse," Donovan hissed. "Do it. We'll hide the H2s down the road. When Joe sees the smoke, he'll come racing back. Then, Hector, you'll kill him."

As Blinky approached the cabin, gas can in hand, a shot rang out from the woods. The man collapsed bonelessly to the ground, his open eyes glazed with death.

Donovan and his men scrambled for cover behind the H2s. More shots rang out, each followed by a familiar ratcheting sound Hector had heard in a dozen Westerns. *Joe's out there with that blasted rifle!*

"Sound off!" Donovan called out. "Who's hit?"

Hector heard eight voices for eight men, including himself. Only Blinky was down. Joe was a crack shot, so what was going on? Could the old man even see in this swirling snow and dying daylight?

Donovan chuckled. He slapped Hector on the shoulder and said, "The bastard can't shoot straight in this, any more than we could! He's firing blind. We'll drive away in the darkness and find him when the sun comes up."

Hector laughed bitterly when he realized what Joe's true targets were. *Hubris.* That was the Greek word he was trying to recall.

"He isn't shooting at us." Hector pointed with his Beretta to what was left of their vehicles' tires. Each H2 was lopsidedly resting on two of its rims, and Joe had even shot the spares exposed on the back. "Joe's shooting the tires on the H2s. *We* are the ones trapped on this mountain, not him. We are the hunted."

Full night fell, and the snow began to come down in earnest. Every so often, the Winchester echoed across the mountains of West Virginia.

BURYING OLIVER
John M. Floyd

On a grassy slope overlooking a pond, Bucky Harper stood up, leaned on his shovel, and wiped his forehead with the sleeve of a blue work shirt darkened with sweat. Ninety-percent humidity will do that, and on this July day the hill country of north Mississippi was as steamy as a rainforest. With a weary sigh Bucky trudged through the Johnsongrass to the dirty Ford pickup parked twenty yards away, propped his shovel against its door, and took a long drink from a Thermos of ice water he'd left on the lowered tailgate. Like his shirt, the truck was multicolored: dried brown mud on the surface, faded black paint underneath. Bucky didn't mind. He was no stranger to mud and dirt, or sweat either. For more than ten years now, he and his cousin Vernon had owned and worked the farm their uncle had left them.

Bucky checked his watch—half past noon—and went back to filling in the hole he'd dug. Fifteen minutes later he used the flat of the shovel blade to tamp the dirt smooth and level. He was still bent over, leaning downhill toward the pond, when he heard a voice behind him.

"What the hell you digging, in this kinda heat?"

Bucky straightened up and turned. Sheriff Parnell Morton,

his round face flushed an unhealthy color, stood there with his fat thumbs hooked into an already sagging gun belt.

"I'm not digging. I'm done," Bucky said. "Where'd you come from? I didn't hear a car."

Morton pointed one of the thumbs over his right shoulder. "I parked my cruiser upair in the woods, where the road ends." He tilted his head and grinned. "Scared you, didn't I?"

Bucky glanced past him and back again. "What in the world are you doing out here?"

"Looking for Vern. Need to ask him about that bass boat he's got for sale."

"I hope you buy it," Bucky said. "Maybe he'd get more work done, then."

"Depends how much he wants for it." The sheriff looked around. "Where is he?"

"Vern? Gone to town."

"He's walking all the way to town?"

"How'd you know he's walking?"

Morton took off his hat and ran a hand through his damp hair. "Same way I knew where to find you. I saw you and him in your truck a while ago and saw y'all turn off in this direction. I was gonna follow you, but I got called back to the office, so I'm just now getting here. Since you was riding together and your truck's settin' right there, I figure Vern must be on foot."

"What a detective," Bucky said.

"I am, at that," Morton said. "But you're pulling my leg if you say he's walking to town, 'cause I just drove here from town and I didn't see him on the road."

"You wouldn't have seen him. He cut through the woods."

The sheriff squinted at the dark wall of trees between here and the town of Sebastian. "I don't think so," he said. "Them woods is so thick a fat squirrel couldn't get through."

"Vern can. Him and me grew up on this land. We know all the shortcuts."

"Is that so." Morton calmly scanned the scene—a green valley surrounded by forest—and then focused on the smoothed-over dirt at Bucky's feet. "I asked you what you was digging."

"And I told you I was through digging." Bucky took a red bandanna from his hip pocket and wiped his face. "If you must know, I just buried my dog."

"Your dog? The big collie?"

"The collie belongs to Daisy," Bucky said. "I mean my beagle. Oliver. A moccasin bit him, when him and me was out rabbit hunting this morning. I shot the snake but it was too late for Oliver."

Morton frowned. "Snakebite don't usually work that fast."

"This was a big 'un. Thick as my arm."

"Is that so," he said again. "How is it I ain't never seen this dog you're talking about?"

"Probably because you never went rabbit hunting with me."

The sheriff snorted, hitched his drooping pants up six inches or so—they slid right back down—and continued studying the dirt covering the hole.

Before he could reply, Bucky said, "We spent a lotta time up on this hill, Oliver and me. I figured it'd be a good place to plant him." He jabbed his shovel upright into the ground and looked down at the pond. The water was as still as glass. Somewhere far away, a train whistle blew, the sound thin and mournful in the heat.

After several seconds Bucky snapped out of his reverie, turned, and said, "I'm sorry you missed Vern. I'll tell him to call you about the boat."

Morton nodded, then tilted his head again and fixed Bucky with a stare. "Know what I think?"

"What?"

"I think maybe it's Vern downair in that hole."

Bucky blinked. "*What?*"

"You and that cousin a yours been fighting over just about ever'thing for years. It wouldn't surprise me a bit if you finally decided to do him in."

"Do him in?" Bucky's eyes narrowed to slits. "I can't believe you're saying that to me."

"Just speaking my mind. Truth is, I think you been lyin' to me ever since I got here."

"Look here, Mort—you want me to dig Oliver up? Show you his poor carcass? I will if that's what you want."

"No need," the sheriff said. "I told you, I think I already know what you got buried here. What I'm saying is, I don't blame you for doing it. I prob'ly woulda done it too, if it was me."

Bucky shook his head. "You don't know what you're talking about. That fight Vern and me had in town a while back? We were both drunk as skunks that night."

"I ain't talking about fistfights. I'm talking about Vern and that little wife a yours."

He froze. "What?"

"You heard me."

A long silence dragged by.

"Vern and Daisy?"

"Come on, Bucky. Don't play dumb. Everybody in the county knows them two been foolin' around. Goin' on a year now."

Both men stayed quiet for half a minute or more, each studying the other. Bucky's cheeks had reddened, his eyes darkened. Off to the east, a crow cawed. A bee buzzed past.

"You got anything to say for yourself?" the sheriff asked.

Bucky cleared his throat. He was clenching and unclenching his fists. "I'll say this. If you're accusing me of murder, then why ain't you arresting me?"

Morton broke out a sly smile. "Because, like I just told you, I understand why you did it. Also...well, to be honest"—he turned and spat into the grass—"I'd like more'n just a used fishin' boat. I'd like a new car, maybe something sporty." He put his hat back on. "But I ain't greedy."

"What does *that* mean?"

"Thirty thousand oughta do it."

Again, Bucky stared.

"Nobody else needs to know, about any of it," Morton said. "Nobody but us two."

"Thirty thousand *dollars?*"

"I'll need it today, though. In cash."

They both fell silent. In the pond below, a fish jumped and splashed.

"I can't do that," Bucky said.

"Sure you can. Look, I know that farm of yours and Vern's—which is all yours, now that he's gone—is one of the biggest anywhere around here." The sheriff waved a hand at their surroundings. "This hill, this little valley, this hid-away pond, all this is still on your land, right? And we're more'n a mile from your house. You're well off, boy—if you ain't got the money now, you can get it." His face hardened. "Bucky? Look at me."

Their eyes met, and held.

"Thirty thousand. I'll be at my office. You call me when you have it."

They stared at each other for several more seconds. Then Sheriff Morton turned and headed back toward the woods.

Bucky Harper sagged down into the grass and sat there motionless, peering into the distance and thinking. Five minutes later he came to a decision. He rose to his feet, walked to his pickup, and spent a while looking through the glove compartment. Then he returned to the grave, where he stripped off his shirt and pulled the shovel out of the ground.

When Vernon Harper got back from town, Bucky was sitting bare-chested on the edge of the open hole, dangling his feet inside. It was much deeper now than it had been, and longer too, with a three-foot-high mound of fresh and fragrant dirt beside it. Something small and blanket-wrapped, thankfully not yet fragrant, lay beside it also. Bucky sat with the shovel across his lap like a shotgun.

"Looks like you musta dug all the way to China," Vernon said. "Bring back any geisha girls?" Then, seeing the wrapped bundle and the look on Bucky's face: "Sorry, Buck. I been treating this like a day off for both of us. I shouldn't joke with a man who's burying his dog."

"It's okay. Come here, I got something to show you."

Vernon walked over, careful to skirt around Oliver, and took a seat on the opposite edge of the hole, across from his cousin. Both were so sweaty their faces gleamed in the afternoon sun. "Before I forget," Vernon said, "Mr. Albritton at the bank said we got a CD coming due next month."

"Whatever. You didn't run into Sheriff Morton, did you?"

"Didn't go to that end of town. I stopped to make our regular deposit, then grabbed a milkshake at Polly's and headed back. Why?"

"No reason," Bucky said. "How about Daisy—did you see her?"

"Why would I see Daisy? Ain't she at the house?"

"Probably."

Vernon glanced at Bucky's pickup, parked a short distance away. "I sure was glad to see you're still here with that truck. I like walking, but I've done enough of it today."

Not that it seemed to have bothered him much. Vernon had always been tougher than Bucky, and better looking too, and never seemed to tire or complain no matter what the task was. And their lives had never been easy. Both had grown up together here in Sebastian County—same school, same church, same friends—and since neither had siblings they'd always been more like brothers than first cousins. After the deaths of both their unlucky fathers and the disappearance of both their worthless mothers during the boys' high school years—what a go-round *that* had been—their fathers' younger and childless brother Aaron took them in. When Uncle Aaron died six years later, Bucky and Vernon found themselves sole owners of one of the biggest farms in this part of the country. Some time after that, Bucky met and married Daisy, Vernon built and moved alone into a second house nearby, and the three Harpers managed a hard-working and surprisingly profitable enterprise. Bucky and Vernon disagreed a lot, but they'd stayed the course. Until now.

Vernon was looking at Oliver's covered body. One white paw was poking out from under the blanket. "Want me to help you lower him in?"

"I'll do it myself," Bucky said. After all, he had already done it once. And then taken him out again.

Vernon nodded. Gazing into the hole, he said, "You know, this is one helluva big grave for a little beagle hound. And way too long."

"I mighta overdone it a little. But if I hadn't"—Bucky opened his right hand. In its palm were two tiny stones, dirty but gleaming in the sun—"I wouldn't have found these."

Vernon's mouth fell open.

"Ever seen a diamond?" Bucky asked.

"What? You mean—"

"I mean a dug-up diamond."

Vernon looked at them again, then at Bucky, then down into the hole. "But—there ain't no diamonds in Mississippi."

"Why not? There are in Arkansas," Bucky said. "And that ain't far away."

Vernon lowered his head and stared again into the hole.

Bucky pointed. "Right down there. On the far end, in that corner." When Vernon hesitated Bucky said, "Climb down, see for yourself."

Slowly, his eyes glittering brighter than the stones in his cousin's hand, Vernon stepped down into the grave and stooped for a closer look. Behind and above him, Bucky put the two stones into his pocket and gripped the shovel in both hands like a baseball bat. As he raised it high over his head, he could hear the sheriff's voice in his mind, just as he'd heard it over and over for the past hour.

I'm talking about Vern and that little wife a yours...

***

Bucky had refilled most of the hole when Daisy showed up. He was surprised to see her. For what he'd always considered to be a remote spot, today this corner of the farm was Grand Central Station. He looked up from his work long enough to notice her jogging suit, which told him all he needed to know about how she got here. For Daisy Harper—transplanted Yankee, fitness freak, marathon runner—a mile was nothing but a hop, skip, and jump. She wasn't even breathing hard.

"Figured you'd be finished by now," she said to him.

"Almost. Took longer than I thought."

"I didn't hear you humming. You always hum a tune while you work."

"Not just while I work. I hum when I'm happy." He went back to filling the grave. "This ain't a happy day."

"No, it's not." She stood there a moment, still and solemn. "I'm gonna miss little Oliver. Not as bad as you will, but I did love him."

Among others, he thought.

As if reading his mind, she looked around, almost exactly as Sheriff Morton had done, and asked, "Where's Vern?"

"Probably getting a bite to eat. He rode this far with me, then hiked into town through the woods. A bank errand. I expect he'll be back soon."

She smiled. "Good old Vern. He likes walking as much as I like running."

"Yep. Good old Vern." Bucky threw another shovelful of dirt into the hole. The one that now contained two of his former friends—one a lot more loyal than the other.

Daisy frowned. "Are you okay, honey? You look a little...put out."

"I'm fine," he said, eyeing the shovel blade as he worked. Nothing like fresh dirt to clean off troublesome stains.

"By the way," she said, "have you seen my diamond earrings?

The fake ones, I mean. I think I might have left them in the truck's glovebox after we drove to that party at the Benningtons' the other night. When my car was in the shop."

He shook his head. "Ain't seen 'em. But," he said, brightening, "I found a whole cluster of four-leaf clovers. Never saw anything like it."

"Are you kidding me? I collect four-leaf clovers."

"I know you do." He straightened up, stretched his back muscles, and pointed. "Right over there, next to the truck."

"Show me."

They walked together to a dark-green swatch of clover. "Where exactly?" she asked.

"Right there." He pointed again, and she bent over. "Look hard and you'll see 'em."

Behind her, he set his feet, flexed his arms, and raised the shovel.

It took less than a minute to load Daisy's body into the front seat, move the gearshift to neutral, and lock the doors. Bucky didn't want one of them popping open at the wrong time. He'd moved the truck earlier, after putting Oliver in the hole on top of Vernon, such that its front tires were positioned at the very edge of the steepest part of the slope. All he had to do now was give it a push and let it roll straight and true all the way down the hill and into the pond. The ground was too dry to allow any evidence of tire marks, and Bucky knew how deep the water was there—he and his cousin had helped their Uncle Aaron dig the pond, years ago. Sure enough, the old black and brown pickup rolled down the hill and sank like a three-ton rock.

Afterward, standing high on the slope and watching the last ripples fade from the pond's surface, Bucky checked his watch. Not yet three o'clock. He took out his cell phone and punched in the sheriff's number.

"You got it?" Morton asked.

"Some of it," Bucky said.

"How much?"

"Three thousand. I had to sell my truck and all my tools."

"That's not enough."

"It's a start," Bucky said. "You'll get the rest by the weekend."
A long pause. Then: "Where are you, right now?"

"Same place as before."

"I don't know," Morton said. "I don't like where I had to leave the car."

Bucky knew what that meant: too visible. "This time, drive on through the woods, past the road's end," he said. "I'll be watching for you. I'll show you where to park." *Exactly where*, Bucky thought.

When he'd disconnected, Bucky put on his sweaty shirt, checked the load in the revolver he'd taken from underneath the seat of his truck, and sat down in the grass to wait.

It was still hot, but the sky was clear overhead, and a slight breeze was stirring the leaves of the trees. He looked again at the white column of clouds on the horizon, the surrounding forest, the steep slope falling away at his feet, the blue-green water of the pond at the bottom of the hill. He was glad they'd dug it deep, he and Vern and their uncle. There was plenty of room in there for another vehicle.

He glanced to his left, at what he now thought of as the gravesite, and made a note to stop by there when this was done, and get his shovel. It was the one thing he wanted to take back home with him, today. A handy tool, that shovel.

He found himself humming a tune.

SLIDE

Ann Aptaker

Legit jobs are hard to come by if you're less than a year out of prison, you've got a jailhouse scar on your cheek on a face not too pretty to begin with, and your recent birthday landed you on the wrong side of young. It took every smile she could fake and every "please" and "thank you" she could muster without gagging to get this gig.

She's been working in the bodega almost six months now, a boring, backbreaking job that barely pays the bills. It's tough to earn decent dough when the boss keeps changing your hours, even cutting them to the bone at the last minute. Sometimes her pay envelope has more lint in it than cash. But the gig's better than prison, and her parole officer says if she can just hang on and stay out of trouble, he can get her into the state's job training program for ex-cons. She could learn computer programming, or maybe healthcare work. Helping people. Okay, she figures, why not? Maybe it's time to start helping people instead of ripping them off.

For now, she squelches her frustration and boredom, just keeps stacking the shelves with salsa and chips, stocks the freezer with microwave chicken wings, tater tots, and tubs of ice cream. She keeps the cooler full of beer, refills the coffee machine, mops the floor.

The only thing she doesn't do is work the cash register. The counter help does that, securely locked behind bulletproof glass.

The boss gave her a job, but he won't trust her to handle the cash. Not that she blames him. Who'd trust a convicted thief? Still, the insult hurts. And scares her. Because like her parole officer says, she has to work hard to earn society's trust, but she's not sure she knows how. Prison never taught her. Her here-today-gone-tomorrow mother never taught her. Her never-there-at-all father never taught her. Best she can do is stifle the urge to steal a few cans of soup.

She's stocking six packs in the beer cooler when she hears, "Slide?" from a guy suddenly behind her. "Angie Slide?"

She knows the voice and she shudders at the sound of the name. She hasn't been called Slide since she got out of prison. She goes by her full name now, Angela Slidell. As far as she's concerned, Slide is dead.

"Bobby," she says, turning to look at the guy. He's still rough and rugged in his short black coat, the collar turned up. Still fast with a pearly smile, the devil's light in his blue eyes. Angie Slide used to get a kick out of his aura of danger. It came in handy when they pulled jobs and some civilian got in the way. Angela Slidell, though, has no use for Bobby or his danger.

"Listen," she says, "whatever trouble you're bringing, you can just march it right out again. I got a legit job here, and you're the last—"

"Hey!" he says, palms up, smiling his do-you-wanna-dance smile. "I just came in for a six pack and a bag of chips."

"And you just happened to come in here, huh? Aren't you a little out of your patch?"

"Look, I didn't know you work here," he says. "I didn't even know you're out of lockup. I'm just passing through, catching a night's sleep at the Night Owl motel until I move on in the morning."

She hears an old familiar music in the way he says it, steady, with confidence underneath. It's not the offhand chitchat of a drifter. It's the way people sound when they have purpose, a goal, a destination. It's the way Bobby always sounded before he and Slide knocked off a store or a gas station or some other joint with cash. Even an out-of-the-way bank.

"Get your beer and chips, Bobby, then go enjoy your night. Have a nice trip tomorrow." She turns away from him, moves to the dairy cooler, straightens up containers of milk, but watches his reflection in the glass door. She doesn't breathe until he walks out of the bodega.

The only good thing about her ramshackle, rent-by-the-week bungalow is the quiet. After eighteen months of prison noise—the barked orders, the violence, the clang of iron bars, women's cries in the night—she welcomes the quiet of this crummy bungalow on a dirt road outside the city.

The view's a peaceful change from prison, too. Outside her window there's nothing but scrub bushes, a few trees, the night sky, the city's lights in the distance. There's no crowded hallways, no parade of tan jumpsuits, no guards with nightsticks they're too eager to use. Outside her bungalow there's nothing and no one.

Inside, there's just her.

Sleep usually comes easy after her backbreaking days of lift, carry, and stack at the bodega, but there's no sleep tonight. She's tried for an hour or so, but all she gets for her effort is prickly wakefulness. She feels like a stranger in her own skin. Even her bed doesn't seem to know her, offering no cozy welcome, no lullaby embrace.

She knows why. It's because of Bobby. Sure, she got over the lure of his pretty eyes long ago, but his confidence, his sense of purpose when he told her he was moving along in the morning, got inside her, seeped deep where Angie Slide has been shut away, sleeping.

Angela Slidell can't sleep because Angie Slide is waking up.

She starts to cry, the way one cries at seeing a long-lost family member who wanders back through the door, the family member who thought you were swell, who respected your talent. Yeah, Angie Slide had talent, all right. One of the best light-fingers and break-in artists around. It's why Bobby called her Slide: she was good at sliding her hands into people's pockets, good at sliding herself in and out of stores or banks or houses, slide like a greased string through a keyhole.

She gets out of bed.

A full moon lights her way along the dirt road. There's no bus on this outside-of-town route after midnight, and it's half past that now. She has to walk to the main road to catch the all-night bus.

The night air feels good on her face. The moonlight, shadowed here and there by drifting clouds or branches of trees, welcomes her, welcomes Angie Slide. Moonlight and shadows are Slide's home. She's missed home.

She's not enjoying the walk, though. Her feet kick up dirt, some of it gets into her shoes, a worn-out pair of thrift-store Nikes. She'll make sure that situation changes after she hooks up with Bobby, gets in on what he's up to, partners up with him again for more jobs. She'll have cash in her pocket again. Forget this walking crap; she'll get a car. Angie Slide doesn't walk; Angie Slide rides in style.

She's smiling. She feels joy for the first time in months. The joy flows through her, warms her, gives her muscles renewed suppleness as she makes her way along the dirt road. She may not like the walk along this dusty stretch but she likes the feel of her legs, likes how smoothly they slide her through the night.

She takes her hands out of her jacket pockets, looks at them in the moonlight, opens and closes her fingers, exercising them, getting to know them again. She rubs her fingertips against each other, brings their sensitivity back to life. The idea of using her hands and fingers to stock shelves and mop floors disgusts her. It's like asking a thoroughbred racehorse to pull a junk wagon.

The light of the main road is up ahead. She walks a little faster to catch a bus that will take her away from Angela Slidell's dreary bungalow and toward Angie Slide's life of cash and kicks.

There's only one other passenger on the bus, a guy in a tan lumber jacket, his tool belt on his lap. He's sleeping in his seat, his head down, his brown cap slipping over his face. He reminds Slide of a bulging potato sack.

The bus drives past the bodega. It's closed and dark for the night. She's tempted to open the window and spit at it or give the place the finger, but decides to just ignore it, pass it by along with the rest of Angela Slidell's boring grind.

The bus glides by a liquor store still open, its red neon sign an invitation to middle-of-the-night oblivion. Next door is a used-car lot. Seeing it dredges up the lousy memory of the night the cops pinched her with her hand in the till. Oh sure, she got into the place okay, picking the lock and sliding in like always, but that night Bobby was laid up with the flu and she used another guy for a partner and lookout. The only thing he looked out for was himself, sold her out before the heist even started. She swore revenge on the creep but was spared the trouble. A freak accident on a rainy night on a slick road took care of it for her. The guy's car was in the middle of the five-car pileup, his body crushed to pulp and splinters. She laughed when she heard about it in prison.

The bus moves into the outskirts of the city. More light seeps into the bus. The Night Owl motel isn't far now. Slide's life isn't far now.

It's as if her fingers sense it. Their tips are warm. An electric tingle slithers through her fingers to her palms. Even her hands are eager to get back to doing what they were once so good at, and never again bear the insult of stacking six packs and mopping floors.

Her fingers curl, impatient. The Night Owl and Bobby are just a few minutes away, but the sleeping potato sack on the bus presents a handy opportunity to try her skills again, maybe score a few bucks, too.

She slides from her seat, focuses on the guy's right front pants pocket. Maybe there's a wallet in there, maybe not. Though a few bucks would be cool, it's the thrill of the lift that calls to her now. There'll be plenty of money later, after she hooks up with Bobby, gets back in the action.

She takes her time, slides into an aisle seat across from Mr. Potato Sack, keeps her eye on his pants pocket. She figures her best play is to make the lift just as she pulls the cord to signal the driver to let her off at her stop.

The light of the approaching city rolls through the bus, the light of streetlamps, colorful neon signs, red and green traffic lights. It's like a dream now, being on the bus. She's calm. Her hands feel supple. She can feel her own blood running through her fingers. She likes the way her hands look in the wash of light streaming through the bus.

The Night Owl is near.

She stands up. She pulls the cord with her right hand, and bends to Mr. Potato Sack, slides her left hand into his pants pocket. Her fingertips feel a wallet.

She smiles.

She waits to look in the wallet until the bus pulls away, gets beyond this block of gas stations, a saloon, and the Night Owl motel, its yellow Vacancy sign flashing.

Jackpot. There's 130 bucks in Mr. Potato Sack's wallet. Slide's not one for New Age-y stuff, but she figures this is a good omen, the universe agreeing that she's wasted her talents long enough. It's time to respect them again.

The Night Owl motel, a single-story row of rooms with the office at the end, is just ahead. Slide's sure the office is still open. These roadside motels get transient traffic at all hours. Truckers, hookers, people like Bobby passing through. She hopes whoever's working the office won't give her trouble about handing over Bobby's room number. After the elegantly delicate lift of Mr. Potato Sack's wallet, she'd hate to have to use her hands for more bluntly brutal work.

She doesn't need to worry about it after all. Among the half dozen vehicles parked at the motel, each in front of a room, she spots Bobby's pickup in front of room number eleven. It's the same green Chevy pickup he had before she went to prison. Same Disney World bumper sticker.

A C-and-thirty in her pocket, and no trouble with a suspicious late-night motel clerk, the night couldn't be running any smoother. She's sliding right back into the life she's missed. Sliding like a greased string through a keyhole.

Sliding into a sudden bright light and vicious pain cracking into her head. Sliding down to the ground in the motel parking lot. She blinks past the light and the pain. Mr. Potato Sack stands above her, his tool belt in one hand, a wrench in the other. The wrench slams down on her face.

She slides into darkness.

SUNSET BRUNETTE
C.W. Blackwell

I hadn't checked the fuel tanks all night.

Most nights, I'd check them well before midnight, when there were still a few customers around to notice if someone jacked me up and robbed the place. It's happened before. Not to me, and not this station, but it happened at the 76 station across the street just a few months back. A couple of meth-heads coldcocked Niles Kopecki with a brick and ransacked the minimart, stole the register and safe. Niles pulled through, but the poor kid still doesn't know what year it is and can't pronounce his own last name. All for six hundred bucks and a tank of gas.

Minimum wage, maximum risk.

It's the goddamn American way.

So I put off checking the tanks until three a.m., and it wasn't until I got my second gauge reading that I heard it: a woman's voice—*crying*. I set the gauge stick on the ground, tightened the tank lid. I thought maybe the voice came from somewhere down the street. I looked up and down the block. No cars, nobody out on foot. Just the traffic lights signaling to a dreaming city.

Then I heard it again. *Closer this time.*

I returned the gauge stick to the rack behind the minimart and that's when I saw her, sitting cross-legged on the trunk of a late-'90s Honda Accord. Brunette, early twenties. Black sweatshirt and jeans. She wore a red bandanna that covered most of her face.

"Hey handsome," she said. She said it like she'd been waiting there behind the minimart all night. "You need some company?"

There was something familiar about her—*something about the eyes.*

"I heard crying," I said. "Was that you?"

"Had to get your attention somehow."

"Well now you have it. Do I know you?"

"You didn't answer my question."

"I've already got two strikes with the boss," I said. "It's a shitty job, but I need it."

"I need work too, Charlie." She pointed to the polyester patch on my uniform. "That is your name, isn't it?"

"That's right."

"Want to see something, Charlie?"

She didn't wait for me to respond—she just lifted her sweatshirt and flashed me. The first thing I thought was that maybe I could use the company after all, and the next thing was whether the boss would check the surveillance cameras when he came in tomorrow. Then I saw the overhead camera had an old T-shirt draped over the unit, blinding the lens.

Next came the metallic ratchet of a revolver.

A gun barrel pressed into my spine.

"Don't move, shithead." A young man's voice behind me, nervous and loud.

I put my hands in the air.

"I'm not going to fight you," I said. All I could think about was Niles trying to say his last name—*Kop-p-p-eck-i*—spit hanging from the corners of his mouth. "Take what you want."

The kid already had my wallet out. He found eight bucks and a nickel bag of shitty Mexican weed in the billfold. An old condom behind my debit card. I wouldn't miss it. "Charles Tillman," he said, reading my license. "Still live on Fairway?"

"No," I said. "That's my parents' house." I regretted it instantly.

"Your parents, huh?"

"Their old house. Nobody lives there anymore."

But I wasn't a good liar. He could hear it in my voice.

"Nobody lives there? So, if it caught fire, nobody would get hurt?"

"Look, man." I felt my cool slipping. They had me right where they wanted me. "Just tell me what you want."

He kneed me in the thigh, causing me to turn. It took all I had not to fall.

"I'll give the orders," he said.

"Take it easy, Scotty," said the girl.

Scotty didn't like this. "You said my name."

With sass: "Sorry, *Scotty*."

"Look, I don't care about any of that," I said. "You want the money in the register? I'll bring it out. I'll throw in a case of beer, too. I don't give a shit. This doesn't have to be complicated."

I took a good look at the kid. Just another low-life mountain tweaker with a scabby face and teeth like wooden pegs. I'd grown up with these kids, seen them waste away in their sun-scarred mountain Hondas, racing from one petty crime to the next. Maybe a part of me didn't blame him. Maybe kids like Scotty took a good long look at the odds and knew they didn't have a chance at playing it straight. So they didn't bother. But you could play the *maybe game* all day long. Maybe the only way to measure a kid like Scotty was by his gram-a-day meth habit and the three good teeth he had left in his head.

"Bring me the money from the register, then bring me the safe." Scotty turned and addressed the girl. "You know what to do."

She followed me around the building to the aluminum double-doors of the minimart. Nobody in the store but us. On a normal night, I'd be making a fresh pot of coffee by now and getting ready to give the bathroom a once-over. Once I got rid of Scotty and Bandanna Girl, I'd still need to get the coffee ready for the PD and the unending questions they'd inevitably ask.

I grabbed a package of breath mints from the counter and swiped it across the barcode scanner.

"What are those for?" she said.

"They're for you. I can smell your breath from under the bandanna."

She crossed her arms. "Oh, can you?"

"Meth mouth is a hell of a thing. When my cousin got hooked, you could smell her from down the street."

"You're screwing with me, aren't you?"

I tapped the register and the cash drawer popped open. "I sure am. I needed to ring something up to get the cash out."

She laughed, one eyebrow raised. "You're a real asshole, aren't you?"

Then I knew.

Becky Santorini.

Back in junior high, we'd hang out after class. Mostly, we'd smoke weed and cigarettes down in the creek with a couple other burn-out friends. We'd fantasize about leaving town one day to some buzzy, neon-lit city. Maybe we fooled around a couple times. I remember thinking she was more interesting than everyone gave her credit for. Sort of quirky. When she didn't show up freshman year, I figured she'd gotten her wish and moved out of the county.

"You always struck me as one of the smart ones, Becky."

She froze when I said her name.

"Forget it," I said, slapping the cash on the counter. "You and Scotty deserve each other. I'll be a nice guy and give you ten minutes before I call it in. For old times' sake."

She gathered the cash, folded it into the front pocket of her jeans. The digital clock above the soda machine read 3:20 a.m. She glanced at the surveillance camera and adjusted her bandanna.

"Listen Charlie, I'm not really with that guy."

I gave a quick shrug. "You didn't say shit when he stuck that pistol in my spine."

"He wasn't going to shoot you. I wouldn't have let him."

"Oh good, I feel better."

"I mean it."

"Was he the one that put Niles in the hospital?"

She looked at her shoes. "It's not what you think, Charlie."

"What am I thinking?"

"That I'm a tweaker. A criminal. I'm not."

"What then?"

She looked at the clock and scanned the windows as if any minute Scotty would come bursting in with his pistol, popping off rounds like firecrackers. From her back pocket she unfolded a red flyer with bold writing on the front and laid it on the counter.

"Scotty's buying dope, but I'm saving for this."

I looked.

An announcement for a downtown burlesque show. I didn't even know they had clip art for pole dancing and latex pants. She folded the flyer and returned it carefully to the back pocket of her jeans.

"So you're knocking over gas stations for some titty show?"

"I'm a dancer, Charlie. I need money for all the expensive costumes."

"What's the point if they just end up on the floor?"

"There's more to it than that. I don't expect you to understand."

"Try me."

Becky rolled the sleeves of her sweatshirt up to her elbows. I'd never seen so many scars. Like she'd dipped her arms in acid. She must have read my expression because her face grew sad and she quickly unrolled her sleeves again.

"There's a cream that covers it up, but it's expensive, too."

"What happened?"

"They call it PMLE. It's a sun allergy. I've got it worse than most."

I'd never heard of such a thing, but it explained why she'd disappeared all those years ago. I couldn't help but feel genuinely intrigued by her strange condition, not to mention her life of crime and exotic dancing. I still wasn't happy about the bullshit she and Scotty were putting me through, but talking to her felt like we'd picked up where we left off in junior high.

A car horn blared and her eyes widened.

"I need the money in the safe, too," she said quickly.

"Tell Scotty I don't know the combo."

"He's really not going to like that."

"Will he hurt you?"

"No, but it'll upset him."

"That's too bad. Maybe you can give him a hug."

Another honk.

"You'll still give us a head start?"

I looked at the clock. "Your ten minutes start now."

I'd been a little too chatty with Becky during the robbery, at least that's what my boss said after he reviewed the tape and fired me on the spot. Of course, I told him I didn't know who she was, told the cops the same. I said she was spun up on dope, talking a mile a minute. I insisted it wasn't much of a conversation at all. They did, however, appreciate when I gave up Scotty's name and description, and it made everyone feel just warm and fuzzy enough to let me walk away from the whole ordeal.

Still, I walked away broke and under a cloud of suspicion.

I spent the next few days filling out job applications and selling old items on the internet. A game console, some sports equipment. I hocked a few pieces of junk silver from a coin collection that I'd had since grade school. I knew it wouldn't add up to much, but it might stave off the worst of it till I landed my next minimum wage job.

If I landed one at all.

While out walking the neighborhood to clear my head, I realized I'd passed Niles Kopecki's house on Whispering Pines Drive. It felt a little strange knowing who had ruined his life, knowing they were still at large, prowling the county for their next midnight robbery victim. Before I knew it, I found myself knocking on the door. It was the middle of fall, pumpkins on the front porch. A wreath of colorful maple leaves hanging in the window. After a few seconds, the door opened, and Judy Kopecki answered.

"Charlie?" She looked surprised, but pleasantly so. Niles and I had played baseball together back in grade school, and I'd gone to a few of his birthday parties. She'd even worked with my mother at the bank for a year or two. "What a surprise— what brings you here?"

"I was just in the neighborhood, thought I'd say hello."

"Niles is in the dining room. I'm sure he'd love to see you."

Maybe he was happy to see me, maybe not. His face didn't leave much to interpret. He sat at the dining table with a bowl of oatmeal in front of him, and by the looks of it, most of it had ended up where it wasn't supposed to.

"Hey buddy, it's been a while." I didn't know what else to say.

"H-hey," he said. He pawed at his messy face and sort of bulged his eyes at me. He tried to say my name, but Judy spared him the effort.

"He has to re-learn how to eat," she said. "Sorry about the mess."

"It's fine. I understand."

"He's able to play a few video games if you want to stick around."

"No, I was just passing through. You heard about the new robbery?"

"Oh my God, yes. You weren't working that night, were you?"

"I was."

She pulled out a chair and had me sit down. I told her what I told the police, about Scotty and the pistol in my back. How the girl never showed her face. Judy hung on every syllable. She watched me with an intensity I'd never seen before in my life, like she'd jump straight down my throat if I opened wide enough.

"It's them, isn't it? The ones who attacked Niles?"

"I think so."

"Oh honey, you got lucky."

Niles dumped another spoonful of oatmeal in his lap.

"I talked my way out of getting hurt, but the owner fired me for it."

"Fired, huh? That figures. Well, you just think about that reward money. When the story broke, it came in from all over the country. We're a Gold Star family, in case you didn't remember. Any little detail might put it all in your pocket, sweetie."

"I didn't realize there was a reward."

"Have you been living under a rock? It's all over Facebook."

"How much?"

"Thirty-eight thousand, last I checked. Everyone feels terrible for my poor boy."

I exchanged glances with Niles. Even he looked surprised.

"Maybe I'll see a hypnotist or something," I said. "Scratch out a new detail or two. I saw a TV show where they did that and it really brought the whole case together."

"Good idea, Charlie. I'll even pay for it." She fished a handful of twenties from her wallet and folded them into my hand. "Think hard."

We exchanged goodbyes and I walked the few short blocks to my studio apartment, cracked open a beer. I'd been covering for Becky since the robbery, and now I needed to reconsider. Sure, we'd been friends ten years back. Maybe more than friends at times. And it's true I felt a little sorry about how she ended up. But the money changed everything. With no job and my reputation in doubt, I'd lose my apartment come wintertime.

Or, I could tuck myself in beneath a blanket of reward cash.

It was time to pull Becky Santorini out of the shadows.

Maybe I'd even give her another ten-minute head start.

* * *

It didn't take long to track down one of the red flyers Becky showed me that night. I found one stapled to a telephone pole outside a laundromat in the gritty beach town of Santa Cruz, just a few exits down the highway. I snapped a photo with my phone and bought a coffee at the little laundromat cafe, sipping carefully and looking over the details. They called the show "Santa Cruz Cabaret," and it listed a few campy names like Hott Waters, Venus La Doll, and Pussy von Plum. I wondered which name Becky would pick for herself, or if maybe she'd been included in the *"...and many more"* category of dancers.

Luckily, I didn't have to wait long.

I pulled up to the Blink Bar a few nights later, hoping I might catch Becky in the crowd before the show started. The door price was more than I'd spend on a night out, but I used the cash Judy Kopecki gave me for the hypnotist. I didn't feel bad about it, either. I told Judy I needed to work out the details and that's exactly what I was doing. Soon, they'd have Scotty tied up in a neat little bow and I'd take a much-needed break from the hellscape of retail shift-work.

Luckily, admission came with a free drink ticket.

And brother, I was thirsty.

I ordered a Jack and Coke and watched the crowd. Mostly young, tattooed twenty-somethings like me with a mixture of middle-aged weirdos and other exotic dancers off the clock. The MC came on stage, a curvy redhead in some kind of skimpy wizard costume. She told a few jokes and introduced the first act, another redhead named Sweet Ginger. She did a thing with fire batons and a boa constrictor that had me genuinely intrigued. I'd ordered a second drink and was halfway through my third when I felt a hand on my shoulder.

"I can't believe you came, Charlie." Becky pressed close, took a sip from my drink. She'd done her hair and makeup for the show, but hadn't yet changed into her burlesque costume. She looked stunning. "Did you come to watch my act?"

I shook my head. "You already showed me your tits, Becky."

"I hope it's not about—"

"The robbery? Of course it is."

"I see," she said, looking me over like a bad deal. "You want to extort me. Is that it? I thought you were a better guy than that, Charlie. I'm not a hooker if that's what you're getting at. The hair and makeup is just an act."

"That's not it either."

"Then what?"

I told her about Judy Kopecki and the reward money, how I intended to turn Scotty in, if I could just get a few more details. Her eyes searched the crowd as I explained it to her, as if she wasn't interested in any of it. When I finished, she checked her makeup in her compact mirror.

"There are lots of Scottys out there, Charlie. The one they want doesn't have a local record. What you're really saying is that you're turning me in to get to Scotty."

"I'm cutting you a little slack is what I'm doing. I don't even know why. Maybe I find this whole burlesque thing kind of endearing. The fact that you can't even go out during the day like some kind of vampire—"

"Don't you dare call me that."

"Give me his last name, Becky. Maybe tell me where he's from. Then get out of town. Once you land somewhere, call me and I'll wire you a couple grand of the reward money. That's at least four gas stations you won't have to knock over. It's your best shot."

She rattled the ice in my empty drink. "You gonna let me finish my act?"

"I'll wait till the morning, but no later."

"That's still not much time."

"I'm doing you a favor, Becky."

"Why doesn't it feel that way?"

"Because you're as guilty as he is, you just can't see it."

The cocktail waitress passed by and Becky lifted a mai tai from her platter, gave the waitress five bucks and a wink. She

drank it halfway down and handed the rest of the drink to me.
"His name is O'Shea. Scotty O'Shea. I met him in Sacramento
while on circuit with the girls. He overheard me crying into my
phone about not being able to afford my own costumes, and we
hit our first gas station that very night."
"He's from Sacramento?"
"No, some methed-up foothill town. Auburn, I think."
"You think?"
"I'm sure."
"That'll do." I scribbled my phone number on the back of a
cocktail napkin. "Buy a prepaid phone and call me. I'll hold up
my end."
"You gonna stick around for the act, tough guy?"
I considered the mai tai. "I'd need another Jack and Coke.
This shit is a joke."
"I can arrange that."

I stumbled out of the Blink Bar a few hours later, half drunk
and without any indication where I'd left my car. I'd blown
through Judy Kopecki's money and even dipped into my own,
downing whiskey and tossing small bills onto the stage with
each act's big finale. Becky came on toward the end dressed as a
sexy street cop, announced with the name "Hannah Handcuffs."
She held the other girls at gunpoint, then cuffed and spanked
them in some comical BDSM routine. I'd never seen anyone have
so much fun. She even pulled me onto the stage and gave me a
square pat on the ass, but I bailed out when she brandished her
baton.
Who knows what she had planned with that thing.
The fog had rolled in by the time I left, the moon just a rumor
beyond the orange haze of lamplights. Street musicians played
old Django Reinhardt tunes and a brimstone preacher stood on a
milk crate, goading the locals with threats of damnation. I
wandered up and down the side streets, thumbing the key fob,

hoping to hear my Toyota chirp. By the time I found the car, I had to piss like a racehorse, so I ducked into an alley and let a greasy old dumpster have it. I wasn't even halfway done when I heard that telltale ratchet of a revolver and felt the barrel press into my spine.

"Are we going to do this every Saturday night, Scotty?" It was just a guess. I couldn't see for sure who had a gun in my back.

Still, it felt too familiar.

"Zip it up, fucko," Scotty said.

"Mother nature says otherwise," I replied.

"I'm not going to ask again." He pressed the piece deeper into my vertebrae and the pain did the trick on its own accord. I zipped and raised my hands.

"All right, now what?"

"Now you drive me somewhere."

"Haven't you heard of Lyft?"

"Don't be cute, just do what I say."

He marched me across the parking lot, and I ducked into my Toyota, Scotty settling in the back seat, gun to my back. He barked directions as I drove: a right on Cedar, another right on Water. I'd received two fix-it tickets for my broken taillight over the past year and now I desperately hoped for a third. But hoping for it only seemed to make the city more desolate. Paper trash tumbled through the intersection. Streetlights blinked in and out. At the end of Ocean Street, Scotty had me pull into an old apartment complex and kill the lights.

"Who are we waiting for?" I said.

"Just wait."

In a few minutes, a late-'90s Jetta rattled into the lot and parked a couple spaces away. The radio played some Top 40 station and when the engine shut off, I could still hear the driver singing along. A woman's voice, not half bad. The car door opened, and Becky stepped out, singing more quietly now. She'd changed from her crazy cop outfit, and she now wore a big puffy jacket and a beanie pulled down to her eyebrows. I watched Scotty in the rearview, gaunt and pockmarked. His sallow eyes fixed on Becky as she trudged up a stairwell to the second floor.

"Look, Scotty," I said. I had the sense that this had little to do with me. "Whatever you're thinking, I'm sure there's a better way out of this."

"I didn't ask your opinion."

"How did you know where to find me tonight?"

He snorted. "I put spyware on Becky's phone. It tells me everything, man. She was texting about you to one of her girlfriends."

"So what?"

"So, word's getting out about the reward money."

"What reward money?"

"Nice try, Charles. I'm not as dumb as I look."

Another car passed on the road—Scotty ducked when the headlights swept over the lot and when all was clear he told me to get out of the car. He stayed close behind as we went up the same stairwell Becky had climbed and nudged me into a flickering alcove toward apartment 2D. He banged on the door with his fist, and I could hear footsteps creaking through the apartment.

Becky opened the door and saw us both standing like a couple of bible salesmen. "What the hell, Scotty?" she said. "Is that a gun in his back?"

Scotty gave me a hard kick. I stumbled past Becky and toppled onto the linoleum entranceway. He gave Becky a once-over and went to the refrigerator, twisted the cap on a bottle of Budweiser. "Sorry to ruin your evening, babe," he said, pointing the gun at me the whole time. "But we need to talk about that reward money. Seeing as you were the one who screwed that kid up, I nominate you to take the fall for us."

Becky made a disgusted face, folded her arms. "Bullshit. I was the lure, Scotty. You hit him with the brick. No way I'm going down for this."

He itched a facial scab with the barrel of his gun. "I don't think that's up to you. See, this dickhead is going to call the police and tell them it was you. Then he's going to wire me the reward. And he's going to play it just the way I want him to."

Becky's eyes heated up, and I wondered for a moment if those eyes were more dangerous than Scotty's janky .38. "Why do you think Charlie will help you?"

"Because I know where his parents live. He told me the other night."

"You're not thinking this through," I said to Scotty.

"I thought it over plenty."

"Really?" I got up from the floor slowly, showing my palms. *Keeping him calm.* I already felt the emotional temperature starting to tick up. "After I call it in, what's to stop Becky from going on the run once you take off? Unless you're planning on sticking around for the cops?"

He considered Becky for a moment, then: "Get your handcuffs, babe."

"That's not happening," she replied.

"Come on, *Hannah Handcuffs*. It's showtime."

She shook her head no.

Scotty thumbed the hammer on the revolver real slow so she could hear every click. "For the last time, babe. Cuff your ankles and give me the key."

Becky went to a cigar box on the coffee table, flipped open the lid. She held up a pair of handcuffs in one hand and a little silver key in the other. She shot me a look when she handed the key to Scotty, and I almost didn't catch it. But when she fumbled the hand-off and the key fell to the floor, I knew what it meant. Scotty set the beer on the kitchen counter, and when he stooped down to pick up the key, I swiped the bottle and cracked it over his head. He rolled forward, beer and blood streaming down his neck.

I went for the gun, but he still had a good grip on it.
Gunshot.
The cupboards burst and dinner plates rained down.

Becky went for the gun, too—all of us scrambling on top of each other, scratching and punching. Scotty nearly gouged my eye before I hammered my elbow over his nose, and then again. He squeezed one more round into the ceiling before softening a little. One more hit and the gun clattered to the linoleum.

Becky quickly recovered it.

She stood, clicked open the cylinder and counted the rounds.

"You're not going to shoot me with that thing, are you?" I said.

"No, Charlie," she said. "Not going to shoot you."

"I guess we're back to Plan A, huh?" I tried to stand but immediately toppled over.

Scotty and I were cuffed together at the ankles.

"Not exactly Plan A, Charlie. Now give me your phone."

I raised an eyebrow at her: *come on.*

"I'm serious," she said. "Scotty's phone, too."

"The cops will be here any minute. Someone must have called in the shots."

"Then you better hurry."

"He's out cold, Becky. I'm not digging in his pants."

"Do it, dammit." She sounded anxious now, eyes shifting to the door. Fight or flight instincts ratcheting up. With her burlesque makeup and the gun flicking out the commands, she looked like some 1970s crime-flick vixen. When I handed over the phones, she powered them down and slipped them into a purse on the counter. "I don't need you to give me a head start, Charlie. This time I'm going to take one for myself."

I watched her scuttle around the apartment, stuffing clothes and toiletries into reusable shopping bags. It didn't take her long. She went to the doorway, and with her hands full, she turned and gave me an apologetic look.

"I'm keeping your cut," I told her.

But she'd already slipped down the hallway and out of sight.

***

The cops didn't like my story, but it all checked out in the end.

Being cuffed to their main suspect raised some eyebrows, no doubt.

Still, they connected Scotty to a dozen robberies throughout the state, and it gave the DA courage to stick him with an attempted murder charge for bricking Niles. Mrs. Kopecki released the reward cash to me a few weeks later, and that's when I sold everything I owned and hit the road. Part of me thought I'd run into Becky Santorini out there on some dark Central Valley highway, or behind a gas station minimart with a gun in her hand. I pictured her changing up her act, sneaking into cabarets in Las Vegas, Denver, St. Paul. Sticking to the shadows where she could find them. I bought a prepaid phone in Bakersfield, and I started getting calls in the middle of the night. There'd be nobody on the other end, just the sounds of cars passing on the road or a hard rain falling. It wasn't Becky. Couldn't have been. My new number was probably an artifact on a stranger's contact list. A jilted girlfriend, maybe. A debt unpaid.

Still, I wondered.

When I reached San Felipe, Mexico, I stopped worrying about everything: Becky and Scotty, Niles Kopecki. Retail graveyard shifts. I wasn't sure how many beach days thirty-eight grand would buy me, but the beer and rent was cheap, and I wasn't planning on going back home with any money in my pocket.

At least I wasn't allergic to the sunshine.

And brother, there was plenty of it.

THE OTHER WOMAN
Nils Gilbertson

The headstone jutted from the ground like earth's decaying incisor. She could make out *In Memory of* etched shallow into the stone, but the rest of the sentiment was eroded by the decades between. Moss and grime crept up its base, obscuring the name. She knelt and double-checked the hand-drawn map of the grounds. They'd assured her this was the one. Leaning forward, she saw faintly through the rot: *Henry Arthur Jensen, 1914-1940.*

The late morning was still and quiet as she stood peering over the cemetery. Old crumbling stones lay scattered in the dead grass. There wasn't a single fresh one, as if no one in the small town had died in the past fifty years. Surrounding the graveyard were tall trees with leafless branches that needled the vacant sky. The horizon looked to her farther than it ever had before. She pulled out her phone and took a picture of the grave. *Henry Arthur Jensen*, she thought. *Poor old Henry.* He was near, yet lifetimes away. She placed the bouquet of white carnations at its base, took one more glance, and started down the dirt path. Aggressive brown weeds, taking advantage of the nutrients deep in the ground, sought to overtake the walkway. The bramble tickled her ankles.

As she walked, she saw a figure at the edge of the graveyard.

The man wore denim overalls over a red plaid shirt. He moved toward the mouth of the path that led to the parking lot. Closer, she saw stalks of straw-like hair growing out the sides and back of his ball cap and a lump on his lower jaw. As he sauntered toward her, he squirted brown juice through the corner of his lips, natural as a breath.

"Morning, ma'am." He kept some distance, fidgeting like a skittish animal.

"Good morning," she said.

He spat. "You visiting someone today?" His voice was coarse like tobacco-stained cowhide.

"Yes, old family."

"Family? Is that right?"

"Yes."

"That's good of you. Some people don't care much for family these days."

"Well, I have to get—"

"You're not from 'round here," he said, like it was news to her.

"I live in St. Louis. I came because I wanted to visit my great-grandpa. He lived here his whole life and I've never been to visit."

"That so? Drove out here from St. Louis?"

"Sure."

"To see a dead man you never met?"

She paused. "How'd you figure that?"

His tongue crept from his mouth and massaged his upper lip as he thought. "Are you sticking around town?"

"For a couple"—instinct brushed her hand against her hip—"of days. It was nice to meet you, but I have to get going."

"Gordy."

"Excuse me?"

"I'm Gordy." The lump on his lower gum migrated from the left to the right side.

"Mia," she said. "I'm Mia Jensen."

He couldn't suppress an amused snort. "Miss Mia Jensen.

How 'bout that."

She turned toward the parking lot, hand steady by her hip. When she got to her car she peered back and saw him approaching the familiar grave.

The humble downtown mimicked the atmosphere of the graveyard. The sidewalks were empty and a few beat-up cars were parked on the wide streets. She slowed to a crawl at the intersection, anticipating a direction but the sign-less roads met her only with apathy. There was a bar, The Cellar, on one corner and a pharmacy on the other. The rest of the drag was a sullen row of restaurants and shops and hollow, boarded-up buildings. The tired Western Bank & Trust anchored the block, lamenting its neighbors. The boulevard was lonely but used to it.

She parked in front of Ruby's, the recommended lunch spot, and locked the car. A bell jingled as she entered. She sat at the counter of the nostalgia-soaked diner and examined the black and white photos that could have been from the day before or fifty years ago. She felt she ought to pay a coin for a milkshake. Instead, she ordered a Reuben with coffee and glanced at the two elderly men in the corner playing dominoes. Besides them, the joint was empty.

The woman behind the counter served her up and said, "Here you go, dear. You need anything else, give me a holler." She was an older woman, sharp eyes contrasting with her soothing tone. She couldn't utter a phrase without chasing it with a wrinkled grin. Wisps of gray streaked her short bobbed hair.

Mia ate the greasy sandwich and the woman refilled her coffee. Hesitating, her professional smile faded to a milder look of genuine curiosity, and she said, "You're not from town, are you?"

"It's that obvious?" asked Mia. "That's about the only thing anyone has said to me since I got here."

The woman put down the coffee pot and leaned on the counter

and nodded toward Mia's purse. "That bag'll give you right away, hun." She stuck out a calloused hand. "Charlotte. Pleased to meet you and welcome to Bigsby."

"Mia. Good Reuben."

"And what brings you here, Miss Mia? Pardon me, but we don't get many visitors these days."

Suspicion needled the young woman, alone, in a foreign town. Years in the city had left her with the sort of reasonable mistrust that can keep you alive—the sort that senses a question from a stranger and regurgitates *what in the hell do they want?* But the woman's face—her tone—was sincere, invested already in the unspoken response. Mia considered spinning a tale worth the woman's keen interest but decided that the truth wasn't a bad one itself.

"My grandpa died recently—"

"Oh, I'm sorry, dear."

"Thanks. He was born here in Bigsby."

"Is that so? Heck, I might've known him. What was the name? My family's been here as long as we can trace it back." A prideful beam crossed her face.

"No," said Mia. "He left when he was very young, a baby. I came from the cemetery. I'm here visiting my great-grandpa's grave. My parents are out west but I'm in St. Louis so I wanted to make the trip. After my grandpa died—and based on the family stories I've heard—I got curious. I wanted to know more about where I came from." Mia felt her face redden and only the twang on the radio and the click of dominoes in the corner interrupted the stillness of the diner. "Anyway, it gets more complicated than that; I won't keep you by going into details."

Charlotte squawked and gestured toward the near-empty diner. "The town's dead this time of the day. Heck, it's dead most times of the day. I bet I don't see another customer for at least a couple of hours when the boys at the processing plant hang up their hats. I'd love to hear a good tale about a family from Bigsby."

Mia sipped her coffee. "The way I heard it from my dad—which is how he heard it from my grandpa and my great-grandma—is that my great-grandpa, Henry Jensen, was a farmer here. When he was eighteen, he married my great-grandma, Violet."

Charlotte's face creased with vague familiarity.

Mia continued, "When they were twenty-five, they had my grandpa, Thomas Jensen. The problem was, Henry was also getting on with another woman in town. I don't know her name."

Charlotte gasped. "Oh, Lord."

"Right. So, Violet worked up the nerve after the baby was born to confront Henry about it and demand he break it off, if nothing else, for the sake of the kid. And he did. But, the mistress didn't like that much. One night, she showed up on the front porch crying, hysterical. Drenched from a summer storm, lightning splintering the sky. Great-Grandma Violet was in the other room with baby Tom. When Henry let the mistress in and went to get her some water to calm her down, she took an ax and buried it into his back. She hacked him to bits while my great-grandma escaped with my grandpa in her arms."

Mia paused to let Charlotte react. Her face twisted into an expression of shock, but intertwined were lines of confusion. "You say she murdered him? The *mistress* murdered him?"

"That's right." Mia sipped her coffee. "And Violet ran and took the baby out west. She had some help along the way and ended up settling in California. She never looked back. Years later, she heard the mistress ended up in an asylum upstate. They buried Henry in the town cemetery. Life went on and, eventually, I was born out in the San Francisco area. Great-Grandma Violet passed the story down to Grandpa Tom, who passed it down to my dad and me. No one's felt the need to come back to visit, until me, I guess."

Charlotte fidgeted with her ring and mouthed the words *Henry Jensen* under her breath. The dominoes had stopped clicking. Mia peered over her shoulder and saw the two old men, their long, sunken faces looking on. She turned back and saw Charlotte's face drained of color.

"You've heard this before?" Mia asked.

"Oh, not how you tell it, dear." She tried to smile. "But we have some old stories that get around town. You know, the darker side of our little history. All I've heard is rumors, tall tales. I'm afraid I don't have anything to add. It was a long time ago, after all," she said, grasping at words only to stumble over them. She took a breath. Dominoes clicked. "Can I get you anything else?"

"That'll be all, thanks."

Mia paid her tab and left a generous tip. As she left, she looked back in through the window and saw Charlotte hustle to the two old men's table. One of them met her eye.

The Cellar was cramped and dark with frayed flags on the wall that Mia didn't recognize and grainy pictures of people posing on the downtown drag like they were famous. A couple of guys sat at the bar sipping slowly, staring at the wall like it might start moving. Mia found a table in the corner next to a drum set and an old Vox amp and sat down in a rickety chair. After a few minutes without seeing a server, she went to the bar and ordered a George Dickel on the rocks. The bartender gave her a piano-key grin and said, "You got it, little lady."

Her phone rang.

"Hi, Mom." She sipped her drink.

"About time you answered. I've been calling all morning."

"I've been busy."

"Busy? In that town?" She scoffed.

"I went and saw Great-Grandpa Henry's grave this morning." Her voice was hushed and she glanced up at the men at the bar. Their eyes were still on the wall. They coughed and rasped and drank like they were stuck on a loop.

"You hear that, Don?" said Mia's mother to her father on

the other end. "She went to the grave this morning."

Mia didn't hear a response. "He say anything?" she asked.

"He asked if you have your…you know."

"My gun? Yeah, Mom, I have it. Saying the word doesn't make it go off."

She sighed. "You and your dad and those darn things. I'll never understand. Any trouble so far?"

"Nope. It's nice here."

"Nice?"

"Quiet, at least. Did Dad say anything else?" Mia asked.

"No. That's all."

"You speak for him now?"

"Your dad doesn't have much to say about you being there, Mia. Neither he nor Grandpa Tom, rest his soul, ever felt the need to go back. Not after the mistress butchered your great-grandpa and your great-grandma ran away and didn't turn back until she got to an ocean. He doesn't have an interest in stepping foot in that town. And I understand you're curious since Grandpa Tom died, but…" the sound of her mom's voice continued to hum through the phone, but Mia's attention turned to the darkened doorway.

"—and lord knows your mind runs wild all alone in that big city apartment. You need to meet someone, Mia, you need to—"

"I'll call you back." She hung up and peered across the dim room, smoke lingering, obstructing the view like morning haze. Standing there was one of the men from the diner.

The old man hobbled toward her. He had an arched back and kept his eyes on the floor as he walked so that his liver-spotted scalp faced her as he approached. His hair was white and stringy and a trembling hand held his glasses in place so that they wouldn't slide from the bridge of his long, slender nose. When he reached the table, he straightened best he could, nodded, and said, "Miss," as if waiting for an invitation.

She gestured toward the chair across and he took the seat and exhaled. Before she could say a word, the bartender had placed a copper ale in front of him. He licked his scabbed lips and dipped the upper one into the frothy head. He lifted the glass and tilted it back and his Adam's apple bobbed under folds of loose neck skin and half of the pint disappeared. "Miss," he said again. Foam clung to wayward whiskers.

"It's nice to meet you. I'm Mia." She stuck out a hand and he examined it before gripping it like a rare fabric.

"Jensen's your family name?"

She tried to recall if she'd mentioned her last name in the diner. "Why's that any concern of yours, Mr...."

"I'm Lester." He leaned across the table. "It's not the first time folks have been hearing that story you're spouting. They never thought they'd have more Jensens coming to town, though."

"So the story's well known around here? What else do you know?"

His beer had disappeared like a magic trick. "I got nothin' to add. Someone might." He slipped a pen from his shirt pocket, moved the empty glass, and jotted something on the damp napkin beneath. "Pleased to meet you, Miss Mia Jensen. You be careful, now." He rose.

"Wait." She started to follow him, but his curved, tired back assured her he'd said what he came to say.

"On the tab, Lester?" the bartender hollered after him.

The old man showed him a bony thumb and left. Sun spilled through the open door, illuminating the smoke that permeated the bar like a dissolving ghost. Mia looked down at the napkin. The bleeding pen marks read: *1221 Elm, Jensen.*

Mia sipped her whiskey as she thumbed the damp, tattered napkin, reading the sloppy address again and again. The potential for danger arose in her mind, but it was soon stifled by curiosity— curiosity about the merit of a story that had been passed down to her, the story of her family's grisly origins. She pondered that, had her great-grandpa's mistress not plunged an ax into his back and neck over and over on that muggy night, lightning streaking the charcoal sky, her great-grandma would never have fled with her infant grandpa, they never would have gone west, her father would never have been born, met her mother, and had her. She took the last gulp of whiskey and felt bumps crawl over her skin like brail and realized she owed her existence to that deranged mistress who, generations ago, graced the same streets she now did.

She pocketed the napkin, paid her tab, and headed for the door. Before she reached it, it burst open and cracked against the adjacent wall. A man with patchy hair and a hollow face dotted with pus-filled sores stumbled in. He was a stick draped in baggy clothes and Mia looked down at frantic, scaly hands. He panted like a rabid dog and his teeth were black and rotting. He shoved Mia aside, grabbed a pool cue, and pulled it tight against the man at the bar's neck, dragging him from his barstool. The man sputtered and gasped for air.

Without a thought, Mia drew a concealed Glock 43 from her hip and held it on the crazed man. Saliva foamed at the corner of his lips and he grunted and pulled the cue tighter. The man had a few fingers wedged between his neck and the cue, and saw the small pistol in the corner of his eye.

"Shoot'im!" he gasped.

The tweaker, engrossed in violence, didn't notice the Glock.

"Hey!" she hollered at him. Nothing.

She glanced up at the bartender, who gave her a look like she had his blessing to decorate his bar with the tweaker. Instead, she sidestepped the writhing bodies struggling on the sticky floor so that she was in the man's line of sight. She held the gun steady on him. He slowed. As he loosened the tense grip on the patron's neck, he smiled, showing her soiled gums. His face was like cracked, rotting leather. He dropped the pool cue and started cackling. He flailed and kicked and the patron stumbled to the corner. The bartender and a bar back approached and gave Mia a nod as she holstered her pistol. "We'll take it from here, missy. Appreciate the hand," the bartender said. "And nice piece." He and the bar back each took a leg and Mia left before seeing where they were dragging him.

The afternoon sun was blistering and the avenue was still quiet and empty. As Mia's eyes adjusted, her mind second-guessed the happenings in the bar, she checked her pocket and found the old man's scribbling still there. She recalled she had an appointment with the records office at the town hall. She checked for the time and the address. It was only a couple of blocks away. As she started on her way, she sensed a figure across the street, watching. The man from the graveyard stood like a misplaced statue in his denim overalls. He stowed his hands in his pockets, his only movement the instinctual twitch of his mouth to spew brown juice to the gutter. He grinned and tipped his ball cap. Mia kept walking.

Town hall was a dignified, rectangular brick building— small, but still the biggest in town aside from the bank and the church. Next to it, and standing out from its red neighbors due to its bluish-gray brick walls, was the records office. The shades were drawn, but Mia's knock prompted a woman's invitation. "C'mon in!"

The clerk was middle-aged but still one of the younger people Mia had encountered in Bigsby. She wore large, thick glasses and a blouse with loud red flowers. "You must be Mia." She rose and walked from behind her desk to greet what must've been her first guest of the month. "Pleasure to put a face to the voice. I'm Elsie."

"Good to meet you, Elsie. And thanks so much for your help over the phone."

"Well," she said, leading Mia to a table with a small stack of papers. "I'm afraid I may not be as much help as I'd hoped. I pulled all the documents I could find about your great-grandfather, but there wasn't much. And very few newspaper clippings. I know it was a long time ago, but, given the nature of the crime—" She stopped like her tongue was caught on the word. "I'm sorry…" she hummed.

"For what?"

She smiled and straightened her blouse. "I thought there would be more."

"I appreciate you finding what you could," said Mia.

"I'll leave you to it, let me know if you have questions."

Mia skimmed through the materials, and her gut was heavy as she realized how little there was. She felt the napkin in her pocket. She contemplated how unusual it was that there were no articles about a grisly murder—but reasoned it was a small town, the recordkeeping didn't seem particularly sophisticated, and, as Elsie pointed out, it was a long time ago.

Then she found the obituary. *On this day August the four-teenth of the year nineteen-forty, Mr. Henry Arthur Jensen was laid to rest. He is survived by his wife, Violet Elizabeth Jensen, and his two sons, Silas and Thomas.*

"Excuse me," said Mia, waving to Elsie. She hustled over. "Is this all there is for the obituary?"

"Yes, that's all I could find. Is everything all right?"

Mia felt the concern on her face. "No," she said. "This isn't right."

"What is it?"

"There's nothing of how he died…"

"Well," said Elsie, "back in those days maybe they didn't want to publish the details."

"There's nothing about who he was, his life."

"I'm sorry."

"And the children, it's wrong."

"What's that?"

"It says he had *two* children," said Mia. "Thomas and Silas. Thomas is my grandfather, but there was no Silas. Grandpa was an only child. I'm sure of it."

Elsie squirmed like she was responsible. "I—I don't know what to say. Tell you what, I can run a search for—"

The old phone clanged in the corner. Elsie gave Mia an

apologetic look but scurried to it. "Hello?"

There was a brief, hushed conversation that Mia couldn't make out before Elsie took a breath and returned.

"I'm sorry about that."

"People are talking, aren't they?" said Mia.

"Excuse me?"

"People have been looking at me sideways, following me, talking behind my back ever since I got here. The whole damn town knows more than they're letting on."

Elsie began to shake her head frantically and Mia immediately regretted the harshness of her tone. "I swear I don't know what you mean. I—I pulled all I could, everything you asked for. In small towns back then there weren't many records, newspapers, documents," she sputtered, uttering any word that came to mind in hopes it would absolve her of the perceived sin.

Mia tried to smile. "It's all right. I didn't mean you."

"I've only lived here for a year," added Elsie. "I swear I don't know a thing about that awful history of your family here. The gals around town take longer than that to let you into the sewing circle."

"I bet." Mia glanced back at the paper. "But this isn't right." She thought back on the many times the infamous family legend had been retold during family gatherings after a few bottles of wine. No Silas. No second child. Only Violet traversing the country with young Thomas after Henry's mistress murdered him. "Mind if I take a picture?"

"Please do."

Mia took a picture and thanked Elsie for her time. Before leaving she asked, "You wouldn't happen to have some time to look up Silas Jensen this afternoon, would you?"

"I've got nothing but time."

Outside, a few heavy clouds had gathered, dimming the town and blotting the late afternoon sun. Mia called her mom.

"I guess now's a more convenient time for you," her mom answered.

"Sorry about that."

"Mhmm."

"Grandpa Tom was an only child, right? It was only him with Great-Grandma Violet when she went west?"

"That's right. He was a baby at the time, not more than a couple of years old. You remember him saying he doesn't remember the ordeal at all, don't you? Lord knows it's for the better. The way Violet told it..."

As Mia walked down the boulevard, she felt the eyes of a few onlookers that dotted the mellow sidewalks. She lowered her voice. "There are records in the clerk's office saying that Henry and Violet had *two* kids, including a boy named Silas."

Her mom let out a dismissive yelp. "No, definitely not. And what year was that record from? It's probably a misprint. Was there anything to back it up? To verify this Silas?"

"The clerk's looking into it."

"What's that?" her mom said, away from the phone. Then back to Mia, "Your father asks how's playing detective."

"Funny, Dad."

"I told him you're finding new family members left and right."

Mia jumped as a squawk resounded from a bench in front of the hardware store as she passed by. "Always on your phones, you kids." She turned and saw an elderly woman with years of tired righteousness molded into the lines of her faces. She chased her remark with a sardonic grin.

"What was that?" Mia's mom asked, her mocking tone transforming to maternal concern.

"It's nothing, there are some real characters in this town. Is Dad still there?"

"He went out to mow the lawn."

"All right. Do me a favor and ask him about Silas when he gets in."

"I will. Be careful, now."

Mia got in her rental car and drove toward the bed and breakfast about ten miles out of town. She marveled at how a mere few streets later she'd left the small downtown and was alone on a long stretch of blacktop, surrounded by nothing but farmland. A few farmhouses scattered the sprawling fields and cows went about their business. Meandering from the main road were nameless gravel paths that led to lives away from it all. It was calm and big and still, and Mia felt belittled as she drove, as though the town didn't care much for her or her life in the city—as though for hundreds of years people came and went and died and were born. The cows and crops grew and died, same as the people, and the town was old and used to it.

Mia heard a heavy thud and the car slowed and pulled to the right. She tried to accelerate but the car's vibration and the sharp flapping noise insisted that she pull over. She stood on the roadside eyeing the flat tire and regretted not springing the five bucks a day for roadside assistance. She glanced down the long, flat road. It rippled in the distance, not a car in sight. She sat on the side of the road and considered her options. Despite the predicament, the unhurried pace of the country calmed her. Time was a passive observer—not an anxious reminder that it was running out.

As evening began to darken the horizon, Mia saw a police car emerge at the end of the road. She stood to flag it down, but as the officer passed, he slowed, gave her a look, and kept on. As she hollered, Mia saw him speaking into his radio. The car disappeared into the country. Soon after it did, Mia felt the rumble of a second car. She turned and saw a pickup truck coming down the long stretch of road, the exhaust from its sputtering engine dirtying the landscape. It pulled over behind her car, and emerging from it was the man in his red plaid shirt and denim overalls.

"Looks like you're in a bit of a jam there, Miss Mia Jensen." He spat on the road.

"What the hell do you want?" She felt the weight of her pistol, ready, on her hip.

"I'm here to help out a troubled traveler."

"That so?"

He adjusted his cap. "That and your great-grandpa."

"Excuse me?"

"You're looking to find out more about him," the man said. "That's why you came to Bigsby, right? That's why you were at the graveyard this morning? I'll tell ya, there's a hell of a lot more to know." He read the hesitance on her face, adding, "Tell you what, you can hold that pistol hiding under your coat on me all you want. May hurt my feelings a bit, but I'd understand." He showed her yellow teeth.

"Let me see an ID," she said.

"Why's that?"

"So I can text someone who I'm with so they know who to come for if I go missing."

He hesitated but pulled out a frayed wallet and a driver's license. Before showing her, he peered down at it as if to make sure it was him. He held it toward her.

It read *Gordon Herman Jensen.*

The ride was quiet except for Gordy's intermittent spitting into a crumpled water bottle. Mia kept a tense hand near her holster but the name on the driver's license distracted her. Questions formed in her mind, but she imagined answers would be waiting at the end of the bumpy gravel path the truck rumbled down. The sky was draped in dark indigo. Pinks and reds and yellows saturated the boundless horizon as the setting sun bled into wisps of clouds.

Gordy turned at a crooked mailbox.

"You got addresses out here?" Mia asked.

Gordy chuckled. "Of course, where you think you are, city girl?"

"Twelve twenty-one Elm?"

He snorted and spat and said to the windshield, "She's a sharp one, no one's denying that."

He pulled the truck out front of an old farmhouse. A rusted barn loomed beyond. The house rested on crooked, tired beams, the white paint peeling and stained black as if burned. Tangled weeds climbed onto a slanted front porch and the upstairs windows were boarded. The shingled roof reminded Mia of the scaled neck of the tweaker in the bar.

"You coming in?" Gordy asked.

Mia followed across the unkempt lawn and up the front steps onto a porch that felt as though it would collapse under any more weight. The second-story balcony above sagged with similar weariness. The front door was ajar and Gordy pulled open the torn, rusting screen door behind it. Mia kept her hand close to her hip as she followed into the dark, stale atmosphere of the decrepit house.

The inside of the home struggled to retain some semblance of nostalgic charm despite the broken furniture and warped, dusty floor. Tables and chairs, covered with antiquated sundries, scattered the house. Mia examined an old banjo with broken, bending strings leaned up against the edge of a forgotten fireplace, its empty opening like a black hole siphoning the remaining light from the already-darkened living room.

"That banjo's been in the family for generations," a voice wheezed from a doorway in the corner. Mia turned and saw an elderly man emerge from the shadows in a wheelchair. Strapped to its back was an oxygen tank, tubes slithering from it and around his ears to his swollen, red nose. He coughed like there was sludge in his throat, raising a hand to catch the spewing phlegm while still wheeling himself forward with the other. "Let me get a look at you, girl."

Mia clenched her teeth.

"She's pretty, ain't she?" said Gordy.

The old man sucked his dentures loose and examined bumps of naked gum with his tongue before popping them back in. "She sure is. And your name, Miss?"

"Mia Jensen. I hear you know about what happened to my

great-grandpa, Henry Jensen." A rasping cackle overcame the old man. It soon turned to a violent cough, prompting Gordy to rush to the kitchen. He returned with a glass of water and knelt next to the old man, comforting him and assisting his eager sips. Mia slipped the cocktail napkin from the pocket of her jeans and confirmed the address. The dark black letters also reminded her of Gordy's ID. Her last name felt foreign.

Soon as the old man stopped hacking, Mia said, "About my great-grandpa? A man down at The Cellar gave me this address. And I got this"—she glanced at Gordy—"man following me around all day. He's not exactly discreet."

The old man slapped Gordy on the back of the head. "Idiot. And I figured Lester couldn't keep his goddamn mouth shut either." He looked at Mia with tired—yet fierce—gray eyes, like stained windows to the past. "I'm sorry if any of this gave you a scare, Miss Mia. I heard you were in town looking for answers about our family history, and I figured you deserved a few. Now, folks in Bigsby like to gossip about our family 'cause not much exciting has happened since that night Henry was murdered." He paused, reflecting.

"*Our* family?" Mia breathed.

He nodded and adjusted the tube in his nostrils. "It was a hell of a storm that night. I was a young boy—six. But I remember it clear as a summer afternoon."

"Silas?" Mia said. She felt her pocket buzz but ignored it.

He hummed with gratification and a fey smile crossed his face, his pale, translucent skin like crinkled wax paper. "That's right. I remember the day your grandpa, just a babe, was stolen from me. I understand why she did it but that don't make it right."

"Are you saying—" Mia shook her head. "You're saying you were Henry's other son, Grandpa Tom's older brother? But that makes no sense. Great-Grandma Violet ran away with Grandpa Tom when the mistress killed Henry. Why would she leave you?"

The old man exhaled peacefully, as though sustained by the

truth. "From what I've heard you've been spouting around town, your family's been fed lies, dear. No, no mistress murdered my pa—*Violet*—his wife, my ma, did. She came back from a church social with little Tom and me, rushing to escape the storm, and found Pa in bed with his other woman. Ma lost it. She'd known about it, but couldn't handle seeing it. There's more to it than that, I figure, but I was only a boy. Ma took the ax to him, and Pa's mistress—Cora—took Tom and me and ran for it. Last I saw was Ma trying to dislodge the ax from Pa's back so she could hack him again." His face creased in agony like he was reliving the boyhood nightmare. "The mistress tried to get us out of there, I remember getting lost as she dragged me through the fields, baby Tom in her arms. I remember her sobbing, lightning jagged in the sky. But I ran from her. I didn't know her and I couldn't go home so I ran and found myself at a neighbor's farm. They took me in. Lived there till I was eighteen. I never left Bigsby since."

Mia absorbed the story, her periphery still on Gordy, but hand relaxing at her hip. "But...you..."

Reading her confusion, the old man said, "I'm Silas Jensen, your great-uncle, your grandpa Tom's older brother. The woman you know who ran out west wasn't Violet; it was Henry's mistress—Cora. When Violet murdered him that night, Cora disappeared. Violet ended up in a sanitarium. Cora took her place. Sounds like she took her name, took baby Tom, started that family of yours out west, and made some changes to the story."

Mia shook her head. "But someone would've gone after her, for kidnapping if nothing else."

The old man sighed. "Not back then, and not when half the town suspected that Tom was hers anyhow."

"What do you mean the town suspected Tom was hers? Which one of them was pregnant?"

"Both were gone for the duration. Pa took care of me alone; Ma went to stay with her family a few towns over so her sisters could help out. And to get away from Pa, I'm sure. I figure Cora's family thought it best to send her away given the circumstances. She went to work for a family out in Braxton. Ma came back nine months later with little Tom. Cora did too soon after. She and Pa picked up where they left off. Nasty rumors started swirling that the whole thing was a cover and that Cora was Tom's mother, and she gave him up knowing what an awful time he'd have growing up a bastard in this town. Cora never suggested so much. And the way Ma looked at that baby, I knew it was hers. But after Ma killed Pa and Cora took Tom, folks were willing to convince themselves it was best to leave things be."

Mia couldn't muster a response.

The old man continued, "I figure Cora wasn't a bad woman. She came from a good family. Pa was dead. Ma was a murderer— I never heard from her again. The town decided to let the mistress go. Start something new, something better." He paused and examined Mia. "Seems like she did. Meanwhile, I was here growing up, tended to the farm best I could, had Gordy, and, somehow, by the grace of God, I'm still alive." He cringed as he coughed into a damp handkerchief, irritated by his longevity.

Mia eyed Gordy.

"Guess we're kin, huh?" He spat tobacco juice into a cup he'd found on a dusty couch-side table.

Mia's pocket buzzed. "So why's everyone in town been so weird? Is this some big communal secret?"

"Nah," said Gordy. "Everyone heard a Jensen's in town and made a big stink about it. Dad here wanted to talk to you." He bowed his head, near embarrassed. "I wasn't sure how to get you out here."

Mia scanned the scabbed walls of the old room, searching her memory for something that would poke holes in the story— for a piece of irrefutable evidence that surfaced during a late-night retelling of the tale by Grandpa Tom that would prove the whole thing a lie. The same tale, a pesky voice in her head reminded, that was first passed down by her so-called great-grandma Violet. As she consulted the urge deep within her that prompted the journey to the depth of the country for her history, she pondered the implications of truly finding it. Either way, it was too late. She saw it in the old, dying man's gray eyes.

"Good to meet another Jensen before I die," the old man croaked. "And to be able to show you where it all started."

"All started?"

The old man rolled across a soiled rug toward the fireplace. He stopped. "Right here. This is where Ma butchered him." He said it like a museum tour guide. "I watched it. Clear in my mind as a summer afternoon."

Mia's phone buzzed.

Gordy nodded toward it. "Go ahead."

"Mom?" Mia answered. "I'll have to call you back...yes, I'm fine...I'll call back when I can." She hung up.

"Should we have her stay for supper?" Gordy asked.

The old man shrugged. "She's kin, ain't she?"

THE DELIVERY
Andrew Welsh-Huggins

Carter drove an unreasonable fifteen miles per hour down the
street, drawing the ire of the driver behind him—at least judging
by the sudden flood of brights in his rearview mirror. Undeterred,
he came to a full stop in front of the two-story wood frame and
made a production of rolling down the windows and squinting
in the darkness to find the house numbers. He took just long
enough to earn an irritated honk from the car whose passage
down East Illinois Street he was impeding. At last, satisfied that
he'd attracted the appropriate amount of attention, on the street
and inside the house, he drove away, picking up speed as he
approached the intersection.

He turned right at the stop sign, circled around, and returned
to the same block a minute later. That first go-around, he had
spied a space practically in front of the house, which might have
worked under different circumstances. Instead, he parked nearly
the entire length down the block. He turned the car off but
didn't exit right away, taking a moment to examine the street.
Not his first time in Urbana, Illinois; he'd made a number of
deliveries there over the years. Lot of business in university
towns, though the packages were always different. Case in
point, his clients tonight. A couple, both retired professors.

Awaiting a small delivery with big implications. Mindful of this, he retrieved the envelope from the Suburban's glove compartment and tucked it into the top left pocket of his utility vest. The envelope was folded in half to the size of a deck of cards, but was not much thicker than a royal flush.

He got out and slammed the driver's side door hard. He squeezed his key fob not once but twice to ensure a double beep locking confirmation. He waited a couple of moments, then walked around the front of the car, stepped onto the sidewalk, and started toward the house. Late August, a humid Midwestern darkness descending over the tree-lined street. His passage lit by the soft glow of streetlamps every few yards. The saw of cicadas in the air like miniature engines on the cusp of running out of gas. Carter looked ahead and nodded to himself. He'd guessed correctly. Even at this time of night and at this distance—several dozen feet down Illinois—he saw the greeting party right away.

Party of one, not that it mattered. The guy was huge. Carter wasn't surprised, given what was in the envelope in the top left pocket of his utility vest, but still. Talk about using a cannon to kill a canary. He must have had eight inches on Carter, and that wasn't even talking shoulder width. Nothing to do about it now. He continued walking. This next bit was tricky. You couldn't screw it up. Conventional wisdom said he should make the move nonchalantly, leave the sidewalk for the alley up ahead as though he just happened to be going that way. No big deal. Nothing to do with the gorilla headed straight for him, hands the size of scuffed-up softballs already rolled into fists. Normally it was a good play, but something told Carter not tonight. The alley was twenty yards away, Greeting Party maybe forty. Closing fast. Alley ten, Greeting Party twenty-five. Alley five, Greeting Party fifteen. Alley one—and Carter darted to his right, letting the fear show on his face as he sprinted down the lane. Making it clear he was trying to get away, exaggerating his footfalls—*clomp clomp clomp clomp*—as he ran.

Of course the guy wasn't just big, he could run too. Of course he could. Carter picked it up a bit, considered his options, and settled on the far side of an alley-facing garage. He looked behind him as he ran, making sure his eyes were wide; it wasn't much of an act when he saw the look on Greeting Party's face as he closed the distance between them. If *Pissed Off* and *This Only Ends One Way* hooked up and had a baby. Carter guessed he had maybe ten seconds to spare as he dove around the corner of the garage. He amped up the sound of labored breathing—*huh, huh, huh*—but in truth that wasn't much of an act either. Five seconds. One.

At any other time the expression on the man's face as he rounded the corner and skidded to a stop might have been comical. Puzzlement wrestled with rage as he whipped his head back and forth, hunting his quarry. He shot a glance into the adjoining yard, but it was bare except for an empty playset. He looked past the garage toward the house to see if Carter had run that way but a tall wooden fence suggested: impossible. He took a step back and examined a plastic garbage bin tucked against the fence. His gaze deliberate, as if judging its capacity for hiding a body with the look of someone who might have experience in that regard. He retrieved a gun from thin air, where guys like that kept guns, raised the weapon with his right hand and flung the lid of the garbage can up and over. Nothing. He leaned forward and peered inside, which was the same moment Carter swung down from the slanted roof of the garage, executing a not-too-shabby arc as his boots slammed into Greeting Party's head with that sound as when you drop a watermelon off the side of the deck just to see what happens.

The man dropped to his knees and then over to his side. He gave a little moan. Carter put a stop to that with another kick to the head. The man's eyes rolled up into his skull and blood foamed at his mouth. Carter knelt beside him and rolled him onto his stomach in case he vomited. He reached into the lower right pocket of his vest, retrieved a pair of heavy-duty zip ties, and pulled Greeting Party's hands up and behind his back. He bound them together, drawing the ties tightly enough that a little white of constricting skin showed but not tight enough to draw blood. He picked up the gun where it fell and studied it. Smith & Wesson M&P. Not what he would have expected, but no matter. He ejected the magazine, examined it, and checked on the chambered round. He made sure everything was as it should be, reassembled the gun, and placed it in his waistband in the small of his back.

Next, he patted the man down and found his phone. He examined the two text messages visible on the screen. What he read was not a good sign, but it was possible he wasn't seeing the whole picture. Carter maneuvered the phone to Greeting Party's hands, positioned the lock button beneath his right thumb and pressed. He raised the phone and checked the screen. Nothing. He tried again. It worked this time. Crouching, Carter scrolled up through the long chain of text message balloons. Counted the number of participants. Not a good sign indeed. Much worse than he'd anticipated, in fact.

The phone buzzed. A text. *What's up?*

Carter checked the time. Nearly ten. Maybe three minutes since Greeting Party left the house and started down the sidewalk. He didn't have long. He tapped through the phone's settings and set auto-lock to never. He placed the phone in his upper right vest pocket. He checked Greeting Party's pulse. Weak but steady. He moved quickly, straining more than he cared to, but the extra push-ups he'd taken to doing each morning helped. Turned out Carter hadn't been entirely correct when he decided against hiding in the garbage bin. It could hold a body after all, but he had to really push to make it fit, ignoring Greeting Party's groans as he lowered the lid.

Finished, he headed back down the alley. Another text. *Where are you?* Okay—he had a minute tops, he guessed. He texted: *Package retrieved. On our way back.* He made it to Illinois and walked up to the house. Light leaking through the drawn curtains, which meant no chance to scope things out from the street. He knew from this morning's reconnaissance that a rear entry was out—it involved both a sticky screen door and a mud room with squeaky floorboards. He might as well come down the chimney for all the cover it provided. So, it was a blind entrance straight through the front door, or nothing.

He looked up and down the sidewalk, mounted the stairs, and knocked.

"Mmmph."

Holly looked at the girl sitting on the side of the bed.

"Shut up."

"Mmmph."

Holly checked her phone. Was it her imagination or was this taking too long?

"*Mmmph!*"

Holly walked to the girl, hooked her right thumb through the tightly coiled red bandanna at the edge of the girl's mouth, and tugged. The girl winced.

"What."

"Too tight," the girl gasped.

"Like I give a shit."

"Why are you doing this?"

"It's just the way things worked out."

"Please. I promise—"

Holly unhooked her thumb and the gag slipped back into place.

"*Mmmph.*" The girl's brown eyes, wide as shucked walnuts, imploring. Holly walked away, thought better of it, returned, and untied the knot at the back of the girl's head. She pulled even tighter, ignoring the whine of pain, and then relaxed the tension a tad and retied the knot. Finished, she checked the lines binding the girl's hands and feet. Nothing to change there. She stepped back, admiring the results.

"Better?"

The girl nodded. Hard to read what was in those eyes. Anger? Fear? Regret? Holly didn't care, having seen it all and more. Loosening the bandanna a real gift on her part. She'd told Jay the girl wasn't worth it. That she complicated an already precarious situation. The old couple was the target; she was just in the way. Better to cut her out up front. Whatever it took. But Jay said no. Said they needed her to make the plan work. What happened afterward wouldn't matter—a little collateral damage never hurt anyone. Holly rolled her eyes, recalling the conversation. What a liar. You'd have to be a moron not to see why Jay wanted to keep the girl around. That ass. Those tits. Those kissy kissy lips. The opportunities presented by a twenty-two-year-old girl's body. He'd never admit it, of course. He was happy with Holly, he said. Happy to fuck her for a month of Sundays and more. Which he often did. Except afterward, driving around, running errands, whatever, it wasn't her he was looking at. It was girls half her age with the tits and asses and kissy kissy lips. If Holly bothered to dwell on it, she felt bad for what Jay had in store for the girl, afterward. But the plan was the plan.

Her phone buzzed. She picked it up and read the message. *Package retrieved. On our way back.*

Finally, she texted in return. She put the phone down and crossed her arms and waited.

"Mmmph."

"Quiet."

"Mmmph!"

Holly walked across the room, right hand raised. Enough was enough, already. She stopped, hand in motion, hearing the knock downstairs. The door opening and Jay's voice, rising with the inflection of a question. A low conversation. Then—a sound. The door shutting? A heavy footfall, maybe involving the errand they'd sent Walter on? Something not entirely right. She lowered her hand, crossed the room, and pulled the bedroom door open.

"Jay?"

A pause.

"Yeah." Voice low and indistinct.

"Everything all right?"

"Yeah."

It didn't sound all right. "You sure?"

Another pause.

And another.

"Jay?"

No answer.

Standing on the threshold, Carter understood right away why they sent Greeting Party. There was a reason you hired out those kinds of jobs. This guy, for example. Not that much taller than Carter, not exactly paunchy but not exactly not paunchy either, like the senior lifeguard who supervises but doesn't actually guard. Brown hair, receding hairline, goatee expanding over his fleshy face like something drawn on a balloon. Maybe the brains of the operation, but definitely not the muscle. He smirked at Carter.

"About time."

Carter didn't say anything. He'd always found it difficult to feign disconcertment and talk at the same time. Instead he waited while the man looked over Carter's shoulder.

"Walter?"

Carter allowed silence to fill up the space between them.

"Where's Walter?" the man said.

"He was delayed."

"Delayed?" The smirk fading now, replaced by confusion.

"More like waylaid."

"What the hell—"

Carter made it quick. Two-finger jab to the man's throat. That itty bitty indentation just below the Adam's apple. No more noticeable than the notch on a leafy branch at the height of summer. You had to hit it just right. Carter hit it just right. The man gasped, staggering back. Carter lifted his right foot as if aiming for the man's groin. The man instinctively hunched to ward off the blow. Carter kneed him in the head instead. The man's knees buckled, and he dropped faster than Carter expected, and it was all he could do to keep him from crashing onto the floor. As it was he landed with a louder-than-ideal thud. Carter took a step back, reached into his utility vest pocket and retrieved more zip ties. He worked fast, wrists and ankles. They wouldn't hold forever but Carter didn't need forever. He knelt.

"Listen."

The man coughed and gagged, trying to catch his breath.

"I said, listen." Carter reached around and retrieved the Smith & Wesson from the rear of his waistband.

"See this?"

The man nodded.

"Recognize it?"

He shook his head.

"It belongs to Walter."

Carter let that sink in.

"Do I have your attention now?"

Another nod.

"Who else? And where."

Despite everything, the man hesitated. Carter pressed the gun's barrel into the soft flesh beneath the man's jaw and pushed, forcing him to tilt his head back like a man following the path of a spider across the ceiling. Carter repeated the two questions. No hesitation this time. Carter thanked him, replaced the gun in his waistband, and pulled a roll of black electrical tape from his vest. Three and a half times around to achieve the proper gag. Just enough to keep him quiet; not that he seemed the talkative sort.

Then, from upstairs, a woman's voice.

"Jay?"

Carter paused, raised his arm, lowered his voice, and spoke

into the crook of his elbow.

"Yeah."

"Everything all right?"

"Yeah."

"You sure?"

Holly fumed. Now what? She had her instructions, not that she agreed with them. *Stay with the girl no matter what.* Fucking Jay. What was that supposed to mean? What if there was an emergency? What if things didn't go as planned? She looked over at Sam. She sat slumped on the bed, eyes dull with resignation. Who could blame her? She wasn't stupid, despite her looks. She had to know what was coming. Had seen the way they treated her grandparents when they barged in—them first, then her. You think she couldn't figure it out, despite everything? Holly almost pitied her, except this wasn't the sort of business where you wasted time feeling sorry for people. Like that would get you very far.

So, what to do? What to make of Jay's monosyllabic replies? Or the fact she didn't hear the sounds she expected to hear when Walter returned with the person, with the deliveryman, he'd been sent to retrieve? Had the plan gone south? That wouldn't be good. But maybe they were just playing it safe. It was a delicate operation, after all. She had an idea. She picked up her phone. She texted. *Everything OK?* She waited. No answer. Glancing again at Sam, she tiptoed to the door and opened it a crack, as if she were five years old again on Christmas morning and she was just, you know, checking. The hall was dark, but all the lights were on downstairs. She made a decision. She opened the door all the way, stepped into the hallway, then stopped as she felt the phone buzz in her hand. A message. From Jay.

Everything's fine. Just wrapping things up. Stay put. Be there in a second.

OK, she replied. She stepped back inside the room and slowly pulled the door shut with a soft click.

Carter found the couple in the back of the house, in a sunken library slash rec room. Either a patio or three-seasons room once upon a time, before a renovation. Each in a separate chair, tied up with line and with duct tape around their mouths. He wrinkled his nose as he stepped into the room. One of them had soiled themselves. No surprise: they were elderly, late seventies or early eighties, and who knew how long they'd been tied up like that. Hours? A day? Her hair still dark, only flecked with white here and there. His hair, what was left of it, the color of snow along a curb in March. Their eyes widened with uncertainty at his appearance. Carter reached into his vest and pulled out a small knife and opened the blade. Their eyes even wider now, searching each other out. He stepped forward and gently pulled the tape from around her mouth, then his. Next, he cut their hands and legs free and pocketed the knife and stood back.

"Oh," the woman said, breathing deeply. Carter realized, this close, it was she who'd had the accident. He hardened his face so she wouldn't know he knew. "Thank you," she said.

"You're welcome."

"Are you...him?" The man, voice whispery. He cleared his throat, trying to regain speech. "The one—"

"I have a delivery for you, yes. I'm the one you hired."

"Our granddaughter," the woman said. "She was here when they showed up. We were just saying goodbye, before the trip and all. They hit her, took her—the things they said." She shook her head, emotions betraying her as she began to weep. "Is she—?"

"I'm about to check on her. But I need you to stay here."

"Should I call the police?" the man asked.

Carter considered the question. It was a common one, despite the fees he charged.

"What about your trip?"

"I don't know. I mean, now? After all this?"

"I thought it was a big trip. Maybe even an escape?"

The couple exchanged glances, hearing the word.

"Something like that," the man said. "But..."

"You can call them if you want." He thought about Walter in the trash bin in the alley and the trussed-up man lying on the living room floor. "But it might change the terms of my contract."

The couple traded another look. After a moment the man slowly nodded.

"Our granddaughter?" he said.

"What's her name?"

"Samantha," the woman said. "But she goes by Sam."

Conventional wisdom was all over the board on this one, and of course he had no time to weigh the options. Go in guns blazing. Go in easy, playing along and acting surprised. Bargain hard. Bargain soft. He'd done them all, and it's not as if one worked better than the others independent of the facts at hand. You just hoped you made the right choice at the right time. He headed up the wooden steps. Upstairs, he approached the closed door. He checked the two phones, Walter's and the one he took from the man downstairs, making sure he had the name right. Satisfied, he stepped forward and knocked.

"Holly? I need you to open the door."

Jesus Christ, Holly thought. Who was that? Not Jay, for sure, and not Walter either. Definitely not Walter. The old man? It didn't seem likely, given what she'd observed of him and his wife, neither of whom seemed capable of doing much more to protect themselves than wave a broom around or throw a book across the room, both of which in fact they'd tried. She would have smiled at the memory had she not been so panicked. If not Jay or Walter or the old man, then who? The delivery guy? But how? And in that case who had texted her? *Be there in a second.*

Hadn't that message come from Jay's phone?

Another knock. "Holly?"

"Who's there?"

"Someone who needs you to open the door before something bad happens."

Holly turned and looked at the girl on the bed. Watching Holly, listening to the voice on the other side of the door. Watching everything play out. Her expression almost smug. Holly wanted nothing more in that instant than to erase that look permanently. To drive home the point that none of the bad things going through the girl's head for the past couple of hours was even remotely close to the really bad stuff that was going to happen to her.

"Holly? Last chance. Open up."

Fucking Jay. She told him they needed a gun. His response so patronizing. "Why? We've got Walter." The pitying look in his eyes as he said it. She crossed to her handbag and reached in and retrieved the canister of pepper spray. She might be crazy but she wasn't stupid. She always had it with her. Even with Jay around. Especially with Jay around. A girl couldn't be too careful. She palmed it, walked to the door, and turned the knob.

"Holly?"

"You got her, asshole," the woman said, misting his face.

He stumbled back, blinking, and wiped the spray from his eyes. He coughed once, but no worse than the man at the symphony with the tickle in his throat who covers his mouth during a pause between movements.

She stared at him as if she'd seen a ghost. He knew she'd been expecting a different reaction. The hacking, the watery eyes, possibly the up-chuck. The reaction the spray garnered from most people. Just not him. Nothing special—he just wasn't affected the same way. Who knew why? Plus, he'd practiced a bit on ways to fight through it. He'd seen the same look of surprise in the eyes of a lot of people with similar canisters in their hands, emptying the contents in his direction as they grew more and more frustrated. Surprise, which he always used to his advantage, springing into action a couple of seconds later. Which was how he made the mistake. He didn't spring fast enough this time. He took the scene for granted. She was on him a second faster.

He knew right away he was in trouble as she hauled him back into the room. It wasn't her size, though she was big enough. The problem was her strength. And the fact she'd fought before—obviously. Not necessarily in the ring, as he had, once or twice. But some place, that's for sure. Maybe in bars or maybe on the street or maybe the bedrooms of girls she'd caught her boyfriend in. It didn't matter at this point. She dropped the canister and kneed him and he grunted and she hit him in the head and he grunted again, flailing, and she drove him backwards and onto the floor and fell on top of him, hard. His breath left him at the impact and he thought he might pass out. Even more so when she hit him again. And again, but this time he raised a hand and warded off the blow. This angered her and she reared back to leverage the impact of her next strike and that was her own error. He scissored his legs and grabbed her right arm with his right hand and pulled and a moment later flipped himself around and onto his knees. Startled, she gave him a half bear hug but like it or not, strength or no strength, the referee's position—hands and knees on the floor—was a tough nut to crack. Now it was her turn to grunt, trying to move him, and he was breathing hard, trying not to be moved and to find some purchase to stand. He reached his right hand out and closed it over the upended canister of spray. He thought he might have her. Then her weight vanished from his back and she was scrambling backward and he sat back on his knees and turned and found himself staring at the wrong end of Walter's gun.

"Stand up."

He did so, slowly. Glancing at the girl on the bed. Examining her bindings. Not good.

Holly said, "Where's Jay?"

"Downstairs."

"Is he alive?"

"Last time I checked."

"Who are you?"

Her posture and the positioning of her hands made Carter think she might also have spent some time at a firing range.

"Just a guy trying to make a delivery."

"In that case you've come to the right place. Hand it over."

"Hand what over?"

"Don't be an idiot. The key. Now."

"I can't do that."

"I said, don't be an idiot. I know all about the safety deposit box. Let's have it."

"And I said I can't. The invoice is clear."

"Invoice?"

"Who receives the delivery. You're not on the manifest. Neither is Jay." He paused. "Or Walter."

"I'm not afraid to use this," she said, extending her arms.

"I can see that."

"In that case, just give me the key."

On the bed, the girl watched the scene before her, eyes round with both fear and curiosity.

"For the last time, I can't. And in fact, I need you to give me the gun." Carter took two steps toward her.

"Stay back. I'm warning you."

"I know." Another two steps.

"Don't make me shoot."

"Sorry."

He stepped forward and extended his right hand and she depressed the trigger.

Click.

Her eyes widened. She swore and tried again. Same result.

She raised the gun to strike Carter but it was too late. He raised his hand and emptied the remainder of the spray into her face. Unlike Carter, she had the reaction that most people do.

He stepped back, patting the loose cartridges—including the chambered round—that he'd taken from the Smith & Wesson and were now tucked safely in a vest pocket, and watched her fall, clawing at her eyes, onto the floor.

The granddaughter descended the stairs in front of Carter. A bit shaky after being tied up for so long—reaching out halfway down to steady herself against the wall—but she made it under her own steam. She gasped when she saw Jay on the floor, and at the way he watched her with angry, wet eyes. Carter gave her shoulder a reassuring squeeze and guided her back to the recreation room.

"Sam."

The grandmother, gratitude etched on her face, stepped forward and embraced the young woman.

"Grandma," Sam said, returning the hug. "Are you okay?"

"I'm fine. Just a little shaken up. And I'm sorry—I think I had an accident."

"It's all right. I'm just glad you're safe."

Ten minutes later they gathered in the dining room. The grandmother changed into a fresh outfit. Three suitcases beside them.

"Are you sure—about the police," the grandmother said.

"I'm sure," Carter said. "If you want to make your flight and all."

He pulled the envelope from his pocket.

"Do you know what that is?" the grandmother said.

"A key, I believe."

"Do you know what it's for?"

"I have a basic understanding—"

"We had to hide things away," the grandfather said. "Our

son, Sam's dad"—he glanced at his granddaughter, shaking his head—"the drugs just overtook him. We tried everything…"

"At least we had a nest egg," the grandmother said. "Stored in the box, at the bank. It seemed the safest place. But we kept the key where we did"—she looked at Carter—"just in case. So thank you. For the delivery."

Carter nodded but didn't speak. It always puzzled him when people thanked him for fulfilling a contract they'd paid him to execute. Thank-yous were for gifts and favors and unexpected kindnesses.

"But somehow these people found out," the grandfather said. "If you hadn't—"

"It's probably time you got going," Carter said. "If you could just sign here."

He produced a receipt book. He filled out the top portion and passed it to the grandmother along with a pen. She examined it, wrote her name, and handed it back. He thanked her, pocketed the book, and handed her the envelope holding the key. The receipt was meaningless—he'd been paid up front, as always, and he'd dispose of it as soon as they were gone—but somehow it comforted people.

"Ready?" Sam said. She reached down and picked up her suitcase. Nice-looking girl, Carter thought. Sweet face. Someone you know would work hard to get ahead in the world.

"Here. Let me help you with that," he said, stepping forward.

"That's okay," Sam said.

"I insist," Carter said, reaching out and taking the suitcase with his left hand. Surprisingly light. As he'd expected. He set it down and reached for the girl's right hand as if to shake it. A quizzical smile on her face, she reached forward to accept the gesture, which gave him the angle he needed to grab her hand, twist her arm up and around her back. He grabbed her other arm and pushed her up against the wall.

"What the—" she yelled, but it was too late. He had the zip ties around her hands a second later and forced her first to her knees, then onto her stomach a second after that.

"Oh my God—" the grandmother cried.

Holding down the girl with his left hand, he pulled a pink phone out of her rear jeans pocket. He asked her for her passcode. She shook her head with a sound like a snarl. He leaned closer and said in the best stage whisper he could manage, "Have you noticed Walter's not here?"

She instructed him to perform an anatomically impossible act. He repeated the question and added: "You saw Jay, right?"

A moment later she told him the passcode.

"My God," the grandfather said. "What are you doing?"

"She was in on it," Carter said, rising and facing the couple. He laid four phones on the dining room table, screens up: Walter's, Jay's, Holly's, and Sam's.

"What?" the grandmother said.

"That's wrong." Carter corrected himself. "She *planned* it. What happened tonight. Holly and Jay and Walter. She arranged it. She and her dad—your son. He's due here shortly, I believe. But she's the one who set it up. Gave them your address. Instructed them to intercept me—to take the key. To take your money."

"That's impossible," the grandfather said.

Carter gestured at the phones. He showed them the entire chain of text messages over the evening. The five-person group chat, counting the son. The *Who cares if they die?* text that Sam sent just a few minutes before Carter pulled onto Illinois Street.

"No," the grandfather said, backing up and steadying himself with his hand on a chair. "It can't be true."

"Oh, Sam," the grandmother said, moving in the girl's direction. Carter blocked her way.

"Probably best to just get going."

"Go?" the grandmother said. "After all this?"

"She was going to let them kill you."

"But—"

"I can drive you to the train station. You'll be fine once you're on board. Chicago's only a couple of hours."

"Fine?" the grandfather said.

"Nest egg?" Carter said.

After a long moment they nodded dumbly. Carter reached down and picked up their suitcases, one in each hand. These were heavy, the way they should be.

"Please."

Sam, gasping from the corner of the room. Squirming, struggling to roll over. Carter wondered what would happen to her when Walter freed himself from the garbage can. When Jay and Holly were back to their old selves. When the son showed up. Not his problem, though he had a pretty good guess.

"I'm sorry," Sam said. "I'm so, so sorry. Please don't leave me here. I promise—"

The grandmother started to cry again. The grandfather looked at his granddaughter on the floor, his face blank. Sam pleaded.

"My car's right down the street," Carter said, nodding at the door. "It won't take but a couple of minutes."

He wasn't exaggerating. He had them at the station in ten. Five minutes after that he was on his way out of town. No point in dallying. Why bother? He'd completed the delivery. And he'd probably be back at some point, anyway. University towns. They always had something going on.

TO RUN AFTER DARK
Jon Penfold

I like to run after dark. While moms and dads are tucking their kids into bed and reading fairytales, I'm lacing up my shoes. I do my left foot first. *Bunny ears, bunny ears into the hole, popped out the other side beautiful and bold.* Then I tie my right. Always left, then right. No special reason, I guess. Maybe it's superstition, though I don't consider myself a superstitious kind of guy. I always double knot them. I didn't use to, but then one time I was running, and my shoe came untied and I tripped and fell. It was on a sidewalk and I scraped up my left elbow real bad. When I got home, I poured rubbing alcohol on it and it burned. And then it took a long time to heal. The next night I was still able to run, but now I always double knot my shoes.

After tying my shoes, I say goodbye to Wilson. He's my cat. I named him after my favorite football player. He's not a pet. He's an emotional support animal, though I'm not sure he really supports me. But he's a good kitty. And when I get home, we'll eat together. He'll have wet food, and when I open the can, he'll rub up against my leg and make funny noises, as if wet food is a special treat, even though I give it to him every night. He's funny like that. Me, I'll have a box of macaroni and cheese. It's my favorite. The directions on the box say to put three tablespoons of butter in it, but I always put more. Sometimes I'll boil hotdogs and slice them up and put them in the macaroni and cheese. I call it hotdogaroni and cheese.

As I leave my apartment, I try to be as quiet as possible. I pretend like I'm in a movie and if the bad guys hear me, I'll get caught. We've only had one bad guy come around here since I moved in. He broke into my neighbor's apartment and stole his TV. I don't know if he ever got caught. But I'm not *really* worried about bad guys. The reason I'm quiet is because I don't want to wake up any of the other people in the building. Some of them work first shift and have to get up real early. Sometimes, when I'm getting home from running, they are just leaving for work. I only pretend there are bad guys.

I keep my key on an old shoestring around my neck. I tuck it beneath my shirt so it doesn't bounce while I'm running. I tiptoe down the hall. And then down the stairs. And then through the parking lot. But as soon as I hit the sidewalk, I start running, because my footsteps, no matter how fast I'm going, aren't as loud as the cars driving down the street.

I always take a left on Division Street. If I were to take a right, it would take me to my work. I have a job at a thrift store that sells used goods. Stuff like clothes and furniture and whatever else people are looking to get rid of. They hire a lot of people like me. I work in the back. People pull up in cars and trucks and vans. They donate boxes and bags full of stuff they don't want anymore. My job is to sort through the stuff and separate it into categories. I work from one p.m. to nine thirty p.m., Monday through Friday. I take my lunch from five to five thirty. It's not the best job in the world, but it has its perks. I found my running shoes at the bottom of a garbage bag full of old clothes. They were barely used. And I get first dibs on all the old VHS tapes. I collect old action movies. The best ones are with Arnold Schwarzenegger and Sylvester Stallone and Chuck Norris. My favorite is *The Running Man*. I have three copies of that one, though only two work. I keep the third one anyway. I'm not sure why. I guess I just don't have the heart to throw it away.

One block west on Division, I pass the bus stop where I get picked up for work. I tried running to work once but I was covered in sweat when I got there and they don't have a shower. Nobody told me that I smelled bad, but I knew that I did because anytime anyone came close to me, they would quickly step away and scrunch up their nose. So I never ran to work again. But the bus is okay. Work gives me a free pass. Plus, there's this really pretty girl that rides it on Monday, Wednesday, and Friday. She has blond hair and blue eyes and always clenches her bag real close to her chest. She's already on when I get on and she gets off before I get off. Sometimes the seat next to her is open, but I've never had the courage to sit next to her. Even if it's the only seat open, I will stand.

About a mile past the bus stop, I pass Franklin High School. My old stomping grounds, as people like to say. They got a new football field recently. The old football field is where my accident happened. There was an interception, and I was chasing down the cornerback who picked off the ball and I was blindsided by a linebacker. At least that's what I've been told. I don't remember anything from the game. I was in a coma for three months afterward. The doctor said I had brain damage and that I was lucky to be alive and that I could never play football ever again, or any other sports for that matter. If I hit my head again, I could die. That's why I'm slow. I know that's not the technical term, but I know that's what people say about me. The funny thing is, I don't feel slow. I just feel like the rest of the world sped up. Sometimes I think I did die that night on the football field and was transported to another dimension where everyone else is just a bit faster than I am. But I don't know.

I might be slow in the head but I'm still fast on my feet. Faster than I used to be even, and I was *fast*. When I woke up from that coma, I was forty pounds lighter. Almost all of my muscle was gone. I was nothing but skin and bones, which it turns out is better for running, especially long-distance running. That's why

I can run so far and so fast now. Every night I run for at least two hours, but sometimes I'll run all night, for five or six hours straight. When I get thirsty, I'll drink water from the water fountains around the city. I'm not sure how many there are but it seems like a lot. And I hardly ever see anyone else using them. Sometimes I like to think the city put them in just for me, for when I go running at night.

It's a few miles from the football field to downtown but it's almost all downhill. Sometimes I'll run a couple streets over, right on the pavement, on roads lined with nothing but houses. But I usually stick to the sidewalks on the main drag because there are more streetlamps, which makes it easier to see. Plus, when I get to the busy intersection, there are crosswalks. I have to push a button and wait for the red hand to turn into a green man, but it's safer than waiting for a break in traffic and sprinting across the street. And I don't mind waiting on the little green man. Sometimes there will be a water fountain at the intersection. If there isn't, I'll run in place or stretch until the light changes. If I'm lucky, I'll time the light just right and I won't even have to stop.

The busiest intersection is Cesar Chavez Boulevard. When I was a kid it was called 39th Street, but then they changed it, which is okay I guess, even though I don't know who Cesar Chavez is. I think somebody told me once, but my memory isn't that good these days. At least not as good as it used to be. After 39th Street, I mean Cesar Chavez Boulevard, I pass more businesses. Most of them are closed for the night, though some are still open, a few restaurants, but mostly bars. One of the bars always has a crowd of people smoking cigarettes outside of it, especially on the weekends. I always cross the street before I get to it because I hate slowing down and walking through all the people. Plus I hate the smell of cigarettes. Tonight it's nice out, with the moonlight shining bright, but even if it's cold and rainy, people will still be standing outside smoking their cigarettes, even if they don't have umbrellas or raincoats. This guy at work,

Tommy, is always stepping out back to have a cigarette. And he's always calling in sick. I don't understand why people smoke those things.

But like I said, tonight is nice and the air is warm and calm, and the crowd, even though it's a Thursday, is as big as ever. From the other side of the street, I can hear the people laughing and talking, even if I can't make out what they're saying. Most of them are about my age and it makes me wonder what would've happened if I didn't have my accident. Would I be standing out there with them, talking and laughing and smoking cigarettes, under the moonlight, in the warm air? Or maybe I'd be a professional football player, getting ready for Sunday's big game. Or an actor, getting in shape for my next action movie. And then I think, maybe I am one of those things, or all of those things, in other dimensions. But here, in this dimension, it makes me sad to think about it, the what-ifs.

After I pass the bars and the restaurants, I follow the train tracks under the highway and cross the river on the new bridge. Only trains, bicycles, and people on foot are allowed to cross the new bridge. No cars. At this time of night, I'm almost always the only person on it, and again, just like the water fountains, I sometimes think the city built it just for me. I always run on the north side of the new bridge because that's the side where you can see downtown, all the buildings lit up, their lights reflecting off the water like a mirror. Sometimes I'll even stop for a couple of seconds and just stare at the view and pretend that it's all mine.

On the other side of the bridge, I take a right and follow a new bike trail that leads to downtown. I pass underneath a gondola, the kind normally used to take skiers and snowboarders up a mountain. I used to snowboard before my accident, but I'm not allowed to anymore, even with a helmet on. This gondola isn't used for skiers and snowboarders though. We almost never get snow here. This one is used to take people to the hospital on top of the hill. You can drive up there too. Or take the bus.

That's how I get up there. Every three months I go see Dr. Simons. It's always the same. He does some tests, asks a bunch of questions, and then tells me to come back in three more months. Then I take the bus back home. Sometimes I think about riding the gondola from the hospital to the bottom and then back up again, just for fun, but I never do.

The bike path takes me into the heart of the city. I don't go all the way downtown. I did one time, but it was too crowded. There were too many people on the sidewalks and too many cars in the streets. I had to keep stopping at red lights. And even if the light was green, it didn't mean it was safe to cross. I started crossing at one green light and a car from behind turned right into me. There was a guy behind the wheel, probably the same age as me. At first, I don't even think he realized I was there. He just saw that the light was green and started to turn. Luckily he noticed me before it was too late and slammed on his brakes. His bumper was only inches from my knees. And then he started honking his horn, like it was *my* fault. That was the last time I ran downtown.

Some nights I follow the path next to the river and then take one of the bridges back to the east side of the city. There are a bunch of bridges to choose from. At one point or another I've taken them all. But tonight I'm feeling good. I'm feeling strong. I decide to stay on this side of the river a bit longer. I follow a sidewalk away from the river, toward the college. I could have gone to school here. They offered me a partial scholarship to play football. Some other schools were also interested. They were bigger schools but they were further away from home. I'm not sure where I would have gone. It was a big decision at the time. Sometimes I'm glad I didn't have to make it. But other times I wonder what would have happened.

I pass a bunch of buildings that must be closed up for the night. Their lights are off and nobody's around. This lasts several blocks before I start hearing the sounds of people laughing and talking real loud and music blaring. I pass a row of old houses.

College kids are on the porches and in the yards and on the sidewalks. They have plastic cups in their hands. Some of them have cigarettes in their mouths. In one yard a bunch of them stand around a table throwing a ping-pong ball back and forth, trying to land it in a cup. Every once in a while one of them screams really loud, the same way people scream at football games when the home team scores. When they see me run by, one of them yells, "Run, Forrest, Run!" Everyone else laughs. I just keep running.

I get to the football field where the team practices. There's a track that goes around it and I decide to take a lap. At first it's very quiet. The only thing I can hear is my own footsteps. But then I hear a strange sound coming from the middle of the field. It sounds like someone is moaning. And there's a noise like someone is slapping someone else. It's steady, like a clock ticking. I slow to a walk so I can listen better. The moaning doesn't sound happy. It sounds like a child crying into a pillow. And then I think I hear the word, "Help."

I walk slowly onto the grass. As I get closer to midfield, I can make out what looks like two people, one lying on top of the other. And then I hear it again. "Help...Help me." I'm about ten yards away when I can finally see what's making the noise. There's a man on top of a woman. Her bra is showing. He has her arms pinned to the ground. Her legs are spread out wide. His pants are down around his ankles. Her hair is blond. I immediately think about the girl on the bus. I know it's probably not her. But what if it is? "What's going on here?" I say it loud enough for them to hear.

The man is immediately startled. He climbs to his feet and franticly pulls his pants up. Now, with the moonlight shining on his face, I can see that he's not a man, but a boy, a college kid who can't be older than nineteen. He has short curly hair and is wearing a T-shirt with the logo from the college on it. And as soon as his pants are buckled, he starts to run. I don't even think about it. I just start chasing him.

The kid is fast. In the comic books they would say he's "lightning fast." But I'm fast too. I can keep pace with him. Across the football field and through the gate, I stay about ten yards behind him. I don't gain any ground, but he doesn't gain any distance. When we're out of the practice facility, he runs right down the middle of the street. If it was daytime, he'd probably get hit by a car. But there's nobody out driving this time of night. He tries to lose me by taking a quick left, cutting through a small park, and jumping up and over a bench. I mimic his every move. I step my right foot on the seat of the bench and leap over the backrest. It feels like I'm an action hero in an action movie. It feels like this is what I've been training for my entire life.

When we get to the row of houses where the college kids are partying, the kid I'm chasing does something I'm not expecting. He runs right up onto the porch of one of the houses. He yells, "Help me! Some lunatic is after me!" And then he disappears through the front door. When I try to follow him into the house, two guys with Greek letters on their chests try to stop me. I have to admit, it probably does look pretty crazy, a thirty-year-old man chasing a teenage boy late at night. But they don't know what I caught him doing. They don't know that I'm the hero in this story. So I plow through them like I would a couple of linebackers in my old football days. They fall to the ground like bowling pins and I stumble through the open front door.

The house is so crowded it doesn't feel like you could fit one more person inside. Everybody has a cup in their hand and the air is filled with smoke. The music is so loud it hurts my ears. I can't believe this is what people do for fun. I spot the curly-haired boy on the far side of the room. He looks right at me, like a deer in headlights. I can tell exactly what he's thinking. He can't believe I had the guts to follow him inside this house. He frantically starts pushing his way through the crowd. I do the same. I follow him through a kitchen where a dozen people are standing around a table flipping cups into the air. I follow him out the back door, onto a small porch where more people are smoking more cigarettes. By the time I'm down the steps, he's climbing over a six-foot-tall wooden fence. I sprint across the small backyard and jump up and over the fence after him. When I land on the other side, I lose my footing and fall face-first into the grass. I quickly spring to my feet and follow the kid across a different backyard, around the side of a two-story house, and down another street.

This kid must be an athlete, because a normal person can't run this fast for this far, even if they're being chased. I follow him toward the river but then he takes a left. He's heading right into the heart of the city. There's no way to run down the middle of the street here, so he hits the sidewalks, dodging people left and right. I follow him, first as he crosses a couple of one-way streets with little traffic and then across a busy two-way street. He nearly gets hit by a small pickup truck and then slides across the hood of a car that squeals to a stop in the middle of the crosswalk. I have to zigzag around the vehicles and he's able to gain a couple of yards on me by the time I reach the other side. But I don't give up. I just keep on chasing him.

He passes a restaurant that has a couple of tables set up outside. He knocks them over onto the sidewalk. I have to jump over them, but I don't lose any ground. If anything, it takes him longer to knock them over than it does for me to jump over them. He crosses another one-way street and when I follow him, I get hit by a car. It takes my legs out from under me and I land on its windshield. The glass turns into a spider web. I bounce off the car and onto the pavement. Luckily, my shoulder and hip take most of the impact and I don't hit my head. I quickly realize that I'm sitting in the other lane of the one-way street. A pair of headlights are coming straight at me. The vehicle slams on its brakes and skids to a halt. Its bumper stops only inches away from my face. Its headlights shine right into my eyes. The driver lays on the horn. My eyes burn. My ears ring. I know this is the point where I should give up. But I don't. I can't.

By the time I climb back to my feet, the kid is rounding the corner at the far end of the next block. I sprint down the sidewalk after him. When I round the corner, I don't see him anywhere in front of me. *How did he get away?* There's no way he made it around the next block already. I head in that direction anyway, but before I can get there, I hear some ruckus across the street. I spot the kid, in the doorway of a crowded bar, arguing with a giant man wearing a tight black T-shirt. The giant man shoves him hard in the chest. The kid falls backwards onto his ass. He climbs to his feet and curses at the man before retreating down an alleyway to the right of the building.

I wait for a couple of cars to pass and then I jog to the other side of the street. The alleyway is narrow, wide enough only for one car to fit down it. There are two dumpsters and three doors. The kid is trying to open the furthest door but it's locked. There's nowhere else for him to go. The alley dead-ends with a brick wall covered in graffiti. The kid looks at the wall, then looks at me, then puts his hands on his knees and throws up. When he's done puking, he stands up straight and says, "What the fuck are you going to do? Call the cops?" He's covered in sweat and breathing hard. "They're not going to do anything. Do you even know who my father is?"

How would I know who his father is? And how would I call the cops? It's not like I carry a phone when I go running. Outside of the closed door is a can full of cigarette butts and a single brick. I know the brick is there to keep the door from shutting when employees come back here to smoke their cigarettes. I know this because Tommy uses one just like it at work. If he doesn't jam the door open, it will shut on its own and lock and he'll have to walk all the way around to the front to get back in. I pick up this brick and carry it over to the kid, who now has his hands on his knees again, looking like he's about to throw up some more. I raise the brick over my head and slam it down hard against the back of his head. The first hit has the same feeling as when two football helmets slam into each other at full speed. The kid immediately falls to his knees. I strike him again. This time I hear something crack. The kid falls to his belly and I drop to my knees. The third time I hit him, it feels like I'm striking a sponge. A wet sponge. This one also makes a mess.

I flip the kid over and place the brick in his hand. I move his arm so it looks like he hit himself in the head. I get to my feet and stand over him. I think about Arnold and his silly accent and what he would say if this were one of his movies: "*Suicide by brick.*" Or something funny like that.

I jog out of the alleyway, down the block, and around the corner. I find a drinking fountain. I take a couple gulps of water and then I wash my hands off. I start running again. I feel good. I feel strong. I feel like I've got a couple more hours left in me. As I head toward the river, I think about the kid. I wonder where he'll go. Maybe he'll end up in the dimension where I used to live before my accident. Maybe there everything will seem just a little bit faster than it used to be.

THE SPORTS AGENT
Janice Law

My name is Adam Hundlow. I am a forty-nine-year-old sports agent, specialty, ice hockey. I'm midlevel, with one real star plus several journeymen NHL players on my books, some AHL lifers, and a handful of quality juniors in the pipeline. Thanks to me, my guys make handsome livings, and until Martha's accident, I did okay, successfully juggling a mega-mortgage, college tuition, and orthodontist's bills in an upscale 'burb with her and our two kids. But when a drunk driver piled into Martha's SUV, leaving her in the hands of an orthopedic surgeon and a PT outfit, my finances got complicated.

My fiscal ace in these difficulties was my one genuine blue-chip athlete: Petey Brovnic, whose career was the surest thing I was ever going to manage. I first saw Petey as a sophomore in a big suburban high school, one of those outfits with a first-class rink and gym, well-groomed athletic fields, and an ambitious coaching staff. He was a late bloomer who had not yet showed the all-important tendency to grow tall. But even several inches short of big-time height, Petey was lovely on skates. It's easy to be impressed by the big hit and the powerful shot, but the ones that are going all the way look easy on the blades and operate with a touch of the poet.

That was Petey and right away I was interested. I got more so when I saw he had anticipation, the extra sense to cut right or left just a second or two before a pass that he would bury in the five hole or loft into the top corner of the net. He was a thing of beauty, I kid you not.

Was I the only one to notice this phenom? Absolutely not, but somehow, on what I considered until recently the luckiest day of my professional life, Petey Brovnic signed with me instead of a big-name agency, and I wound up with a potential NHL all-star in my pocket.

Recent events have led me to assess that day differently. At the time, I naturally credited my reputation for getting young players onto good teams, for steering my second-tier guys through the maze of college choices, and for seeing that any loose cash from ambitious junior owners flowed to my real prospects. *Petey will be in good hands*, I promised his father, a heavy man with the big frame that suggested Petey would add the weight and muscle he'd need to make the big time. *I know you'll see he gets all he deserves,* his dad replied.

'Course, his dad was talking in terms of playing time and awards and, down the road, a seven-figure signing bonus and multi-million-dollar contracts. I was on board with that. I saw myself bringing along a young player and positioning him to reap the rewards of genetics plus hard work, because Petey was a worker.

Every team he ever played on from mites to NHL had the same report: he's first on the ice and last off and work, work, work every minute in between. Gym, too, and cross-training to keep him fit and give him an edge. He covered all his bases— even the books. Plan B if he blew out his knee or took a bad hit to the head: the college game and something in business. He'd have been fine; he was that smart.

So, you're thinking a paragon, huh? Student athlete and hockey player of genius. He sure looked the part, and on the ice, he never let me down. Off ice, well, now we get to the heart of the matter, but I want you to understand that when you are offered a once-in-a-lifetime prospect, you aren't keen to kick the tires. It was only later that I began to suspect that it wasn't my reputation for hockey sagacity that had put Petey's signature on my agency agreement.

I think, rather, that the high-powered player reps spotted some warning signs and cooled off. I saw a few myself, but nothing that a few years of growing up couldn't cure. Petey had a bit of a temper. Lost it occasionally on the ice. So work to do there. And we did, me and his dad, though Dad was of the macho rough and tumble school with dubious contacts in trash haulage and dodgy construction. He was prone to shouting *Let the kids play* at the ref and defending even the most flagrant boarding as *just a clean hit*.

Still, Mr. Brovnic was ambitious for Petey and big enough to enforce any edict that would promote the boy's career. Petey came in one day with an unexplained black eye, and after that, his off-the-puck fouls and roughing penalties dropped markedly. Good behavior made Petey more valuable. He was signed by one of the top junior clubs and departed at sixteen for Canada to make his fortune. And mine.

At the time I was a little surprised that his dad was so eager for Petey to go north when we had reasonably good junior teams closer to home. I mentioned this during negotiations. *Change of scene,* said his dad and gave me to understand that the topic was closed. Okay. No doubt Canada takes its juniors seriously, and Petey was going to the very best, a perennial championship contender.

He stayed for two years before he was abruptly traded to a team in the Maritimes. I called his original coach, because Petey's stats had been nearly off the charts. *Well,* the coach said, *Petey's new team's building up for the Memorial Cup, and they made an excellent offer. This is business, Adam,* etc., etc. I told him to cut the bullshit.

There'd been an incident, the coach said finally. Boys being boys, basically, but the feeling was that Petey might benefit from being in a smaller city. Beyond that the coach wasn't saying except that, personally, he was damn sorry to see Petey go.

Not girl trouble, I said then.

No, he said, *nothing like that.*

I heard warning bells, because the next most likely thing was drugs of some sort. Using, obtaining, selling, the usual possibilities. I sounded out Petey's dad and had a heart-to-heart talk with my star prospect.

No, no, Mr. Hundlow, Petey said. *It was all friend of a friend stuff. Just trying to fit in with the older gang.*

I'd have been entirely sympathetic if I hadn't caught his cool and appraising look, not like a kid being called on the carpet but like a savvy adult checking to see if his story would fly.

After I gave him the usual warning not to blow a big talent on short-term gains and dubious pleasures, he packed his gear and went off to rack up big numbers in the Maritimes. Thanks to him, his new club got to the Memorial Cup finals and that they didn't lift the trophy wasn't Petey's fault.

He spent that summer filling out his frame and by the time he was eighteen, he had NHL written all over him and a draft bonus to prove it. He got himself a sharp car, which worried me a little. I hate to see a good portion of my income tooling around in a vehicle that can cruise at 120 miles per hour. But either he was careful or the local cops cut him some slack, because there were no troubles with the car.

He left the rest of his signing bonus for me to invest, and I thought that he was growing up, despite a complicated social life that occasionally required my intervention to keep girlfriends happy. I should really have been worry free, but over the next couple of years, I couldn't help noticing that Petey was a big spender for a player whose bonus I'd invested conservatively in index funds and a small condo. He was getting a reputation for lavish out-of-season parties at pricey restaurants, and I could have paid off my mortgage with what he was spending on threads and shoes.

He upped his dating budget, too, with a skinny beauty who pulled down four figures per hour on the runway and had a serious yen for the finer things in life. I warned him about going into debt, and then when he saw that reassurances wouldn't cut it, he added that he was a silent partner in a garage that did top-of-the-line body work.

I should have put it to him then that if he wanted a different financial advisor, I could give him the names of some honest guys. But Martha's rehab was long and expensive, Sue needed a bundle for some summer program abroad, and Joey's orthodontist remained a man of great ingenuity, so I let it slide. Old friends are not always the best friends where big money athletes are concerned, but I told myself that Petey was a nice suburban kid and ignored the fact he was living close to Bridgeport, not to mention the assorted mobs of New York.

You can probably guess that there were some worries in the back of my mind. The cautious part of my brain was adding up little details—Petey's still edgy temper, his frequent need for changes of scene, his old pals with lucrative businesses, even his father's reputed mob connections—and coming up with a big picture that the rest of me was ignoring.

Then came the morning when he called me early. This was rare. Morning was for crack-of-dawn workouts in season and for sleeping in during the off months. *Adam,* he said, soon as the preliminaries were over, *I need a little favor.*

Sure thing, I said, and he launched into a complicated story focused on Delphine—the skinny model of the expensive tastes. Seems my man had been cheating on her with a lady packing a little more flesh on her bones. Unsurprising but awkward because Face Fabulous and Skater Supreme were about to be featured in a pricey ad spread. *Complications, Adam,* he said, and I could see them landing on my desk.

To cut to the chase, what he needed was for us to have been together the night before. Late meeting at the office—okay, I'd been there alone—followed by a drive back to my suburban manse. Possible. I'd taken the train that morning. *All right,* I said. *But if anyone checks—*

Naw, he said. *Delphine knows you're my main man in finance.*

I took out my appointment book and added Petey's name to my previous schedule. Then I went through and told my secretary I'd seen him the day before. *Late,* I told her. *A late call. Just put it in the calendar for the record.*

Romantic troubles avoided, the ad was shot. Perhaps you've seen it—it won some kind of award and they both wound up on the cover of *People:* "Glamor Couples of the Millennium." Right.

Petey spent that off season being glamorous, and I began to think I might just have the next David Beckham on my hands, when a little of the old Petey showed its hand. This was just before training camps started, and he was out very late clubbing with Delphine. Their chosen locale was dead fashionable but edgy, and late in the evening, a drunk accosted Petey, who flattened his assailant but broke a bone in his hand in the process. When another man joined the fray, my client pulled out a Glock and fired into the air. He shattered a couple of fancy lights and cleared the dance floor quite nicely.

Petey's hand took six weeks to mend, setting back his on-ice preparation and producing bad vibes from his team that required yours truly to go into damage control mode, especially since the Glock lacked the proper permit. Petey claimed it was an old family handgun, picked up because Delphine had been troubled by a stalker. A general belief in the tooth fairy would have come in handy at this point, but I put Petey in touch with a good criminal lawyer and things were settled with a hefty fine.

At the time, I surmised that some money must also have passed to the club and to the assailant of the evening, because no charges were pressed. Big relief! Delphine of the skinny hips and gorgeous face found herself a hedge fund magnate and left the Petey scene. Another relief. My man was back on the ice, scoring goals right and left, and I signed checks for orthopedists, therapists, school trips, and pricey dentists with a lighter heart.

So when the corpse turned up—"Body Discovered in Brant Quarry"—my eyes slid right over the story and on to the sports pages. The follow up, however, got my attention. The deceased had been identified, and the best guess was that the late Kyle Galen had been murdered by criminal associates. I called Petey. "Wasn't Kyle Galen in high school with you?" I asked him.

"Name's familiar," he said. Petey in cool mode. "But just barely. He get a contract?"

"Maybe," I said, "but not the right kind. They fished him out of the quarry."

"He was the guy they found? Poor Kyle! I haven't seen him since—I think it was middle school."

"I hope not," I said, "because your old friend had a record as long as my arm."

"You worry too much, Adam," he said. "If I didn't know better, I'd think you didn't trust me."

Feathers to be smoothed. "You must realize it's still unfortunate," I said. "And I hope you've properly registered that handgun. You did take care of all the legalities, right?"

"Would have," he said casual as could be. "Some dirtbag broke into the Porsche and stole the Glock. Right out of the glove compartment. Can you believe that?"

Frankly, I could not.

"I don't know what we pay taxes for. So, no. It's long gone."

"You tell anyone about this?"

"I'm reminding you now, Adam." There was an edge to his voice I didn't much like. "I'm sure I sent you a text the day it happened. But you've a lot on your mind, what with contracts coming up. Better check your emails," he said and hung up.

I had a bad feeling right then that I was being put on the spot, and after a bit of hard thinking, I called a cop I know. I'd helped his boy to a free ride at a Division One college, and he was willing to share a little info, like how long the late Kyle

Galen had been dead. "Hard to say for sure, but probably six, seven months. And just so's you know, he was shot with a Glock 17 C. Bullet still in the cranium."

"That's—" I am not a gun enthusiast and I'm vague on makes and calibers but *Glock* rang a bell.

"Yeah, Petey Brovnic's model." I was worried before he added, "His and a couple hundred thousand other folks.'"

I felt better until the blogosphere discovered a connection between Petey and Kyle Galen. Overblown, sure, but putting together one thing and another, I realized that Petey's move to our big neighbor to the north must have been designed to put some distance between him and Galen and other associates, high school punks who were even then moving a lot of marijuana and ecstasy.

Petey had retained his entrepreneurial spirit up north, hence the move to the Maritimes, not to mention that oh-so-profitable, specialized garage investment. Just what they'd been cooking up there, I'd like to know. Or not. At least until Martha was walking like normal on her new artificial foot, Joey lost the metal in his mouth, and Sue had her BA and a job, total ignorance seemed the best bet.

Anyway, that's how I handled the detective who arrived a week later. This was not my friend Mark with the talented winger. This was a little shrimp of a guy who probably didn't even play table hockey. He didn't want to talk sports at all which pretty much deprived me of my usual ice breakers.

"I don't know what I can tell you." I was sitting behind my big desk with star photos and posters and award plaques on three walls. "I manage the off-ice stuff of a big career. Endorsements, promotions, contracts, investments, that's what I do. Petey takes care of business on ice, and I see that we maximize his profits."

"Mr. Brovnic seems to have some other sources of money," the detective said carefully; he had the kind of expressionless face that can win at poker.

"You can check my books. I have Petey in growth stocks and

real estate. Nothing fancy, nothing too speculative. Athletes tend to be risk takers; I favor mostly conservative investments."

Gospel truth but maybe not the right tack because right away he asks, "Would you say Mr. Brovnic was a risk taker?"

A key question I did not intend to address. "All I can speak to is his career, and I'd say he manages that very shrewdly."

He cleared his throat. "Mr. Brovnic tells me that he was in a meeting with you on the night of June sixteenth this year."

"I meet Petey frequently," I said, casting my mind back. June sixteen? Was that the day he called me for *a little favor*? I really hoped not. "He takes an active interest in his investments and in the details of his contacts."

"But June sixteen in particular?" the detective asked.

"We'll have to check my calendar. Jane keeps me up to date." My normally easy laugh sounded nervous. "August, July, June. Here we go, June sixteen. Yes. *Evening conference with P. Brovnic.* I remember now, he called late in the day and stopped by the office. Kept me so long I missed my train and he drove me home." Whoa, I thought, watch that impulse to elaborate.

The detective took a careful look at the entry. "Looks like your secretary's handwriting."

"If I have a late meeting, I ask her to enter it the next day. Keeps the record straight."

"I don't suppose you remember what was so urgent?"

"With big-time athletes everything is urgent."

"Whatever you can recall would be helpful," he said and handed me his card.

I promised to do my best and asked, as casually as I could, why June sixteenth was of such interest.

"That was the last day Kyle Galen was seen alive," he said.

After he left, I called Petey, who didn't want to talk on the phone. "I'm driving, man, and you're always on about automotive safety. I'll stop by, okay? Meet you at the coffee shop."

But when we got there, he didn't want coffee and he didn't want to sit. "A walk," he said. "Let's hit the park."

Alarm bells for me. "The detective," I began.

"I know about him. Tell me something new."

"June sixteenth is new."

His expression was bland. "We had a late meeting. I drove you home. With that detour, I wasn't at the condo until ten."

"Except you called me and asked a favor. We didn't meet at all."

"No one needs to know that. Really, Adam, you called me for a meeting about this?"

"Small stuff," I agreed, "unless you were in Kyle Galen's vicinity that night. I'm your alibi, Petey, and you're asking me to lie for you."

"And I'm your alibi, too," he said. "Remember that."

This was brazen even for a star athlete. "You're kidding me. I never met the man."

"He was dangerous," Petey said coldly. "He wanted to trade on old times and own a piece of me. So maybe you were worried about your star client. Plausible, right?"

Well, yes, it was, but I didn't have longstanding ties to criminals like Galen. I should have told him right then to get a new agent. Instead, I thought about bills outstanding and said, "You don't pay me enough for this kind of grief."

"I'm sometimes out of line," Petey said, reaching for the charm. "But I trust you, Adam. Who else can I trust? Not the old gang, that's for sure." He gave a bitter smile and reached into his pocket for an envelope. "I don't want you thinking I'm not grateful."

I hesitated. Let the record show I hesitated and there were various bad vibes from Petey before I took an envelope fat enough for the new prothesis Martha would probably need. Real generosity was one of Petey's virtues. But, though the money was welcome, even necessary, the amount raised enough concern that when a West Coast team started angling for him, I urged him to make a change. Petey wasn't interested. He liked the East, and even after I upped my percentage, he apparently liked—or at least, trusted—me.

So we went along together, pretending everything was fine. Sometimes I got to thinking, hoping really, that he might switch agencies, because I lacked the willpower to dismiss him as a client. This was usually after another of the dubious favors he seemed to need with increasing regularity. Other times, when Martha's bills came due or the kids needed this or that for school, I worried that he might leave my modest stable.

What Petey thought about the situation, I don't know, because he appeared to have outsourced any worries to me. And why not? I was the one who followed the Kyle Galen case, paid the lawyer's bills, and kept the hockey beat men sweet. While I gobbled antacid pills, he skated with careless abandon as if lethal associates and a potential homicide charge had simply evaporated.

I made every effort not to know whether Petey had dropped his dodgy off-ice associates, and I lived in passable ignorance until the night he called for a meeting. "This is for *business*, if you get my meaning." I couldn't miss the heavy tone of voice. "Business that involves you, too, Adam."

Events had taken the turn I'd been dreading. Somehow a few little favors, starting with lies to pacify Face Fabulous, had entangled me in some *business* I wanted no part of. I did not respond until he added, "Look, Adam, you're known. Your family, too."

I believed him, though perhaps I shouldn't have. "Okay," I said. I was still at the office and I asked when I could expect him. Or did he prefer the bar across the street?

Neither. Petey gave me an address of an auto body shop, no doubt the garage that had supplied his extra income and been the haunt of the late Kyle Galen. I found it on a deserted industrial street, a nondescript building of several bays. Cars in all states of repair crowded a lot surrounded by a chain-link fence with razor-wire topping. All it needed was the classic junkyard dog. I pulled to the curb but kept the motor running. This was not my scene at all. *Where are you?* I messaged. *The place is all dark.*

Door's unlocked, he replied instantly.

I liked that even less, but I switched off the motor. Mine was the only vehicle on the street, and I wondered what had persuaded Petey to leave his red Porsche behind and risk some telltale ride service. I was approaching the office door before I saw a dented black SUV squeezed close to the building.

Not a typical Petey ride for sure, but I had my hand on the doorknob before the strangeness kicked up a warning. I walked over to the car and touched the hood, still warm despite the chill night. My heart jumped. The dossier that the canny part of my brain had been assembling was suddenly open in front of me: I was in deep shit.

I stepped back from the door, edged past the SUV and tried to see through the dirty and clouded side windows. Was that a light? More than one? I moved to another window and caught the distinctive blue rectangle of a cell phone: Petey, texting me to see what the holdup was! Then a white circle of LED light revealed that this was a stranger and he wasn't alone. I dropped below the window, and I barely had time to wonder what sort of game my star center was playing before the familiar red Porsche slid into the yard.

Petey stepped out, looking big and determined and carrying what I guessed was that "stolen" Glock. He straightened his jacket and strode toward the garage. I was visible beside the SUV but he didn't glance my way. Why would he? He expected me to be inside. *Door's unlocked,* he'd said, meaning, *Go right in, Adam.* So the only question was, had he known about the two guys inside?

I stood up. With an impulse to warn him? To call, *Petey!* Or thump on the hood of the black SUV? Or give a silent wave? He'd have seen the motion; his peripheral vision was superb, the key to his "blind" passes and effortless teamwork. I'm sure I opened my mouth, but no sound came out, because he had deceived me, because despite charm and generosity, he was a homicidal son of a bitch.

He opened the door to a fusillade. I froze, then lunged toward my car, stumbled into the driver's side, and screamed away. Stupid, of course, but maybe they'd been deafened, because when I got up the courage to look behind me, there were no lights. I didn't think about Petey or his career or even my percentage, just the need to get out of the nightmare.

Eventually, I was shaking so badly that I stopped at a highway rest area, turned off the motor and put my head on the steering wheel until I was breathing normally. I fought shock with a cup of coffee and a highly sugared donut and drove home.

There was nothing in the morning papers nor on drivetime news. I finally caught a broadcast at work: a shooting in an auto body shop, name withheld until the next of kin was notified. By afternoon, the story had broken. No anonymous punk. No wannabe gangster. No honest mechanic gunned down in a robbery gone wrong. It was Petey Brovnic, the glamorous all-star center, dead at twenty-eight. My phone started to ring. You can be sure I said all the right things—I was shocked, sick at heart, stunned, filled with sorrow—and most of them were sincere.

The next day the non-sports fan detective arrived. Of course, he had Petey's phone records and questions.

"Yeah, he called me. I was worried."

"Had you been to the garage before?" The detective wanted to know. His name was Herman, and the bland, noncommittal expression that had irritated me during our first interview now struck me as soothing. He wasn't deeply invested in Petey Brovnic or his reputation or the fate of his memorabilia.

I shook my head. "But he had mentioned it. He was a silent partner in the business."

The detective took that under advisement. "You knew about the business?"

"I knew he had more money than I was able to make for him. That's all."

"So. You went to the garage."

"You've got the calls."

"You assumed he was in the building, but you didn't go in. Why not?"

I told him about the dented SUV beside the garage, and the detective stopped the interview to pass on the description to the traffic and surveillance people.

Funny, isn't it, how fate can turn on the smallest detail. My cooperation and observant eye secured his goodwill, and, eventually, my handprint on a ditched SUV led back to two of Petey's old high school associates. With them secured, my transgressions were minimized, and, given that I had fortuitously insured my big breadwinner, you could say that I landed on my feet. My name is certainly known now and I have almost more prospects than I can handle.

Of course, there's a downside that I've kept from the kids and minimized with Martha, because I'm hoping that I'll be okay. I have a top-of-the-line security system and vary my routes and routines, very necessary since apparently either inquiring minds think I know a lot more than I do or feel the need to complete Petey's plan. To forestall them, I also keep in touch with Herman, who's not a bad guy. Most days the detective's sympathetic, and he keeps me in the loop on dangerous characters, including Petey's grieving dad, who feels I should have walked through that garage door and into permanent residence at St. Benedict's Cemetery.

Unfair of him. Thanks to me, Petey probably got what he deserved, but I really do miss him and not just for my percentage. Why is that when he was treacherous and selfish and a menace to society?

Because he was a prince on skates.

COMES AND GOES
Alan Orloff

"He begged you to bring him along, didn't he?" Drew Simms asked from the passenger seat.

The driver, Cory Harford, glanced into the rearview mirror at his uncle Pete in the back, who was staring straight ahead, blank expression on his stubble-covered face. Cory lowered his voice and answered Drew, his partner in crime. "He hates being left alone. And something might happen, you know?"

"Something better not happen here," Drew said.

"My father and Pete taught me everything I know about the business. Cut him some slack. It's not his fault he's...the way he is."

"Going soft in the melon?" Drew said, a little too loud for Cory's taste. After all, Pete wasn't hard of hearing, he was just declining mentally. And the decline seemed to be accelerating.

"Keep it down, will you?" Cory looked at Pete in the rearview mirror. His uncle—his father's brother—had directed his empty stare out the side window. For the hundredth time, Cory wondered what was going through the old guy's mind. Was he remembering when he was in Cory's place, riding off to pull a heist? Or was he just thinking about this morning's breakfast of buttermilk pancakes? Did he have any inkling about the state of his mind? Did he realize he would keep deteriorating until he couldn't remember his own name? Cory sure hoped not; he wouldn't wish that on his enemies. The man deserved to go out on his own terms.

"He better not screw things up," Drew said, hammering home the point.

"Don't worry. If anything, he'll be an asset. He used to run with this crew, years ago, before they had a falling out. Maybe he can help us if things go sideways. He's not always confused. Sometimes he's lucid enough to remember some detail or answer an important question. It comes and goes, you know?"

"I *don't* know. Having him along still makes me nervous."

"He'll stay in the car and keep watch, warn us if something happens while we're inside taking care of things." Cory had been tipped off by his fence, Big Dog Bohannon, who'd been approached by another gang to buy some stolen jewelry. Big Dog owed Cory a debt, and alerting him to an easy score was his way of paying it off. All cool with Cory. In many ways, it was less risky ripping off other thieves—they'd never report it. To put the cherry on top, they'd be taking down a long-time rival crew led by royal douchebag Norb Fletcher.

"He really can't remember what happened five minutes ago?" Drew sounded skeptical, but Cory knew that after spending some time with his uncle, he'd believe it, in spades.

"The mind can be a tricky thing, all right."

Drew addressed Pete in the back seat. "Do you know where we're going?"

Pete shrugged. "For a ride?"

"A ride where?"

"The zoo?"

"Ha! Naw, man, we're going to see old friends."

"Don't be a dick," Cory said. "One day, you could be like him."

"Hell, no. Kill me first." Drew engaged Pete again. "Hey, where are we going, Uncle Pete?"

Pete frowned, then shrugged. "For a ride? To the zoo?"

"Bingo. To the zoo. To see the lions." Drew let out a little roar, then laughed.

"Will you fucking cut it out? This isn't some freak show." Cory turned on the car stereo, hoping to prevent Drew from harassing Pete any more.

A minute later, Drew reached over and switched off the radio. "How is it, day to day, living with him?"

After Cory's father died last year, Cory had taken Pete in— the poor guy had nowhere else to go. "It's bizarre, at times. Sometimes he remembers who he is and what he's done, and other times, I could tell him he's the Good Humor man and he'll try to sell me a Creamsicle. Like I said, comes and goes."

"That's messed up."

"Yeah, it is."

One half of Drew's thick unibrow arched. "And he's going to be like this until…"

"Who knows? Since my old man died, Pete's been on a steady decline. Things seemed to take a sharp turn for the worse, about two weeks ago. Right around the time we started planning this job, in fact." Cory lowered his voice. "His long-term memory isn't too bad. He can't remember what happened twenty minutes ago, but he can tell long stories about shit that happened twenty *years* ago."

"Oh yeah? I'd like to hear some stories." Drew swiveled to the back seat. "Yo, Uncle Pete."

"Leave him be." Cory checked the rearview. His uncle kept his gaze focused out the window. Cory was pretty sure Pete heard Drew and was ignoring him. Maybe his uncle still had some brains, after all.

"Relax. I'd like to know anything that might be pertinent to our job here," Drew said to Cory. Then, "Hey, Uncle Pete. This could be important. What happened with Fletcher? What caused you guys to part ways?"

Cory examined Pete in the mirror. He hadn't moved. Then,

slowly, he turned his head to face Drew. "Ruined my life, the fucking bastard."

Drew snapped his fingers. "I knew you were listening to me. How did he ruin your life?"

"Come on, man. Don't get him riled up," Cory said. Trying to get a rise out of an old, memory-impaired man was just like Drew. Sometimes Cory wondered why he worked with the dipshit.

"Don't crush the man's dignity. He wants to answer my question, let him answer. I'm sure Pete doesn't want to be treated like a child. Ain't that right, Pete?"

"Fuckin' bastard. Screwed me, but good." Pete spoke in an unsettling monotone, as if he'd been popping downers like Tic Tacs. "We'd just pulled a job and were divvying things up, when Fletcher—the self-proclaimed boss, really just a big asshole— declared that he got half, right off the top, before the split. I called bullshit, and the rest of the fuckers took his side. Sent me on my way with zilch. Fucking fuckers!" Then, seemingly out of nowhere, Pete pulled a gun and began waving it around.

"Holy shit, put that down!" Drew held both hands in front of his face, as if that would protect him. "Easy, now."

Pete pointed the gun directly at Drew, right between the eyes. Where his hand had been shaking like a crazy man's before, now it was rock steady.

It was Cory's turn to laugh. "Don't worry, I made sure it's not loaded. Having it makes him feel like part of the gang again. Gives his life meaning. Got to try to do nice things for him when you can, you know?"

"Well, there's such a thing as being *too* nice." Drew's face had gone pale.

In the mirror, Cory watched Pete gently put the gun in his lap and stare out the window again, a faint smile on his lips. Cory whispered to Drew, "He's harmless. Back in the day, he was a mean SOB, but now, he wouldn't hurt a fly."

"It's not the insects I'm worried about," Drew said, then

turned and stared out his own side window.

They drove for another twenty minutes, through the outer burbs into a more rural area, leaving behind the blight of strip shopping centers and cookie-cutter housing developments in favor of untamed vegetation.

Cory hoped Big Dog hadn't been lying when he'd said Fletcher had confused isolation with security. According to Big Dog's source, there were only two members of Fletcher's crew holding down the proverbial fort: Fletcher and his right-hand man, Marty Vinson.

Cory had met Fletcher once before about fifteen years ago, when he, his father, and Pete found themselves working together with Fletcher and his cronies on some giant insurance fraud scheme, sort of like subcontractors on a huge construction project. To be honest, Cory and Fletcher hadn't exchanged more than a passing nod then, but Cory had heard stories—from his father and Pete—about how much of a shithead double-dealer Fletcher was.

It would be sweet to screw him, but good, on this one.

A few more turns down increasingly narrow roads until Cory pulled over on the dirt shoulder. "Fletcher's place is right through these trees, about thirty yards." He unbuckled his seat belt and shifted to face the others. Drew mirrored him in the passenger seat. "It's showtime."

Pete stared out the side window.

"Uncle Pete?"

He didn't move.

Cory reached back and gently touched him on the shoulder. "Uncle Pete. Time to go over the plans. For the job, remember?"

Pete slowly swiveled to face Cory and Drew. "What job?"

"Jesus Christ," Drew said under his breath.

Cory ignored him, spoke directly to Pete, calm and steady. "The job. We talked about it. Ripping off Fletcher."

A blank stare from Pete.

Cory licked his lips, swallowed. "How about if I go through it again, okay?"

"Sure," Pete said. "Again."

"Okay, here's the plan. According to Big Dog, these guys are soft and they're not expecting any trouble whatsoever. Drew and I are going in through the back door, ski caps on, guns drawn. We'll surprise them, tie them up, take their loot. All goes right, we'll be back in about five minutes." Cory tapped Pete on the shoulder again to make sure he had the man's attention. "Here's what you need to do, Uncle Pete. Stay here in the car. Be the lookout. If you see anyone at all, use this to call me on my cell." Cory handed another phone to Pete. "Got it?"

Pete nodded.

"Remember. Stay in the car, no matter what, okay?"

Pete echoed the instructions robotically. "Stay in the car. No matter what."

"Okay then. Let's go."

Cory and Drew hopped out and met in front of the car. "You sure he's going to be all right here by himself?" Drew asked.

"Don't worry, nothing will go wrong."

"What if he calls us, just for the hell of it? How will we know if there's really someone coming?" Drew said.

"First off, no one's going to wander by the car, way out here in Bumfucksville. Second, even if he knew how to use the phone, there's no juice in the battery. And he's not going anywhere because I put the child locks on. Trust me, he'll just sit in the car and hum to himself. Besides, we'll be back in five minutes." Cory slipped his ski mask over his head. "Come on, let's get this over with."

Cory and Drew hustled through the trees until they had eyes on Fletcher's house, a nondescript, two-story, piece-of-crap shack. Peeling paint. Trash in the yard. Country manor living at its finest, it wasn't.

Keeping to the tree line, they circled around toward the rear of the house. Then, staying low, they dashed ten yards through a small clearing to the wall, taking up positions next to the back door. Cory reached out and turned the knob. Unlocked. So Fletcher was an idiot, in addition to being a shithead.

Confusing isolation with security. Cory bet he would never make that mistake again. Holding his gun tightly, he jerked his head toward the open door, waited for Drew to step in, then followed.

They quickly passed through a small laundry room and snuck into the kitchen. Sounds of a television blared from the adjacent room. Cory peeked around the corner, saw Fletcher and Vinson lounging in a family room, watching some old movie on a big flat screen TV.

Cory shrank back, stared at Drew through the cutouts in the ski mask, then gave him a thumbs up. *Go.*

Together, they burst into the TV room, screaming and brandishing their weapons. Fletcher threw the remote control at Cory's head, but Cory batted it away. "Don't fucking move!"

Fletcher cussed and put up a token fight, but Cory had the older man subdued and on the floor, hands zip-tied behind him, in twenty seconds. On the other side of the room, Drew had little trouble tying up Vinson.

Big Dog had been right; Fletcher and Vinson were soft. Of course, everything was easier when you held the guns.

Cory fished a roll of duct tape from the pocket of his hoodie, along with a knife. He and Drew used virtually the entire roll to tie up the thieves. They taped arms to torsos and legs together. By now, Fletcher's threats had petered out. Hard to sound tough when you were wrapped head-to-toe in duct tape.

"Where's the stuff?"

Fletcher and Vinson kept their lips pressed together.

"You know we'll find it. If you want us to trash the place looking, that's your choice." Cory waited a moment to see if Fletcher would cave; Fletcher just stared daggers at him. Cory wished he could take off his mask and show Fletcher who was ripping him off, but he knew better. No sense starting some kind of never-ending feud. "Suit yourself."

Cory used the last of the duct tape to cover their mouths.

Cory sent Drew upstairs, while he searched the floor they were on. A few minutes later, Drew came storming down the stairs carrying two Nordstrom shopping bags.

"Bingo, baby. All packed up and ready to roll." Drew turned to the two saps lying on the floor and saluted them with the barrel of his gun to his forehead. "A pleasure doing business with you, losers."

Cory and Drew hustled from the house, this time through the front door. They ran straight through the woods, no longer worried about stealth.

When they reached the car, Cory stopped short. "Oh shit."

The driver's door was wide open.

"Oh shit is right," Drew said. "Where's your fucking uncle?"

Cory spun around, hoping to spot Pete chasing butterflies or smelling flowers or entranced by some nature shit, but he was nowhere to be seen.

Drew's eyes bugged out. "Where the fuck is your goddamn uncle?"

"I guess he climbed into the front seat and got out."

"I thought you said he wouldn't go anywhere. You said he couldn't get out of the fucking car. Child locks, my ass." Spittle flew from Drew's mouth.

"Calm down, he couldn't have gone far."

"Okay, smart guy, where would a guy with dementia go?"

"Anyplace," Cory said. "Let's split up. I'll head toward the road, and you go—"

"Oh fuck me." Drew bent over and picked up something shiny. A bullet. Then he took a closer look underneath the car. He dropped to his knees and pulled out a half-full box of ammo. "I think you've been played, man. Big time."

A gunshot rang out, and although it was difficult to pinpoint the origin, Cory figured it must have come from the house. Had

Uncle Pete somehow doubled back on them? Cory took off at a dead run, with Drew close behind, and as they sprinted, another gunshot boomed. When the house came into view, Cory skidded to a halt, and Drew pulled up next to him.

Pete stood on the porch, holding his weapon at his side.

For a moment, nobody moved. Then Cory whispered to Drew, "I'll take care of this. Go back to the car. Get it started and ready to roll. We need to get the hell out of here."

Drew narrowed his eyes, opened his mouth to speak, but thought better of it and loped back toward the car.

Cory approached the house, climbing the two stairs to the porch extra slowly. He spoke quietly, trying not to spook his uncle, who remained motionless, still gripping his gun. "You okay?"

Another faint smile formed on Pete's lips. "Fine."

"Did you...? Are they...?"

A curt nod. "I did what I came to do."

"You sure you're okay?" Cory asked.

"Yep. Never better, in fact." He stood there with a grin on his otherwise blank face.

"You sure you're okay?"

"I'm fine now. You know, it comes and goes." Pete's grin melted away. "But I'll be bad again. Real bad. Real, *real* bad."

As far as Cory knew, Pete had never killed anyone before. Maybe he was in shock. He figured they could sort things out later, deal with the inevitable emotional fallout. Right now, Cory needed to get his uncle back to the car without further incident, and they all needed to leave the scene of the crime. He gently put a hand on Pete's shoulder. "Let's go, okay?"

Pete didn't move, but a change seemed to wash over him. Cory stared deep into his uncle's eyes, noticing something he hadn't seen in a long time. A spark of life. Then a glint of more: *satisfaction. Relief.* There was a shift within, and Cory detected a deeper emotion. Something darker. *Fear.* Finally, after one last inner transformation, Cory was met with a look he couldn't quite identify, but if he had to guess, he'd peg it as *acceptance*.

"Come on, we need to get out of here. Quickly."

"Okay," Pete said. "Let's go."

Cory took off for the car, leading the way.

Before he'd gone ten steps, another gunshot sounded behind him.

He hesitated for a second, then kept on moving, didn't turn back, just kept going, faster and faster toward his escape, knowing that Uncle Pete had finally, mercifully, found his.

VIKING BLOOD

Adam Meyer

It's all my mother's fault, you understand. If she hadn't gone around running her mouth about our Viking blood, I wouldn't be in this mess. But she did and I am and that's all there is to it.

When I was eight or nine and those bigger kids would try to push me around at the bus stop, my mother would say, "You don't let them do that, hear me? You're a fighter, Miles." I never felt like a fighter with my glasses pushed back against the bridge of my nose and my coat collar damp with fear-sweat. But my mother looked me right in the eye and said, "We got Viking blood in our family, you know. And the Vikings were some of the toughest people that ever lived."

Of course, that didn't do anything to stop those shitheads from tying me up with the straps on my backpack, or stealing my lunch money and using it to buy Pokémon cards. But within a month of hearing my mother repeat those words again and again—"We got Viking blood"—I felt a little bit stronger, more powerful, more confident. One day, when I shuffled up to the bus stop and saw Jason Delaney moving in, I heard my mother's voice as loud as if she was standing right there. A red-hot wave scorched my chest, and my arms and legs hummed with energy. I watched beneath the brim of my baseball cap as Jason rolled

129

up, and then I charged him, fast as I could, bringing my head up under his chin.

In the end, he got eleven stitches, and I had a quiet time at the bus stop for the rest of the year. All thanks to my mother telling me about our Viking blood.

My mother was all I had, really, since my father had left years before. "He was a mean son of a bitch and lazy, too," she often said. "Didn't want to change a diaper or give you a bottle, never lifted a finger around here. We're better off without him."

"Can't I at least meet him sometime?"

"Afraid not. He moved west years ago, didn't say where or how to find of him. And he hasn't got any family, no idea where he came from." She ruffled my hair, like I was still a preschooler or something. "But what's that matter when we got each other?"

That might've been true, but when I was growing up, there always seemed to be someone else around too. One guy or another. Funny thing was, they all acted like they were going to be Mr. Forever. I knew better. When they tried to buddy up to me, I just laughed and turned on the TV. That used to bug them but I didn't care. By next week or next month or next year, they'd be gone, and it would just be and my mom again.

Then when I was twelve, Carl moved in. He wasn't my mother's usual type. He was a little heavy and had kind of a big bald spot and wore glasses to read, which he did a lot, usually novels about cops or criminals. One day, I went into the kitchen to pour myself a bowl of cereal and saw one of Carl's books on the counter. This didn't look like the boring stuff we read in school. The cover had bold colors and a drawing of a woman sprawled across a bed, dark blood staining the sheets.

"What do you think?" he asked.

I froze at the sound of Carl's voice, thinking he was going to backhand me like the last guy had done when I took a sip of one of his beers.

"Sorry. I didn't mean to touch it." I backed away, like the book was radioactive. "It was just lying there, that's all."

"You ever read Jim Thompson?" he asked, smiling.

I shook my head no,

"Go ahead," Carl said, nodding at the book. "Borrow it, see what you think."

He held the old paperback out to me. I glanced down at the title, *The Nothing Man.*

"I don't know if my mom'll want me reading it...I mean..."

"It's a book." He smiled at me as if we were sharing a secret. "It's educational, right?"

Shrugging, I tucked the book under my arm and headed off, listening to the sound of Carl flicking on the TV behind me. I woke up that morning around three, the way I sometimes did, and when I couldn't get back to sleep, I turned on a flashlight and got the novel out. I read nonstop until I was done and when my alarm went off the next morning, I was so tired I could barely roll out of bed.

When I gave *The Nothing Man* back to Carl after school that day, he asked me how I liked it. "It's okay," I told him, and he nodded.

"If you thought that was okay, then you ought to try this."

He gave me another Thompson book, *The Killer Inside Me*, and this one was even better. Soon he had pulled out a whole stack of novels for me, and instead of just watching TV during breakfast, we ended up talking books. I could see it bugged my mom that she didn't know what we were going on about, but that was part of why I liked it.

I liked a lot of things about having Carl around.

Unlike some of Mom's other boyfriends, Carl didn't leave dirty dishes in the sink and he was pretty good about doing stuff like mowing the lawn and raking the leaves. He even painted the bathroom once when Mom said something about all the chips flaking off. Carl started taking me to the movies once a month, on Fridays, when my mom had to work late. We'd go out for pizza after and talk about the action scenes and the crazy stunts, and we'd laugh until we had root beer shooting out our noses.

Everything was great with Carl around, except the fights.

It was my mom, really. She was on Carl for spending too much money on books and movies and pizza, saying that was why he never had enough to help her cover the rent. Sometimes me and him would be having fun, watching TV or talking books, and my mother would just lash out at him about this or that. As soon as she started in on him, I'd slink off to my room, turning my music up so loud that I couldn't hear them.

Then one day I came home from school and saw Carl loading boxes in the rear of his hatchback. They were full of books and DVDs, which was pretty much all he owned.

"Hey, buddy," he said, holding his hand up against the sun. It was only four thirty but darkness had started to creep in. "Glad I caught you before I head off."

My throat was so tight I could barely get the words out. "Head off where?"

Praying he was going to say the movies or a job interview or Home Depot...

"Well, look, Miles...it's not gonna be any shock to you, I'm sure, that things just aren't working out."

"What do you mean?"

He ruffled my hair, even though I was too old for it. I didn't mind.

"Me and your mom...it's over."

"You can still try." My toes went numb and my mind raced as I tried to think of ways to keep them together. They could see a therapist, right? That was the kind of thing people did on TV, but it might work in real life too.

"I don't think so, buddy. Your mom's just got...a lot of feelings. Not saying it's her fault, you know, but she gets a little crazy sometimes."

"It's just...it's her Viking blood."

Carl looked at me like he was trying to decide whether to say something or not, and finally he nodded. "Yeah, well, that Viking blood of hers...it can make her hard to handle sometimes."

I nodded, the numbness in my toes curdling into something hotter, more intense. Soon I could feel that red-hot tingle burning through my veins like wildfire, driving me to do something, anything, to let it out. My mother wasn't the only one with a temper that could turn on like an overheated furnace, but I fought it down. Tears sprang to my eyes.

"Here, you keep this, Miles." Carl reached into the back of the hatchback, pulled out one of his novels. It was *The Nothing Man*, the one he'd handed me months earlier. "You keep this, read it again. And maybe I'll see you around sometime."

I stood there, clutching that thin paperback so tight my fingers hurt, as Carl's car backed out of the driveway and streaked off.

After that it was just me and Mom for a while. That was lucky, because if some other guy had come along, I probably would've made his life hell. With no one but us around, I turned my anger on my mother. For weeks I stomped up and down stairs, slammed dishes into the sink, and answered questions with a simple "yes" or "no" and said as little else as I could.

"I know you're mad at me," she said one day, as we sat in front of the TV eating cold pizza. "But did you ever stop and think maybe it was Carl's fault things didn't work out?"

"That's a lie." I took another bite of my pizza, the cheese tasting like a blob of old glue. "He was a nice guy."

"To you, maybe." She narrowed her eyes at me. "You don't know what he was really like."

But I had, hadn't I? Carl was someone who'd sit and talk old books for hours, and buy an extra-large popcorn at the movies, and smile at me when I came into the room. My mother's other boyfriends hadn't done any of those things, and she hadn't cared a bit. Besides, Carl had made it clear who was to blame here. She was. Her and her Viking blood. Couldn't she learn how to control herself? Couldn't she be just a little bit nicer sometimes?

After Carl, my mother decided she was going to "take a break from men" for a while. At first I was glad there wouldn't some other random guy in our house, and then I started to wish she'd go find some new boyfriend, even if he was no Carl. I hated coming home to an empty house, and having those dinners with Mom where no one talked except the people on TV, and hearing her whisper into the phone late at night like she was making a confession.

One time, I told my mother how much I missed finding Carl in the kitchen drinking black coffee and reading an old Cornell Woolrich or John D. MacDonald and pulling up beside him. Shrugging, she said I ought to make some friends my own age. I tried to tell her how the kids at school were hard to talk to, how they acted like I was too dumb or too dorky or too weird, and it seemed like I just didn't fit in.

She didn't listen. Of course, she never did.

About midway through my sophomore year of high school, I overheard some kids in my homeroom talking about how they'd stolen a bottle of wine from their parents and gotten drunk. I'd never been wasted but I'd seen my mom that way plenty, and she seemed to like it well enough.

I knew I could never sneak a whole wine bottle from her; she was always tracking how much she had and whether she needed to buy another. But there was liquor in the basement that one of her old boyfriends had left behind that she hardly ever touched. Every day, I'd take a little from one or another, pour some into a glass of Coke, and watch TV, usually some movie with Vin Diesel or The Rock.

In my junior year, I got the idea of bringing my "special soda" in to school in a plastic bottle and that was how I met Hannah. She was tall and skinny with big teeth and too-pale skin but she had shiny blond hair and legs as long as algebra problems. She found me at study hall one day and asked me what I was drinking. I gave her a taste.

After that we sat together nearly every single day, and soon we were going to her place after school too. She told me she was so glad she had a friend like me, and that was all we were, friends. Only I could tell she wanted more, and the truth was so did I.

One afternoon we were doing our social studies homework when I put my pencil down and leaned in and kissed her. She acted surprised, but I wasn't fooled that easily. I kept on going until she started to scream, and when she threw my textbook at me, I stared in disbelief. "Get out!" she howled, tears running down her pale cheeks.

When the principal called me into his office the next morning, he asked me about what happened with Hannah. I told him the truth: we were hanging out and things started to get hot and heavy and she freaked out. He explained that wasn't the way he'd heard it. He also warned me that because he'd found a bottle with alcohol in my locker, he was going to expel me. I told him that wasn't fair, but he said life isn't fair and the sooner I understood that, the better off I'd be.

My mother was pissed, especially after she found out how everyone had taken Hannah's side over mine. When she asked if I'd gone too far with "that girl," I shrugged and said maybe I had, just a little.

"What can I say? Must be my Viking blood."

"Yeah, Viking blood…" My mother swirled the wine in her glass, brought it to her lips. "That and teenage boy hormones are strong stuff. But I know you didn't mean to hurt her."

She said it as if she meant it, but then she looked at me like she was asking a question.

"Of course not. She's my friend."

My mother took a long sip of her wine and nodded. "You're a good boy, Miles."

After that I could've gone to another school, but I didn't bother. I'd never liked math or science or even reading except for those books Carl used to share. But after a while my mother got tired of me sitting on the couch and playing video games all day and told me I had to go out and get a job. There were lots of things I could've done but no one was hiring, and those that were kind of wrinkled their noses when they heard I didn't have a high school diploma. That was how I ended up working at the burger joint.

It was too bad I never got to do the fun stuff, like take people's orders. They let the girls do that, 'cause they could smile and stick their boobs out and get these poor slobs to order a super-sized everything when all they wanted was a cheeseburger. No, I was in the back, suffocated by the smell of old grease and fresh dirt. I dragged in big bags of frozen fries and boxes of ground meat and hunched over those fryers as tiny specks of hot oil sizzled on my skin.

"You know I'm better than this," I told my mother one day as I finished putting on my work uniform. My black pants smelled of grease no matter how many times I washed them. "I mean, I got Viking blood. You think our warrior ancestors would've been flipping burgers? They would've been out there sailing to faraway places and taking whatever they wanted when they got there."

My mother looked at me in the bathroom mirror, her makeup brush in hand. "Miles, you gonna hunt and trap our food like some Viking warrior?"

"Well, no but..."

"Then we need money to pay for it."

"You've got plenty of money. You just don't want to spend it on me."

She put her makeup brush down, glaring. Her hair was carefully combed and sprayed in place, and she wore her red skirt, the one she always saved for first dates.

"Is that what you think?" she asked.

"Sure. You're always looking out for yourself, not me."

"Miles, you have no idea how much I've given up..." She put a hand to her head but her sprayed hair barely moved. "You really believe that?"

"I believe the truth, which is all you've ever cared about is yourself and trying to catch a man."

She squinted at me, as if seeing me for the first time. "You know, you can be real a son of a bitch sometimes, just like your father."

"Yeah, well, I'd rather take after him than you."

My mother's face turned red, her Viking blood rising into her face, and her manicured fingers curled in toward her palms. I'd pushed her too far and I knew it. But if she turned her anger on me, I'd beam it right back at her. Maybe she knew that. Maybe that was why she gritted her teeth and turned.

"I've got to go, Miles. We'll talk about this later."

We didn't talk about it later, because my mother didn't get back until well after midnight, her makeup and carefully combed hair all mussed. That was her first date with Lance, but it wasn't the last. He moved in two months later.

Lance was tall with white hair and a bit of a belly, but he was strong as an ox, hitting the gym at least five times a week. Maybe it was all that muscle, but he walked with a cowboy swagger my mother seemed to love. He worked in construction and made good money, and for the first time in my life my mother had a guy who seemed to take care of her more than she took care of him.

You'd think I'd be happy for her. I guess I was, for a little while. I liked that they went out to dinner a lot and took long weekends upstate, because I had the house to myself and could leave things where I wanted with no one nagging me. But then one day my mother came around and said, "We're thinking maybe it's time you get your own place."

At first I had no idea what she was talking about. The only "we" in that house had ever been me and her.

"You're nineteen years old, Miles, I can't take care of you forever."

"You don't take care of me."

"Yeah? Who cooks your meals? And does your laundry? And picks up after you?"

There's no point in getting into what I said next, or what she said back. Both of us with our Viking blood, we got pretty worked up, as you can imagine.

We each said some things we probably didn't mean to, and for a couple weeks after that we both kind of ignored each other. That was all right, in a way. I did my thing and she did hers, and most days we hardly even saw each other. We could've gone on like that for months, I suppose, except for me getting fired from the burger joint.

The manager said it was on account of me showing up late every other day, but it was always slow in the afternoons when my shift started, so I didn't see why that ought to matter. No, it must've had more to do with that girl Lily, the one who worked the cash register.

She kept chewing me out for trying to put a move on her, and whose fault was that? She was the one who never wanted to move when I had to haul in a load of frozen burger patties, and it was an accident I opened the stall on her while cleaning out the girl's bathroom. But somehow she ended up employee of the month and I got canned.

I didn't make a stink of it, since I never liked that job anyway. Besides, I figured I'd bought myself a few more months of not fighting with my mom about moving, since she couldn't very well pressure me to get my own place when I didn't even have a steady paycheck. Still, I liked the people at the burger joint and I was kind of bummed. I stopped to pick myself up a case of beer on the way home that day to help me feel better.

I only drank a couple on the walk from the store, and they were too damn warm, so I headed into the kitchen to put the rest of the cans in the freezer. I'd seen Lance's car in the driveway, no surprise since he started his days early and was always home by three thirty. Mom had bankers' hours and didn't usually get back until after five. When I got inside, however, I heard the faint sound of a woman's voice. Surprised, I glanced back outside just to be sure, but my mom's car was not in the driveway. I heard some more sounds after that, and I don't have to tell you what they were like.

"What the hell?" Lance said, looking up from the bed he shared with my mother but was now trying out with some other woman. "How long you been standing there?"

"Long enough to see what the hell kind of bastard you are."

I slammed the door on them and went to get myself another beer. There were some cold bottles in the fridge, the fancy stuff Lance liked to drink, and I took one of those instead of the piss-warm cans. I went out in the yard and waited for Lance to come find me. About ten minutes later, he did, sitting down on the back steps. A hot rush of anger shot through me, but I said nothing, just clutched my beer bottle so hard I could feel the glass as hard as stone.

"Look, you want to tell your mom about this, you think you're doing her a favor, but you're wrong about that." He shook his head at me like I was the one in trouble. "You're just gonna hurt her. And what's going on with me and Nora, that don't mean anything anyway."

"Here's what's gonna happen, Lance." I put down my half-finished beer and looked at him closely. "You're gonna pack all your shit and tell my mother things just didn't work out, you're sorry, but you feel like it's time to move on."

"And why the hell'm I gonna do that?" Lance smirked. "She pays the bills, she cooks and cleans, and best of all, she's not bad in the sack. Not to mention, she thinks I'm the best damn thing that's ever happened to her."

I could feel the heat in my veins, the thrumming in my legs and arms. My Viking blood was starting to stir.

"You're a freeloading piece of shit, Lance, and a cheater, and a liar." I stood up, looking down at him, and clutched my beer bottle so tight my fingers hurt. "She may not know it, but she's a hell of a lot better off without you than she is with you."

"That right, Miles?"

Lance stood too, a power play, because he knew he was half a head taller than I was and stronger too. He wore a thin white

T-shirt that showed off his muscles, the veins bulging out of those curved biceps like worms burrowing from the earth. I felt that tingle in my fingers, that wildfire in my belly, and I knew something I'd learned back when I headbutted Jason Delaney down at the bus stop: yeah, this guy might talk tough, but in the end, he was no match for me.

"See you around, Lance."

"What the hell're you—"

I smashed the bottle against the side of his head, hard as I could. My hand moved so fast I could barely see it, and my fingers hummed with the force of the impact. The bottle didn't break—I suppose that kind of thing only happens in the movies—but it busted the side of Lance's head right open. Blood streaked down his close-cropped white hair and one of his too-big ears. He stared at me in disbelief.

"You want to mess with me, Lance?"

"Your mother's right, you know. You're a fucking nutjob."

He stormed off, holding his shirt sleeve against his bloody head.

By the time my mother got home from work that day, he was gone. "Where's Lance at?" she asked. She hadn't gone into the bedroom yet and seen all his clothes missing.

"Must've had someplace to be," I said, shrugging.

My mother figured out what was going on soon enough, and she called Lance on his cell. He didn't pick up. She left a bunch of messages that night, and a few more the next day, and sooner or later she got the idea he wasn't going to call her back. She must've figured I had something to do with Lance taking off. Funny thing was, she never came right out and asked. I didn't tell her anything, either. I figured Lance was right, after all. No point in hurting her if I didn't have to.

After that, my mom and I settled into a routine, just the two of us. She'd go to work and I'd sleep in, get up late, play some video games. I did look for a job, and I even got close a couple times. But when the hiring people called over to the burger joint to check my references, they must've gotten an earful, because they never called me back. I didn't mind. I did some odd jobs around the neighborhood, painting and mowing lawns, enough to put a few bucks in my pocket. I still needed some help covering expenses, and I always took whatever I needed to make up the difference.

One night, I came in from doing some yard work—my mother had been nagging me about trimming those hedges for weeks—and I was too dead tired to make myself dinner so I reached into Mom's purse. All I wanted was a few bucks for a pizza. Her wallet was empty, however. I rummaged around because usually she had some loose bills, a couple fives or even a twenty. I didn't find any cash, but when I was pulling some things out of her purse—a crumpled tissue, a dry cleaning ticket—I found something that surprised me. A receipt for a shrink.

I found my mother in the mud room, sorting a load of my dirty socks and underwear, and held the slip of paper out.

"What the hell's this?" I asked.

"That's...what're you doing in my stuff?"

"I asked you what it is."

My mother put down a pair of boxers and sighed. "It's just as well you found it, I suppose. I've been going to see Dr. Addison the last few weeks. He's been telling me I need to bring you with me, but I keep saying no."

"Bring me with you? I don't get it."

"He says you're sick, you got problems. Some kind of, I don't know, attachment disorder. Guess it's my fault." My mother sounded sad, her voice huskier than usual. "I didn't raise you right. Tried my best, just me on my own, but it wasn't enough. You needed more."

"I got all I need. You did fine."

"Oh Miles...I finally talked to Lance. He told me what you did."

Good old Lance. You know, I could've kept whacking him

with that beer bottle until he couldn't get up, but I didn't. That's not the kind of guy I am. Besides, I'd warned him not to say a word about what I'd done or else.

"Lance is a goddamn liar," I said. "He tell you what he did, too?"

"He told me everything, about him and that woman. It doesn't make what you did right. Besides, he didn't tell me anything that I didn't already know—that you're...that you ought to talk to someone."

I felt the faint heat rising in my neck and ears. "Oh yeah?"

"Miles, don't be like this...please..."

The sound of her trying to calm me down turned the heat inside me from a simmer to boil. It was in my back now, too, and moving up my legs. I could feel the energy rushing through my whole body, pushing its way to the surface like lava inside a volcano.

"Dr. Addison is right. You need help, Miles. More than I can give. Maybe we need to take you in to...to stay someplace for a while."

"I haven't got a problem. You know what I got 'cause you gave it to me. I got Viking blood, that's all."

My mother was sniffling and wiping her nose with the back of her hand. She looked pathetic.

"Miles, that's just some nonsense I made up when you were little, so you'd feel better about yourself when those bullies beat up on you. And I guess I just...well, I couldn't stand to tell you the truth, so I let you keep on believing a lie."

I moved in closer to my mother. The open washer door thunked as she bumped against it. She looked at me the same way that girl had when I walked in on her in the stall at the burger joint: eyes as big as stuffed olives, fear oozing out along with tears.

"You're lying," I said.

"No, Miles, that's the truth. I swear. Now please, put those down."

At first I wasn't sure what she meant. Then I saw I had the pruning shears I'd used to do the yardwork earlier clutched in my hands. I opened the blades, just a little, so my mother could see how sharp they were. Bits of chewed-up leaves still stuck to the shiny silver metal.

"You're just mad at me on account of Lance, that's all. That's why you're saying these things, that's why you're lying like that."

I felt the heat rising all along my back, a tidal wave of hot, cleansing energy that washed out into my arms, my wrists, my fingertips. I felt my whole body hum, and I knew that it was too late, whatever my mother had said or not said, there would be no stopping what came next. She must've known it, too, because she grabbed that pile of dirty socks and flung them at me and started to run.

You know, maybe my mother was right, that she really didn't have Viking blood. I looked at it spilled out all over the floor, and it was just as red and sticky as any other blood. And it took a long while to mop up, I can tell you that. Maybe she was right about me, that I was just like my father, a mean son of a bitch. Still, I can guess where he got that mean streak.

Must've been his Viking blood.

HOMETOWN HEADLINES

Stacy Woodson

Jett sat in an office of the Brinkman Talent Group—a group that consisted of his agent, Clyde, and an aging bulldog named Stallone—and hoped for good news.

But Clyde was eating sunflower seeds, a habit he'd picked up when he'd quit smoking. Repurposed water bottles, filled with discarded hulls, lined his desk like empty beer bottles in a college dorm room window. And Jett knew the news couldn't be good.

"I didn't get the part," he said quickly, wanting to avoid Clyde's ass-kissing windup before he delivered the punchline.

"Sorry kid." Clyde paused to spit out another hull. "The casting director decided to go in a different direction. You know how these things go."

Jett thought after his two-time appearance on a hit television series that things would get easier. But no luck. Now, the bills were piling up—rent, utilities, union dues, head shots. "Let me guess, I'm not tall enough?"

Clyde shook his head.

"Not fit enough?" Jett tried again.

"Not good enough."

Jett flinched. "Damn, Clyde. Nothing like breaking it to me gently."

"Look, kid, it's been rejection city for the past twelve months. The time for gentle is over." Clyde picked up the bag of sunflower seeds, corner torn, and offered it to Jett like it was a consolation prize.

Jett waved it away. "Did they say anything else?"

"They loved your look"—*crunch, spit*—"you just didn't feel connected to the character."

Clyde continued to talk while Jett's mind drifted back to the day he told his mother he was leaving for L.A. to pursue his dream to become an actor.

Norma had sat on their couch, glass of gin in one hand, newspaper in the other. "Oh, son," she'd laughed. "God, you're stupid. You'll never amount to anything. The men in our family never do."

A muscle in Jett's jaw flickered, the humiliation still fresh like it had happened yesterday.

And now another failure.

Maybe Norma was right—

"Are you listening to me?" Clyde asked, water bottle poised for another discard. "They said it *seemed* like you were acting."

"I know what *not connected* means," Jett snapped, his mind still on Norma—how he hated that woman, how he desperately wanted to prove her wrong.

"The important thing is to take the note and move forward." Clyde cleared his throat. "And I have something in mind."

Another audition. Jett straightened, the excitement already starting to build. Another audition was just what he needed—something new, something fresh, something to put this recent setback behind him. He wondered what the role would be.

Another *Walking Dead* spin-off?

A Marvel movie?

Or maybe it was—

"School," Clyde said.

Jett blinked. "What?"

"Method acting classes. You need to hone your craft, kid."

Jett's stomach tightened. "You don't think I can act?"

"I didn't say that." Clyde sighed. "I wouldn't have agreed to represent you if I thought you couldn't act." He reached behind his desk to pet Stallone. "I just think, based on the notes we've been getting, right now, this is the best move for you."

School. Jett's mind reeled. Where would he find the money?

Clyde's computer pinged. He glanced at the screen, frowned, continued to talk. "The definition of insanity is doing the same thing over and over again and expecting a different result. We need to try something new."

Another reinvention speech. Now it was Jett's turn to sigh.

Clyde was big on new approaches, reinvention. When Clyde told him that his name, Jethro, wasn't commercial enough, he changed his name to Jett. When Clyde told him that he didn't look tough enough to audition for an action movie, he got a tattoo.

Now this?

Even if he could afford classes, it wouldn't guarantee work. The only thing it would guarantee was missed auditions and debt—debt he didn't need. "Hollywood is filled with successful actors who didn't go to acting school," Jett said.

"And you're not one of them, kid."

Norma laughed.

Jett's face flushed. He pushed up from his chair and walked over to the window. "I can act," Jett said, more to reassure himself than to echo Clyde. "I just need to hone my skills."

"This is what I'm saying."

Jett looked through the window at the parking lot, a slab of cracked asphalt faded from the sun, and tried to decide what to do. Clyde had a reputation for knowing the business, securing auditions, booking clients. Something he couldn't ignore. Just like he couldn't ignore Clyde's painful advice now. He faced Clyde, again. "I'll try school," Jett conceded.

"A reputable school," Clyde said, his tone no longer collegial. "Don't waste your time or *mine* with something else."

Jett narrowed his eyes. "What are you saying, Clyde?"

"If you want me to continue to represent you, this is what I need you to do."

"I said, I'd do it." Jett folded his arms. "But then, I expect auditions."

"You do school. I'll get you the auditions."

"I'm talking real roles," Jett pressed. "Something big."

Something Norma couldn't miss.

Something that would finally prove her wrong.

And maybe—finally—the voices would go away.

Payment failed.

Jett stared at his phone. Sent his credit card through again. Had the same result.

In between shifts washing dishes at Luanne's diner, a hole-in-the-wall-joint in West Hollywood, Jett tried to register for a method acting seminar—a six-month course that taught psychological techniques to help artists behave realistically under imaginary circumstances.

Whatever the hell that meant.

And now, it looked like Jett would never know because Clyde's must-have class exceeded his credit limit.

He minimized the payment screen and tried a few other reputable schools—the cost nearly the same. Shoulders slumped, he pocketed the phone, and returned to the sink in the kitchen. Clyde wouldn't find him auditions until he finished school. That was the agreement. And Clyde was big on agreements.

Jett had to figure something out.

A loan was out of the question. His credit rating sucked, and he was already working two jobs. He didn't think he could handle a third. Even if that were a possibility, he only had a high school diploma, and it was unlikely he'd make more than minimum wage. It would take months to save enough. Tack on time for school—it would be a lifetime before he would see another audition.

A lifetime with Norma in his head.

Maybe he should buy a lottery ticket. Or rob a bank.

He laughed at the idea.

Norma laughed, too.

Jett yanked at the wall-mounted hose, blasted a plate, placed it into the dish rack, grabbed another.

"This is the last of it." Luanne plunked a tub of dirty dishes in front of him. A former Hollywood stunt woman, Luanne had a body that showed it. Her face was weathered. She had a scar on her cheek and limped when she walked. But she had kind eyes.

Not like Norma's.

He picked up one of the plates, thumped it against the garbage can, and watched chunks of fried chicken tumble inside.

"You alright?" Luanne asked, cigarette bobbing between her lips.

Jett shrugged.

"That bad?" Luanne leaned against the sink, took a drag, and seemed to study him.

He cycled through a few more dishes before he finally told her about his day—about the part he didn't get, his mounting debt, Clyde's reinvention plan. "I just don't know how I'm going to swing it, Lu."

"Talent agents." Luanne shook her head. "Frigging gatekeepers. Such a pain in the ass."

Jett couldn't argue with that. He sometimes wished he could do things on his own, but that wasn't the way Hollywood worked. When an agent signed a client, it was an endorsement of his talent and the only way the community took you seriously. An agent also had access to casting directors, access someone like Jett couldn't get on his own.

He loaded the remaining plates. Pulled the hood to the dishwasher. Pressed a button. The water *whooshed*. "I feel like I'm on the edge of something—that big break. I just need to get this class behind me."

Then, he had an idea. Maybe he didn't need another job. Maybe, he could just work more at the diner. "Any chance I could get more hours? I'd be happy to work out front. Anywhere, really."

Help me, Luanne. Help me, Norma sing-songed. You're pathetic.

Pathetic like your father.

Jett's face flushed. He turned back to the sink, started on another batch of dishes.

"I'd love to help, really I would…" Luanne began.

See, she thinks you're pathetic, too.

"…it's just…I sold the place."

A plate slipped from his hands and thudded into the sink.

"Sorry for telling you like this," Luanne continued. "I just accepted the offer today. The diner was my retirement plan. And now, I can finally move to Florida." Her hand went to her bad leg. "Rest a bit. You know?"

Jett never considered how difficult things were for Luanne working on her feet all day, waiting tables, managing people.

"The diner will be open for another week. Then, we will have a few weeks to close things out—sell the kitchen equipment, furniture, that kind of thing." She took one last drag from her cigarette, crushed the butt against the heel of her boot, and flicked it into the trashcan. "The new owner plans to gut the place, turn it into a day spa. Can you believe that crap?"

"Happy for you, Lu." He forced a smile. But Jett wasn't happy. He'd lost two jobs today. The part he didn't get and now the diner.

He was a two-time loser.

Norma agreed.

Luanne limped toward the back office, and Jett returned to the sink. An hour later, he finished, more depressed than ever. Not only did he need another job, but Luanne had become a friend—his only one, really. And now, he would lose her too.

He cinched up the trash bag and went through the back door

to the alley outside—a tight space between buildings with just enough room for a graffitied dumpster, Hal-the-homeless guy, and Luanne's rusted-out-Mustang. Jett didn't own a car.

He tossed the bag into the dumpster, turned back to the diner. In the darkness, he could just make out Luanne. She leaned against the building. A cigarette glowed between her fingers. The light trailed to her mouth, stopped, and then returned to her side.

"Finished?" she asked.

"Pretty much." He found two plastic crates, flipped them over. Offered one to Luanne, sat on the other.

She pulled out a flask, unscrewed the top, took a swig, handed it to Jett.

He hesitated. The smell reminded him of Norma and her boozed-out-binges.

Be a man. Drink it.

"I better not," he said.

Norma groaned.

They didn't say anything for a stretch. A nearly burned-out streetlamp buzzed nearby, and Jett watched two rats scurry along the sidewalk.

"Did I ever tell you how I got into stunt work?" Luanne crushed out her cigarette, pulled out a pack, shook out another.

Stunt work had seemed like such a perfect fit for her that Jett had always assumed it was the natural order of things. He shook his head.

"I was an actor."

He laughed. He couldn't help it. A gymnast he would have believed. Some kind of ninja warrior would have been plausible. But an actor? He struggled to see it.

"Actually, I was pretty good."

"No kidding," Jett said.

"Had success in supporting roles. Television mostly. But I wanted more. I wanted to be the next Sigourney Weaver," she said, her tone wistful.

"*Aliens* Sigourney Weaver or *Working Girl* Sigourney Weaver?"

She narrowed her eyes. "You seriously have to ask?"

Aliens, Jett decided. Luanne as gritty Ellen Ripley—now that he could see.

"Anyway, many Oscar-winning actors used method acting. So, I enrolled in a class." She put the cigarette to her lips, lit the tip, inhaled. "The techniques they teach you—stuff is dangerous."

Jett eyed Luanne skeptically. She wasn't prone to exaggeration, but there were times, after she'd been drinking—

"I'm serious, man. They teach you to evoke sense memories, to tap into dark places from your past. To suffer inwardly so you can perform outwardly." She paused, made air quotes with her fingers, cigarette still tucked between them. "At least that's the crap they tell you." Her voice turned brittle. "You're suddenly faced with emotions, confronting crap from your life that you thought you'd put behind you."

She went back to the flask, took a long swig. "I completely lost it during an audition," she continued, her voice even again. "I was so messed up, I had to go away for a while. Get my head right. When I returned, I decided stunt work was better for me."

"Damn, Lu." He touched her arm.

She jerked away. "Don't do that."

"Don't do what?"

"Feel sorry for me," she said, clearly irritated. "That's not why I told you. I just want you to be careful, okay?" She flicked her cigarette into the alley. "I know it doesn't matter what I say," Luanne continued. "That you're going to take that damn course, anyway. No one could have stopped me back then. So, I'm not going to pretend I can stop you, now."

She reached behind her, pulled an envelope from her waistband. "I did some research on the cost of reputable courses. I want you to have this." She handed him the envelope.

He looked inside—a stack of bills. His breath caught. Luanne had given him the tuition. He stared at the money not sure if he should take it, not sure what he should do. "Luanne, I—"

She raised her hand, cutting him off. "You need to know this money comes with a condition."

"Of course, Lu. Anything."

"If you feel yourself slipping, you call me."

Jett frowned. "Slipping, how?"

"When it happens, you'll know."

The next day, Jett went to the bank, deposited Luanne's money, and registered for Stanley Studios' method acting seminar. In two weeks, he would start the six-month course, and he would be one step closer to that breakout role—the one that Clyde had promised.

The role that would prove Norma wrong.

Then, maybe Norma would stop haunting him, and he'd finally have some peace.

Now, he sat on his futon in his studio apartment and scrolled through the *Hollywood Underground*, a website that published industry-related news, and tried to predict which studios would cast major movies soon. The possibilities were endless. And he was hopeful. Nearly happy.

Until his cousin Beaufort called.

"Hey cuz." Beaufort's twang was thick, a twang Jett had worked hard to lose. "Make it big yet, or are ya hardly making it?" Beaufort snorted—the sound like a pig having a seizure.

Jett pressed his lips together.

"I'm sorry. I shouldn't be laughing." Beaufort paused, took a drink—the *gulp, gulp, gulp* bleeding through the phone.

"What do you need, Beaufort?" Jett asked, already irritated.

"Your mama...she's in the hospital."

Norma in the hospital wasn't breaking news. Her ER history was long and distinguished, something Jett had stopped worrying about the day he left Georgia. "Let me guess, alcohol poisoning? Another blackout? Or is it stitches this time?"

"No, man," Beaufort's tone somber, now. "She's bad off."

Bad off in his cousin's world could range from a heart attack to the TV in Norma's hospital room not working. It was tough to tell with Beaufort.

"She's bad how?" Jett asked.

"Doc says she's got osmosis."

Osmosis? Jett frowned, tried to process the word. "You mean cirrhosis?"

"Yeah. That there's the one." Beaufort took another drink, crushed a can—at least that's what it sounded like on Jett's side of the phone. "Old girl needs a liver transplant. With her age and history—basically being a drunk and all—doc says she ain't gettin' one."

Wise move. Given a chance, Norma would pickle that one, too. "How long she got?" Jett asked.

"Maybe six weeks."

His mother was dying.

He tried to imagine Norma in a hospital bed, her body frail, skin yellow, struggling to live. And he waited to feel something—sadness, loss, empathy, some form of compassion that a person who had a normal childhood would feel.

But there was only anger.

The old bat was going to die before he had a chance to prove her wrong.

Jett paced between his futon and the kitchen while he tried to come up with a plan. He couldn't live the rest of his life with Norma in his head—poking, prodding, mocking.

Clyde's school was out of the question, not when Norma could die before he finished. Still, Jett could land a role tomorrow, and it was unlikely she'd live long enough to see him on the big screen. Producing a film took time. From the movie announcement, to pre-production, filming, post-production, and release, it was at least two years.

But he wasn't giving up.

He still had a chance to prove her wrong.

If he landed a role in a big film, there would be a news release—an announcement about the part, an announcement that would make headlines in his hometown newspaper, headlines Norma couldn't ignore. And that had to be enough.

It *needed* to be enough.

Now, the biggest hurdle—his promise to Clyde. He wouldn't find Jett auditions until he completed school. He needed a class. Something quick. A class that taught a new tool or technique that would improve his next audition. Something that would fool Clyde into believing Jett had attended a reputable school. That he had upheld his end of their agreement.

Jett had just the thing. Something he'd seen on the *Hollywood Underground* before Beaufort had called.

A washed-out '80s movie star, Cory-something-or-other, taught a two-week method-acting course online. He scrolled through, clicked on the link, prayed the cost wouldn't be an issue. Luckily, it wasn't.

Now, he had to convince Clyde—a man who had an unparalleled ability to detect BS—that he was enrolled in a "reputable" program that happened to be shorter than any other advertised.

Heart jackhammering, he took a deep breath and dialed Clyde's number.

Clyde picked up on the first ring. "Kid! How's the school thing coming?"

"I found a course," Jett said. *Not a lie.*

"That's great, kid. Just great. Which studio?"

"Stanley," Jett said, *still the truth.* He had registered for their seminar—a seminar he wouldn't be attending. *Now for the lie.* He gave Clyde the dates and held his breath.

"Stanley is good," Clyde agreed. "But a two-week course? That doesn't sound right."

He doesn't believe you. Norma laughed. What kind of actor are you?

Jett's face flushed. "The course is some kind of pilot program," he said quickly, cursing how uncertain he sounded. He waited, expecting Clyde to push back, to say something more. But Clyde's computer pinged.

"Sounds good, kid," he said, dismissively, fingers tapping on his keyboard.

"Clyde?"

"Hmmmm…" Clyde said, still tapping.

"Remember our agreement. I want auditions."

"Agreements are my business, kid."

Jett was relieved the conversation with Clyde had gone better than he'd expected. He nuked some ramen, went back to his futon, and clicked on the first acting video. He expected some close-up of Cory or a wide-shot of an actors' studio. Anything, but a cup of herbal tea.

"You must use experiences from your life," an ethereal voice said. "Everyday rituals, something as simple as this cup of tea, can enhance your acting."

Woo-woo classes, Norma said. This, is your plan?

Jett ignored her, looked for something hot. He didn't have tea, but he had ramen, and the bowl would have to do. He cupped it between his hands.

"Look at the cup. How big is it? How much space is there between the liquid and the rim? What's the color? Feel the weight in your hand. Now, place the cup down, close your eyes, visualize the cup, recreate each sensation."

Jett dutifully followed each step. And when the class was over, he went to the next one. Each session went deeper, each exercise more personal. And Norma's voice grew more powerful, so powerful that it became harder and harder for Jett to push her away. At the end of the day, the experience left him edgy and emotionally wrung out.

Two weeks and things would get better, Jett reminded himself.

They had to.

Because he didn't know what he'd do if they didn't.

Two weeks later, Jett was at the diner, supervising the final sale of Luanne's kitchen equipment, when Clyde called.

"Kid! You finished that class, right?"

Jett swallowed, nodded.

"Kid?"

"Yeah, Clyde. It's done."

"Good. Because I've got that audition—the movie I promised you. A smaller role, but with a major star—great exposure for you."

Exposure was all he needed. Something that would show he'd finally made it.

Something that would finally silence Norma.

"What's the movie?" Jett asked.

"*Yuletide Zombies.*"

As in ho, ho, ho? Norma laughed.

Jett didn't. He hated Christmas and the crappy memories that came with it.

"Studio is billing it as *The Walking Dead* meets Santa Claus. It's going to be epic, kid. Zombie elves will be all the rage. They want you to audition for the role of Wilbur."

Wilbur—like the pig? Norma laughed, again. This just keeps getting better.

"When?" Jett asked, ignoring Norma.

"It's a taped audition. So, I'll need you in my office, *early*, tomorrow." Clyde tapped on his keyboard. "I'm sending you the sides. Trust me, kid. This is the one." Clyde ended the call.

Yuletide Zombies—Jett played the title over again in his head. He wanted to trust Clyde, but it was hard to see the possibilities. Still, he thought about other oddball Christmas movies that somehow made it big—*Christmas Vacation, The Elf, A Christmas Story.* They weren't exactly traditional. *Yuletide Zombies* could be one of those movies, too.

Fat chance, Norma said.

Jett wished Luanne were here so he could ask her opinion. But she'd gone to Florida to look at condos and wouldn't be back until tomorrow.

Norma hummed "Let It Snow," her favorite Christmas song, while Jett toggled through his phone. He found Clyde's email, looked at the section of the script sent by the casting agency. They wanted to see a taped audition rather than have Jett attend a casting call. One of Clyde's filmmaker friends would record Jett, at Clyde's office, auditioning for the part.

Jett read through the scene. Wilbur was on a fire escape, a sea of elf-zombies on the street below. It was night, winter, in Boston. His feet were bare, clothes thin, arms wrapped around his girlfriend. They fought to stay warm.

The lines that followed were simple, easy to memorize. Delivering the emotion, the right subtext would be the key. He thought about the exercises he'd learned from his classes, and he knew what he had to do to prepare.

When it was dark, Jett went outside to the alley behind the diner, took off his shoes, sat on the ground, and leaned against the building. He watched a rat climb up the side of the dumpster, then another—the rat parade no different than what he'd lived through in the trailer park where he'd grown up. He closed his eyes and forced himself to go back there.

He was six years old. It was Christmas Eve. He'd done his best to be good that year. But no matter how hard he'd tried, it had never seemed good enough for Norma. Still, he'd hoped Santa would know and that maybe, this year, he'd get a present. He'd stepped outside, wanting a better look at the night sky— hoping to see Santa's reindeer—but there was only fog. When he'd turned to go back in, the door was locked.

He'd pounded, over and over.

Santa never came.

And neither did Norma.

She'd passed out on the couch in front of the TV, credits to *Die Hard* scrolling through the screen. At least that's what Jett had seen when he pressed his face up to the window. In his pajamas, he had returned to the stairs, hugged his legs to his chest. He could hear "Let It Snow" playing through the trailer's thin walls.

The longer he'd sat there, the colder he'd felt. His six-year-old fingers and toes had turned blue, his skin—gooseflesh. And— God—he'd felt scared.

So scared.

He was alone, forgotten outside with the rats.

He started to scream.

When he opened his eyes, Homeless Hal was shaking his shoulders.

Clyde said the audition went well, the best he'd seen from Jett. But Jett had no real memory of it. He was back in the trailer park on that terrible Christmas Eve, and he remained that way until Clyde's filmmaker friend said, "Cut."

After the audition, Jett took a walk, tried to shake loose the feelings the audition had brought to the surface. But despite his best efforts, his mind dipped back to the past. And the fear, the anger he felt, only intensified.

He was slipping.

He needed Luanne.

When Jett arrived at the diner, Luanne was outside in the alley— cigarette in one hand, bottle of gin in the other—the smell oozing from her pores.

Just like Norma.

"Luanne?" Jett said, cautiously.

She turned toward him, the effort too much, and she slid down the wall onto the ground. "The sale fell through, man."

Stacy Woodson

She exhaled a cloud of gin.

He wrinkled his nose, tried to block out the smell and the anger that came with it. "What sale?" he asked, his mind going back to her recent trip, and the condo she had intended to buy.

"What sale?" Luanne laughed—a sarcastic laugh—like Norma's. "Where the hell have you been? Jesus. Are you stupid or something?"

Stupid. Jett's jaw flickered, the anger continuing to build.

"The diner." Luanne thrusted her arm toward the back door. "Damn property inspection. Some environmental issue—rat infestation. Can you believe that shit?"

Jett tried to listen. He wasn't sure if it was the smell of the booze, the words she used, or the way she tripped over them. But instead of Luanne, all he could see was Norma.

Norma's beady eyes. Norma's disapproving scowl.

Norma. Norma. Norma.

He closed his eyes, tried to fight it. When he opened them, Luanne was back.

"I offered to fix it," she paused, took a swig of gin. "They didn't care. Real estate agent thinks the buyer was looking for a reason to walk."

Jett wanted to say something helpful, comforting. "Maybe you can reopen the place?"

"Jesus, Jett. Didn't you hear what I said? Damn, man. Maybe, you really are stupid."

Jett bristled, again.

"I've sold everything. I don't have enough to start over, and it's not enough to retire. I still can't believe I gave you money for that stupid class. You are going to be just another washed-out actor in this shitty town. You won't amount to anything, just like the rest of us."

You won't amount to anything.

And just like that, Luanne was Norma again—the mother he could never please, the mother who had torn him down, the mother who had locked him outside with the rats that Christmas

160

Eve. And the emotions he'd felt—the fear, the anger from years of abuse and neglect—rose to the surface. He hated her for it. He hated that every twisted choice he'd made in his life was with the hope of somehow pleasing her.

He wanted it to stop.

Her to stop.

He lunged forward, knocked her to the ground, wrapped his hands around her neck, and squeezed—tighter and tighter and tighter—until the lights went out.

Until he was no longer staring into Norma's eyes.

He was staring into Luanne's.

Jett wasn't sure how long he'd stayed in the alley with Luanne. He wasn't sure when he'd found Luanne's keys, climbed into the Mustang, and drove to Clyde's office. But he stood there, now, staring through Clyde's window at Luanne's Mustang in the parking lot.

"Glad you're here, kid. Just got a call from *Yuletide Zombies*. Director loved the audition. Wants to meet with you next week." Clyde continued to drone on about contracts and Jett's five-year plan.

But Jett's focus wasn't on Clyde. It was on the two police cruisers that pulled into the parking lot. He was going to jail.

Maybe jail was where he was headed all along.

Uniforms walked into Clyde's office, slapped cuffs on Jett.

Clyde made a show about promising to call his lawyer, which Jett knew was all an act. Jett wasn't a big enough actor for Clyde to care. Apparently, he wasn't big enough for Stallone to care either. The dog never emerged from behind Clyde's desk even during the commotion.

As the police walked Jett outside, he overheard one of them talk about the homeless man who had witnessed Luanne's murder, the man who had led them here.

You're going to make headlines now, all right. Norma

laughed. As a jailbird, just like your father. Told you, you'd never amount to anything. The men in our family never do.

I warned you about slipping, Luanne whispered.

As the police cruiser pulled away, with Jett tucked inside, Norma started humming, "Let It Snow."

MOTEL AT THE END OF THE WORLD: END OF TOUR

Trey R. Barker

Two bros argue, yell, shove. Throw drinks, yell some more. Woman at the far end of the bar, just beyond the bros, looks surprised. Her date pulls her away from the bar and the idiots. First punch leads to a flurry of violent, almost manic punches. Her date pulls her into the safe corner but scoots back for her drink.

Same bar fight he's seen his entire career. No victims, just drunken idiots. Same as it ever was. Someone starts a fight, gets their ass beat, calls the cops to have the other guy arrested. More than twenty-three years behind the badge and there isn't anything new...even his exhaustion at working the job is old news.

Her date gets her drink into her hand, urges her to drink as idiot blood spurts. Tilts the drink back as one of the idiots finishes the night by KO'ing the other.

Both idiots were gone by the time Sergeant Hickman arrived. Bored and annoyed at the service call, he gathered witness statements and a copy of the vid. Hickman watched it three times before he noticed the man and woman; four times before he registered the man's urgency. The fifth time, Hickman ran the video back to five minutes before the fight started. At 1:13 before the fight, he saw it.

A pill; a little Mickey Finn cocktail. Roofie. GHB. Special K, maybe. Something he'd seen eighty hundred times since he was a rookie copper.

God, I am so tired of this shit. This is not the job I wanted.

His phone rang; Harry Connick, Jr.'s melancholy version of "If I Only Had a Brain."

"Yeah?"

"Hickers." Hickman's lieutenant.

"Don't call me that."

"You walked out of the patrol meeting this afternoon."

"Yeah."

"Any particular reason?"

"Uh...hate my job get it done for you?"

"Funny man. You coming back?"

"Haven't decided yet."

"Well...since you haven't retired yet...you still belong to me."

Hickman stopped, his hand on the motel door. The fight had been seventeen days ago and this was the last place anyone knew Taco might be.

Why you here, boy? he could almost hear his Gramps asking. Gramps, the forty-one-year fire veteran who saved thousands of people. *Why you chasing a woman you don't even know is missing? You hate these empty calls when you're on duty. Why chase one when you're off duty? You're making no sense. Retire, boy, put in those papers you're carrying around and get out.*

"Taking a comp day, Loot. Thanks."

"Hickers, what the—"

Hickman hung up and shoved his way into the motel.

The woman on the video was just some college chick, cruising the bars for drinks and easy humps. She'd never called for PD, never been reported missing. She got roofied, probably got nasty with him on the couch or against the bathroom wall, and went home.

These were the bullshit calls that filled his day: custody calls with no court-sanctioned co-parenting agreement, harassment calls where baby mama was posting mean things about baby daddy on social media, neighbor disputes over a tree limb hanging over a property line.

So why the hell was he creating a call, an empty call at that, where none existed?

Because something about her kept his attention. Ultimately, he went to narco division to see if the pill-dropper was a known quantity. *"Yeah, that's Taco. Cheap mutt likes to get over on girls who ain't smart enough to see his bullshit. I'll get you a list of his known hangouts."*

The funk of the motel, one of Taco's hangouts, was heavy. A mix of body odor and rancid nightmares, of blood and piss and shit. The old, cracked plaster fell away in places and allowed the rotten stink of the motel's innards to leak out. It was a last-stop motel. The clients paid sometimes by signing over their entire monthly government check and sometimes by whatever they could panhandle.

At the front desk stood a used-up woman who looked Hickman up and down. "Missing your costume, Officer."

After leaving the patrol meeting, he'd stripped to his blue pants and white T-shirt but had been only vaguely aware he'd done it. Hopefully, his uniform and gear were in his car at the station and not just dropped in a garbage can...or worse, sitting in the floorboard of the cab he'd snagged to the hotel, ready for just anyone to steal.

He laid a picture of the woman from the video on the counter. The woman said nothing, her eyes empty. He set down a picture from narco. "Okay. What about him?"

The woman nodded. "Yeah, but I don't want your trouble."

"No trouble. I'm old and tired and way too close to the end

to cause trouble."

Her face lit up. "Retirement? We could use a security guy. Ours got...well...got busted. Drugs and...stuff."

"Hard pass but thanks. Not interested in working a shithole like this."

"Straight-up shithole and ain't got anybody with half a ounce of human. Street name is Taco. He's squatting downstairs and ain't no man around here with enough sac to get him out."

"Downstairs? Thought this place went up, not down."

"Old building. Basement, couple of subbasements, I don't know what all."

Hickman frowned. "Ain't you the desk clerk? Shouldn't you know what all?"

"*Desk* clerk. Don't pay me enough to go downstairs."

"Don't pay me enough for any of this, sister," Hickman said.

On his way downstairs, his phone rang. "Yeah?"

"I rejected your report on the bar fight."

"Okay."

"Fix it first thing tomorrow."

"Okay."

There was a long silence. "I know you want to be done. Feel like you haven't done anything, but—"

"My entire career, Loot, my entire fucking career. Not a damned thing. Never made a difference for anyone. Never made detective, never made lieutenant, never made SRT. Nothing."

"You're the ICAC investigator. That's something. Saving kids from sexual exploitation."

"Never saved any kids. My cases were peer-to-peer kiddie porn via the internet. Never found a kid being trafficked or molested."

And when cases of molested kids did come along? Investigations had refused to call him and utilize his specialty training. Turf wars.

"Loot, thanks for trying, but I spent twenty-three years cleaning up after people who don't know how to live. And warehousing them at the pokey. Just paperwork, man, nothing else."

"Yeah, but you had some fun, too."

"Sure. Loved most of my fellow coppers, but I never got to help. I don't know why, but lately that's been eating at me. Maybe I'm just tired."

"We're all tired."

At the basement, the landing was lit by three forty-watt bulbs yellowing into death, scattering bad light over putty-colored walls. There were four rooms and across from the stairs were more stairs leading down.

He snapped on his phone's flashlight, checked the three rooms without doors. Scanned with veteran cop eyes: enough to see he wouldn't be killed but uninterested in anything else. They were storage rooms crammed with old beds and lamps, rolls of forgotten carpet.

But in the fourth room, Hickman found someone. A guy walking loose circles, who startled when Hickman appeared. In the dim light, his eyes were red and swollen, his face covered in snot and tears.

"Devin?"

"Uh...no, I'm Hickman."

"Did you bring Devin?"

"No. Sorry. Don't know Devin."

The guy's arms were spindly and bloody, the skin shredded from wrist to elbow. His right arm was dried to brown while his left arm glistened beneath a constantly moving right hand.

"Hey, man, looks like you got a problem."

"Won't when Devin gets back."

"Want me to call the doc?"

"Waiting on Devin, be like waiting and waiting and waiting, man. Probably waiting forever. Friggin' purgatory. Never get outta here."

"Yeah, huh." Hickman saw a small couch, covered in dried blood. Empty beer and soda cans were everywhere. "Devin going for some medicine?"

The guy's eyes shot suspiciously toward Hickman. "*You* got any?"

"Fresh out."

"Ain't that the shit?" He stopped walking suddenly, played with his school ring, missing the stone. "You the cops?"

"Looking for someone. A young woman. Heard she might be down here somewhere."

"Drugs are legal, man. Can't bust me. I ain't doing nothing wrong. Drugs are totally legal."

Holding his hands up, palms out, Hickman said, "Not looking for you. Get me? Do what you gotta to get to tomorrow. Ain't nothing to worry about from me, I'm just looking for this woman. Maybe with a guy called Taco."

His nod was lethargic. "Asshole. Never shares his stash. She's with him. I guess, I don't know. Was last night, anyway. Heard them fucking, man. Screaming so good. He must have the all-time best dick."

"You know her name?"

"Maria? Marla?" He kept scratching, fresh blood over old, and walked his circle faster, coming closer to Hickman. "I don't give a crap, get outta here, cop. Fucking shooting people in the back, standing on their necks! You wanna kill me?" His voice wound up into a scream. "You wanna kill me? Huh? You wanna kill Delilah's baby boy?"

He lashed out and the ring caught Hickman's hand. A sting rocked up through Hickman. He looked and there was a tiny seep of blood, too.

"Son of a bitch." Hickman moved the guy away from him and left the room.

"You cain't kill Delilah's boy. I'm immaterial...I'll fucking live forever."

As Hickman headed down toward the subbasement, there

was a second or two of silence before the man spoke again.

"Devin? Can you tell Devin to hurry, please? I've been waiting so long."

At first, Hickman had tried to help everyone. Every situation was new and he was fierce to fix it all. Even off duty, he watched how the angry diner interacted with the waitstaff, or how the driver at the intersection got sideways with the homeless man panhandling.

I just do my thing, boy. Gramps again. Voice broken and scratchy from smoking his entire life. *Try to be the person everyone should be.*

Hickman snorted. The immutable lesson *he'd* learned was that the world always won, and she was a bitch kitty of a mistress.

Wiping his bloody hand, Hickman moved down the stairs, phone as flashlight to keep the dark at bay. The stairs creaked, a few of them bowing beneath his weight. The handrail, painted upstairs, wasn't even varnished this far down. Just raw, rough wood.

On the wall, two heavy lines ran just above the handrail, as though escorting him down. Halfway down to the subbasement, the top line was interrupted by a crudely drawn cock and balls. Stick-figure but hard as steel. Covering the tip of the cock was a mass of lines in a different colored ink. Pussy, Hickman realized. Another seven or eight steps and the lower line was interrupted by bumper stickers for a pizza place—Bukka's—whose main attraction was a huge buffet. "Eat Until You Explode...Only 9 Bucks."

That's a good day, Hickman thought. A little lust, a little gluttony.

When Hickman made the landing, he heard some random conversation—

"...took your cut, you greedy asshole."

"Bullshit. Left every cent, muthafucka, ain't touched nothing."

—and came around the corner.

In an instant, he was slammed against the wall, his nose crushed, his right arm pretzled behind him. Pain stomped him as a gun damn near punctured his skull.

"Hang on, *hang on.*"

"The hell're you?"

"Don't shoot."

"Tell me who you are or I will shoot, muthafucka."

"Stop, stop—"

"*Who are you?*"

The guy with the gun, holding Hickman's wrist damn near at his shoulder blade, yanked that arm upward once. Gold stars spotted Hickman's eyes—though he caught a glimpse of the athletic bag crammed with cash—and his legs sagged beneath the pain and the warm leak of blood from his nose.

"Hickman. I'm Hickman."

Humiliation slid down his throat. Veteran cop and he got caught like this? By a couple of thieving junkies? Wandering along, thinking of retirement, paying attention to crap-all. Now sweating blood, wanting to piss himself, furious he'd been so oblivious.

God, I hate this. She wasn't even a damned service call and now I'm bleeding. What the hell am I doing here at gunpoint with some junkies?

"Means shit to me."

"Joseph H. Hickman. Looking for Marla. Or Marie. She's with Taco."

"Yeah?" The guy raised Hickman's arm again, incrementally, and pain threatened to erupt down the front of his shirt. "Taco's an asshole. All his goddamned computer gear. Fuck him. Maybe I'll kill you *and* him and sell Marla Marie."

"Hang on, Bellsy." A new voice. "Don't be shooting anyone we don't have to."

"Don't have to. Just want to."

The other man moved close to Hickman. His breath smelled

black and rotted. "Got a bloody nose, mofo."

"Courtesy of your boy there."

"My boy is a greedy son of a gun that keeps me rolling in dough. What you rolling in, copper?"

"Looking for the girl. That's all."

"Ugh. Taco got nothing but skanky chicks. I wouldn't fuck one with Bellsy's tiny wiener."

"Fuck you, Jemmson."

They both laughed.

Hickman took a deep breath. Pain whistled through his broken nose. "Not one of his regulars. He kidnapped this one. Roofied her and stole her right outta the bar."

The gun Bellsy held lessened slightly against Hickman's skull. "Stole her? Like a six pack or a box of pepperoni sticks?"

Face still against the wall, Hickman nodded. "Yeah, exactly like that."

"You wanna arrest him?" Jemmson said.

Hickman tried to turn, to see who he was dealing with. But Bellsy pinioned his arm up again and his shoulder screamed. "Okay, okay."

"Remember arresting me, cop?"

A long moment of silence. Eventually, Hickman said, "No. Honestly, it all runs together after a while."

Bellsy laughed. "Not even important enough to remember."

"So you're just out looking for this chick?" Jemmson asked. "One of his 'models'? Down in the basement of this shitty hotel filming porno scenes? Just happened to be here, huh? Ain't got nothing to do with us counting out?"

The light snapped on for Hickman. Not down here scoring, but down here divvying up. Couple'a thieves, burglars most likely, maybe robbers. Cashing out like waitstaff at night's end.

And you stumbled into them.

"This is our place, cop. This is where we put away the Benjamins."

Bellsy laughed. "Usually Hamiltons, Jacksons, and maybe a

Grant or two."

"Jemmson, listen, I don't remember who you are, or why I arrested you, but—"

"Like fifteen years ago, dude. Once a cop...always a cop."

"Ain't a cop anymore."

Bellsy spun Hickman around. "Bullshit."

"Got my retirement letter in my pocket. Off the job."

There was a letter in his pocket, rewritten and updated every couple of months since he'd hit twenty years. He'd been praying he could make twenty-five years—a better monthly pension check—but that was a pipe dream. He just couldn't stack any more time on that monthly payoff.

And yet, neither had he turned in the letter yet. Easy peasy...just file with HR and all this was behind him, the broken glass swept outta his head.

Get out, boy, it's way past your time.

But you did forty-one years. And you helped.

Guess my fire hose is bigger than your cop hose, ain't it?

Funny stuff, Gramps.

Sweat rolled from Hickman's brow. "Cash out. I could give a crap. All I want is the girl."

"Madelyne," Bellsy said.

"Or maybe Tricia," Jemmson said. "Anyway, they like games. Domination, submission. 'Yes, sir,' 'No, sir.' Zings my ol' crank." Squeezing his balls, he made a slurping noise. "Smacks and chokes and beats. Gets that blood flowing. She loves it. When they going at it, she knows just how to put some juice in her screams."

Hickman bit his tongue. Maybe he was chasing a phantom.

"Show me the paper." Jemmson shoved a hand into Hickman's back pocket, went to the next pocket, and found the letter. He opened it, read it, and nodded. "Son of a bitch ain't a cop no more."

"So we could kill him and not have no problems?" Bellsy asked.

Jemmson stared at Hickman.

"All I want is her. You have my word."

"The word of an ex-cop."

"How did I treat you when I arrested you? Did I do what I said I was going to do?"

"Yeah."

"Treat you with respect?"

"Better than any other cops treated me."

"Then give me a little rhythm."

"And you don't care about any of that cash?"

"Let's say I did. Let's say I wanted to return it all. How I'm gonna do that? That cash, for all I know, has been sitting down here for how long? How do I track down when and where it came from? See?"

"So...like a found item. Like a syringe in the street." Jemmson rubbed his chin.

"Not even that. A found item wouldn't have anyone attached to it. That cash has someone attached, someone who says it's theirs. I don't remember ever arresting either of you for anything, so I don't have any reasonable suspicion, much less probable cause, to go sniffing around."

"But you do for the girl?"

"I *saw* that on video. More than enough PC."

Jemmson smiled but Bellsy frowned and shifted foot to foot.

"And your nose?"

Hickman took a few tentative steps toward the stairs and wiped at the blood on his lip. "Cost of doing business in your house, I guess."

"Bellsy," Jemmson said. "Leave him go. We can pass on that trouble, we got our money to get back to."

"'S bullshit, man."

"No, what's bullshit is you saying you left your cut here. I saw you take it, you greedy-ass son of a bitch."

Their words slipped away in the dark as Hickman headed further down the stairs.

* * *

His phone tried to ring, but had barely a bar for a signal. He ignored it, concentrating on the pain in his nose. Maybe broken, maybe not, but it hurt pretty serious. His hand hurt now, too, where the junkie had scratched him. God alone knew what diseased nightmare he'd picked up in that contact.

His foot caught a broken step and he shone his phone light over it. The wood was cracked near the edge and some of the other steps were completely gone. As was the handrail. But the lines on the wall continued. Like a spiritual handrail down and yet further down a guide to the world beneath the motel.

And you keep going, don't you, boy? Keep on a'chasing. But you 'bout to throw up thinking about going back to work tomorrow, ain't you?

A shitty job, getting shittier; busting up arguments over control of the TV remote and the Wi-Fi password and who got the table when baby daddy moved out.

There were different interruptions this time, though. The first line was broken by a scraggle of graffiti: *We Are Angry. We Will Rise Up In Anger* in sharpened letters, a fist next to them.

A few steps further, the second line was broken by a taped-up picture of a Renaissance-style painting of priests.

Setting people on fire.

"What the hell?"

Heretic just a man who sees with his own eyes.

Open ur eyes.

Get woke.

There burning us.

Hickman stumbled down the last few broken stairs, in pain, confused by the violence of the artwork plastered on the walls from ground level down. Near the landing, he heard someone calling. Faint and weak.

"Help. Please help."

Hickman sucked a hard breath and kicked the only door on

this level, secured by a shiny new padlock. The door rattled and on the other side, someone screamed. He kicked again and the door popped open in a shower of broken wood.

"Holy shit."

On the far edge of a dirty and blood-streaked mattress, the woman he'd been searching for lay curled into a fetal position almost as an afterthought.

Gear filled the room. Cameras and light stands, light curtains and backdrops, lenses galore, and hundreds of SD cards strewn all over like the endless paperwork that accrued on a case. But also four computers, two running porn, one with some sort of fight club with crude-edged weapons.

And one showing her.

In real time.

Fear rocked her eyes and she scooted away from him. Rather than immediately going toward her, Hickman held up his hands, palms out, and then he pulled his wallet and showed his badge.

"Oh, my God. A cop. A fucking cop. Oh, Jesus, thank you." Hope, a magnesium-heated fire the opposite side of what he'd seen when he walked in, blasted through her face. "You found me. Please, get me out of here. I wanna go—" She stopped when she realized he was bloody.

"Don't worry about the blood. We're going home right now. Hang tight."

Before anything else, he checked his phone but had no signal this deep.

Her clothes were piled in the corner, and he grabbed them before untying her hands. She dressed slowly like someone with chronic pain.

"What's your name?"

"Ashlee Thomas. I was..." She coughed. "I'm so thirsty." Croaked out a bitter laugh. "That's funny. That's what got me...here. I was thirsty. Went to a bar. Met this guy and he—"

Hickman shooshed her. "I saw it on the video."

She looked confused.

"I got called for the fight. You were behind them and the guy—"

"Taco." She stood. "I don't know his real name."

"Taco basically forced the drink down you. I saw that. Did some investigating and found you. I'm sorry it took so long."

She stared, amazement ripe in her eyes. "Is that a joke? I didn't think anyone would ever find me. I figured I was bound for Russia or Europe or somewhere to fuck until the drugs killed me."

"Mother*fucker*."

A new voice, followed immediately by a shot. Then a second. Ashlee yelped and ducked, trying to stay out of the line of fire. Plaster on the far side of the room exploded.

Hickman plowed over Taco just as Taco fired another round.

Pain exploded in Hickman's arm, a ball-peen hammer hard against his bone. Hickman yelped as they slammed against the wall and hit the floor. He tried to keep the gun pointed away even as he also tried to gouge Taco's face or eyes or knee his nuts or something.

Taco's teeth snapped down hard as he tried to sink them into Hickman's skin.

Setting his feet, Hickman turned the pair closer toward the wall and managed to pin Taco's legs between him and the floor.

"Son of a bitch, get off me."

Hickman bashed his head back and forth, trying to find Taco's skull. Taco moved quick and Hickman only cracked the wallboard, sending new waves of pain through his nose. When Taco rolled away from Hickman, his ribs and kidneys were exposed, just for a split second, like a fighter who'd gone too far around on a punch.

Hickman blasted his fists against Taco as hard and fast as he could. Yelling, Taco tried to roll against the wall to protect himself.

And then Hickman found himself in a shower of metal and

plastic and glass.

Taco was out cold, blood spattering the top and side of his skull.

Ashlee stood over them, a busted light stand in her hand, the rest of it on the floor. Her face was empty and tired. "Your arm. He shot you."

"Winged me." Yeah, a scratch, but it hurt like mad.

"I want to go home."

Hickman held his wounded arm gently, cradling it. Blood had spattered up and down his arm and chest. "I'll call...son of a bitch that *hurts*...my guys."

"No. No police."

"What? Of course, the cops. This guy needs to see some jail."

"No, he doesn't."

Hickman's entire career rolled through his head. It had been a hollow twenty-three years. Abuser and victim. He'd filled out this exact paperwork so many times, dutifully putting in the various inboxes and case folders. He'd arrested abusers and victims had gone back. Or he'd thrown abusers out and they'd never faced anything more serious than finding a new address. Or the district attorney had pleaded down to simple battery rather than domestic.

Or or or...

So many copies, useless copies, of this paperwork.

With a nod, Hickman said, "No more paperwork." He retrieved Taco's gun and kicked him back to consciousness.

"The fuck, asshole?" He glared at Ashlee. "You fucking hit me? You fucking hit *me*? You goddamned bitch. Get ready, you cunt. Was gonna film a BBC double-penetration scene with you today but fuck that noise. Now I'm gonna have my black boys jus beat your ass. We'll live-stream that shit and probably make more money."

"Shut up."

"Whoever the fuck you is." Taco looked surprised at all of Hickman's blood. "Nut up, streetfighter, 'cause my boys are going to eat you alive."

Hickman leaned in. "I'm a cop but I'm so close to the end that I don't care. Get it? Close enough to done that no one will give fuck one if I shoot you. You shot me…I shoot you. Fair is fair. Nobody will investigate any too close. See? I get a freebie."

"You're nuts."

"Okay, nuts it is." Hickman lowered the gun to Taco's crotch. "I'm sure that'd make Ashlee happy. I've always believed there are people who need killing. I think you're one of them."

Taco spoke but Hickman didn't hear him over the shot. It was a crappy little .25 but a shot in the belly is a mean wound that would take hours to do its damage.

Screaming, Taco writhed on the floor, blood leaking from the hole. "I'll kill you both. My boys are coming. Both of you fucks."

Hickman shoved him over and tied his hands behind his back the way he'd found Ashlee. He tore a cord from a light stand and tied up Taco's feet.

While he did that, Ashlee shoved a ball gag deep in Taco's throat, muffling his rage. She then repositioned his live-stream camera, glanced at the computer screen. When she saw Taco bleeding, she walked out.

Two hours later, he sat on his front porch, sipping lemonade and eating aspirin.

He'd put them in a cab and gotten them both home, looks but no questions from the cabbie. Ashlee had no roommate or family, no pets. Her apartment was exactly as she'd left it, as though the last three weeks hadn't happened, a sliver of time easily erased by the mechanics of routine.

His phone rang. "If I Only Had a Brain."

"Hickers."

Hickman said nothing, rubbing his self-bandaged arm.

"Uh…just wanted to touch base about tomorrow. I've got you holding hands with some politicians from Austin."

"I've been doing this twenty-three years. You realize that?"

"I know how long you've been up. Been a helluva career, too."

"Been a shit career."

"No, Sergeant, it has not. You've done good work and have respect from everyone—"

"Oh, stop. Some people respect me, some don't. Could care less about that."

"Dude, what is the *problem*? What the hell is going on in your head?"

Along the block, nothing moved. No one mowing or watering, no one playing with kids or walking a dog or anything else. Certainly no one shooting a trafficker and leaving him to bleed out on his own live-stream.

Hickman tried to crunch the ice from his drink, but it shot jolts of pain through his head.

"My mom used to get beat. A string of violent boyfriends. I think that's why I hired on. Maybe thinking I could help whoever couldn't help themselves. Fucking corny as that sounds."

"No, it doesn't. It's why all of us serve. And you have arrested people like that."

"A few. Kept them from beating on whoever for a few days. Nailed some thieves but no one ever got their stuff back 'cause it was already sold for drugs. We don't help, we babysit and clean up the shit mess and I really wanted to help. I wanted to do for someone what no one had done for my mother. Even one person would have been enough, Loot. Then I could have retired happy."

"Joseph, come on, let's think about this—"

"I'm done. Resignation letter's in my desk drawer. Signed and dated two days ago."

Hickman hung up, stood and stretched, and went inside. He put on some music and opened a book he'd wanted to read for a while.

He *was* retiring happy. He had his one person; unknown,

unheralded, but acknowledged enough for him. *Good enough for one career, boy, damned good job.* Thanks, Gramps.

CUT MAN

Sam Wiebe

"I tell you the time I played with Ike and Tina?" Joe Ricky said. "Oil Can Harry's. Nice little club. Might've been the Fairgrounds, now I think about it. I was seventeen."

One of Vancouver's best scenic views can be eyed from the bleachers at Hastings Park. We were closer to the top bench than the bottom, looking down on the racetrack. Beyond that the docks and the water and the North Shore mountains. A late morning in June, still twenty minutes before the first race.

In the last few years, young suburban couples had discovered the track, dressing up for it in the outfits they wore to prom, massing at the beer garden or the picnic tables near the finish line. A cluster of pink and yellow dresses, cowboy denim and tooled leather. The disreputables, whose Sunday finery tended to sweatpants and warmup jackets, clung to the stands or the gaming rooms inside. Fewer of them all the time. If I had a reason for being there on my day off, that was it.

Below, I could see Donna Lum waiting by the beer tent as the vendor tapped the kegs. To the right of the track, Doc Pedersen paced the fence of the parade ring, interrogating a jockey in pink silks about the hind leg wraps on Short Term Gains.

"What happened, Dave," Joe Ricky said, "their tenor got

caught wrong at the border, turned back. So there I am, seventeen, sneaking backstage to fill in. Probably told you this before."

"Sure," I said. Meaning sure, I'd heard it, and sure, tell it again.

He smiled, his fingers curling over invisible keys. Joe Ricky—Ricci, his last name Anglicized into a stage name and alias—had a blond-gray surfer's mop and a tobacco-colored horseshoe 'stache that bristled at the end. He looked something like a deflated walrus. Joe Ricky had played tenor sax and bass clarinet, and he'd once beat a man with a brick to settle a feud over a ten-cap bundle of heroin. Manslaughter and trafficking and a dozen short stints inside. Both careers now a long time in his past.

"Imagine, Dave, you're standing die-rectly behind the most beautiful chick in the world. I mean my God. We do 'River Deep,' we do 'Proud Mary.' I'm playing, and watching Tina, and then corner my eye I catch Ike watching me watching her. Set ends, he crooks a finger at me. *Over here, kid.* Know what he says?"

Joe Ricky's shoulders pistoned up in anticipatory laughter. In that moment Donna reached the bottom stair and called up, "How 'bout a hand, gents?"

I walked down, took the tray of beers from her, and gave her a steadying elbow. We took the steps one at a time. When we reached our bench, Donna slid in next to Joe Ricky and unlidded the first of her beers, setting the tray by her feet. She adjusted her champagne-colored wig.

"Don't let me interrupt," she said. "Ike and Tina again?"

Donna Lum had been a special constable in the West Van police, married to a sergeant and now widowed. Her husband had worked patrol with my father, had been my Little League coach. Before I was kicked out of Little League.

"Where's the Doc?" Donna asked.

I pointed him out, now charging toward the betting machines

before his inside info dissipated. Joe Ricky finished telling me what Ike had said.

My early memories of Hastings Park were of sitting in the stands, holding a seat for my father while he conferred with the Doc or another of his informants. A track is a great social leveler. Dead more than a decade now, my father. Sitting here, sometimes I felt he'd only stepped away momentarily. He'd be back to nudge me over, sitting down with a black coffee and a roast beef sandwich. I never missed him so keenly as I did here.

We watched the Doc take his slip and jot something in pencil on his form. He kept track of his bets like a chess player recording moves. In his seventies now, Aaron Pedersen had been a heroin pusher and draft dodger, a pimp and an abortionist, and maybe at one time even a doctor.

Donna stood up and waved. The Doc spotted us and walked over to the stairs. From the washroom, a stooped shaggy man in a green army jacket staggered toward him. They collided.

"That look like Attila to you?" Joe Ricky asked.

I'd heard stories but had never seen him. Attila the chemist who'd blown himself up half a dozen times. Who'd patented some food preservative bought by Kraft. Who cooked clear acid and crank for the Exiles Motorcycle Club out of his mother's laneway garage. I'd assumed he was dead.

But there he was, bulling into the Doc, the two fumbling on the ground, entangled. Attila sank down and the Doc wrangled free. A bystander helped him to his feet, then shrieked, seeing what was in the Doc's hand. Attila flopped onto his back, the front of his jacket stained dark and wet.

I was down the stairs two at a time.

Security was good. At the sight of the knife, a tall blond guard moved to cut the Doc off from the swelling crowd.

"Please put that down, sir." The guard took a step forward, arms at her side. "No weapons on the premises."

The Doc looked down at the bloody knife in his hand. Opened his fingers and let it fall.

"I merely removed this," he said.

Two guards in black polo tees each seized a spindly forearm. The Doc sank back as they dragged him toward the building.

"Holding cell?" I asked the guard in charge.

Her nametag said *Blake*. She was hunched down, feeling through Attila's mane for a pulse. The jacket gave off a warm, visceral smell.

"We'll just keep an eye on him till the police come," Blake said.

"It's possible he didn't do this. The dead man came out of the washroom, I think."

"You know it all," Blake said.

I dug out a card. "My name's Wakeland. I'm a PI."

"Explains it," she said. "You mind stepping back?"

The fabled Wakeland Charm wasn't going to prevail over Blake and her protocol. I backed off and jogged to the men's room. No one inside, but sure enough, a faint patter of blood across the green tile, smeared by at least one shoeprint.

Being stabbed is excruciating—I have the scars to vouch for this—but it's not always immediately fatal.

"A good cut, man, you're ten minutes dead before you feel a thing," my father had said. A beat cop for life, and not outwardly afraid of much, Matt Wakeland kept his guard up when it came to knives.

Attila had been stabbed here in the washroom. By the time Blake realized this, the Doc would be in a hard interview room at police HQ. Told sure, he could have a lawyer, he really wanted one, but why not talk this through with us? My guess, you probably didn't wake up this morning thinking today you'd stab a guy. Or maybe you did. I see you have a record.

The video cameras might have caught the killer's image, but if and when that was confirmed, the killer would be gone. Did they leave in the confusion? Or were they still here?

I knocked the lid off the garbage, pawed through the crumpled paper towels. No blood, no clue of any kind. I washed my hands.

Joe Ricky and Donna Lum had made their way to the bottom of the bleachers. Security had the crowd pushed away from the dead man. Someone had draped a coat over Attila.

"Why'd the Doc do it?" Joe Ricky said.

"He didn't, he's a conscientious objector," Donna said.

"Dave, what's going on?"

I explained what I thought, how the killer might not have left. More people were streaming in than out. Donna said she'd post up at the gate.

"Who am I looking for?" she asked.

"Guy soaked in blood carrying a sign, *I Did It*, would be nice," I said. "But could be anyone. Hands in his pockets, coat zipped up all the way. Anyone like that."

"Might not be a he," Donna said. "Just 'cause it's the men's room doesn't rule it out."

"Anyone suspicious," I said.

Donna smiled and nipped from her flask. "Like old times."

Joe Ricky had vanished. The crowd around the body had densified, couples pushing to see the corpse, beating a queasy retreat once they had. Over the speakers a voice apologized for the brief delay in the race.

The betting machines, the beer garden, and the ground-floor casino were all a short walk from the washroom. Attila had been inside, I reckoned, since Joe or Donna would have spotted him from the stands. Which meant the killer had also been inside, watching the chemist for the right moment.

The Hastings Park gaming room was all nickel slots and red velour stools. Emptied out in the rush to see the body. The remaining diehards fed their tickets into the machines. To them, a dead man was nothing to give up your lucky seat for.

I tapped a lady on the shoulder and endured a scowl of such vehemence I wondered if I'd poisoned her child in another life. As I unspooled my questions she smacked the Spin button mechanically, joylessly. No, she hadn't seen anyone strange. That it?

A few stools over, a woman in coveralls swore. She stood up, saw me, and said, "I'm coming right back, don't steal my machine."

"I guard it, will you talk to me a minute?"

She shrugged. The woman looked about fifty, her red hair in a ponytail. I watched her hit up the ATM and then turn its spew of bills into a fresh slip of barcoded paper. She reclaimed her seat in front of BC Gold. Above the machine, a white-bearded miner held a pickax and a melon-sized nugget of ore. The miner grinned like an idiot god. The only one grinning in the room.

"Don't you miss quarters?" I asked. "Wouldn't it be more satisfying, hearing that change spill out?"

"I hear change all day," she said. "Vending machine repair."

The screen flashed *YOU WIN* and her balance rotated up seventy dollars. Her good fortune didn't alter her style of play.

"Someone was killed," I said. "You see anything suspicious?"

"Nope."

"Hear anything?"

"No. Well."

After losing the next spin, she paused to unscrew the lid from a Thermos. Leaning down, she pulled a spoon from a knitted handbag, and ate soup as she talked.

"I didn't really see them. The guy who was yelling had a beard and real long hair. On the hefty side. Looked kinda like the guy who directed *Apocalypse Now.*"

Attila. "Who was he yelling at?"

"I just saw the back of her head. She was in a black uniform. Taking him out the door."

"Hear what they said?"

The woman in coveralls scowled in thought. "Something about her father—he was saying he'd get better treatment from her old man. She kind of shrugged this off and said, 'I already asked you to leave.'"

"Color was the guard's hair?"

"Yellow," the slot player said, with minor resentment.

When I left, she was still up twelve dollars.

A tent was being raised over the body of Attila, the same one they put up when a horse snaps a leg and the Euthasol comes out. Blake oversaw the tent. She spoke into an earpiece, saw me, and shook her head, "Not now, Magnum PI."

"You spoke to Attila before he died," I said. "What about?"

"Only to—" Blake caught herself. "How'd you know?"

"How did you know Attila?" I countered.

"My job to be familiar with our regulars."

The police were approaching, two uniformed constables. Blake moved to greet them.

"Heya, Dave." Joe Ricky had appeared behind me, holding half a hotdog and a paper cup. Mustard on his top lip. "Blood sugar was getting low. Got you a coffee with a little moo in it." He waved at Blake. "Heya, Suze."

"You know her?" I asked.

"Since ages. Tommy Blake's little girl. You ever meet Tommy?"

I shook my head. The crowd was pressed backwards and the tent raised to its full height.

"Your dad sure knew him." Joe Ricky laughed. "This one time, he picked Tommy and me up outside Guys and Dolls, the pool joint on Main—"

"Tell me later," I said. "Tommy Blake have any run-ins with Attila?"

"Bet your boots." He scoffed as if it was a silly question. "Tommy spent three years in Oakalla off Attila putting him next to some undercover cop. Tommy sold the guy a brick of weed, couple guns. Was bringing the guy around for weeks, some big deal they were putting together, wholesaling crank."

"What happened to Tommy Blake?"

"We lost him pretty young," Joe Ricky said. "Never the same after prison. Tommy jumped off the Lions Gate. This was eighty-eight, maybe eighty-nine."

"And his daughter works security here," I said.

If it was her, she'd done it cleverly—the first to the body, the one to take charge. Any last-minute tinkering that needed to be done, Blake could write off as a lifesaving measure, or preserving evidence for the cops. Security cameras might show her entering the washroom after Attila. Circumstantial evidence at best.

I headed for the tent. Tommy Blake's death was several decades ago. Would his daughter hold a grudge that long?

And longer. I thought of my own father, dead eleven years from a hit and run. No, time wasn't an issue.

I waved over Blake again, who was talking to one of the officers. Announcements said the races would begin shortly, we're sorry for the delay.

"You're lucky I haven't thrown you out," Blake said. "What do you want, Wakeland?"

"Nothing at the moment, Suze. You planning to tell the cops how your father knew the dead man?"

From startled to pissed to self-conscious, the muscles of Blake's mouth set and curled, a lenticular image given a sharp turn.

"That's not germane to the task at hand," she said. "Which in any case does not involve you."

"I'm not leaving till I see the security tape," I said.

Blake smiled. This was a fight she could win. Her head turned as Joe Ricky bounded up to us, out of breath.

"Donna got the guy," he wheezed.

Blake and I ran shoulder to shoulder over the hardpacked dirt around the side of the stadium. Donna had her knee pressed into the shoulder of a scrawny teen who was trying to rock his face out of the dirt.

"Who's got spare cuffs?" Donna asked.

"Offa me," the teen shouted. "S'not even mine, lady planted that."

"Kid had a knife," Donna said.

I helped her up. Her wig was askew. The kid crabbed away from her and stood, shaking.

"Drunk old bat," he said. "She just tackled me, no reason."

"I saw the weapon in question," Donna said. "Little three-inch blade. Have it here somewhere." She patted her jacket.

"The Doc was holding the knife used on Attila," I said gently. Blake pulled something glinting from the dust, smacked it. Donna's silver flask made a hollow *pling*.

"Incredible," Blake said. "A man's dead and I'm pissing away time with a lush and a half-assed PI." She pointed up the sloping ground to the parking lot. "Stay the hell out, the both of you."

Security nodded and began herding us, pausing when Blake held out the flask. Donna took it sheepishly.

We walked to my Cadillac in the parking lot between the track and Playland. I tried to think of ways to sneak back in, but nothing came to mind short of spirit gum and Hollywood latex. Security would be watching for me on Blake's orders.

And in the meantime, Blake would be selling the cops her version of the official story. Why would the police believe anything else? They had a body, a knife, and a known felon to connect the two.

"Got any cigarettes?" I asked Donna.

We leaned against the passenger's side and blew smoke at the cement-colored clouds. Out of ideas. At least until I saw Joe Ricky shambling toward us.

"If you're not up to it," I said, after explaining what I wanted him to do.

"Hell, Dave, I was sneaking into clubs time I was fourteen. One time, I'm at the Penthouse—"

"What're you going to say if they stop you?" I asked.

"That Suze told me wait by her office 'cause I'm a witness."

"And if she's the one that stops you?"

"It was the police told me to wait."

I nodded and adjusted his lapel. Joe Ricky headed back across the lot and disappeared down the sloping entrance.

I'd wired him with a lav mic, and was listening on a Tascam recorder I kept in the trunk. One headphone in. All I could hear was Joe Ricky's breathing and the rustle of his Members Only jacket.

I burned another cigarette. Donna rustled her pockets for her lighter and came up with a clasp knife with a black carbon blade.

"Knew that little bugger was carrying," she muttered.

"You know Attila, back in the day?" I asked.

"Knew of," Donna said. "Craig used to bust dealers moving clear acid. Always a couple steps removed from the chemist. But he knew it was Attila."

"Your husband ever work undercover?"

Donna shrugged. "Thirty years with the Mounties, Craig had all sorts of assignments. Died two years after taking his thirty."

Donna shook the flask, empty, and pulled on her cigarette.

Joe Ricky's breathing was picking up. The background noise took on interior tones. Slot machines, music. Inside the gaming room.

"This the way to security?" I heard him ask, loud, for the benefit of the room. "I was told all witnesses should report to security."

"You mind?" I heard someone say.

The electronic bells of a jackpot went off as he moved through the room. A hollow, tinny sound over the mic.

He asked for directions twice more and finally found the security station. I heard him talking to a guard, asking for Blake. Busy, he was told. Wait here.

Message delivered. I tossed the cigarette and started toward the exits.

There were taxis lined up along the curb, the cabbies eating or on their phones. That's where she came out, heading for the closest cab, urgency in her step, handbag flapping against her coveralled hip.

I interposed myself between her and the passenger door. "Spare another minute to talk?" I asked.

Call it intuition. I wasn't surprised it was her. My witness to the argument between Attila and Blake recognized me. Her free hand darted out and when I moved to block, she swung the bag down at my head.

Smooth. I staggered back and by then the woman in coveralls was striding across the parking lot as if that had always been her destination. Heading toward my car, toward Donna.

She was bigger than Donna, younger, and sober. But the older woman snagged her arm and held on as she fought and struggled, the two of them spinning and falling like ice skating doubles recovering from a botched camel spin.

The woman's arm extended to the side. Donna wheeled her around, sinking her weight onto the shoulders, forcing the woman to the ground.

But the time I got there, Donna had straddled the woman's back and was asking me again if I had cuffs.

"Twice in one day," she said. "The old lady's still got it. Anyone want to buy me a drink at the Press Box?"

From the window of Blake's office I watched Butcher's Crossing leg out an easy win. Blake had her back to the window. After a while she hung up the phone.

"Woman's named Maggie Callway," Blake said. "Know who she works for?"

"I can guess."

"The Exiles like their meth cooks honest and exclusive. Attila had told them he was retired. But then, last year or two, the chemist started freelancing. I guess he thought it was still an open market."

"Short-term gains," I said.

Blake nodded. "Callway's the old lady of an Exiles sergeant-at arms. She's been inside for distribution, for assault causing bodily harm. The police would've got to her eventually. Maybe. How'd you figure it?"

"Just a guess that whoever did it would be patient," I said, "and would know they'd be on camera. After stabbing Attila," the worst thing she could do was run. So she went back to what she was doing, with an eye to leave later."

"Why talk to you?" Blake asked.

"Less suspicious than not talking to me. Plus she could put suspicion on someone else. You."

"But why leave when she overheard your friend?"

"A witness is different," I said. "She couldn't know what he might have seen. And enough time had passed, her escape wouldn't be noticed."

"It nearly wasn't," Blake said. Which was as close to a "Thanks, Dave, heck of a job" as I was going to get.

On my way back to the bleachers I put twenty on Curry on Top to win and twenty to place. A sucker's bet, according to the Doc. The smart money was on Gran's Collectible.

"It's a free country," I said.

"Guess it would have to be, they let you make bets like that."

Joe Ricky made space for me to sit down. "I tell you the time I opened for The Collectors, Dave?"

I sat down, thinking of a Chinese proverb about how at the gaming table, there are no fathers and no sons. I looked at my slip. We'd see.

PRE-PROCEDURE TIMEOUT
C. Matthew Smith

Daniel said, *"Let's go through it again."*

The words made Tomás frown. He shifted in his plastic chair and looked out on the parking lot of the Take It EZ Extended Stay Motel. At the far end of the pavement, beyond two rows half full of beater cars and trucks, the "No Vacancy" sign flickered and sizzled. He could hear it from where he sat. To his right, the sun was dipping behind leafless trees, trying, but failing, to conceal the interstate.

"We've been through it already. Twice."

"That's not enough. We need to have it down. Automatic."

"You talk shit to death like this at the hospital?"

Daniel breathed in deeply and nodded. The air was grainy and thick with the scents of manure, old blood, and ammonia. Though you could only see it from the rear of the motel, still the poultry complex made its presence known. He'd hated that smell as a boy, but this evening he found its familiarity oddly comforting. It was the odor his father brought home every evening when Daniel was in grade school, before a heart attack left the man slumped beneath one of the plant's conveyors.

"We talk a lot," Daniel said. "Pre-procedure timeouts. Multidisciplinary rounds. Care conferences."

"Amazing you ever get around to treating patients."

"When we do, we know exactly what we're doing and how we're doing it. Talking reduces the chance for errors."

A sound erupted from Hector's belly, angry and loud, and they both turned to look at him.

Hector bent over and folded his arms. A tattooed rose stem twined all the way down his right forearm, encircling his gut with thorns. The bloom on the back of his hand had his son's name in the center. "If we're gonna go through it again," he said, "let's do it already. I'm hungry as a motherfucker."

"Here." Daniel unzipped his black Swiss Army backpack, removed a breakfast bar, and held it out.

"The fuck is that?" Hector asked.

"It'll fill you up. I promise."

"You just walk around with a bag of snacks all day?"

Daniel shrugged. "When I'm working, I never know when I'll get time to stop for a meal. So I bring stuff I can eat on the move."

"Why you got it with you now?"

"I'm on call tonight."

"My little brother," Tomás said, smiling. "Too busy saving lives to eat."

"What's it taste like?" Hector asked.

"It's chocolate. You'll like it."

Hector sighed but took it and fumbled with the wrapper.

"Okay, then," Daniel said, zipping up the pack and turning back to Tomás. "One more time, from the top. Step one."

"Fine," Tomás said. "Step one is when Frankie calls from the airport. Lets us know it's on a truck and headed out."

"You're sure Frankie's in? He backs out on us, we're back to square one."

"His abuelo works in one of the orchard packing plants," Tomás said. "Trust me, Frankie's in."

When the truck appears, Tomás is just stuffing the burner back into his pocket. The car they boosted early this morning is parked on the side of the road, hood up, sporting new plates. They've been leaning over the engine compartment for a while now, pretending to fiddle with something. Tomás knows a thing or two about vehicles from having to keep the only ones he can afford running. He knows how to make the fiddling look real.

He straightens himself and looks toward the access road. He waits for the truck to turn onto the road so the logo on the side is visible, then taps Hector's shoulder and motions in its direction.

Hector raises the binoculars he'd set on the coolant tank.

"What's the plate number?"

Hector reads it off.

"That's it."

Tomás lowers the hood, wipes his hands on his jeans, and climbs into the driver's seat. Jet fuel tints the air, bitter but also hopeful. The smell of escapes and new beginnings. As he cranks the engine, a thought flits across his mind. He's never been on an airplane before, but one day he'd like to take a trip somewhere far away. He's heard Jamaica's nice.

"How will we know it's the right truck?"

"Frankie helps load the trucks at the distribution center, looks over the paperwork before they leave," Tomás said. *"We want the one that's headed to the hospital."*

"And when it gets into downtown?"

"I turn off on Hardy Street, haul ass around a couple blocks the other direction, end up coming down Whittier past the back side of the hospital."

"Then?"

"We park the car in the alley and wait for the truck."

"North end of the street, two blocks beyond the hospital loading docks. Why?"

"It's an old, abandoned building there," Tomás said. *"No security cameras."*

* * *

The driver takes one look at the two men—one running toward the driver's side door, the other in the middle of the road with a shotgun trained on the windshield—and raises his hands.

"Get out of the truck," Tomás says, tapping his pistol on the window. "And keep your hands where I can see them." The words echo in his ears behind the Bugs Bunny mask he's wearing for the occasion. His own breath blows back hot on his cheeks.

"Please," the man says, climbing down from the cab.

"Don't do nothing stupid," Tomás says, "and you'll be fine. Give my friend here your phone."

The man complies. Hector, in a Wile E. Coyote mask, throws the phone on the asphalt and smashes it thoroughly under his boot.

The driver winces, makes a noise somewhere between a groan and a whimper, then looks back up at them. "I don't have what you think I have back there. No TVs. No PlayStations."

"Is that right," Tomás says. "Well shit."

"This is different," the man says. "It's really important I get it delivered."

"You will. We just want a little before you go."

The driver looks confused. "I don't understand."

"Just open up the back."

Tomás turned toward Daniel and leaned in close. "You sure you want to do this? You get caught and—"

"That's what the preparation is for. So we don't get caught."

"I know," Tomás said. "But if—"

"Do you know how to give someone a shot?"

"How hard can it be?" Tomás said. "Pinch and poke, right?"

Daniel decided it wasn't worth getting into the weeds of proper injection technique with Tomás. Instead, he asked, "Do you know how to look for side effects?"

"You know I don't."

"Do you know how to treat anaphylaxis?"
"I don't even know what the fuck that is."
"Sounds like something this girl gave me one time," Hector
said, his face scrunched tight. "I had to go to the clinic."
Daniel looked at Tomás and cocked an eyebrow.
His brother just shrugged.

They take city back roads east, making sure downtown security cameras capture the car heading that direction. There are public housing developments on the eastern border of the city, and given any excuse, the police will search there first. Tomás feels a twinge of guilt for this part of the plan. He knows plenty himself about living beneath a veil of constant suspicion. But they need the misdirection to buy time.

Several miles outside the city, beyond the reach of the municipal surveillance system, they hook north. The rendezvous is an hour away along a county two-lane with few houses and even less traffic—beyond the bedroom communities with homes on treeless one-acre lots, but not yet to the orchards the postcards depict or the migrant worker camps they do not.

Ahead on the road, Daniel's BMW proceeds slowly, a sightseer's pace. A city dweller in search of fresh air, perhaps, or a speculator scoping out cheap real estate to develop. Nobody the police or highway patrol would bother with.

Daniel puts on his hazard lights when they're close, and both cars pull to the shoulder. As Tomás and Hector approach, he opens his trunk and sets the jack and tire iron out in plain sight.

"Any problems?"

Tomás shakes his head. "It was easy."

"Were you followed?"

"No chance," Hector says. "I been watching the rearview the whole time."

"You did it like we talked about?"

"And talked about and talked about," Tomás says. "Yeah.

Your damn voice was yapping in my head the whole time."

"Good. Now let's move."

Hector carries the cooler to Daniel's coupe and sets it down in the open trunk.

"We clear?" Tomás asks.

This particular stretch of road is flat and straight, with visibility for miles in each direction. Daniel scans both ways, shielding his eyes from the sun.

"Clear."

Tomás lifts a red gas can from the back seat of the stolen car and splashes the fuel onto the cloth upholstery and carpeted floorboards. He lights a match and tosses it into the cab as Daniel and Hector climb into the BMW. By the time Tomás has joined them, black smoke is seeping from cracked windows and billowing from the open door. He winks at Daniel from the front passenger seat and puts on his seat belt.

"I'm just looking out for you, little brother." Tomás wasn't letting it go.

"Yeah, you've told me that before," Daniel said. "Right before you went away for ten years. You need to stop trying to protect me and let me help."

"You bringing up ancient shit?" Tomás blew air out through his pursed lips, almost a whistle. "That was twenty years ago."

"So why does it feel like it's happening right now?" Daniel said. "You cutting me out of the job all over again."

"You were fifteen. You had your whole life ahead of you."

"And you were nineteen, Tomás. Maybe if you'd taken me along as lookout like you promised, you wouldn't have spent your twenties in prison."

"Bullshit." Tomás stepped toward Daniel and faced him squarely. "You weren't there, so don't talk like you were. That job was fucked. A stupid idea. I know you wanted to help. But if you'd come along, I'd still end up doing ten, maybe more for

having a minor with me, and you'd've ended up in juvie. The only thing I did right that night was leave you out of it."

Daniel opened his mouth, then shut it again just as quickly.

Tomás shook his head and backed off, allowed his shoulders to slump. "You got out of the shit, got yourself a nice thing going. No more wondering how the rent gets paid, when the debt collectors will call. I don't want to see you waste it. Life in prison's a bitch, and life after isn't much better. You get out after a few years, you think they give you back that sweet job at the hospital saving lives?"

A pickup with a creaking exhaust bounced into the motel parking lot, splashing through leftover puddles of rain. When it came to a squeaking halt, two men jumped out of the bed and walked toward a room at the far end of the building. Their gait was ginger, their faces slack with exhaustion.

Tomás waved at the men. Each raised a weary hand in return and kept walking.

"No," he said, answering his own question. "You go to work next to those guys, doing whatever the fuck it is they do. Whatever you can find to make ends meet."

Daniel rested his head back against the motel's exterior wall and closed his eyes. "Hector, you remember the nitrogen leak at the plant last year?"

"Hell, yeah," Hector said. "That shit was scary. People passing out all around me. A couple of them died."

"How many people you know got exposed?"

"Twenty, thirty."

"And how many went to the hospital?"

Hector shook his head. "Most were too scared. They think ICE hangs out at the hospital to pick them up or will go through the records for their addresses."

"So, then, how many do you think are going to go wait in some line for the hospital or county health department to give them the vaccine?"

Neither of them said anything.

Daniel turned to look down the row of motel room doors

stretching out away from him—behind each a family making do, or perhaps a collection of men sharing quarters in order to save every penny they could for families back home. Two boys about seven or eight had come outside and were kicking a half-deflated soccer ball.

"They won't bring the vaccines here," he said. "The farms and plants need the cheap labor, but the government can't afford to admit they let undocumented workers slide. So if you have a different idea, now's the time. But I don't have the patience to wait for some miracle I know isn't coming. And we can't afford for it to catch on in one of those plants or the farms while we're sitting on our asses."

"Okay, okay." Tomás laid an appeasing hand on Daniel's shoulder. "I get it. It's on us."

"All of us this time," Daniel said.

About five miles from their destination, the county road runs by the town's oldest cemetery. When the entrance comes into view, Tomás sits up in his seat and points. "Turn off up there real quick."

"What? No."

"We need to tell her." Tomás sticks his hand out the open window, splays his fingers, and feels the cool air coursing between them. "She'd be proud of us."

"She'd whip both our asses," Daniel says, "and you know it."

Tomás laughs. "With that wooden spoon. You remember? Hurt like a bitch."

"Remember?" Daniel squirms in the driver's seat and grimaces. "She hit me so hard one time, I still can't straighten my leg out all the way."

"Well, now's your chance to get onto her about it. She can't beat your ass no more."

"We need to get where we're going."

"Just five minutes," Tomás says. "Promise. When was the

last time you were there?"

"Don't start that. I paid for it all. The plot, the stone, the funeral. I've done plenty."

"I know that," Tomás says. "But how long's it been?"

Daniel exhales noisily, brakes, and turns at the entrance.

The brothers make their way to the farthest corner of the cemetery, well beyond the mausoleum with its ionic columns and row upon row of graying headstones. On foot, Daniel moves in a straight line through the grass, businesslike and efficient, the shortest route between two points. Tomás weaves his way among the graves, careful to step on none. They stop at last in front of a rose-colored tombstone, the marble still shiny, glinting beneath the electric blue sky. Over the past four months, the ground has settled and the edges of the cut sod have melted back into the brown grass.

Daniel looks at the name etched on the stone and thinks again how this would not have been possible here even twenty years ago. A *Villareal* among a sea of venerable *Sullivans*, *McFaddens*, and *Baileys*. A housekeeper and apple picker, this invisible brown soul, nestled in eternal rest among the gleaming white citizens of the town. The "good families." Daniel had paid top dollar for the privilege.

"*Hola, mamá,*" he says.

The quiet that surrounds them in response is a void. It's the hole that was left when her laughter and singing stopped. It's the absence of sound in her hospital room after the monitors and ventilator were turned off. The weighted silence between Daniel and Tomás as they sat in the chapel down the hall, each man all the family the other had left. Both faces asking the same question.

How could we ever make this right?

When they arrive at the motel, already a line has formed on the back side of the complex. Trusted sources in the community have spread the word. Daniel parks at the rear edge of the property, behind the buildings and out of view from the road. Through the leafless trees, he can make out the roofs of the chicken coops down the long hill, each as wide as a house and as long as a football field.

Daniel tosses Tomás and Hector each a surgical mask and walks toward the motel. Hector follows after him, carrying the cooler into the first of two rooms with their doors propped open. One for injections, one for observation, just as he has instructed.

Daniel sets his backpack down on the bed nearest the door and begins to remove its contents—alcohol swabs, Band-Aids, and syringes he's siphoned from hospital supply closets over the last couple of weeks, one lab coat pocket-full at a time. He arranges them on a clean towel he spreads over the foot of the bed.

"You got any more of those bars in there?" Hector says, watching him. "I couldn't eat nothing last night or this morning, but now I'm starving."

Daniel finds one in a smaller pocket, a little mangled but wrapper still intact, and tosses it to Hector.

When his supplies are laid out, he washes his hands in the bathroom sink and snaps on a pair of gloves. The vial he pulls from the cooler is bitterly cold to the touch. It sparks a buzzing in his brain, a current darting across his skin. Reminds him of the night during his fellowship when he repaired some poor kid's femoral artery where a stray bullet had torn a ragged hole. Snatched the kid back from death by his fingertips. That was the first time it all went right and he knew he was exactly where he was supposed to be, doing exactly what he was supposed to do.

Tomás stands guard by the door, hands folded in front of him, his eyes narrowed and intent. "You ready?"

"Just a minute." Daniel tears open an alcohol swab and motions his brother over. "You first," he says.

WINE COUNTRY
John Bosworth

Charlie sucked in his gut and shimmied sideways into one of the country store's narrow aisles. There was nothing on the shelves, nothing at all, that he could see himself buying with a straight face. Orbiting the store in a pointless scavenger hunt, his patience was wearing thin. He already knew what he was going to leave with. It just did not happen to be for sale yet.

The shelves held an odd collection of sun-bleached and dusty items. It wasn't clear if some of them, like a cracked ceramic bowl he lifted from its resting place on a yellow newspaper, were part of the inventory or just misplaced personal items belonging to the old woman behind the register.

"Hot one today!" he said as he passed her for the third time.

He was practically shouting over her radio. Christian rock and mariachi music divided the airwaves in the area. She had elected for the latter, and at exceptional volume. In an exhibit of business acumen which he felt explained the emptiness of the store, and maybe even the desolation of the surrounding acreage of farmland, she had positioned her plastic radio so that the trilling speakers would face out at the paying customer, had there been any. Charlie tapped his foot irregularly to the battalion of panicked tin horns ricocheting around the tiny one-room store, guessing at the rhythm.

He noted with professional disgust the cheapness of the countertop the radio sat on. It wasn't even a veneer. Thin laminated stickers meant to look like a varnished walnut finish peeled away from the edges, showing dull gray aluminum underneath. Absolutely worthless.

The folded hands that lay next to the radio on the countertop were tanned to nearly the same shade of brown as the fake wood covering, like a lizard that had evolved to match the rock she lived on. She reached one out and turned the volume on the radio down an imperceptible amount.

"Help you find anything?" Her voice was young and strong and did not match a face that had been puckered by the sun.

Charlie adopted one of his most well-practiced facial expressions: an openly moronic grin he called The Agreeable Dolt. Smiles and idiots tend to have a disarming effect, even on naturally distrustful people, and Charlie's idiotic smile was, in his opinion, among the best in the business.

"Just rustling up a few essentials, ma'am!"

He carefully inspected a can of expired chili with a rusted rim, and then set it back down next to a row of dusty, unrefrigerated beer cans. Most of the six pack holders had lost a can or two over the years. The empty plastic rings drooped impotently, matching the mood of the blighted cropland outside.

But it was as good as anything else there, and he had browsed long enough. He grabbed one of them by an empty ring and swung it onto the fake wood countertop with a dull clang.

"I thought everyone sold wine in this area," he said. "You must be some kind of conscientious objector." The Agreeable Dolt beamed a guileless smile at her.

"Wine?" She seemed amused. "I never even thought to stock it, to be honest. I only drink brandy myself. Besides it wouldn't be right, me sitting here stocking a store brand wine while all my neighbors grow the grapes for the wineries."

Charlie winked. "Well, I wouldn't want to get you into any

trouble."

"We look out for each other," she agreed, quite seriously. "Everyone's real neighborly out here in wine country." She tapped the sales tax into a pocket calculator. "Seven fifty."

Every few moments an oscillating metal fan on the countertop would churn some stale air past them and stir the limp strands of colorless hair that hung by each side of her face.

"Goll-ee, that air feels nice," he said, handing her a ten.

She let the comment pass and handed back his change. Charlie counted it slowly, making no progress toward the door. He could feel her looking at him.

His bumpkin accent sounded terribly fake to him when it went unreturned. A little rattled, he decided to retire The Agreeable Dolt for the day.

But it was not yet time to give up on the all-time favorite topic of conversation for Agreeable Dolts everywhere: the weather. Was it possible she was unaware the drought had put the grape farms around her out of business? The desolation for miles around was hard to miss. But then again, she seemed to be fairly isolated. There certainly weren't any regular customers to keep her up on current events, as far as he could tell.

"I would guess you're used to the heat by now, though," he prompted.

She still said nothing.

While he poked at the coins, he pulled together a blend of two facial masks—the wide eyes and wrinkled forehead of The Earnest Citizen combined with the welcoming smile and slight head tilt of The Understanding Confidant—and screwed them into place.

With this particular expression, Charlie found that he could take a breather while the face itself came alive and took over the interaction. The character intuitively knew what to say to forge a deeper relationship or move a conversation toward a profitable end, even when he himself had no idea. He was a bit surprised to find himself deploying it ahead of schedule.

When the coins were neatly arranged in his palm, he swung the gaze upward, leveling it just over her hairline. It was sometimes hard to look people in the eye until he was a few sentences into a character transition.

Just above her head, he found himself staring into a pair of eyes anyway. They belonged to a stuffed pheasant mounted high on the wall behind her, its wings splayed wide open like it was catching an updraft and its head cocked downward to survey the room below.

The plumage around the neck was a beautiful iridescent green that shimmered from under a thin film of dust, but the handiwork on the bird's head suggested it was the effort of a hobbyist. A bright pink plastic tongue stuck far out from between its gaping beak and two oversized glass eyes popped out of either side of its head, like it was in the throes of asphyxia.

Charlie was a little breathless himself at the providence being handed to him. He let out a low, appreciative whistle.

"Now *that* is a remarkable specimen. Majestic, really."

She turned to join him in admiring it.

"It is a beautiful bird, isn't it? It was my husband's. He finished it just before he passed on. Shot it himself, too. Just out in the backyard here." She gave the bird a wistful look, like she expected it to share her fond memory of the event.

A large four-pane window speckled with dirt made up most of the wall behind the counter, and as Charlie peered through it, he tried to imagine the yard as a teeming hunting ground. Fifty yards behind the store was a collapsing shed. He guessed that was where the old woman slept. In between the store and shed was a field of dust and rocks with a few clumps of tall yellow grass that had dried to straw. A copse of denuded apple trees held their blistered arms up in a shrug. No birds had any reason to stop there for quite some time.

"He must have been quite a man," Charlie said. "Both a marksman *and* an artist. I would have sworn that was done by a professional. Heck, it's so lifelike I half thought it would pick up and fly right off the wall at me.

"And I should know," he said. "I'm a bit of a collector myself."

"You collect trophies, do you?" She regarded him now with the interest of a fellow enthusiast. "Selma Bryant." She held out her hand, a weightless strip of leather, which he shook.

"Charlie. Glad to meet you. And to answer your question, not just trophies. I happen to collect antiques, curiosities, and collectibles of all kinds. But only when they meet a high standard of quality such as this piece, of course." He paused, then went for it. "I don't suppose you would ever consider selling it?"

He pulled a thick sheaf of neatly folded cash out of the back pocket of his slacks and made sure that she saw the top bill was a hundred. Her eyes fell upon the money and stayed there. She reached out a hand and snapped the radio off.

"Oh, I don't know. It really is an heirloom. It was Barney's. He shot it himself," she repeated.

"Of course. I understand. There's no replacing sentimental value." He rapped the sheaf of bills delicately on the countertop in front of her hands, squaring the edges, and returned the money to his pocket. Her gaze remained on it even as it passed from view. "It was selfish of me to ask."

"Then again," she said, "I don't suppose he's around to enjoy it anymore. And it really should go to someone who would appreciate it."

"It's a beautiful specimen," he said reverently.

"Well," she said, "if I ever were to sell it, it would need to go to someone who was capable of keeping it in good repair. Perhaps to a collector. Such as yourself." Her eyes then raised to meet his. "But I can't just give it away, you understand."

"Oh, of course not, Mrs. Bryant. I wouldn't dream of taking advantage."

A smile collected dryly around her tile-colored dental plate. "Perish the thought. It never crossed my mind. Would you say...two hundred dollars is fair?"

He pretended to consider this. "To be frank with you, Selma, I think two hundred is not at all fair."

She looked like he had slapped her.

"For a bird in such excellent condition? For delicate craftsmanship of this quality? I would insist on paying no less than three hundred," he said, breaking out his smile again.

This time it was returned.

He quickly thumbed three bills off the outside of the stack and made a small pile in front of her. They were new bills, fresh from the bank that morning, and she looked like she wanted to authenticate them by smell.

Charlie was sure to move his remaining cash back into her line of sight as he returned it to his pocket. He waited a beat to allow his generosity to sink in, and then adopted a look of surprise.

"Well, hey, would you look at that."

He walked over to the end table beside the counter. Underneath it, half covered by a gray canvas drop cloth, was a thin tower of varnished dark wood, lined with rotting leather straps. It stood about three feet high, a narrow, arm-length restraint on a wide base. At the top, a long wooden handle connected to a geared wheel. A twisted spike of rusted metal jutted downward from the opposite side of the gear.

Charlie casually tossed the drop cloth aside to inspect it closer, and as it fell the entire structure exhaled a draft of moldy air past his face.

"Huh. Where did you find this funny-looking old thing?" he said.

It was indeed very old. But it was by no means funny to him. Hand-operated presses used to cork wine bottles were not exactly a rarity in the collecting world. But the medieval French monastic style, like the one in front of him, was in a class of its own. Very old, very rare, and very, very expensive.

"That thing?" she said. "It's always been there as far as I recall. Barney might have brought it back from the war for all I know. Hideous, isn't it?" Then she remembered herself. "But I suppose it's handsome. In its own way. Or historical, more like?"

Now it was his turn to let the silence hang in the air, to let her come to him. And of course she did. She had to.

"Do you happen to collect historical things, Charlie?"

"From time to time," he said, disinterested. "It's not usually my thing. There's just not a lot of value in it, if I'm being honest."

"Oh," she said. "And how much would you suppose this one might be worth? If you had to guess."

"I make it a policy to not offer free appraisals," he said. "People tend to take advantage."

She looked aghast. "I didn't mean to—"

"That rule," he smiled, "doesn't apply between friends, of course. I'd be happy to take a look."

Charlie drew a squinted eye close to the press and began to mutter as he poked at it.

"Hmmm...fittings badly corroded...broken clamp...purely decorative."

He straightened up.

"Well, Selma, I'm afraid this just isn't in very good shape at all. You see in my business there's a very fine line between collectible and just plain junk."

"Oh. I see. Of course." She was crushed.

"But don't you worry. Seeing as that we have such good working relationship established, I'd be happy to give you a hundred dollars for it. Maybe I could use it for scrap. A hundred dollars is a far sight better than having to pay someone to come in here and haul it away, wouldn't you say?"

"Well, that's very generous of you, and I'll certainly take it," she said. "But it's too bad you don't have much use for old winemaking things. I have a whole mess of it down in the cellar."

"Oh, really?" A flash of hunter's adrenaline shot through him and, worried his mask might slip, he turned his face to a spot of imaginary rust on the machine beside him. "What sorts of things do you have down there?"

"Just more old junk I would guess. It probably wouldn't

interest you. Barney had a whole mess of stuff. 'Vintner's tools,' he called them. Old barrels and bottles. Presses. That kind of thing."

"You don't say."

"Oh, sure. But as I said, it's just old junk like that thing there. You wouldn't be interested."

"Selma," he said, "you're right, it's almost certainly junk. But I'd be happy to take a look for you, just to be certain. As a friend."

"Where in the hell did you get that thing?" Charlie said.

A steep flight of stairs punched in the floor behind the counter had dropped them into a cold fog of damp air and mildew below the store. It caused Charlie to shiver, partly from the wet chill, and mostly from his awareness of what such an atmosphere can do to antiques.

But those concerns were forgotten when Selma found the light switch, popping on a naked low-watt bulb that hung on a long wire dangling from the ceiling. It spread a dim circle of greenish yellow light on a room that matched the footprint of the store above, but dug so deep into the earth it felt cavernous. It was packed on all sides with shadowy stacks of furniture, tools, books, clothing, and crockery. Just the mainstays of an average estate sale in a below-average zip code.

With one obvious exception.

Against the far wall, a massive oak wine barrel, a several-thousand-gallon tun, stood just on the edge of the light. It lay on its side, nested in a series of wood braces that created a platform underneath it. Even on its side, Charlie guessed it reached more than fifteen feet in the air. A tall, narrow ladder leaned against the front.

A small wooden spigot was hammered into the bottom, just above the base, with a glass tumbler collecting a slow drip of thick golden liquid below it.

Overall, the barrel appeared to be in immaculate condition.

The finish was still on, the wood unwarped, and there was no obvious rusting on the hoops. It was, without question, one of the most unexpected, impressive, and valuable things that Charlie had seen in his entire career. All that remained to do was to tell her the exact opposite.

"Is there still wine in there?" he said casually. "It must be vinegar by now. I can't imagine the wood has held up well on the inside at all. I couldn't possibly sell a barrel soaked with rotten wine."

He wished he hadn't wasted his best derision on the corking press.

"There's some brandy in it," Selma said, "but it's not too old and it's far from vinegar. I start a fresh batch every now and then. I told you how it's the only thing I'll drink."

She stooped to pick up the tumbler.

"It's very sweet. Try it and see."

The glass was filthy and smeared with grease. Charlie's mind whirred through an index of frightening-sounding diseases that he associated with rural areas: botulism, rickets, diphtheria. He didn't know what they were, exactly, but he knew he didn't want one.

"I'm sure it's wonderful, but I'm afraid I never indulge before getting behind the wheel."

"Suit yourself." Her look told him that sober driving was the prissy affectation of a city dweller. She drained the glass and licked the rim.

"This was such a good batch, and it's nearly gone already," she said. She looked terribly sad staring into the empty glass, but then perked up suddenly. "But that means you can buy the barrel, right? That's what you said. You said that it needed to be empty. How much could you give me for it?"

She seemed eager, almost desperate, like the drink had unlocked a need in her.

Perfect, Charlie thought. *A motivated seller.*

He had already moved in close to inspect the condition of

each barrel stave. The lighting was terrible, but even in the dimness he could tell the specimen was exceptional. Miraculous preservation, really. He climbed the first two steps of the ladder looking for any blemishes he could point out as ruinous, but couldn't find a single one. It was flawless.

"I imagine I could find a buyer who would use it for scrap wood," he said. "I could give you, say, eighty dollars for it. Oh, what the heck, let's make it a hundred. Plus I'd waive the standard haul-away fee. That's usually charged by the pound, so I'm afraid it would be very costly for an article of this size if you hire somebody else to do it."

"Only a hundred for the whole thing?" She drew another ounce or two of brandy into the glass.

"I'm afraid the resale market just isn't very strong for a piece like this," he said. "Maybe I could give you one-fifty if the interior condition is better than expected."

Selma didn't say anything right away, and he felt the deal slipping away from him. It was his own fault, too. He had not greased the skids enough upstairs, and now she was cooling on him. It was time to introduce her to his old negotiation deputy, The Distracting Conversationalist.

"Say," he said, "how did you get so devoted to brandy anyway?"

"There is a winery a ways away from here," she said, looking into her glass. "It's called Vecchio. Have you heard of it?"

"Can't say I have," he said quickly. He turned back toward the ladder, which he continued to climb, inspecting each knot as he rose. "They make a good brandy, do they?"

"No, no. Not the point," she said. "I've never visited it, and from what I hear, the wine they produce isn't anything special. But the whole operation sure *looks* special. Very old and important. In truth, they've only been open a few years. But the whole place is built from old wood and glass. It's lit by hundreds of candles. Not one electric light in the place. You walk in there, you'd think you had somehow ended up in

Renaissance France."

"Huh," Charlie said. "What a crazy idea."

"Crazy like a fox," she said. "The wine is nothing special, like I said. But you couldn't convince a tourist of that once they're in there, feeling like they've traveled back in time. Vecchio sells out every season. They have a wait list for members."

"You were going to tell me why you like brandy so much," he reminded her.

"Was I?" She had refilled her glass again and looked into it.

"I guess what I meant was, maybe people don't really know why they like the things that they like. Someone will pay a hundred dollars for a bottle of wine at Vecchio, and they'll be grateful for the opportunity. And what are they really buying? A ten-dollar bottle of wine and a ninety-dollar story they tell themselves while they drink it. Put them together, and it tastes like a hundred bucks to them. And as long as the math adds up, there's no harm to them in believing it, I guess."

"That's quite a theory," Charlie said, continuing up the ladder, peering at the wood, searching for flaws and finding none.

"Well, that's all it is. A theory." She swirled her glass. "After all, I drink this stuff and the only story I know about brandy isn't a very pleasant one."

"Oh, no?"

"I'm afraid not. Have you ever heard of Horatio Nelson?"

"I don't think so," he said. "Does he live around here?"

"Not hardly. He was an Admiral in the British navy around 1800."

"Well now...how about that." Charlie found himself wondering what legal vagaries he would be inviting by closing a sale with someone with advanced dementia. He shrugged. He had contracts out in the car. As long as she could still write her name, or make her mark, or whatever she did, that was good enough for him.

"He was their bravest and most respected officer," she went on. "And a brilliant strategist."

"And he liked his brandy, did he?"

"Probably not as much as he ended up getting. He was shot in the spine by the French at the Battle of Trafalgar. A mortal wound. His loyal crew was devastated. They dragged him into the belly of the ship to die."

Charlie tried to inject some levity back into things with a dry laugh, but the Distracting Conversationalist was failing him. Selma's oddness was hard to read, and he was running out of techniques.

"Well. I guess anyone would need a drink at a time like that."

"The Admiral most of all," she agreed. "The agony was terrible, but it didn't last long. And after he died, they packed his body in a barrel full of brandy to preserve it for the voyage home."

"Ah, I see, that *is* a quite unpleasant story." As he neared the top of the ladder its feet dug unevenly into the packed dirt floor and the uppermost rungs shifted slightly, scraping along the barrel's edge. Charlie grit his teeth, praying he wasn't damaging the finish.

"Oh, that's not the unpleasant part," she said. "The most terrible thing happened as they sailed back to port. Just wretched, actually."

Charlie reached the top of the ladder and gripped the edge to steady himself. The wood on top, which he had feared would be scarred or water damaged, was perfect. About two feet from the edge, a circular trap door was neatly cut into the top where new wine could be added for aging. Its latch was clamped into place by brass hinges that matched a narrow handle screwed into the top.

"What happened," Selma went on, "was the ship was delayed returning home. They were sailing through the Mediterranean and they got lost. You can just imagine what it must have been like, tossed around by the ocean with no idea where you are going or where you have been. No idea if you would ever see your family again, but fairly certain that you would not. Pretty quickly they ran out of supplies, and they suffered terribly in the punishing heat."

Charlie grabbed the handle on the trap door and tugged on it. It was stuck firmly in place, and he nearly lost his balance. He carefully nudged forward, leaning his forearm on the top of the barrel. With his knee propped on the edge and one foot planted firmly on the top rung of the ladder, he leaned in and grasped the handle again, giving it a powerful jerk and wrenching it halfway up before it stuck. He wouldn't have enough leverage from the ladder to pry it all the way open.

"It's just terrible, what happened next," she continued. "But you can hardly blame them, lost and adrift out there with no guarantee of ever making it home for anyone to notice."

Charlie noticed an expectant silence from below. He called down, "What? What happened to them?"

"Well, after a long, horrible ordeal, they miraculously made it back to their home port on the Thames. Everyone was waiting there, thrilled to see their men again and then equally devastated when they heard what had happened to the Admiral. They immediately set out to give him a burial befitting a war hero.

"But when they pried open the brandy cask, they found that some thirsty devil had secretly tapped the barrel with their dear Admiral in it. Nobody had noticed. They probably had other things on their minds while they were out there pitching in the waves with no land in sight. And it must not have hurt the flavor any, because whoever tapped it drank every last drop before sealing it back up and leaving him in there to rot."

Charlie shuddered again, this time not from the cold in the cellar.

"Well?" Selma called up. "How's the interior condition?"

"Ah, just checking that now," he said.

He placed his elbows on the barrel and heaved his torso onto the top. Then one knee, then the next, scrabbling forward until he was hunched over the door. Even stooped to half his height, his hair collected a turban of spider webs from between the crossbeams.

He squatted with one foot on either side of the trap door for leverage, wrapped both hands around the handle, and threw his weight behind him violently. As the door flew open and out of his hands, his body rocketed upward, delivering the crown of his skull solidly into one of the rafters. An explosion of light came around the edge of his vision and pulsed brightly in the gloom of the basement.

He knelt by the barrel's edge, holding the top of his head in his hands. Dampness spread through his interlocked fingers. Shrill ringing flickered in and out of both ears. He swore. He had enough of this weird old woman and her awful, decaying store. It was time to climb down, close the deal, and get on the road while there was still an hour or so of dusk left. He could send a U-Haul back later to collect his winnings.

He could make out the top of the ladder through the bursts of strobing light in his eyes and he reached out for it.

How he missed it, he wasn't sure. With one half-blind swipe of his hand, he was closing in on it, and with the next he had somehow passed it, as if it had moved away from him on its own.

As he lurched forward, he threw his forearms against the edge to keep himself from pitching face-first to the ground below. He thought he had caught himself, but he must have continued falling because the ladder seemed to jab upwards at him, the pointed top of the runner hitting him hard in the teeth.

This time he lost his footing entirely, stepping backwards once, twice, and the third time onto the black air of the open trap door.

His hands shot up over his head, his fingers gripping the metal track that ran along the edge of the opening. Pain screamed through his wrists and knuckles. The rest of him dangled heavily in the blackness inside.

"Selma," he screamed, his voice loud and close to him in the dark of the barrel. "Help me!"

The air inside the barrel was humid and it choked him with a powerful odor. It didn't smell exactly like wine. It was gamy, sickly sweet, and made breathing hard.

Using all of his strength he managed most of a pull-up and thrust the top of his head back into the light. Just far enough to see Selma's face hovering at the top of the ladder, looking at him.

"Thank God! Can you climb on top and pull me out?" The tendons in his wrists and shoulders were on fire.

But she did not seem to hear him. She was saying something to him, talking so quietly he could barely hear her.

"There is more to that Vecchio story, too," she said. "And I'm afraid this one doesn't have a very happy ending either."

"Just give me your hand, all right?" His legs kicked under him as he struggled to keep his head above the opening.

"It's the story of a young man who loves wine. He saves all of his money and opens a winery of his very own. It's his dream. But, Charlie? A terrible thing happens. Nobody wants his wine. The sad fact is, he just isn't very good. Soon the time comes when he realizes it's over. He's going to have to close.

"But then he has an idea. People don't want his wine, it's clear to him that's not where his talents lie. But maybe, he thinks, he can sell them the *feeling* of enjoying a rare wine, without having to make any himself. Using the last bit of money he could borrow, he redecorates with old wood and glass and renames the place...and just like that, Vecchio is born."

Bolts of numbness shot through the pain in Charlie's arms, his strength failing, his whole body shaking with effort.

"And it's a hit! Before he knows it, he has more people showing up than even fit in the place. And it practically breaks his heart to have to turn away paying customers every day after he struggled so hard just to get off the ground. So he hits upon another idea, a brilliant one that's going to make him quite a lot of money: he'll make a whole chain of wineries, all around the region."

"Selma." Charlie's breath was failing him with the strain of keeping himself eye to eye with her. "Please."

"But if he's going to build a whole chain of new stores, he'll need a lot of antiques and bric-a-brac to furnish them. And antiques take longer to make than bad wine. A lot longer. He's in a bind. And do you know what he does to get out of it?"

"Please—"

"He goes out into the countryside. He visits farmhouses and country homes. He meets with the people there. Makes friends with them. But he doesn't go just anywhere, there's something similar about all these places. Do you know what makes them special? No? He likes droughts. Wherever he finds droughts, he always finds plenty of homes that are just a few months away from foreclosure. He finds these people—desperate people—and makes them lowball offers for every antique gewgaw he can find there.

"These people have no choice. They're practically giving away anything that isn't nailed down. But he'll take even more than that. He'll take up the floorboards if he thinks he can use them. He's taken a front door right off the hinges with the family still inside. He takes the plumbing fixtures. He picks the bones clean before the estates can go to public auction. He's a buzzard."

Charlie suddenly remembered what the smell in the barrel reminded him of. He had been nine years old. His family had spent all day in the car driving to their cabin in the mountains. It was August, and the heat was intense. When they finally arrived, they all ran inside at once, fighting for position to be first in the pool. But after taking two steps inside, they ran back out again, gagging. A possum had crawled under the floorboards to die. It was stewing in the heat, filling the house with the smell of rot, gamy and sickly sweet.

"Now my husband, Barney," Selma said, "he wouldn't ever shoot a buzzard. What's the point? You don't eat them. You certainly wouldn't stuff one, hideous as they are. They're worthless. Might as well let them fly on by. Live and let live, he used to say. But things have changed now—the buzzards won't just fly by anymore. They circle.

"One was here just last week, trying to tape his foreclosure notice on my front door in front of God and everybody. You can probably smell him in there. Not too pleasant, is it? But you really should have tried the brandy. It's much better than it smells, I promise you."

"Selma," Charlie said again, but more to himself. His face was damp with sweat and tears of effort.

"Now, not a week later, another buzzard flies in for the last little bit I have to my name. Waving hundred-dollar bills around like it could do me any good at this point. Like he hasn't been all over the county already, cleaning folks out. Like we wouldn't talk. Like I wouldn't know."

She put her face an inch from his, the drink still strong on her breath.

"Of course we talk. *Of course I know*. Goddamn it, I already told you. We're real neighborly out here in wine country."

"Now, Selma." Charlie's mind was back and racing. He had a plan. "Just think about this, alright? Just *think*. I have money. Real money. We can work something out. I can go to your bank, I can give them whatever you need. You'll keep the house, you'll have it all—it will—" he broke off.

She wasn't listening to him. She looked like she was not exactly there anymore. She seemed miles, or maybe even decades, away, a foggy, unfocused smile on her face. She looked happy, like she was standing out in her yard when Barney was still alive and birds still flew by. Back when they had rainy springs, and things still grew there, and she could stand out in the tall, lush grass, just taking it all in.

She reached out a hand, as if to pull a ripe apple from one of her trees, and gripped the collapsible hinge of the trap door instead, rocking it gently back and forth to close it.

STELLA BLUES

Steve Liskow

"It sounds too good to be true. So maybe it isn't."

Phil Teach sits in his dressing room backstage at the Grasso Entertainment Center while blues fans pack the auditorium for the Connecticut Blues Showdown. The winner goes on to the finals in Memphis in the fall, and the anticipation is thick enough to chew. Teach has won twice before, including last year.

"How'd you even hear about it?" Anastasia Brandywine stands across from him in jeans and a black tee that downplays her chest. The other guys have offered her a seat, but with her blond hair falling halfway down her back, it's easier to stand. Besides, the dressing room is the size of a card table.

Teach blows steam off his coffee mug and sips before he answers.

"The guy called me last week. Said he wanted to sell it and he knew I was a collector."

"How can you even check to be sure it's real?" Win Mason asks. "I mean, Blind Lemon Jefferson used a lot of guitars, but nobody seems to know what they were. Or if they're even still around."

Teach nods. "Yeah, there are pictures of him playing different ones, but one's definitely a Stella, and that picture is the right year, 1922."

"Shit." Hermano Vega is the cynic of the group, as if they need one. "Nobody copied his songs because his style was so far ahead of everyone else. But he's been dead—what, almost a hundred years?—and nothing's ever turned up before. His manager probably just sold his shit to a pawnshop when he died. Nobody's got anything like reliable records, right?"

"I agree," Anastasia says. She and Teach used to be an item on the local blues circuit, but he has the loyalty of a rabbit and the attention span of a gerbil on crack. One morning, she came out of her shower to find him getting room service from a hotel chambermaid.

Teach holds up a file folder. "I went online and found the serial numbers for Stellas and Washburns from 1920 to 1925," he says. "When the guy shows up, I'll see what he's got. If it's not on the list, sayonara, kid, have a nice day."

Blind Lemon Jefferson sang early versions of several songs that folk and rock performers covered in the '60s: "C. C. Rider," "Matchbox Blues," "See That My Grave Is Kept Clean." In the 1920s, he made enough money to buy a car and hire a chauffeur to drive him around. Stories about him—mostly bullshit—are more plentiful than ants at a picnic. Ninety years after his death, Teach is one of his biggest disciples.

"That's not much to go on," Win says.

"Well, I know enough about the period so I can work with whatever the guy shows me," Teach replies. "You know, the bridge, the neck joint, the glue. If something's wrong, it'll stick out like Annie's tits."

Everyone laughs except Anastasia, who flips him off. She's the only woman to make the top six tonight, and her combination of originals and classic Memphis Minnie and Big Mama Thornton kicks serious ass.

Tom Lawson, the MC, taps on the doorframe.

"Fifteen minutes, boys and girl."

"How much does this guy want?" Hermano asks.

"Fifty large, in cash."

Annie's eyes widen and the room goes silent around her.

"You're carrying that kind of money around? Are you out of your mind?"

"Don't be stupid. It's not here. But I can get it right away if I need it."

Lawson clearly wants to hear more, but he has to go back to warm up the crowd, like two thousand fans need juicing for the hottest blues gig in the state. The other performers return to their dressing rooms for last-minute tune-ups or bathroom calls.

By the luck of the draw, a duo of guitar and piano will open, Phil Teach will follow, and Annie will close the first set. After a twenty-minute intermission, three more performers will compete, with Hermano Vega, who doubles on guitar and harp, wrapping things up. The judges will tally their score sheets and announce the results a few minutes later.

Annie paces up and down the cramped hallway talking to herself, the ritual she's used since she played her first open mic a decade ago. Some people swear she channels the female singers she now covers and talks to herself in their voices.

She smells cigarette smoke and looks up at a tall man in denim. The brim of his Stetson hides his face.

"Phil Teach?" he asks. She points at the door. When he goes in, she sidles over to listen.

"Bring it in so I can look at it," Teach says.

"It's locked in my car," the guy answers. "You want to see it, you come out and look."

"I'm on a second, I don't have time until after my set. Call it an hour."

"Whatever." The guy pushes past Annie, his cigarette smell so thick she imagines a blue-gray aura surrounding him. He disappears outside again, and she taps on Teach's door before she pushes it open.

"Are you going to buy it?" she asks.

"Like you care." He wears his lucky cap and tunes a thirty-year-old Martin D-28.

"I think you're asking for trouble," she says.

"I think it's none of your business." He squints at his tuner and adjusts a string.

"Phil, if that's really Blind Lemon Jefferson's Stella from a hundred years ago, it's worth a lot more than fifty grand. If that's all the guy's asking, it's a fake and he figures you'll go for it because it's a bargain."

"Remember what I said a while ago?"

"Everyone already knows I've got great tits, but thanks for the endorsement."

"I'll bet every guy in this contest has seen them up close and personal, hasn't he?"

Annie steps back. "I'd forgotten what a prick you can be."

"Miss it, don't you?"

"Sort of like diarrhea." She takes a beat and forges ahead. "If it's a fake, you probably *will* spot it. But if it's real, the only reason I can see for the guy wanting cash is because it's stolen, and he doesn't want to leave a paper trail."

"That's what I miss about you, Annie," Teach puts his guitar back in the case. "Your eternal faith in human nature."

"I had a good teacher." She walks back to her own dressing room. She knows he's checking out her ass, but she's been there before, too. She puts on a white T-shirt and drapes her plaid flannel over it because she wants the pocket for her finger-picks. She tunes her National steel resonator to open G like Memphis Minnie used and clamps her capo on the headstock. Then she tunes her own Martin. She'll use them both during her set. The opening act will be on in five minutes, which means she has another hour.

Half an hour later, she stands in the wings and watches Riley and Lucas bow to enthusiastic applause. They wave to the crowd and edge by Annie, who mouths "nice set" at them.

Guys tell her that, too. The seats are packed and the sound is perfect. Well, that's why they use this venue: great acoustics and a first-rate PA and crew. Two stools and a straight-backed chair sit on stage, along with the mic on an adjustable stand.

Lawson introduces Phil Teach, and Annie steps back so he can go on.

"Break a leg, darlin'." She keeps her face neutral.

Tonight, he's hot enough to fry eggs on his back, and someone's going to have to be touched by the blues gods if they're going to beat him. The guy in the Stetson appears in the hall again and Annie sees Lawson head him off.

"When's he gonna be done?"

"Ten more minutes," Lawson says. "Twenty-five-minute sets. You run over, you're disqualified."

"Harsh."

"This is the big kids' table, Jack."

Phil finishes with a Charley Patton song in an altered tuning that brings the crowd to its feet. He ambles off-stage waving his cap and walks by Annie without a word. He nods at the guy with the Stetson and she strides toward the mic stage center. She puts her Martin on the guitar stand next to it and plugs in her resonator as Lawson says her name and the long vowels echo through the auditorium.

She doesn't use a stool or chair. Phil told her she could breathe more easily standing up and it would help her hit the high notes. The only useful thing she ever got from him. She feels good through "Me and My Chauffeur" and "When the Levee Breaks," using slide and incorporating some of Led Zeppelin's licks on the second one, and the crowd laps it up. When she switches guitars, she feels the heat coming off the seats and finishes her set with her T-shirt sticking to her back.

Twenty-minute intermission. Annie tucks her babies away in their cases and joins the crowd outside watching Phil Teach and the guy selling the guitar. Phil sits on the open trunk of the guy's SUV and holds a guitar that looks small from that distance. And old. He peers inside the sound hole, then opens the file folder beside him and runs his finger down the list.

"Guy's name is Jones," someone says. "Original, huh?"

Phil checks the list and looks into the sound hole again. Then a third time. He turns the guitar over and studies the joint where the neck meets the body. He said that might be a giveaway if the guitar was a fake. He turns it every which way to look at the spot from different angles, and runs his fingers over it. Annie remembers when he used to touch her that way, too.

A burning smell wafts across her nostrils. Win Mason fires up a joint and she shakes her head.

"Seriously, Win? You're going on in half an hour, and you're toking?"

"It's my glaucoma medication," he says.

Everyone stares at him. Win can't be over forty.

"I didn't know you had glaucoma."

"I don't," he says. "It's working."

Over by the SUV, Jones shakes his head and Phil sights down the guitar's neck. The instrument almost certainly needs work, maybe serious work, and that means a really good tech who knows how to treat old instruments without fucking them up. Annie wonders how much Phil will pay on top of the fifty grand—assuming he buys the thing. Brand new, the guitar probably cost fifteen bucks.

Lawson joins them and frowns at Win and his weed.

"Five minutes, people."

The men straggle back inside. Annie stays to watch Phil and Jones approach with the guitar in a beat-to-shit case. Their hats bury their faces in deep shadow. She cocks her eyebrows at Phil, and he brushes by her without a word again. When they're inside, Annie goes to her own car and rummages in her glove compartment. Then she walks over to Jones's SUV with the Illinois plates. Blind Lemon Jefferson died in Chicago, so maybe that makes sense. She crouches behind his bumper for a minute, then walks back to the stage door.

Phil and Jones come out again, without the guitar, and Phil walks over to his own SUV. He pops the hatch and comes up with a reusable grocery bag. Jones sits next to him on the back bumper to count packets of green. They count twice, then they shake hands and Jones carries the bag back to his SUV and turns west out of the lot.

Annie wishes Win left the roach outside so she could finish it off. Phil comes back looking like he just got the world's best blow job from Miss Universe.

"You did it, huh?" Annie says.

"Bet your sweet ass." He disappears inside, where he'll play that guitar until the judges do their thing in another hour and a half.

Annie joins the others watching from the wings. Everyone's playing well, and it's going to come down to each judge's vision of "blues" to determine the winner.

Hermano adjusts his harp rack around his neck and makes sure all his harmonicas are in the right loops on his special belt. Lawson announces him and he walks on stage to close the show.

When the applause follows him off, Lawson encourages the crowd to buy food and drink while the judges tally their scores. Annie knuckle-bumps Vega and goes back to Phil's dressing room, which is packed.

Phil plays a parlor guitar, smaller than most of the guys play now, and everyone leans forward to look at the worn frets, the thick neck, and the purling that remains around only half the sound hole.

"The guy say where he got it?" someone asks.

"Found it in a pawnshop, South Side Chicago. Thought it might be worth something and bought it. Then he checked it out and discovered what he had."

It's so clearly bullshit that nobody even bothers to comment.

"Got a decent sound," Win says.

"Yeah." Phil plays his way up the neck. "I'm surprised it sounds so full. Some of these old parlor guitars, they get tinny."

"Needs lots of work, though," someone says.

"Well, *duh.*"

"Guitars and women," Riley the piano player says. "Both real high maintenance."

"Yeah," Phil says. "But a good guitar won't get fat."

Annie wants to shove his new toy straight up his ass.

Everyone wants to play it a little, but Phil's reluctant. Who can blame him? He tries several different songs and riffs but doesn't change the tuning because he's not sure how the neck will handle different tension.

"Anyone got a string gauge?" he asks. "These strings feel heavy."

"Old guitars used heavier strings."

"Thank you, professor."

Nobody has one. Everyone carries extra sets of their preferred strings with them so they don't need to check such issues.

Lawson appears. "The judges are ready, so come on out if you care."

They all hover in the wings and wait to hear their name. Win Mason is Second Runner-Up and walks out with a big grin that might be part delight and part weed. He waves at the crowd, takes his trophy, and returns.

Lawson looks at his score sheet and waits for the crowd to calm down.

"First Runner-Up is Ms. Anastasia Brandywine."

Annie strides onstage and squints in the stage lights. The crowd cheers from the shadows, and she gives them her best smile and a wave before going off with her trophy.

"Is that your real name?" Riley the piano player asks.

"It's as real as the rest of her," Phil says. Annie flips him off again.

"And the winner of the Connecticut Blues Showdown, for the third time, and second in a row, the incomparable Phil Teach."

Phil sidles out on stage. The blues fans rise to their feet, and he sucks it up like mother's milk. Finally, they quiet down enough so he can lean into the mic.

"I'd like to thank the judges for this honor, but I really need to thank all of you out there, too. You're the best fans anywhere, and without you, we couldn't hold this event year after year. Let's keep the blues alive."

More applause and Teach waits. When they settle down, he goes on.

"You may not know it, but this trophy is all I get. No money. I have to pay for my trip to Memphis and my hotel room for the finals. I hope you'll all go to the GoFundMe site I'll be setting up in the next couple of days, help me bring the big trophy back here to share with all of you."

The crowd goes apeshit, and he rejoins the others offstage.

"Great day, today," he comments. Everyone forces a smile and the men fist-bump him or clap him on the shoulder. Annie gives him a low-key hug to show there are no hard feelings. She even kisses his cheek without biting his nose off.

She watches the excitement surge back to the dressing room and the first bottle of champagne appear before she takes her guitars outside. She lays them in her back seat and wonders if she should go back to the celebration.

Why? She has her trophy. She has other places to be and other people to see.

She slides behind the steering wheel and powers up her GPS tracker. Then she turns west. Half a mile down the road, she stops at a package store and searches the aisles for a bottle of Wild Turkey, 112 proof. By the time she returns to her car, the sun is sinking and she lowers the visor to keep the red ball out of her eyes. She eases back into traffic and checks the GPS again.

Two hours later, she passes a motel and eases her car into a space at a strip mall, near a laundromat and a convenience store. She locks it and walks back to the motel with the bourbon in a paper bag. The SUV with Illinois plates sits directly across from room 114, so she knocks on that door, *shave and a haircut, two bits.*

Jones opens the door and his eyes widen.

"Uh. Hi."

"Hi." She walks in with a smile on her face and the bottle in her hand. "Sorry I'm late, but you made a wrong turn."

"Um, no, I—"

"It's that right-left thing again, isn't it? Other right. Well, never mind. You've got it and here we are."

"Annie, I—"

"You've got the money."

"Well, yeah—"

"So let's celebrate. There must be an ice machine here somewhere, go get some."

His mouth moves like he's trying to figure out how to talk. She holds up the bourbon and raises her eyebrows.

"Uh, yeah." He leaves and she looks around the room, one step up from a cardboard box. A fresh pack of Marlboros and his Bic lie on the bureau, and the ashtray on the nightstand has four butts in it.

She brings two glasses in their shrink wrap back from the bathroom and drapes her flannel over the back of the chair. The coverlet on the bed is scratchy and she suspects the sheets will be even worse.

Jones returns with a bag of ice, his face still bewildered. Annie drops cubes into both glasses and covers them with the bourbon.

"Why don't you put the bag in the sink."

When he returns, she hands him a glass. They clink and sit on the bed.

"I didn't think he'd go for it," Jones says. "He knows his shit, I thought he'd spot it for sure."

"He probably will tomorrow." Annie raises her glass to her face and pretends to sip. "Or the next day. But I knew if I warned him off, he'd go through with it just to piss on my shoes."

Jones drinks deeply and Annie pours him more. The bourbon smell almost hides the cigarette smoke that drives her sinuses crazy. They drink again.

"What I'd really love," Annie says, "I'd love it if he takes the thing to Memphis to show off and someone else sees it's a fake in front of the whole frickin' crew."

"Harsh." Jones shakes his head.

"Hey," Annie says. "Life is how we learn."

She kisses her fingers and touches them to his lips. "You do really good work. I told you that before, and now you know it for sure."

"Six months," he says. "Finding old pieces, distressing them even more, watering down the glue...God, what a pain."

"But it worked." She pretends to sip again and refills his glass. "Now, it's payday."

He doesn't get it for a minute so she repeats it. Then she clears her throat and stares at him.

"Oh. Yeah. I guess...yeah. Right."

He puts his glass on the nightstand and shambles over to the bureau that looks like it could collapse any second. He finds the bag of cash in the top drawer and brings it back.

"Fifty-fifty, right?"

Annie nods. He dumps the packets of hundreds on the bed and Annie picks one at random. She riffles through it and counts. Yes, it's complete. She does it with a second, then a third. They're all full. If Teach shorted any of the others a little, it's not enough to matter anyway.

"He really thought you stole it, didn't he?"

"Must have." Jones drinks and Annie refills his glass again. So far, she's had one sip and he's had about six shots.

They each take five packets of bills. Annie puts hers on the chair near the door and Jones returns the bag with his share to the drawer. He looks at Annie's chest and she can read his mind from years of practice.

She stands and leans toward him. "This is a good day. I won second place in the Showdown, I screwed my asshole ex-boyfriend, and I got lots of money for it."

He stands and pulls her against him. "And now you're gonna

231

get something even better."

She kisses him and lets her hand slide down to the front of his jeans. They undress each other and she pushes him back on the bed. They kiss for a long time, his mouth tasting of Wild Turkey and Marlboros. He's not as good a kisser as Phil was, but he's better than nothing. She moves her lips down his neck and chest, and across his stomach. She goes lower and he groans. She uses her mouth and both hands until his hips hump her chin.

"You want me, baby?" she whispers.

"God, yes."

She moves up and guides him between her legs. His hands clamp around her waist and she closes her eyes and rides him hard.

He thrusts quickly and she knows he's going to finish before she does. She grinds her hips on him and takes what pleasure she can with the time they have left.

"Harry," she says.

He brings his hands up to her breasts, his eyes half-closed and his red face shiny with sweat. His breathing comes faster.

"Annie," he whispers. "God, Annie."

She jams her thumbs into his larynx, rocking forward and leaning her whole weight on them. His eyes pop open and he tries to push back, but she's already ruptured his windpipe and he's starving for oxygen. She pumps her hips and rocks forward again, her thumbs sinking even deeper, and he gasps and gargles, his eyes bulging and his face fading from red to bluish-gray. His hands cup her breasts to push her off, but she rocks back and forward one more time, his breath a thin rasp she can barely hear.

His hands fall away and his eyes roll back. She keeps rocking until she's sure he's dead, then eases off him and stands naked by the side of the bed. She licks her palm and holds it under his nostrils.

Nothing.

She dresses again and pulls the bag of bills from the bureau, dropping her share back into it and putting it on the chair. She pulls the sheet up over the body, puts the ashtray next to it, and pours most of the bourbon over the covers. She waits until the smell fills the room before she lights a cigarette, then she takes a drag and holds the orange tip a few inches above the soaked bedding.

A small flame grows, like a leaf breaking through the soil. She drops the smoking butt next to the ashtray and steps back to watch the flame move across the bed, getting bigger and stronger. She picks up the bag of money, turns off the lights, and closes the door behind her.

She pulls the GPS tracker from under the Illinois license plate and returns to her own car, where she watches Harry's room until her heartbeat is back to normal. The faintest flicker of flame appears behind the blinds in room 114, but not enough so anyone will turn in an alarm.

Anastasia Brandywine heads east, back the way she came. On her front seat, she has a trophy for First Runner-Up in the 2019 Connecticut Blues Showdown. In the back seat, she has a Martin 000-15 and a National steel resonator. In the trunk, she has fifty thousand dollars her ex-lover spent on a piece of junk.

She's got the key to the fuckin' highway.

THE VIOLENCE OF HER TOUCH
Michael Wegener

The Man was watching her from the shadows outside. She was sitting in a small bar not unlike the one Hopper had painted—spare and naked behind high and wide windows that poured yellow light into the darkened street. There was even a lonely man in a fedora, sitting hunched over a bottle of beer at one end of the bar.

She was sitting by herself at the other end, sipping a colorful drink. The place suited her, thought the Man. Or, it was more like she suited the place, adorning it with her understated class while matching its naked confidence. It was almost as if the place had been built around her for the sole purpose of her presentation, and when she left, the place would again be like a pleasant but empty room in a small midtown gallery, with only the faded outline of a frame marking the spot where a beautiful painting once hung.

Entertaining himself with such musings, the Man kept watching from the darkness until she finished her drink, put money on the bar, and slipped from her stool. As she left the bar, the man in the fedora looked up from his beer and followed her exit with his eyes. The Man noticed this and his pulse quickened. The urge rising. Oh how he wanted to take those eyes...

But no. Not for this. He had to pace himself. Otherwise, he would have to lay waste to half the city before the night was out. Luckily, the Man knew how to rein himself in. Stay in control.

Control was survival.

She was now outside on the sidewalk and moving away from him. With a last vengeful look into the bar, he moved to follow her. Taking the shadows with him.

How different she was from the others of her kind. From the girls and women peddling their corporal crafts a little further up the road on the fringes of the city. Faces garishly made up like walking Picassos, barely dressed in a degenerate's vision of female eroticism—and all of them shamefully oblivious to the fact that their appearance and their posturing and their whole sexual charade did little else but announce to the world their collective subhumanity.

She wasn't anything like that. Her allure was a natural thing, and she knew how to accentuate it with grace and subtlety; like she did now by wearing a short, tan trench coat, blood-red pumps, and the illusion of nothing else. With her coat tightly belted at the curve of her waist, her shoes tapping rhythmically on the cobblestones to the sway of her hips, she seemed like a vestige of some bygone era, a place in time so boldly magnificent, it had probably never existed.

He followed her through nocturnal streets as she made her way toward the expanse of railroad tracks leading to and from Central Station. The streets were almost deserted. Maybe it was the—so far unkept—promise of bad weather that was keeping people at home that night; maybe some of them thought it was a bad idea these days to be out at night on this side of town.

They veered south as she led them up an extensive ramp and onto a bridge for cars and pedestrians that spanned the rows of railroad tracks. Below the bridge, the tracks glinted in the artificial light like a bundle of silvery veins feeding into the heart of the city to the east. Up on the bridge, there was hardly a shred of shadow left alive by the streetlamps. He feared she would detect his presence while he crossed the bridge, so the Man fell back to let the distance between them grow.

He caught up with her just as she was rounding a corner on the southern end of the bridge. Returning to the comfort of the dark edges and corners of the urban nightscape, he followed her down the side road until it brought her to a parking lot in the moonlit shadow of the old customs complex. The Art Nouveau buildings with their touch of Reform architecture stood tall and proudly, like old gentlemen long past their prime but still unmatched by what came after. The Man settled in among them as she walked to a lonely car at the far end of the parking lot. Her next client of the night.

The Man watched her slip into the back seat of the midrange Ford sedan. Soon, there was the slight rocking of the car and the fogging of the windows and the taste of bile at the back of the Man's throat, and by the time the rear door opened again, there were cramps in the Man's tensed-up muscles and an ache deep in the joints of his jaws and a lightness in his head and an open straight razor in his hand.

His eyes tracked her walking away from the car and exiting the parking lot. As she did, a dog crossed her path, some Mastiff breed taking a shrunken, half-asleep woman for a walk. The Man waited for the pair to pass out of sight, before he made his move.

The guy in the car didn't notice the Man approach, even as the guy climbed out of the back seat and returned to the driver's seat, rolling down the window to release the smell of himself from the car. The Man made quick work of it, thrusting his arm through the open window for one violent swipe of the blade. He felt something warm and wet on his form-fitting latex glove and was already moving away from the car as the windshield filled with blood—a red curtain closing on a life abruptly forfeit by a hungry touch of flesh.

He hadn't even lost sight of her. Already he was back in her wake, following her onto a broad and quiet residential street lined with trees and widely spaced streetlamps. She walked in the middle of the street, her shape slipping from one pool of light to the next, creating the illusion that she slipped in and out of existence. As if the universe were blinking incredulously at the sight of her. The Man, in turn, kept clear of the light and remained lost in the darkness, unseen. As if, upon his entering its sight, the universe were covering its eyes in horror.

On their way to her next stop, he passed a newspaper box. Under its cover, a screaming headline addressed the string of murders that continued to haunt the city's Westend district, denouncing the lack of progress in the police investigation with as much outrage as could be fit above the fold. The Man knew all the details of the coverage, of course. One of the most troubling aspects impeding the investigation was the fact that not a single connection had so far been found between the victims, leaving the police groping in the dark, stumbling over one grisly death after another.

Of course, there was one person who could deliver the desperately sought connection, the one clue that would kickstart the investigation and change everything. But, so far, she hadn't.

The Man was pondering this, hardly for the first time, as he watched her stop in front of a bakery's dark window. She put a cigarette between her lips, flicked a lighter, and for a moment, a phantom of her face flared to life in the windowpane. He saw her meet her own flickering eyes as she set fire to her smoke— then the glass went black again.

On she went, wading through one street after another drowned in yellow sodium light. It hadn't taken him long to get a good idea of where her next stop would be, and she confirmed his idea when she approached the entrance to a charmless chain hotel that occupied a corner of a drab mid-rise postwar building, one of many that traversed the city like a disfiguring scar.

The Man remained hidden outside but kept her in his sight through the lobby's picture windows. When she entered one of the elevators, he moved in closer to make out the digital display of the floor numbers above the elevator doors as she ascended. When the display stopped counting, he moved. He had never...operated in this hotel before, but he had identified it as a possible location early on and thought it prudent to case it accordingly. That's how he knew to slip through a narrow alley into a backyard, and from there to enter the building through an emergency exit that opened onto a cramped, unrenovated staircase. He found the right floor and crept into the hallway. He was at the end of it and knew that from here, he had an unobstructed line of sight to almost all the rooms' doors on this floor. A housekeeping storeroom was opposite the staircase he'd come from. He settled in there, leaving the door slightly ajar, and waited.

From time to time, he heard a woman moan in the room next door. But it wasn't her.

This time, almost one excruciating hour passed before he spied her leaving a room all the way on the other end of the hallway. Gathering himself, he waited for her to leave the floor. He knew he could let her get away. This late, he knew where she was going, where he could catch up with her. So now, he could take his time.

When she was gone, he sneaked down the length of the hallway. He planted himself in front of the door to the room he'd seen her leave, slightly bowed his head, and set about opening the door the easiest way possible.

He knocked.

He heard feet being dragged across soiled carpet.

The turn of a lock.

And even as the door was pulled open to reveal a bald, stocky figure in boxer shorts and a rumpled wifebeater—the look on its pudgy face both hopeful and confused—he tore into the room with hardly a sound and descended upon the defiler.

Later, when it was done, the Man stood in the room, the door once again closed and locked, his tools safely returned to their various hiding places in his clothes, his gloves replaced with fresh ones—and took a deep breath. Briefly removing the hood of his jacket, he mopped sweat off the top of his head, his scalp as hairless as the rest of his body. The used kerchief joined the discarded gloves in one of his many jacket pockets. Then he allowed himself a moment to savor the sight of his work. How he'd painted the room with the insides of the fat man's body. The hues of carnal life. The bloody reds and visceral grays. The ironic vividness of it.

When he was satisfied that he'd committed the most beautiful parts to memory, he removed a small spray bottle of bleach from another of his jacket pockets and got to work erasing his presence from the room. Well, at least the physical traces of it. Even when, later, every square inch of surface had been scrubbed, the carpet removed, the furniture burned and replaced—even then, something of him, of his essence, would forever linger in this place, like the restless ghost of a lost love.

At that thought, the Man smiled.

He arrived at her home with a delay of no more than an hour. She was living, with several other working girls, in an ugly four-story block of an apartment building that once upon a time had been mercilessly covered top to bottom in gray plaster.

A sleek Mercedes beefed up on steroids was parked in front of the house. The Man knew who owned the car. The girls' pimp had come, probably to collect. Usually, he also took his time to rough up some of the girls who he thought had come up short. Dealing out some physical motivation. Even to her. But the Man didn't mind. He appreciated the firm hand. It was what women needed. Also, the pimp tried to never hit her face or leave any other permanent marks. The Man approved of that, too. Of course, sometimes, things got out of hand. Once, the Man had witnessed one of girls being carried away in an ambulance, never to be seen again. But, alas, there was nothing to be done about a thing like that. The instruments of violence would always be imperfect ones.

He sneaked into the decrepit apartment building next door and made his way to the third floor and into the small, empty apartment that he'd appropriated for his purposes. Once again, there was no one to take notice of him; the lowlifes who inhabited this place tended to keep to themselves. Tonight, even the drunk who'd regularly pass out in the small lobby was absent.

From the window of what had once been some poor soul's feculent living room, he had a good view of the building on the other side of a broad alley, and in particular, of her apartment, which she shared with another girl.

Now, all the drapes were pulled open. He could see her clearly. Her roommate appeared to be out—but she was not alone. The pimp was with her, sitting on a chair in the small but neat kitchen, only partly visible because he was leaning away from the window frame, but still recognizable to the Man by those ridiculous cowboy boots. She was standing with her back to the sink, now wearing a too-large men's dress shirt, arms crossed below her breasts.

The Man had been watching their inaudible conversation for about ten minutes when she moved away from the sink to the kitchen window. She gazed down to the little herb and vegetable garden that some of the girls maintained in the alley below. Then her eyes roamed over the façade of the building on the other side, never quite touching the Man's dark window.

Then the Man watched in astonishment as she turned around and put her hands on the man in her kitchen—caressing his face, pulling at his clothes, grabbing at his crotch. At first, the pimp seemed, even without being in full view, to be as astonished as the Man felt. As far as the Man knew, the pimp never had relations of that kind with his girls. Certainly not with her. That was something the Man had come to respect him for. He'd even entertained the idea that the pimp might be queer.

Not quite. When she pulled up the hem of her shirt to reveal her bare hips, any principles or reservations the pimp might have held melted away like snow in hell. He roughly pulled her close, waited impatiently the two seconds it took her to open his pants, and brought her down on himself.

The Man turned away in disgust.

Started pacing the room like a predatory animal freshly caught and trapped in a cage.

Why would she do this.

Give herself to this man. Voluntarily. For nothing.

Why...

Moments drained away like honey before the Man dared a glimpse out the window again. When he did, the pimp was gone.

The Man moved quickly. To do what had to be done.

Outside, the pimp's car was still parked in front of the house. The Man slipped into the alley, through the small garden, and was melting into the shadows on the building's wall where it was untouched by the streetlights, next to the building's exit, when the door flew open and the pimp stepped out.

For the pimp it must have felt like the hand of God had reached down to crush him as an unseen force hurled him against the wall and pounded his head into the rough and horrid plaster, once, twice, three times, before he was allowed to crumple to the alley floor. The Man stepped from the shadows and plunged his foot into the pimp's crotch the same number of times. Then he moved up the length of the pimp's torso and did the same to his head, again and again and again, until the skull inside was a skull no more.

Panting heavily, the Man looked down at the mess of a body at his feet. A living, virile organism just moments before, now an inert lump of flesh. Before he could begin to lose himself in an appreciation of how he'd turned its head into an abstraction, survival instincts took over.

The body had to go. This was her home. He couldn't allow anything to lead back to her. Immediately his eyes were drawn to the garden beds. Some vegetable beds might just be big enough. If he dismembered the body...

A noise from the door made him turn around.

She was standing in the doorway, her too-large dress shirt clinging to her in the slight draft pushing into the building. Looking down at the remnants of her former panderer, full red lips forming a small, beautiful O. Then, when she managed to peel her eyes away from the corpse, for the first time ever, her eyes were on him.

It's you, she said.

And with that, she stepped close and grabbed his hand and guided it under her shirt and between her legs. His gloved fingers felt warmth and, for once, a different kind of wetness, and the sensation of it sent a numbing wave of heat up his arm and deep into his chest even before the realization of what was happening hit his brain. When it did, the Man tore his hand away as if she'd dragged it through burning coals. He staggered backwards and ripped off the glove and held up his hand and looked at it as if it were a foreign thing.

No!

But, the glove...

You didn't really...it wasn't really you you didn't really touch her it was her your thoughts are pure you are pure you can save yourself be lenient with yourself you are pure you...

With this storm of voices gathering in his head, he looked at her. She had pushed herself against the wall and stood there with one hand covering her mouth. But her eyes were watching him intently, almost expectantly, and the feeling of them boring into him made the Man's heart ache.

Without him quite realizing how, one of his knives had appeared in his other hand, its handle cold, the serrated blade gleaming. A little wooden table stood by a raised bed of thyme that was intensely fragrant in the cool night air. He put his hand on the table, next to an overflowing ashtray, fingers splayed out. He set the blade to his skin.

His hesitation, the Man noted with some pride, was so brief, it might not have been there at all.

MONDAY, TUESDAY, THURSDAY, WEDNESDAY

Sean McCluskey

Monday

The men introduced themselves as detectives Harris and Amenguale, but refused to sign the visitor's log. That would have irritated the doorman, even if they hadn't shown up just before midnight.

"It's awful late, fellas," said the doorman.

"I know," said Detective Amenguale. He tapped the badge on his lapel. "They taught us to tell time at the police academy."

"It's important we speak to Mr. Schulman upstairs," said Detective Harris, with an irritated glance at his partner. "Urgent, actually."

"Legal matters are handled by his attorneys," said the doorman. "I'm sure Mr. Schulman will want you to contact them. I have his law firm's card here." He reached for a drawer in the podium he stood behind.

"If Mr. Schulman tells us that, we'll leave," said Harris. "But it's vital we speak to him."

"Otherwise, you're obstructing justice," said Amenguale. "Then you'll need a lawyer's card for yourself, pops."

The doorman scowled. He was mid-sixties, not fat. His thick white hair and squared-off nose made him look like he should be engraved on Roman coinage. But Amenguale was forty years younger, six inches taller, and muscular under a cheap suit. Harris was shorter and older than his partner. But he had flat eyes, dull like driveway gravel, that his tight smile never reached.

The doorman said, "I'll call him for you, officer." He lifted the podium's phone and tapped *Penthouse West*.

Amenguale glanced at Harris. Pursed his lips and nodded—*That's how you do it*. Harris shook his head and turned away, looking at the lobby's polished marble and dark glass.

"Mr. Schulman," the doorman said into his phone. "It's Silvio, downstairs. I'm sorry to call so late, sir. There're two police officers here, who say they need to speak to you." He listened. "I told them that, but they said it's urgent." He listened, woolly brow furrowed, then covered the mouthpiece. "May I tell Mr. Schulman what it's in reference to?"

Harris turned back. "His daughter."

"Sir, they say it's about Miss Apollonia." Silvio listened, nodded, and hung up. Jabbed buttons on his desk. "Please go right up." He pointed to gilded elevator doors, already opening.

"Thanks," Harris said. He strode toward them, Amenguale following. "Top floor, right?"

"I'll send it up," Silvio said. "Detective? Is she okay? Are you allowed to say? I've known her since she was little. She's a wonderful girl."

Harris shook his head. "I'm not allowed to say." The doors shut.

The elevator rose smoothly as a champagne bubble.

"Don't talk to these people like that," said Harris. "It's not productive."

Amenguale snorted. "Guy's dressed like Captain Crunch, says I can't go upstairs? Fuck him."

"Just let me talk to Schulman."

The elevator doors opened. Not into a hallway, but an entry foyer almost as big as the lobby. Alon Schulman was there, in a terrycloth robe over bare feet. His hair, gray and bald on top, was pulled into a ponytail. "Police?" he said. "Let me see your identification."

Amenguale tapped his badge again, but Schulman shook his head. "The cards. With the pictures." So they hauled out the wallets and flipped them open. Showed him laminated cards with photos and signatures. Miguel Amenguale and Ronald Harris. Detectives, 12th Precinct, New York City Police Department.

"NYPD?" said Schulman. "What are you doing in Connecticut?"

"We'll explain, Mr. Schulman." Harris motioned toward the apartment door. "May we come in?"

"No, we're fine here. What's the matter with my daughter?"

Amenguale pursed his lips again. Harris reached into his overcoat pocket and pulled out a flat slab, inside a plastic bag. Held it up. "Do you recognize this?"

Schulman squinted. The bag, *EVIDENCE* stamped across it, was hard to see through. "It looks like my daughter's computer tablet."

Harris turned the bag over. The tablet's screen was underneath. He tapped through the bag. The screen lit up.

An image appeared. A woman, young, with thick dark hair and light coffee skin. She was seated under harsh light. Silver tape bound her wrists to the chair. Her mouth was open, and her eyes were wide.

"That's my daughter," said Schulman.

Harris jabbed the tablet's screen. The picture sprang to life.

"Daddy!" the woman shrieked. "Please! Give them what they say! What they want!"

A gloved hand appeared in the picture, holding a small rectangular box with little metal spikes on top. A blue spark sizzled and popped between the spikes. The hand dove out of frame.

The girl thrashed in the chair. *"Daddy!"* she wailed over the electric crackle. *"Tell them! Tell them about the—aah! Stop!"* She slumped forward, motionless in sudden silence. The hand reappeared, empty. It lifted her head. She breathed in shallow gasps, eyes shut. The video ran for several more seconds, then froze.

Schulman snatched the tablet. "Who did this? Who took her? Do you know?"

"We do," said Harris.

"Who? What do they want?"

Harris took the tablet back. "Mr. Schulman, it's important you do everything we say." He leaned in. "Because if you don't, we're going to kill her."

Tuesday

"They said don't call the police," said Alon Schulman. "So I called my lawyers, and they called you."

Crenshaw, seated across the desk, nodded. "I've worked for Banks & Stokes in the past. Reputable firm."

"They spoke highly of you. Said you're an excellent investigator who's extremely discreet."

"I am."

Excellent remained to be seen, Schulman thought. But Crenshaw definitely looked *discreet*. Somewhere between thirty-five and fifty-five. Medium height, slender build, brown hair and eyes. Nondescript. He looked...vague. Like a hasty police sketch.

"I hope you're also fast," Schulman said.

Crenshaw nodded. "You mentioned a deadline."

"Thursday. They told me that's all the time Apollonia has."

"Let's not waste any. Tell me what happened."

Schulman described the previous night, detectives Amenguale and Harris, and the video of his daughter. Crenshaw didn't take notes—his clients didn't like written records.

"There is no NYPD 12th Precinct," Schulman said. "I Googled it."

"It's from *Barney Miller*," said Crenshaw. "So are the names they used."

"The TV show? Why?"

"When I find them, I'll ask."

"Find them? I was under the impression you'd be negotiating the ransom and release."

"That's an option the firm is considering. But I'll have to find them to negotiate."

"They said they'd call."

"They also said they were cops."

"*Can* you find them?"

"Of course," said Crenshaw. "The trick is to do it without your daughter getting killed."

Schulman shook his head. Muttered something in Yiddish.

"What happened next?" Crenshaw asked.

"I brought them here, to my office. Harris asked about a courier service I use. He wanted details of a particular shipment."

"Tell me what you told them."

"There's a kid flying in Thursday night, from Dublin, to Stewart Airport, over in Orange County, New York. Those cheap flights Norwegian Air runs. He swallowed merchandise in Ireland. When he arrives, our people pick him up and bring him where he can...you know."

"Relieve himself," said Crenshaw. "Of the merchandise."

"Exactly."

"Drugs?"

"No. What do you take me for? Diamonds. From Antwerp."

"Then what?"

"They told me, you know, don't call the cops. Don't cancel the courier. If you do, she's dead. They left me the tablet. Dumped it on the desk. Said watch it all you want; see we're serious. The big one laughed. They said keep it close. We'll email you on it, to arrange giving her back."

Crenshaw looked at the desk, bare except for a Banks & Stokes business card. "Is the tablet still in here?"

Schulman looked around, red-eyed. Seven a.m., Tuesday, and he'd been up since just before midnight. "I think I left it upstairs. I was walking around, upset. I think I left it in her old room. I kept watching." He stood. "What are you thinking? Fingerprints? I don't think they touched it."

"No," said Crenshaw. "I'm thinking they left you a surveillance device."

"What?"

"Tablets have cameras and microphones, for video chat. Was it in the room when you called Banks & Stokes?"

Schulman screwed up his face and thought. "No."

"You're sure?"

"I couldn't find the number." Schulman tapped the business card. "I had to have the doorman bring it up. And I never call the firm from my cell phone. Always the desk."

"I need to see that video," said Crenshaw. "Without them seeing me." He walked around the desk, where shelves flanked a broad window. Sunrise glittered off the Long Island Sound, Manhattan hazy in the distance. Crenshaw took out his phone and tapped its camera to life. He propped it against a cut geode on a low shelf, aimed at the desk. Checked the angle onscreen. "Take the card away, please."

Shulman put the business card into his robe's pocket. "What are you doing?"

"I'm going to go out. After I do, get the tablet. Hold it on the blotter, lower left, and play the video. Then go put it someplace else. I'll watch the video from my phone."

"You're going to record in here?"

"After I watch, I'll delete the recording in front of you. In fact, I'll leave the phone here. You can smash it with this rock, if you want. Banks & Stokes will replace it."

"I don't like records of my business floating around. I'm sure you understand."

"I do." Crenshaw walked out of the office, through a living room big enough to play volleyball in. Schulman followed.

"When you watch the video, try to seem upset," Crenshaw said.

"I *am* upset."

"Perfect. Tell me about your daughter,"

"She's twenty-three. Lives in Boston, where she went to school—she dropped out. 'Finding her truth,' or some damn thing. I don't like the boyfriend she's living with."

Crenshaw opened the penthouse door. "Tell me about him."

"I only met him once. Scrawny, dresses funny. With a beard. His name's Aiden something. He's in a folk band. Their logo sticker's on Apollonia's tablet. That's how I recognized it." Schulman frowned. "Could he have something to do with this?"

"If he turns up, I'll ask. When you sit down, hold the tablet so I can see that sticker."

"All right."

"Is Apollonia's mother still around?"

"No, we divorced when she was little. Banks & Stokes took care of it."

Screwed her on the settlement, too, according to the file Crenshaw had read. "Are she and Apollonia close?"

"I'm not sure. I haven't spoken to my ex-wife in years, and Apollonia…" He sighed. Rubbed his eyes. "We've had arguments. Drifted apart."

"About her mother? The boyfriend?"

"Yes. And my business. Why is this relevant?"

"Right now, everything's relevant." Crenshaw pressed the elevator button. "Is Apollonia's mother part-Greek?"

"No, she's black. Why would she be Greek?"

"I was curious about your daughter's name."

"Her mother named her after a woman in a movie she liked."

Crenshaw thought for a second. "*The Godfather*?"

"*Purple Rain*."

The elevator arrived. Crenshaw stepped aboard.

251

"Where are you going?" Schulman asked.

Crenshaw said, "What's your doorman's name?"

"They were real assholes," said Silvio. "Pardon my French, sir, but they were extremely unprofessional. The big one, especially."

Crenshaw nodded. "They were the same with Mr. Schulman. Tried to push him around."

"No way," said Silvio. "Not Mr. Schulman. He's tough."

"I know. I'm with his law firm. We're going to file a complaint against those detectives." He nodded at the lobby cameras, up by the onyx molding. "I'll need to see any recordings."

"No problem, sir. I got the big one's badge number, too. They wouldn't sign the guestbook, but I wrote down their names."

"Good work." Crenshaw leaned over the counter as Silvio pushed buttons on the surveillance screens. "Is that a USB port? I'd like to download the footage onto a thumb drive."

"I don't know about computers, sir," said Silvio. "They just taught me to push buttons."

"You got their names. Didn't need a computer for that."

The older man beamed at the praise. "I got their license plate, too. From the outside camera. They tore ass outta here. Nearly hit some people in the crosswalk. That's on video, too. For the complaint."

"Mr. Schulman's going to be very happy with you, Silvio."

"Sir, it's none'a my business, but can you tell me if Miss Apollonia's all right? She's a sweetheart. I can't believe she's in trouble."

"She's not. They think her boyfriend's selling drugs, and the police want Apollonia to testify. But she said no, so they're pressuring her father. It's a common tactic."

"That's bullshit. 'Scuse me for saying, but they shouldn't be allowed to do that." He jabbed a button, and one of the screens froze. It showed a dark SUV darting from the curb. Moving fast, but the cameras were high-end. The license plate was clear.

"I hope you can do something about those guys, sir," said Silvio.

"I definitely will," said Crenshaw.

Crenshaw's office was in Manhattan, forty miles west of Stamford. The interstate was packed with commuter traffic at eight on a weekday morning, but Crenshaw didn't care—he was on company time.

While driving, he used his laptop to watch the surveillance footage. Amenguale and Harris wore dark suits and overcoats. Harris had accessorized his with a trilby that helped hide his face. Amenguale had long hair, with sideburns. Harris had a mustache; Amenguale, a goatee.

Then Crenshaw watched the recording of the tablet video, which he'd surreptitiously emailed to himself before leaving his phone with Schulman. Despite the angle and distance, the quality was good. Banks & Stokes issued pricey phones, with high-resolution cameras.

On screen, Apollonia shrieked. Crenshaw watched as she struggled, then slumped. He frowned. Rewound the video and ran it again. *"Tell them!"* she screamed. *"Tell them about the—aah! Stop!"*

Crenshaw opened the car's center console. Inside was a cell phone, identical to the one he'd sacrificed to Schulman. While it powered up and downloaded his contacts from the cloud, he watched the video again. *"Daddy! Please!"*

His new phone buzzed—ready. He touched the icon for *B&S.*

"Good morning, Mr. Crenshaw." Nicole, his assistant, sounded impossibly peppy for eight a.m.

"Hello, Nicole. As a millennial computer genius, can you run a tag for me?"

"Let me have it."

Crenshaw recited the SUV's license plate and heard a keyboard rattle. Back when he was a cop, he'd have called it in to a bored or irritable dispatcher and waited for them to get around to it. But Nicole would have his information in seconds.

"It's registered to Car Horizons Incorporated, a vehicle rental company," Nicole said. "Not a chain. Business filings only show one location."

"Makes sense. They'd be looking for someplace that takes cash and isn't diligent about record keeping. Where is it?"

"Up in Newburgh. I'll text you the address."

"Thanks, Nicole. You rock, as young people say."

"Aw, so sweet. You want me to try and bust into Car Horizons' records? It's easier with the big companies, but sometimes we get lucky."

"No, I'll go and talk to somebody face-to-face. A *conversation*. That's what we old people call it."

"I may be quicker."

"That's okay. We've got until Thursday."

Thursday

"'Bout fuckin' time," said Amenguale.

"They're on schedule," Harris said. He glanced at the dashboard clock: 10:57. "Hell, they're early. Norwegian Airlines must've caught a tailwind."

They were in their rented SUV, outside the terminal at Stewart International Airport. A herd of people shuffled out the doors. Mostly young, casually dressed, pale and fair. Two stood out.

One was a short guy with a patchy beard. He wore shiny slacks and a wrinkled shirt, a yarmulke pinned to unkempt black hair. He carried a cardboard sign with *Mr. Stone* on it.

Which meant the kid with him was the courier. Tall, athletic, about nineteen, wearing a track suit and lugging two backpacks. Stumbling like a zombie, after his seven-hour flight. He dragged a rolling suitcase. His escort made no move to help.

"Why's he carrying luggage?" Amenguale asked. "He *is*

luggage."

Harris didn't answer. His partner had two modes: asshole and silence. Amenguale—Harris still thought of him as "Amenguale," because he didn't know his real name—hadn't impressed him in the five days they'd worked together. The people who'd set up the job had paired them off. They didn't impress Harris much, either. What impressed him was his promised share of a million two in diamonds.

The escort led the courier to the parking lot. They got in a faux wood-panel minivan, two rows from the SUV. Amenguale shifted it into gear.

"Don't follow too close," said Harris.

The minivan pulled out of the lot. Amenguale followed, cutting off a car leaving a spot. He swung onto the airport service road, a hundred yards behind the minivan.

Harris pulled on a baseball cap, a cheap blue novelty with POLICE printed across the front. With his windbreaker and cargo pants, it approximated a uniform. Amenguale was dressed the same, plus tactical gloves with solid knuckle guards.

The minivan turned onto International Boulevard, a two-mile stretch of road with the airport on one side and a state forest on the other. Nice and empty at eleven on a weekday.

Harris lifted a flat plastic box from the floormat and stuck it on the windshield with suction cups. There was a smaller box, hand-sized, in the cup holder. Harris picked it up. A wire trailed from it, out a back window, onto the SUV's roof.

The minivan kept right, going slow. The SUV followed. A stream of traffic from the just-arrived flight flowed past on their left. It thinned to a trickle. Then nothing.

"Let's do it," said Harris.

Amenguale accelerated. Harris flicked a switch on the windshield box, and the red strobe lights on it started flashing. He tapped a button on the hand box. The siren they'd clamped to the SUV's luggage rack whooped.

The minivan jerked. Harris saw the driver looking back in

the mirror. Amenguale stomped on the gas, closing the gap. "Pull over, you prick," he muttered. Harris held down the siren button, a sustained blast. The minivan wallowed into the breakdown lane and crunched to a grudging halt. Amenguale pulled close behind.

Harris got out and strode to the minivan's passenger side. The window was down, the courier getting some breeze after seven hours of recycled plane air.

"What's this about?" the driver demanded of Amenguale, who had arrived by his window. "You have to tell me what this about."

"Gimme your license," said Amenguale.

"Why? I wasn't speeding."

The courier was watching them. "Hey," Harris said. The kid turned. Bleary eyes and milky skin. "You speak English?" Harris asked.

"Yeah," said the courier. "I do." His Irish accent was almost cartoonish.

"Why are you talking to him?" the driver asked, turning from Amenguale. "You don't need to speak to him."

Harris opened the door. "Get out," he told the courier.

"He doesn't need to get out," the driver said. "You can't make him. I need to call somebody. You have to let me make a call." There was a phone in his hand, but Harris knew there was no cell service there. All electronic signal was drowned out by the shriek of the airport's radar. That was one of the reasons they'd chosen the spot.

Amenguale clamped a massive hand on the back of the driver's head. He shoved the small man forward, toward the steering wheel. Amenguale's other fist crashed into the base of his skull, enhanced by the reinforced glove. The driver slumped. Amenguale leaned in to hit him again.

"Holy shit!" the courier cried, his accent turning it into *hooly shyte.* Harris hauled him out by the warmup jacket. Shoved him against the minivan's flank, face-first.

"Put your hands behind your back," Harris said. The courier

did, hands shaking as though palsied. Harris looped a zip tie over his wrists and pulled it tight. He led the courier by the arm back toward the SUV.

"I didn't do anything," the courier gasped, stumbling along.

"Relax," Harris said. "It'll be over soon." He bundled the kid into the back seat and belted him in. With another zip tie he secured his ankle to a seat stanchion.

At the minivan, Amenguale shoved the driver over into the passenger seat and bulled in after him. The taillights flashed, and it pulled away. Harris hustled around to the SUV's driver's seat and got in. Dropped the shifter into gear and followed.

They drove along International Boulevard until it ended. An airplane roared low overhead. Then onto a busy main road, cruising north. Harris tossed his cap onto the seat next to him. Yanked the box off the windshield and dropped it on the cap.

"Sir, am I in some kind'a trouble?" the courier asked.

"Just do what we tell you. It'll be all right."

"I don't really know that other guy. He was just givin' me a ride."

"It'll be all right," Harris repeated.

"Sir, could I use the toilet someplace?"

"Soon as we get where we're going. It won't be long."

"Could we please stop before that? A petrol station, maybe?" The kid squirmed. "I really gotta go."

"You will," Harris said. "Soon."

They turned east. Harris lowered his visor against the late-morning glare. Ahead, the minivan swerved in its lane and recovered. Harris shook his head. He wasn't impressed with Amenguale's driving, either.

After ten minutes, the minivan turned into the parking lot for the Lakeside Lodge motel, a squat concrete blockhouse, painted faded yellow. There was one other car in the lot, a battered pickup that had been in the same spot since Harris arrived on Sunday to rent their room.

Amenguale parked in front of room 17. Harris pulled in next

to him, killed the engine, and got out. He went around and opened the passenger door.

"This isn't a police station," said the courier.

"You need the bathroom, right? The management lets us use them here, as a courtesy." Harris took trauma shears from his pocket and cut the zip tie on the kid's ankle. "Come on."

He led the kid to room 17. Amenguale was already there, fumbling in his pocket for the key. With his other arm, he held up the driver. The small man's eyes were ringed with bruises, nose and mouth bloody.

"Oh, my God," the courier moaned.

"What the hell'd you do?" Harris asked.

"He got mouthy," said Amenguale. He tossed the key to Harris. "Get the door, will ya?"

Harris opened the door. The room's signature stink of cigarettes and crack cocaine rolled out. He shoved the courier inside. Amenguale dumped the driver into a chair by the window. Harris shut the door and locked it.

The driver groaned. Blood and saliva bubbled from his mouth. Behind split lips, it looked like he had a couple of teeth missing.

"You've got to be kidding me," Harris said.

Amenguale laughed. "Serves them right for killing Jesus." At Harris's look, he raised his hands and sighed. "What difference does it make?"

Harris pointed at the courier. "Take him into the bathroom and get him started." He looked at the blood on the carpet. "This job was supposed to be clean."

Amenguale dragged the courier toward the bathroom door. "Clean? We're about to be elbow-deep in this dude's shit. What, they're gonna keep our security deposit?" He opened the bathroom door. "Relax. It'll be—who the fuck?"

In the bathroom, Crenshaw raised his rifle. It was short, small-caliber, molded polymer and aluminum. It had an adapter on the muzzle to attach an automotive oil filter, as an untraceable suppressor. He aimed at Amenguale's face and fired.

The range was short, but Amenguale was big, and the small bullets were slowed by the filter. So Crenshaw pulled the trigger five times. The suppressed gunshots were no louder than enthusiastic hand claps. A brisk round of applause, and Amenguale went down.

Crenshaw stepped out, shouldering the courier aside. He turned and swung the rifle.

Then a number of things happened, very fast.

First, the courier tried to run. But he tripped over Amenguale and stumbled into Crenshaw, knocking him off-balance. Just a bit, but enough.

Harris dropped to his knees behind the chair. As he moved, he swept aside his jacket and pulled a gun from the holster on his belt.

Crenshaw aimed, struggling to steady the rifle. It had an electronic sight that superimposed a red crosshair where the bullets would hit. He centered it on what he could see of Harris's head and squeezed the trigger three times.

The first bullet went wide, because Crenshaw was off-balance. It hit the driver in the eye.

The second shot was better aimed, but by that time Harris had his gun raised, sighting in. The bullet meant for his head struck his hand. Blood sprayed, and the pistol tumbled away.

The third shot was off, because of the recoil from the second. It hit Harris in the head, but just barely. It skimmed his temple and clipped the tip off his ear.

Harris crashed to the floor. The driver slumped in the chair, blood pouring from his eye like a punctured wine cask. Crenshaw stood still, rifle aimed. He had two rounds left in the gun, and another magazine in his pocket. He wasn't worried about anybody outside hearing the suppressed shots—the place was built like a bomb shelter, and the closest occupied room was eight doors down.

Harris's pistol lay where he'd dropped it. He was on the floor behind the chair, grunting and moaning, legs kicking at nothing.

Crenshaw glanced at Amenguale. His nose was a cratered ruin. His eyes bulged, forced from their sockets by the hemorrhages behind them. It made him look both astonished and drowsy. No doubt he was dead.

The courier was on his knees. He tried to stand, awkward with his hands tied behind his back. Crenshaw hit him in the head with the rifle butt, knocking him on his ass. "Don't move," Crenshaw said, voice muffled by the neoprene mask he wore. The kid nodded frantically.

Crenshaw moved toward Harris, rifle aimed. He edged around the chair. Harris was on his back, head against the wall. Blood streamed down his face. He clutched his wounded hand, staring up at Crenshaw. At the gun.

"Wait," Harris said. "Just wait. That kid has a million bucks worth of diamonds in him."

"I know."

"It's all yours. I give up. I won't say anything to anyone."

"I need to ask you something," Crenshaw said.

"Yeah, I'll tell you. She's in—"

"Why *Barney Miller*?"

Harris gaped at him. "What?"

"When you talked to Schulman. The precinct, the names. I told him I'd ask."

"I...I watched it as a kid. With my mother. My name actually *is* Harris. But it's my first name, not my last. I made the ID cards, so they let me pick the names." He shrugged, awkward with the angle. "It was a joke. We all thought it was funny."

Crenshaw thought about it. "I guess you had to be there." He aimed at Harris's face and squeezed the trigger twice. *Clap-clap.*

Crenshaw pulled the window curtain open a bit. No nosy maid or curious tourist walking by. The parking lot was empty in the noonday sun. He reloaded his rifle as he walked back to the courier.

The kid looked up. A bruise was forming where Crenshaw had hit him, harder than he'd intended. He'd been angry about having his shot spoiled. Sloppy. Unprofessional.

"You speak English?" Crenshaw asked.

"Yeah."

"Stand up." The kid braced against the wall and struggled to his feet.

"Turn around," Crenshaw said. The courier started to, then hesitated.

"If I wanted to shoot you, I'd shoot you in the face," Crenshaw said. "Like everybody else in this room. Now turn around." He did, and Crenshaw took a knife from his pocket. Flicked out the blade and cut the zip tie. "Go in the bathroom." The courier went, rubbing his wrists. Crenshaw followed.

"Look in the tub," Crenshaw said. The kid pulled the grimy curtain aside. Saw the contractor garbage bags and the rolls of silver tape in there.

"That's where you two were going," said Crenshaw. "Afterwards."

The kid mumbled something that sounded like *Hooly shyte*.

"Those men worked for a big organization," Crenshaw said. "They're everywhere. So if you're thinking about going to the police—"

"No way," said the kid. "I won't tell anybody. Swear to God."

"Don't interrupt me."

"I...I'm sorry?"

"It's rude."

"I'm really sorry."

"All right." Crenshaw pointed at the toilet. There was a plastic kitchen strainer in the bowl. Then to the sink, where a plain white box labeled *Bisacodyl* sat.

"What's that?" the courier asked.

"Laxatives."

The courier picked up the box. "How many do I eat?"

"They're suppositories."

"Oh."

"They work faster."

"I've never done it that way before."

"Then this must be a big day for you."

"Last time, they had one I could drink," said the courier. "Grape flavored. It was pretty good."

"You can't live in the past," said Crenshaw.

Wednesday

The cabin was supposed to look like it was made of logs, but the vinyl siding was too even, too regular. It reminded Crenshaw of the icing on a cheap snack cake he'd liked as a child. He couldn't recall the name.

He lay in gloomy woods and looked at the cabin with binoculars. Its windows shone in the dusk, making halos in the fog. There was a car beside it, a Subaru with Massachusetts plates. Nicole had worked her magic and told him it was registered to an Aiden Gillespie, with a Boston address. A long way from home, here in western Pennsylvania.

The car had a bumper sticker, a skull and crossed fiddles, same as on the back of Apollonia's tablet. The band was called Silas Morning. The music on their website was like Woody Guthrie, with more bass and less talent.

Nicole had found tax records that said the cabin was owned by a Joseph Robson, who also lived in Boston. He and Gillespie had old addresses in common.

The SUV that Amenguale and Harris had driven wasn't there. That was okay—Crenshaw knew where it was.

The porch light snapped on. The front door opened and a scrawny man stepped out, wearing a sheepskin jacket against the early fall chill. His gaunt face and bushy beard made Crenshaw think of Civil War photos. The man shouted something over his shoulder as he slammed the door shut.

Crenshaw had a collapsible rifle in his backpack, but he hadn't assembled it. He was two hundred yards from the house, beyond the lightweight gun's effective range. So he watched the man stomp to the Subaru. He had a phone in one hand and a cigarette in the other. At the car he flicked the cigarette away, raised the phone to his ear, and yanked the door open. He sat behind the wheel for a minute, talking on the phone. Then he drove off, spraying gravel and pine needles.

Crenshaw waited until the engine noise faded. When the crickets returned, he crept toward the cabin. He drew his pistol from under his coat. It was a tiny semiauto, .22 caliber, like the rifle, with a threaded barrel and a homemade suppressor.

As he reached the steps, the porch light went out.

Crenshaw stopped. There was a flicker of movement in the front window, a silhouette. Then nothing. He counted to twenty. Saw nothing.

He moved to the front door, pistol aimed, and tried the latch. He hadn't seen the man lock the door behind him, but it was locked now.

He peeked in the window. Saw a rustic living room, tweedy, rough-hewn furniture around a stone fireplace. An open pizza box on a coffee table, with one gummy-looking slice inside. Empty beer bottles on the table and floor.

Crenshaw circled the house. Found a side door, also locked. Looked in a window and saw a dim empty bedroom. The next window was an empty bathroom. Past that was a bigger window, lights on.

Crenshaw looked in, and saw Apollonia.

She was sitting on a bed, a laptop computer on her thighs and headphones on her ears. She was wearing a BU sweatshirt and flannel pajama shorts. Bobbing her head to whatever she was listening to. A cell phone lay beside her.

Crenshaw circled back to the front door. He opened his backpack and took out a chrome tube with a thin, narrow blade protruding from it. An electric lockpick. Imported German engineering. Pricey, but only the best from Banks & Stokes. He slid the blade into the keyhole, eased a tension wrench in beside it, and tapped the pick's button. The motor buzzed, and the blade vibrated against the lock pins, hammering them into position. Crenshaw turned the wrench The lock clicked open.

He walked through to the back bedroom, checking doors on the way to make sure he hadn't overlooked anybody. He hadn't. The bedroom's door was partially closed. He pushed it open.

Apollonia jolted when she saw him. The gun and the mask tended to do that. He pulled the mask off and kept the pistol by his side.

Apollonia took the headphones off.

Crenshaw said. "Your father sent me."

"Thank God," she said, in a loud whisper. "We have to get out of here. The men who kidnapped me are in the other room. They've been drinking, but they might wake up." She moved to get up. Her hand, the one farther from him, darted under a pillow.

Crenshaw aimed his gun at her. "Stop."

She froze.

"Bring your hand out. Slow. And empty."

She did.

"There's nobody else here," Crenshaw said. "And no kidnappers I've heard of leave their victims with a phone."

She sighed. "Who told you? Aiden? Or those two assholes?"

"Nobody needed to tell me." He motioned to her sweatshirt with the pistol. "What did you study at Boston University?"

"Business. I'm my father's daughter, after all."

"I figured it wasn't drama. Your acting in that video was the first clue."

"What?" She sounded stung.

"The screaming at first—'Daddy, daddy, tell them'—wasn't too convincing. But then it changed. Much more realistic. I guess the guy with the stun gun's hand slipped?"

She shook her head, blew thick, glossy hair from her eyes. "Aiden. He wasn't supposed to actually hit me. Those things *hurt.*"

"I know. They also don't work like the phasers on *Star Trek*. Nobody passes out from them. Just the opposite, actually."

"Well, they do on TV."

"And it was sloppy of your two detectives, not putting new plates on that SUV they rented."

"But those just lead to the rental place, right? And they paid cash, with a fake name and address."

"That wasn't too bad," said Crenshaw. "But one of the problems with those smaller places is that they can't just eat the loss the way a big national chain can, if somebody doesn't bring the car back. So they put GPS tracking in all their vehicles."

"Shit," said Apollonia. "Is that even legal?"

"Buried in the fine print. Legal enough."

"Seriously?"

"Trust me—I work for a law firm."

"So what did you do? Hack their computers?"

"I gave the kid behind the counter five hundred dollars for the login password to their tracker. That's the other problem with the small places. They don't pay their employees very well. The tracker stores the car's movement history. So I watched the SUV go from the rental lot to some fleabag motel near the airport on Sunday. Then out here, then over to your father's building Monday night, then back here for two days. And this afternoon it went back to the motel, where they're presumably staying until Norwegian Air 1842 lands at ten thirty tomorrow morning."

"Is there anything you don't know, Sherlock Holmes?"

"You could fill books with the things I don't know. For starters, who are your two phony cops?"

"The big Spanish-looking one was a bouncer at a club I liked. I used to fool around with him. The other guy was a bodyguard for one of my friends at boarding school."

"You fool around with him, too?"

"God, no. He's, like, forty."

"None taken," said Crenshaw. "And who's Joe Robson? The

guy who owns this place?"

"Aiden's stepfather. They used to come out here every summer. Their vacation paradise."

"Where'd Aiden go? To supervise the robbery?"

She scoffed. "I wouldn't put Aiden in charge of watering a cactus. We had a fight, so he flounced out. There's some skank bartender in town. He thinks I don't know they're screwing. Probably have been since they fell in love at thirteen, or something."

Crenshaw nodded. "Now I know everything."

"Bullshit. You don't know why I did it."

"You're angry about the way your father treated your mother. So you decided to break his heart, steal his money, and maybe get him killed by the people he does business with. Is that close?"

"Would they really kill him?"

"It's a distinct possibility."

"Hmm." She didn't look particularly horrified at the thought.

"If the diamonds actually got stolen, of course."

She sighed again. "It was still a pretty good plan. Yeah, a couple of missteps, but it would've worked just fine."

"Still is a pretty good plan," said Crenshaw. "Still can work, just fine."

She narrowed her eyes. "What are you saying?"

"Like I said, I'm with a law firm. We hate to see a good crime go to waste."

"I thought you worked for my father."

"I wasn't hired to guard his diamonds. I was hired to save you from kidnappers. But there aren't any. So I guess I'm here to save you from yourself." He walked around the bed, keeping the gun trained on her, and lifted the pillow. Saw a shiny little .38 revolver, which he picked up. "For example, I wouldn't want you to have a sudden attack of conscience and do something drastic."

"So what happens now?"

"It was a long drive out here," said Crenshaw. "I'm going to go in that other bedroom and take a nap. Around six a.m., you'll brief me on the plan you all came up with, and I'll drive over to New York to supervise the robbery. Then I'll bring the merchandise back. I assume you've arranged some way to sell it? Smart business major that you are?"

"Yeah. I have."

"Then it's all set." He dropped the revolver in his coat pocket. "When Aiden gets back, explain the new arrangement to him. If he has trouble understanding, come get me."

"I'll take care of Aiden," she said. Something in her voice. Her father's daughter.

When he got to the door, she said, "But maybe I'll just kill you while you sleep."

Crenshaw turned back. "Maybe. Or maybe those kidnappers murdered you before I ever got here. Then they stole those diamonds and found their own buyer for them. Either way, it'll be interesting."

"Or maybe I'll run away with Aiden while you're in New York," she said. "We'll start a new life together someplace."

"Without the diamonds?"

"We could live on love."

"Don't make me chase you," said Crenshaw. "Even doves have pride." He shut the door. He walked through the cabin to the smaller bedroom, which smelled of a pine air freshener that reminded him of Christmas. He locked the door behind him. Then he unlocked the window, eased it open, and slipped out. The ground behind the cabin sloped up, making it an easy step down to the dirt. He lowered the window behind him. Apollonia's room was around the corner; he wouldn't be seen.

Brisk steps brought him to the tree line. He crunched through the scrub and crouched behind taller growth, at an angle that let him see the spare bedroom's window and the spot where Aiden's car had been. After he got comfortable against a tree, he dug his rifle from his pack and twisted it together. Settled in to wait.

The best way to find out if you can trust somebody, Ernest Hemingway had said, *is to trust them.* All due respect to Papa, but Crenshaw disagreed. In his experience, the best way to find out if you could trust somebody was to let them *think* you trusted them. Then sit back and see what they did with it.

Maybe Apollonia really wanted to see this thing through, badly enough to let Crenshaw crash the party. Badly enough to *take care* of Aiden, too. Or maybe she was calling Aiden at that very moment, telling him there was a new problem to take care of, so hurry back with your gun, baby, and we'll kill him in his sleep.

Either way, it would be interesting. *A life without risk isn't worth living*, as Charles Lindbergh had said. And if you couldn't trust an adulterous Nazi sympathizer, what had the world become? Crenshaw inserted a magazine into the rifle, pushed until it clicked, and chambered a round.

Probably, though, the interesting part wouldn't happen that night. It probably wouldn't happen until after the diamonds had been sold and the money got split. That's when people usually got silly. So no sense trying to surf a wave before it arrived.

He'd worry about it on Friday.

ECHOING

Joseph S. Walker

Fixing the leak under the bathroom sink in a vacant unit at Meadow Villas was a five-minute job, but Addison stretched it out to half an hour. His next stop was a top-floor apartment at the Pinewood complex. He had a feeling the water heater was finally going to have to be replaced this time, a bitch of a job for one man. If he got there late enough, he could put off the actual work until tomorrow, maybe get Rogers to help. And if he had to hang around the office waiting for Rogers, he could talk a bit with Jeannie. Maybe suggest doing something this weekend. She was twenty years his junior, but her divorce had left her shaken and lonesome. She might welcome a bit of company.

Long time since Addison had a bit of company.

That's all he was thinking about as he finally backed out of the cabinet, grunting as he pushed off the toilet to get to his feet. He closed his toolbox and opened the door and saw a man standing in the bedroom entrance, fifteen feet away, pointing a gun at him. He held it the way people with badges were trained to hold guns, a two-handed grip, close to the body, over a balanced stance.

Twenty years ago, Addison would have thrown the heavy metal toolbox at him, charging in behind it with a midbody tackle. Twenty years ago, he'd had quicker reflexes, better knees, and a fading but stubborn belief that he couldn't really be hurt.

"Lower the toolbox," the man said. "Slowly. Then sit on the floor next to the head of the bed."

Addison crouched and put the toolbox down, watching to see if the man would relax. The gun stayed steady. Addison's own emergency piece, the .22 that almost disappeared in his hand, was in the bottom section of the toolbox. It might as well have been on the moon. He stepped into the bedroom, put his back against the wall next to the bed, and slid down until his ass was on the floor.

The man took a pair of handcuffs out of the pocket of his sport coat and tossed it between Addison's feet, keeping the gun fixed on him. "Left wrist," he said. "Other end on the headboard."

Addison put a cuff around his left wrist and anchored himself to one of the heavy wooden slats of the headboard. He held the hand up to demonstrate.

"Cute," the man said. "Click that a couple more notches."

Addison reached up with his right hand and tightened the cuff.

The doorway the man was standing in opened into the apartment's kitchen. He took a step back, picked up one of the kitchen chairs, and moved it into the doorway. He straddled it, resting a forearm on the back. He was holding the gun loosely now, not pointing it at anything but not putting it away. Underneath the sport coat he wore a white shirt, open at the collar, and dark slacks. Business casual. He stared at Addison in his stained coveralls like the handyman was something unpleasant he'd found in his plate of food.

Addison didn't try to keep his gaze. He looked at the floor between his feet. "You after copper pipe?" he asked.

The man snorted. "Do I look like a junkie?" He pulled a leather case from his breast pocket and flipped it open. Addison was too far away to read the ID, but he didn't have to. "David Young," the man said. "FBI." He put the case away. "Why don't you tell me who you are?"

"Look, you want something with the guy who lived here, he moved out last week. I'm just the handyman. Rick Gibson."

Young smiled. "That's one lie," he said. "You're not going to like what happens if you get to three."

"Sir, I'm not—"

Young held up a warning hand. "See, if you tell me you're not lying, that'll be your second lie. You'd better save that. Remember, three's the magic number."

Addison licked his lips. "I don't know what you want me to say to that."

"Let's try the truth and see how it flies," Young said. "Your name is Richard Roy Addison. In 1985, you and three other upstanding citizens hijacked an armored car in St. Louis and scored one and a half million dollars. You've been a wanted man ever since. Ringing a bell?"

"You got the wrong guy."

Young shook his head. "That's two, Addison. That's all the lies you get."

"I want a lawyer," Addison said.

"Now that I believe," Young said. "I don't give a fuck what you want, but I do believe you're not lying."

"I know my rights," Addison said. "You gotta give me a lawyer if I ask."

"That's not the game we're playing," Young said. "We're not playing good cop bad cop, or mercy of the court, or pleading out. We're playing twenty questions, except I'll ask as many goddamn questions as I want to."

Addison rattled the cuff in frustration. "Man, you're gonna get in a lot of trouble for this. I never stole a damn dime."

Before the last word was completely out of his mouth, Young was up out of the chair. He knocked it aside and charged across the room, a big man moving faster than Addison would have thought possible. The point of his shiny black shoe hit Addison's ribs like Young was trying to kick a field goal from fifty yards out. Air exploded from the cuffed man. He fell to the side, fighting to get a breath, stunned by the blast of pain. For several minutes he couldn't do anything but gasp. He clutched his right arm against his side, his left stretched out uselessly by the handcuff.

Young was still holding the gun. He put it in his shoulder holster, picked up the chair, and straddled it again in the doorway. He put his arms on the back of the chair and rested his chin on them and watched Addison fight for breath.

After many minutes, Addison pulled himself up into a sitting position. His chest still heaving, he looked at Young with hooded eyes.

"Now we start from zero again," Young said. "Tell me three more lies and I'll do something worse. You believe me?"

Addison managed a nod.

"Okay, then," Young said. "Question and answer time. Who started shooting at the cops?"

They staged the accident on a long stretch of nearly empty road. Julie and Hector, shouting and pointing, stood by their cars, the hoods crumpled together. As the armored car got close, Hector knocked Julie to the asphalt and stood over her, brandishing a big wrench. The guard driving jammed on the brakes and jumped out. Addison popped from the trunk of Hector's car with the M16 as Hudlow roared out of a nearby parking lot in the van. In ten seconds, the driver had four weapons pointed at him, and in less than a minute they had the back of the armored car open and both guards on the ground.

The police cruiser appeared at the end of the block and turned their way just as they got the two big money bags moved to the van. Addison dropped to one knee and started firing. A cop rolled out of the passenger side, returning fire. Addison felt the recoil pushing back against his shoulder again and again.

* * *

"The cops shot first," Addison said. "We just defended ourselves."

Young made a tsking noise. "That's one," he said. "Before I ask again, old man, keep in mind that I'm the FBI agent in charge of this case. I've seen every witness statement, every scrap of evidence."

Old man stung. "Agent in charge," Addison sneered. "Now who's lying? What were you, ten years old when this went down?"

"Five," Young said evenly. "I was five."

"Agent in charge, my ass. Who are you really? Give me a better look at that ID."

"What the fuck do you think happens when agents retire? Cases get reassigned. I've had this one for five years. This many bodies, this much missing cash. This kind of file doesn't get closed."

"Bullshit." Addison turned his head and spat on the floor. It was red against the beige carpet. "You were a fed, I wouldn't be sitting on the fucking floor tasting blood. I'd be in a cell waiting on my lawyer."

"Think what you want," Young said. "I'm the guy with the gun. Who started shooting at the cops? Who had the M16?"

This time Addison was ready. "Hudlow. He was always too quick on the trigger."

"For the moment, we'll pretend I believe that. Now get to what happened at the warehouse."

The empty warehouse where they'd stashed the clean cars was a mile and a half from the crash site. By the time they got there, Hudlow was done screaming. He was barely moaning, pushing his hands down against the dark blood bubbling up from the cop's bullet in his stomach. Julie was doing close to sixty as she brought the van in through the big cargo doors, and she had to stand on the brakes to keep from slamming into the opposite wall.

"Get him into my car," Hector yelled as they popped the van doors. "I got a guy I can take him to."

Addison was the last to get out. When he walked around the back of the van, Hector and Julie were ten feet ahead of him, supporting Hudlow between them as they walked toward Hector's car. Addison hadn't planned what happened next. He'd been on jobs before and always played square. But there the three of them were, backs to him, none of them even holding a gun. The big money bags were still in the van, and the rifle was slung over his shoulder.

They had almost reached the car when he started pulling the trigger. The sound in the hollow, confined space of the warehouse was like an assault, a barrage of heavy booming thuds melding into a reverberating echo that lingered for long seconds after he stopped firing.

Thirty minutes later he was across the river in Illinois, the money bags in the trunk. It wasn't until he saw his mugshot in a newspaper the next morning, outside his ratty roadside hotel somewhere in Tennessee, that he learned he'd stopped firing too soon.

"Hector double crossed us," he said. "Pulled a gun and tried to take the whole score for himself. Everybody pulled and started shooting. I was just the lucky one."

"There are lies and stupid lies," Young said. "That right there was a stupid lie, and you're back up to two. Your buddies were all shot in the back, and there was only one weapon fired in that warehouse. Same one that erased the cops."

"Oh, fuck you," Addison said. "Go ahead and kick me again, you snot-nosed punk. Think I'm going to sit here and cop to three murders?"

"Two murders," Young said. "One attempted. You must know Hudlow lived."

Addison's shoulders tightened. "I know the son of a bitch gave me up."

Young laughed. "You think he had a lot of choices? He was

in the hospital close to three months, had God knows how many surgeries. Then he did eight years in Leavenworth. Would have been longer, but coming up with your name bought him something. Let me tell you something, Richie. That man hates you like most people hate VD."

"You talked to him? Where is he?"

"Planning a reunion?" Young smirked. "He slipped parole after a couple of years. Runs a bar in a pissant town in Montana and deals meth. He probably thinks he's safe. Criminals are stupid that way."

"How'd you find me?"

"I just said," Young said. "Criminals are stupid. Thirty years of hiding out, and then a couple months back you ran a red light. Automatic camera took a picture of you. Facial recognition program tags it and I get an automated email with the whereabouts of my fugitive. It's an exciting new era in law enforcement, Mr. Addison."

"Sounds more like you being lucky than me being stupid," Addison said. "Thirty years is a pretty good run."

"Pretty good run?" Young raised his eyebrows. "Enjoyed the last thirty years, did you? I've filled in most of the gaps. You've been a hobby of mine, Addison. I've seen the shithole apartment in Jacksonville you lived in for three years while you were working at a gas station. Sam Waters was the name then, right?"

Addison turned his head away. He looked at the toolbox, just out of his reach.

"Of course, the Jacksonville place was a palace compared to that little clapboard shack up in Wisconsin. That must have been pure hell in the winters. I didn't think much of the accommodations in Kentucky or Nevada, either. Maybe I missed a couple places, but I'm good at my job. I even talked to Lynn Weathers, in Toledo. She still doesn't know what the hell happened to Kevin Hoffman."

* * *

Lynn. The one bright spot in three decades. The one woman who wasn't a hooker or barroom easy. A librarian, of all fucking things. He felt a peace in her bed that had nothing to do with sex. Then one day he turned into her street and there were three black-and-whites parked on her block. Maybe it was nothing to do with him, but he idled on past and didn't stop until he was two states away. He told himself he'd go back someday. He always knew it was a lie.

"So you found me," he said. "Good for you. They'll have a parade when you haul in a janitor on a thirty-year-old beef."

"Let's finish our own business first," Young said. "As far as I can tell, the last thirty years have been sheer misery for you. Shitty job after shitty job, terrible apartments, beat-up cars. Damn few women and no kids. You sure as hell haven't been living like a man with more than a million dollars." He leaned forward. "Back to the questions, Addison. What happened to the money?"

Addison smiled. "So that's it," he said. "All this crusading, master detective bullshit. You just want to drop me in a hole and take whatever's left of the score."

"Answer the question. And remember, you've already had your two lies."

Addison laughed. It drove a spear of agony into his side, so he stopped. "There is no fucking money," he said. "You know what one point five million dollars is in hot cash? Maybe, *maybe*, you can get thirty cents on the dollar, if you've got a guy to change it who has the right contacts and can be patient. Except I didn't even have a guy. Hudlow had a guy."

"Seems like something you should have thought of before you shot him."

It was the weight of the bags that did it. When he moved them from the armored car to the van, the sheer heft of them, the idea of so much cash that you had to sweat to move it, dug into his brain until it was all he could think of.

They were ten feet in front of him, their backs turned. Not even a gun in any of their hands. The continuous rolling echoes off the walls split the world in two.

He didn't think about the price.

He tried, just once, to walk it back, to get back to the life he'd had. He called Poole from a pay phone two hours from the town he was living in. Poole always knew the jobs coming up, knew who was looking for an extra gun or a driver. He was quiet for a long minute after Addison identified himself.

"You're looking for a job?" he said. "Everybody knows what happened in St. Louis, Rich. Hudlow had a lot of friends. Most of the people in the life would shoot you on sight. Don't call this number again."

"So what do you do?" Addison made a face. He hooked his fingers into the cuff fastened to the bed, trying to ease the discomfort of his extended arm. He wasn't really talking to Young, just dealing out the cards he'd been shuffling for three decades, trying to will himself a hand. "Can't leave the country without a passport. You need a money guy and an ID guy, and if you show up in a new city and just start asking around about people like that, you end up facedown in the local river. So you bury the money and get whatever work you can with no real ID and you poke around, quiet. And maybe eventually you find a money guy, but he's strictly small time and he won't do more than ten or twenty k. Not enough for the kind of ID you need. So you trade in a chunk of the money, enough to move on to the next town. Maybe you stop somewhere on the road, risk trading in a few thousand at a casino." He brought his eyes down to Young and sneered. "I suppose an asshole your age wouldn't have any problem these days. Turn it into Bitcoin or gift cards or some shit. I'm old school. I understand cash."

"Christ," Young said. "You expecting me to feel sorry for you?"

"Point is, it's gone," Addison snapped.

"You pissed it away," Young said. "Because you assumed we had the serial numbers."

"Had to," Addison said. "They got Capone on taxes, right? And there's nothing to kick me about because I'm not lying, you son of a bitch. I haven't got a dime to give you. So what the hell are you going to do now? Take me in and let me tell your bosses you tried to shake me down?"

"I could just shoot you."

"Go ahead," Addison said. "Be doing me a favor."

"I've got a better idea," Young said. He reached into his breast pocket and pulled out a syringe.

Addison didn't waste energy crying out. He yanked as hard as he could on the cuff, lunging to his right. The thick wood cracked and bowed out toward him but didn't break. Young got up out of his chair and moved it aside. Addison dug his toes into the carpet and pushed forward, dragging the heavy frame of the whole bed a few inches. His left arm stretched out and twisted behind him. The middle finger of his right hand touched the cold metal latch of the toolbox just as Young plunged the needle into the meaty part of his thigh. A chilled numbness radiated outward from the shot. His hand waved for the toolbox again, but it was a million miles away now, a red dot at the end of a closing tunnel. His body fell away from him.

He shot Hector first. By the time he shifted his aim to the others, the echo was booming through the big empty space. When all three were on the floor, he stopped shooting, but the echo didn't stop. It fed on itself, built, a constant jackhammering that would never end. He dropped the gun and put his hands over his ears, but it didn't matter. He was inside the echo. He'd never be outside it again.

Addison was staring at a cinderblock wall painted dusty red. He felt like he'd been staring at it for a while. It was about ten inches in front of his nose and the pits and ridges in the surface seemed huge, a Martian landscape he was gliding over.

There were things that were wrong, but he wasn't thinking about them.

A torrent of icy water hit his cheek, some of it going up his nose. He sputtered and tried to jump back away from it and was brought up short by a yank on his left wrist. Feeling the cuff brought everything back. Young. He rolled to his other side and managed to get into a half crouch, his right fist clenched.

They weren't in the apartment. They were in a low cinderblock room, lit by three bare bulbs spaced across the unfinished ceiling. It was about thirty feet by fifteen and completely bare except for a staircase going up in the middle of one of the short walls. He was in a corner at the opposite end of the room and Young was standing a few feet away, holding a bottled water. He'd taken off the sport coat and Addison's eyes went straight to the automatic in his shoulder holster. He made an unthinking lunge forward and was brought up short again. His left wrist was still cuffed, now to a big metal staple driven into the wall.

"What the fuck," Addison said. His mouth was dry and sticky and his side ached where Young had kicked him. "Where the hell are we?"

Young didn't say anything. He turned and Addison saw another man sprawled out on the floor in the other corner. His face was turned to the wall and his own left arm was tethered the same way Addison's was. Young stood over him and poured some water on his face, and the man went through the same convulsions Addison had, cursing and yanking against his chain before managing to roll to his knees.

It was Hudlow.

The face was older and battered. One of his eyes was almost swollen shut and there were ugly purple bruises on both cheeks. A crust of dried blood circled his nostrils.

"I had to teach Hudlow the three lies rule a few times," Young said. He'd backed away and was now standing halfway down the room. He took a swig from the bottle of water.

Hudlow was staring at Addison. He didn't say anything.

"Hudlow," Addison said. "Whatever problem we got, this asshole has to be dealt with first. I don't know what kind of sick fucking game he's playing, but we don't have to go along."

"I can't believe you've got the balls to talk to me," Hudlow said. He wrenched uselessly at the chain. "I'm gonna make you hurt bad before you die."

"It's really touching to see you boys reconnecting," Young said. He finished the water and tossed the bottle over his shoulder. "I even got you gifts to mark the occasion." He fished in his pocket and underhanded something to each of the chained men. Addison tried to catch whatever it was, but it deflected off the side of his hand. He picked it up. A switchblade. He flicked it and the blade popped out, six inches, slim and bright and sharp. He wasn't surprised to see Hudlow holding its twin.

"This isn't funny, Young," Addison said. "Take me in. I'll confess."

"Unlock me, Young," Hudlow said. "Give me five minutes. Then you can do whatever you want."

"I'm going to do whatever I want anyway," Young said. "Just give me a minute to look at the two of you. You have no idea how long I've been waiting for this."

"What the hell is this?" Addison said. "You're no FBI agent."

"I am, though," Young said. "I really am. Thanks to you." He walked to the staircase and sat down on the bottom step. "Let me tell you what's about to happen," he said. "I'm going to toss each of you a handcuff key. Then I'm going to go upstairs and draw my gun and wait, just in case you dangerous felons decide to team up and try to take me. If you both come up, I'll kill you both."

"And if one of us comes up, we get hauled in for killing the other," Addison said.

"No," Young said. "If one of you comes up, I let you go."

That brought Addison up short. "You went through all this to let one of us go?"

"Sure," Young said. "I'll give whichever one it is two months. Sixty days to run again, try to find a new life again, another name you forget half the time, another nothing job paying under the table. Then I'm coming for you. In two months you can start looking over your shoulder, but you'll never see me coming, and next time I'm going to do things so much worse than this."

"Why?" Hudlow demanded. "What the hell is wrong with you?"

"A lot of things, I'm sure," Young said. He looked at Addison. "You asked how old I was in 1985. I was five. Five years and two months. I was sitting on a seesaw in my backyard and my mother was on the other end. Then somebody a quarter mile away, in the middle of robbing an armored car, started firing an M16."

Addison slumped against the wall. "Oh, Jesus," he said.

"I don't know which of you it was," Young said. "You both swear the other guy shot at the cops. I don't guess it matters. Either of you would have. A neighbor found me six or seven hours later, still holding her body, trying to get her to wake up. Hell of a weapon, the M16."

"It was an accident, Young," Addison said. "Thirty years ago. For the love of God, I'm a different man now."

"You were never a man," Hudlow growled. He spit in Addison's direction.

Young went on as though they hadn't said anything. "I never knew my father," he said. "I got farmed out to some cousins in California. They adopted me, gave me a different name. They hoped I'd forget. I pretended that I did so they'd leave me alone, and I went to school and made myself into the perfect recruit for the FBI. Once I was in, it was easy to pull a few strings and get assigned the case." He turned his gaze fully on Addison. "I wanted the man who got away. And I got him."

"You did," Addison said. "You got me. Take me in."

Young ignored him. "For a long time I figured you were some criminal mastermind. I imagined you on a tropical island, planning more jobs. I thought I'd be lucky to ever see you. And what do you turn out to be?" He shook his head. "Pathetic." He waved his hands at them vaguely. "A janitor. A two-bit meth dealer. Both of you miserable and alone. It was like I was already punishing you."

"Enough talk," Hudlow said. "You told us what you're going to do. Do it. Maybe you won't find me so easy to deal with, coming up those stairs with two knives."

"I'll kill you if I have to," Young said. He stood up. "But I won't have to. You'd rather have another few months crawling."

"Give me the key," Hudlow said. He stared at Addison and slowly waved the open knife. Blood pumped in Addison's ears. A roaring noise, an endless noise. The echo of gunfire in a big empty building.

"I lied, Young," he said. "There's a lot of money left. I can take you to it."

Young didn't bother replying. He had a handcuff key in each hand. He tossed them, underhand, one in each direction. They were still in the air as he turned and started up the stairs. Addison missed again, saw the key skip several inches across the concrete floor. He scrambled for it and began trying to jam it into the keyhole without dropping the knife, teeth bared, frantic, listening for the sound of Hudlow's chain or his footsteps coming but hearing only the roar of an echo that didn't die away.

ABOUT THE EDITOR

MICHAEL BRACKEN (CrimeFictionWriter.com) is the editor of *Black Cat Mystery Magazine* and has edited several previous crime fiction anthologies, including the Anthony Award-nominated *The Eyes of Texas: Private Eyes from the Panhandle to the Piney Woods, Groovy Gumshoes,* and the three-volume *Fedora* series. With Gary Phillips he co-edited *Jukes & Tonks,* and with Trey R. Barker he co-edited the serial novella anthology series *Guns + Tacos.* Stories from his projects have received or been shortlisted for Anthony, Derringer, Edgar, Macavity, Shamus, and Thriller awards, and have been included in or named among the year's best by the editors of *The Best American Mystery Stories, The Best American Mystery and Suspense,* and *The World's Finest Mystery and Crime Stories.*

Also a writer, Bracken is the Edgar- and Shamus-nominated author of eleven books and more than 1,200 short stories, including crime fiction published in *Alfred Hitchcock's Mystery Magazine, Black Cat Mystery Magazine, Black Mask, Ellery Queen's Mystery Magazine, Mike Shayne Mystery Magazine, The Best American Mystery Stories,* and *The Best Mystery Stories of the Year.* In 2016 he received the Edward D. Hoch Memorial Golden Derringer Award for Lifetime Achievement in short mystery fiction. He lives, writes, and edits in Texas.

ABOUT THE CONTRIBUTORS

ANN APTAKER's (AnnAptaker.com) Cantor Gold series has won Lambda and Goldie awards. Her crime stories have appeared in the *Fedora* anthologies, *Switchblade Magazine, Mickey Finn: 21st Century Noir, Black Cat Mystery Magazine,* and *Punk Soul Poet.* Her novella *A Taco, A T-Bird, A Beretta and One Furious Night* was published as part of Down & Out Books' *Guns + Tacos* series.

TREY R. BARKER (TreyRBarker.com) is the author of the Jace Salome novels, the Barefield trilogy, a few standalone novels, and hundreds of short stories spanning every genre from horror to crime. Once a journalist, Barker is now a patrol sergeant with the Bureau County Sheriff's Office, and—along with his wife Kathy—a produce farmer in Illinois. They give most of their produce to those who can't afford it, and they can be found at BarkerFarm.org.

JOHN BOSWORTH's short stories have appeared in *Mickey Finn: 21st Century Noir, Mystery Weekly, Switchblade,* and *Shotgun Honey.* He lives in Seattle and can be found on Twitter @JGBosworth.

C.W. BLACKWELL is an American author from the Central Coast of California. His recent work has appeared with Down

& Out Books, Shotgun Honey, Rock and a Hard Place Press, and Fahrenheit Press. He is a 2021 Derringer Award winner. His debut novella, *Hard Mountain Clay*, was published by Shotgun Honey earlier this year.

JOHN M. FLOYD's (JohnMFloyd.com) work has appeared in more than 350 different publications, including *Alfred Hitchcock's Mystery Magazine*, *Ellery Queen's Mystery Magazine*, *Strand Magazine*, *The Saturday Evening Post*, and four editions of Otto Penzler's best-mysteries-of-the-year anthologies. Floyd is also an Edgar nominee, a Shamus Award winner, a four-time Derringer Award winner, a Golden Derringer Award recipient, and the author of seven collections of short mystery fiction.

NILS GILBERTSON is a crime and mystery fiction writer and a practicing attorney. A San Francisco Bay Area native, Gilbertson currently lives in Washington, D.C. with his wife. His short stories have appeared in *Mickey Finn: 21st Century Noir*, *Mystery Weekly Magazine*, *Rock and a Hard Place*, *Pulp Modern*, and others. You can find him on Twitter @NilsGilbertson.

JAMES A. HEARN (JamesAHearn.com) is an attorney and an Edgar Award-nominated author who writes in a variety of genres, including crime fiction, science fiction, fantasy, and horror. His fiction has appeared in *Alfred Hitchcock's Mystery Magazine*, *Black Cat Mystery Magazine*, *The Eyes of Texas*, *Guns + Tacos*, *Mickey Finn: 21st Century Noir*; *Monsters, Movies & Mayhem*; and *Peace, Love, and Crime*.

JANICE LAW (JaniceLaw.com) is an Edgar-nominated and Lambda-award-winning novelist, as well as short fiction writer whose stories have appeared in *Alfred Hitchcock's Mystery Magazine*, *Ellery Queen's Mystery Magazine*, *Sherlock Holmes Mystery Magazine*, and *The Best Mystery Stories of the Year*. Her most recent novels are *Mornings in London*

(MysteriousPress.com) and *Homeward Dove* (Wildside Press).

STEVE LISKOW's (SteveLiskow.com) stories have appeared in *Alfred Hitchcock's Mystery Magazine, Black Cat Mystery Magazine, Mickey Finn: 21st Century Noir, Mystery Weekly,* and several other publications. He was the first to win the Black Orchid Novella Award twice (along with two Honorable Mentions) and has been a finalist for both the Edgar Award and the Shamus Award.

SEAN MCCLUSKEY is a federal agent on a fugitive task force, living and working in upstate New York. His short stories have appeared in *Crime Spree Magazine* and *Spinetingler Magazine.*

ADAM MEYER (AdamMeyerWriter.com) is a screenwriter, novelist, and short story writer. His TV projects include several Lifetime movies and true-crime series for Investigation Discovery. His short fiction has been nominated for the Shamus Award and appeared in *Groovy Gumshoes* and *Magic is Murder.* He is the author of the thriller *Missing Rachel* and the YA novel *The Last Domino.*

ALAN ORLOFF (AlanOrloff.com) has won two ITW Thriller Awards, including one for "Rent Due" (*Mickey Finn: 21st Century Noir,* vol. 1). He's also won a Derringer Award, been a finalist for the Shamus and Agatha awards, and had a story selected for *The Best American Mystery Stories.* His latest novel, *I Play One on TV* (Down & Out Books), won both an Agatha Award and an Anthony Award.

JON PENFOLD (JonPenfold.com) is the author of three books—*The Last Indians,* his first novel, *The Road and the River: An American Adventure,* and *A Long Walk on the Beach: A Thru Hike on the Oregon Coast Trail*—and has had work published in numerous anthologies.

C. MATTHEW SMITH (CMattSmithWrites.com) is the author of *Twentymile*, a crime novel set in and around Great Smoky Mountains National Park. *Mystery Tribune*, *Mystery Weekly*, and *Close to the Bone* have published his short stories. He lives near Atlanta with his family.

JOSEPH S. WALKER (jsw47408.wixsite.com/website) lives in Indiana. His short fiction has appeared in *Alfred Hitchcock's Mystery Magazine*, *Ellery Queen's Mystery Magazine*, *Mystery Weekly*, *Tough*, and many other magazines and anthologies. He has been nominated for the Edgar Award and the Derringer Award, and has won the Al Blanchard Award and the Bill Crider Prize for Short Fiction.

MICHAEL WEGENER makes his fiction debut in *Mickey Finn: 21st Century Noir*, vol. 3. By day he is a chemist and medical writer who writes hard science instead of hard-boiled fiction.

ANDREW WELSH-HUGGINS (AndrewWelshHuggins.com) is the author of several novels featuring Andy Hayes, a former Ohio State and Cleveland Browns quarterback turned private investigator. Andrew also edited the anthology *Columbus Noir*, and his short mystery fiction has appeared in *Ellery Queen's Mystery Magazine*, *Mystery Weekly*, *Mystery Tribune*, and other magazines and anthologies.

SAM WIEBE (SamWiebe.com) is the author of the Wakeland novels, one of the most authentic and acclaimed detective series in Canada, including *Invisible Dead*, *Cut You Down*, and *Hell and Gone*. Wiebe's other books include *Never Going Back* and *Last of the Independents*. He has won the Crime Writers of Canada and Kobo Emerging Writers awards, and been shortlisted for the Edgar, Hammett, Shamus, and City of Vancouver book prizes.

STACY WOODSON (StacyWoodson.com) made her crime fiction debut in *Ellery Queen's Mystery Magazine*'s Department of First Stories and won the 2018 Readers Award. Since her debut, she has placed stories in several anthologies and publications. Winner of two Derringer Awards, she has also been a finalist for the Bill Crider Prize for Short Fiction and in Screencraft's Cinematic Short Story Competition.

BOOKS

On the following pages are a few
more great titles from the
Down & Out Books publishing family.

For a complete list of books and to
sign up for our newsletter,
go to DownAndOutBooks.com.

Fortune's Favor
A Thriller
Thomas Locke and Jyoti Guptara

Down & Out Books
November 2022
978-1-64396-286-3

Imagine a world where privilege is stolen and handed down from generation to generation—supernaturally. When a disgraced accountant is hired to shadow a mysterious Indian couple, she partners with them to steal an ancient object that has kept Asia's elites in power for generations.

The first collaboration by bestselling authors Thomas Locke and Jyoti Guptara, the international, intergenerational writing duo.

Getting Dunn
Tom Schreck

Down & Out Books
November 2022
978-1-64396-287-0

Discharged from the army and back in the States and unable to cope, TJ Dunn spirals into an emotional daze, spending her days working at a suicide hotline and her evenings moonlighting as an exotic dancer. Her only outlet for her anger is a punching bag at the local boxing ring where she works out with a handsome trainer, Duffy.

Just when she thinks she's reached her limit, an anonymous phone call shocks her back to life and gives her a new mission, justice for those she loves and she won't stop at anything to do it.

Edgar & Shamus Go Golden
Twelve Tales of Murder, Mystery, and Master Detection
from the Golden Age of Mystery and Beyond
Gay Toltl Kinman and Andrew McAleer, editors

Down & Out Books
December 2022
978-1-64396-278-8

Edgar & Shamus welcomes mystery connoisseurs to the Golden Age of Mystery and Murder—Twelve original tales of mystery and suspense written exclusively by Edgar Allan Poe Award and Shamus Award-winning authors.

As if picking up where Sir Arthur Conan Doyle, Dame Agatha Christie, and Dorothy Sayers left off, the who-dun-it, why-dun-it, how-dun-it, and unshakable alibi are all afoot in *Edgar & Shamus*. Travel back in time with an all-star cast of some today's leading experts in the art of crime fiction.

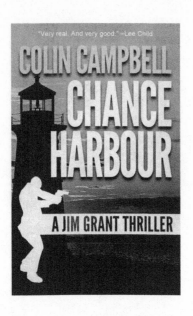

Chance Harbour
A Jim Grant Thriller
Colin Campbell

Down & Out Books
December 2022
978-1-64396-277-1

Dementia is robbing the old man in the ICU of any coherent thoughts until his face finally clears. "Okay. I know what happened. I need you to call my son. He's with the Boston Police at Jamaica Plain."

But Jim Grant isn't at Jamaica Plain; he is getting over being resurrected. Until he gets a call to say his father is seriously ill. But Grant arrives too late. His father has been abducted. A bomb has exploded outside a diner. And the FBI wants to know how his father knows a Russian oligarch who is even older than he is. For father and son it could be the last chance to reconcile their differences. It might also be the last chance for everything.